ACCLAIM FOR MICHA
THE BLACK ICE

"Hard-bitten...complex and convincing."
—*San Diego Union-Tribune*

"Connelly flips the reader's expectations upside down with a surprise ending."
—*Cleveland Plain Dealer*

"A terrific yarn, extending the boundaries of the police procedural in the ingenuity of the plot and the creation of character... Connelly's command of police workings and his knowledge of the turf from L.A. south and across the border, combined with a fertile imagination, give the book a high readability."
—*Los Angeles Times Book Review*

"gripping...One of the finest police procedural novels...Miss it at your peril."
—*Virginia-Pilot and the Ledger Star*

"A solidly constructed novel...persuasive in the depiction of the police ecosystem and relentlessly faithful to the tradition."
—*Philadelphia Inquirer*

"Strong and sure...This novel establishes Connelly as a writer with superior talent for storytelling."
—*Publishers Weekly*

"Bosch is a fully realized and intriguing protagonist."
—*Houston Chronicle*

THE
BLACK
ICE

ALSO BY MICHAEL CONNELLY

THE HARRY BOSCH NOVELS

The Black Echo
The Black Ice
The Concrete Blonde
The Last Coyote
Trunk Music
Angels Flight
A Darkness More than Night
City of Bones
Lost Light
The Narrows
The Closers

Echo Park
The Overlook
Nine Dragons
The Drop
The Black Box
The Burning Room
The Crossing
The Wrong Side of Goodbye
Two Kinds of Truth
Dark Sacred Night
The Night Fire

THE LINCOLN LAWYER NOVELS

The Lincoln Lawyer
The Brass Verdict
The Reversal

The Fifth Witness
The Gods of Guilt
The Law of Innocence

OTHER NOVELS

The Poet
Blood Work
Void Moon
Chasing the Dime

The Scarecrow
The Late Show
Fair Warning

NONFICTION

Crime Beat

E-BOOKS

Suicide Run
Angle of Investigation
Mulholland Dive

The Safe Man
Switchblade

THE
BLACK
ICE

MICHAEL
CONNELLY

GRAND CENTRAL
PUBLISHING

NEW YORK   BOSTON

Copyright © 1993 by Hieronymus, Inc.
Preview of *The Dark Hours* copyright © 2021 by Hieronymus, Inc.

Grand Central Publishing
Hachette Book Group
1290 Avenue of the Americas, New York, NY 10104
grandcentralpublishing.com
twitter.com/grandcentralpub

Originally published in hardcover by Little, Brown & Company in June 1993
First trade paperback edition: August 2021

Grand Central Publishing is a division of Hachette Book Group, Inc. The Grand Central Publishing name and logo is a trademark of Hachette Book Group, Inc.

The publisher is not responsible for websites (or their content) that are not owned by the publisher.

The Hachette Speakers Bureau provides a wide range of authors for speaking events. To find out more, go to hachettespeakersbureau.com or call (866) 376-6591.

Excerpt from "La Pistola y el Corazón" by David Hidalgo and Louie Perez copyright © 1988 Davince and No Ko Music. Administered by Bus Music. All rights reserved. Used by permission.

ISBNs: 978-1-5387-3796-5 (trade paperback), 978-0-7595-2578-8 (ebook)

Printed in the United States of America

LSC-C

Printing 1, 2021

This is for Linda McCaleb Connelly

THE
BLACK
ICE

One

THE SMOKE CARRIED UP FROM THE CAHUENGA PASS and flattened beneath a layer of cool crossing air. From where Harry Bosch watched, the smoke looked like a gray anvil rising up the pass. The late afternoon sun gave the gray a pinkish tint at its highest point, tapering down to deep black at its root, which was a brush-fire moving up the hillside on the east side of the cut. He switched his scanner to the Los Angeles County mutual aid frequency and listened as firefighter battalion chiefs reported to a command post that nine houses were already gone on one street and those on the next street were in the path. The fire was moving toward the open hillsides of Griffith Park, where it might make a run for hours before being controlled. Harry could hear the desperation in the voices of the men on the scanner.

Bosch watched the squadron of helicopters, like dragonflies from this distance, dodging in and out of the smoke, dropping their pay-loads of water and pink fire retardant on burning homes and trees. It reminded him of the dustoffs in Vietnam. The noise. The uncertain bobbing and weaving of the overburdened craft. He saw the water crushing through flaming roofs and steam immediately rising.

He looked away from the fire and down into the dried brush that carpeted the hillside and surrounded the pylons that held his own home to the hillside on the west side of the pass. He saw daisies and wildflowers in the chaparral below. But not the coyote he had seen in recent weeks hunting in the arroyo below his house. He had thrown down pieces of chicken to the scavenger on occasion, but the animal never accepted the food while Bosch watched. Only after Bosch went back in off the porch would the animal creep out and take the offerings. Harry had christened the coyote *Timido*. Sometimes late at night he heard the coyote's howl echoing up the pass.

He looked back out at the fire just as there was a loud explosion and a concentrated ball of black smoke rotated up within the gray anvil. There was excited chatter on the scanner and a battalion chief reported that a propane tank from a barbecue had ignited.

Harry watched the darker smoke dissipate in the larger cloud and then switched the scanner back to the LAPD tactical frequencies. He was on call. Christmas duty. He listened for a half minute but heard nothing other than routine radio traffic. It appeared to be a quiet Christmas in Hollywood.

He looked at his watch and took the scanner inside. He pulled the pan out of the oven and slid his Christmas dinner, a roasted breast of chicken, onto a plate. Next he took the lid off a pot of steamed rice and peas and dumped a large portion onto the plate. He took his meal out to the table in the dining room, where there was already a glass of red wine waiting, next to the three cards that had come in the mail earlier in the week but that he had left unopened. He had Coltrane's arrangement of "Song of the Underground Railroad" on the CD player.

As he ate and drank he opened the cards, studied them briefly and thought of their senders. This was the ritual of a man who was alone, he knew, but it didn't bother him. He'd spent many Christmases alone.

The first card was from a former partner who had retired on book and movie money and moved to Ensenada. It said what Anderson's cards always said: "Harry, when you coming down?" The next one was also from Mexico, from the guide Harry had spent six weeks living and fishing and practicing Spanish with the previous summer in

Bahia San Felipe. Bosch had been recovering from a bullet wound in the shoulder. The sun and sea air helped him mend. In his holiday greeting, written in Spanish, Jorge Barrera also invited Bosch's return.

The last card Bosch opened slowly and carefully, also knowing who it was from before seeing the signature. It was postmarked Tehachapi. And so he knew. It was handprinted on off-white paper from the prison's recycling mill and the Nativity scene was slightly smeared. It was from a woman he had spent one night with but thought about on more nights than he could remember. She, too, wanted him to visit. But they both knew he never would.

He sipped some wine and lit a cigarette. Coltrane was now into the live recording of "Spiritual" captured at the Village Vanguard in New York when Harry was just a kid. But then the radio scanner—still playing softly on a table next to the television—caught his attention. Police scanners had played for so long as the background music of his life that he could ignore the chatter, concentrate on the sound of a saxophone, and still pick up the words and codes that were unusual. What he heard was a voice saying, "One-K-Twelve, Staff Two needs your twenty."

Bosch got up and walked over to the scanner, as if looking at it would make its broadcast more clear. He waited ten seconds for a reply to the request. Twenty seconds.

"Staff Two, location is the Hideaway, Western south of Franklin. Room seven. Uh, Staff Two should bring a mask."

Bosch waited for more but that was it. The location given, Western and Franklin, was within Hollywood Division's boundaries. One-K-Twelve was a radio designation for a homicide detective out of the downtown headquarters' Parker Center. The Robbery-Homicide Division. And Staff Two was the designation for an assistant chief of police. There were only three ACs in the department and Bosch was unsure which one was Staff Two. But it didn't matter. The question was, what would one of the highest-ranking men in the department be rolling out for on Christmas night?

A second question bothered Harry even more. If RHD was already on the call, why hadn't he—the on-call detective in Hollywood Division—been notified first? He went to the kitchen, dumped his plate in the sink, dialed the station on Wilcox and asked for the watch commander. A lieutenant named Kleinman picked up. Bosch didn't know him. He was new, a transfer out of Foothill Division.

"What's going on?" Bosch asked. "I'm hearing on the scanner about a body at Western and Franklin and nobody's told me a thing. And that's funny 'cause I'm on call out today."

"Don't worry 'bout it," Kleinman said. "The hats have got it all squared away."

Kleinman must be an oldtimer, Bosch figured. He hadn't heard that expression in years. Members of RHD wore straw bowlers in the 1940s. In the fifties it was gray fedoras. Hats went out of style after that—uniformed officers called RHD detectives "suits" now, not "hats"—but not homicide special cops. They still thought they were the tops, up there high like a cat's ass. Bosch had hated that arrogance even when he'd been one of them. One good thing about working Hollywood, the city's sewer. Nobody had any airs. It was police work, plain and simple.

"What's the call?" Bosch asked.

Kleinman hesitated a few seconds and then said, "We've got a body in a motel room on Franklin. It's looking suicide. But RHD is going to take it—I mean, they've already taken it. We're out of it. That's from on high, Bosch."

Bosch said nothing. He thought a moment. RHD coming out on a Christmas suicide. It didn't make much—then it flashed to him.

Calexico Moore.

"How old is this thing?" he asked. "I heard them tell Staff Two to bring a mask."

"It's ripe. They said it'd be a real potato head. Problem is, there isn't much head left. Looks like he smoked both barrels of a shotgun. At least, that's what I'm picking up on the RHD freek."

Bosch's scanner did not pick up the RHD frequency. That was why he had not heard any of the early radio traffic on the call. The suits had apparently switched freeks only to notify Staff Two's driver of the address. If not for that, Bosch would not have heard about the call until the following morning when he came into the station. This angered him but he kept his voice steady. He wanted to get what he could from Kleinman.

"It's Moore, isn't it?"

"Looks like it," Kleinman said. "His shield is on the bureau there. Wallet. But like I said, nobody's going to make a visual ID from the body. So nothing is for sure."

"How did this all go down?"

"Look, Bosch, I'm busy here, you know what I mean? This doesn't concern you. RHD has it."

"No, you're wrong, man. It does concern me. I should've gotten first call from you. I want to know how it went down so I understand why I didn't."

"Awright, Bosch, it went like this. We get a call out from the owner of the dump says he's got a stiff in the bathroom of room seven. We send a unit out and they call back and say, yeah, we got the stiff. But they called back on a land line—no radio—'cause they saw the badge and the wallet on the bureau and knew it was Moore. Or, at least, thought it was him. We'll see. Anyway, I called Captain Grupa at home and he called the AC. The hats were called in and you were not. That's the way it goes. So if you have a beef, it's with Grupa or maybe the AC, not me. I'm clean."

Bosch didn't say anything. He knew that sometimes when he was quiet, the person he needed information from would eventually fill the silence.

"It's out of our hands now," Kleinman said. "Shit, the TV and *Times* are out there. *Daily News.* They figure it's Moore, like everybody else. It's a big mess. You'd think the fire up on the hill would be enough to keep them occupied. No way. They're out there lined up on Western. I gotta send another car over for media control. So,

Bosch, you should be happy you aren't involved. It's Christmas, for Chrissake."

But that wasn't good enough. Bosch should have been called and then it should have been his decision when to call out RHD. Someone had taken him out of the process altogether and that still burned him. He said good-bye and lit another cigarette. He got his gun out of the cabinet above the sink and hooked it to the belt on his blue jeans. Then he put on a light-tan sport coat over the Army green sweater he was wearing.

It was dark outside now and through the sliding glass door he could see the fire line across the pass. It burned brightly on the black silhouette of the hill. It was a crooked devil's grin moving to the crest.

From out in the darkness below his house he heard the coyote. Howling at the rising moon or the fire, or maybe just at himself for being alone and in the dark.

Two

BOSCH DROVE DOWN OUT OF THE HILLS INTO HOLLY-
wood, traveling mostly on deserted streets until he reached the Boulevard. On the sidewalks there were the usual groupings of runaways
and transients. There were strolling prostitutes—he saw one with a
red Santa hat on. Business is business, even on Christmas night. There
were elegantly made up women sitting on bus benches who were not
really women and not really waiting for buses. The tinsel and Christmas lights strung across the Boulevard at each intersection added
a surreal touch to the neon glitz and grime. Like a whore with too
much makeup, he thought—if there was such a thing.

But it wasn't the scene that depressed Bosch. It was Cal Moore.
Bosch had been expecting this for nearly a week, since the moment he
heard that Moore had failed to show up for roll call. For most of the
cops at Hollywood Division it wasn't a question of whether Moore was
dead. It was just a question of how long before his body turned up.

Moore had been a sergeant heading up the division's street narcotics unit. It was a night job and his unit worked the Boulevard
exclusively. It was known in the division that Moore had separated
from his wife and replaced her with whiskey. Bosch had found that
out firsthand the one time he had spent time with the narc. He had
also learned that there might be something more than just marital

problems and early burnout plaguing him. Moore had spoken obliquely of Internal Affairs and a personnel investigation.

It all added up to a heavy dose of Christmas depression. As soon as Bosch heard they were starting a search for Cal Moore, he knew. The man was dead.

And so did everyone else in the department, though nobody said this out loud. Not even the media said it. At first the department tried to handle it quietly. Discreet questions at Moore's apartment in Los Feliz. A few helicopter runs over the nearby hills in Griffith Park. But then a TV reporter was tipped and all the other stations and the newspapers followed the story for the ride. The media dutifully reported on the progress of the search for the missing cop, Moore's photograph was pinned to the bulletin board in the Parker Center press room and the weight of the department made the standard pleas to the public. It was drama. Or, at least, it was good video; horseback searches, air searches, the police chief holding up the photo of the darkly handsome and serious-looking sergeant. But nobody said they were looking for a dead man.

Bosch stopped the car for the light at Vine and watched a man wearing a sandwich board cross the street. His stride was quick and jerky and his knees continuously popped the cardboard sign up in the air. Bosch saw there was a satellite photograph of Mars pasted on the board with a large section of it circled. Written in large letters below was REPENT! THE FACE OF THE LORD WATCHES US! Bosch had seen the same photograph on the cover of a tabloid while standing in line at a Lucky store, but the tabloid had claimed that the face was that of Elvis.

The light changed and he continued on toward Western. He thought of Moore. Outside of one evening spent drinking with him at a jazz bar near the Boulevard, he had not had much interaction with Moore. When Bosch had been transferred to Hollywood Division from RHD the year before, there had been hesitant handshakes and glad-to-know-yous from everyone in the division. But people generally kept their distance. It was understandable, since he had been rolled out of RHD on an IAD beef, and Bosch didn't mind.

Moore was one of those who didn't go out of his way to do much more than nod when they passed in the hall or saw each other at staff meetings. Which was also understandable since the homicide table where Bosch worked was in the first-floor detective bureau and Moore's squad, the Hollywood BANG—short for Boulevard Anti-Narcotics Group—was on the second floor of the station. Still, there had been the one encounter. For Bosch it had been a meeting to pick up some background information for a case he was working. For Moore it had been an opportunity to have many beers and many whiskeys.

Moore's BANG squad had the kind of slick, media-grabbing name the department favored but in reality was just five cops working out of a converted storage room and roaming Hollywood Boulevard at night, dragging in anybody with a joint or better in his pocket. BANG was a numbers squad, created to make as many arrests as possible in order to help justify requests for more manpower, equipment and, most of all, overtime in the following year's budget. It did not matter that the DA's office handed out probation deals on most of the cases and kicked the rest. What mattered were those arrest statistics. And if Channel 2 or 4 or a *Times* reporter from the Westside insert wanted to ride along one night and do a story on the BANG squad, all the better. There were numbers squads in every division.

At Western Bosch turned north and ahead he could see the flashing blue and yellow lights of the patrol cars and the lightning-bright strobes of TV cameras. In Hollywood such a display usually signaled the violent end of a life or the premiere of a movie. But Bosch knew nothing premiered in this part of town except thirteen-year-old hookers.

Bosch pulled to the curb a half block from the Hideaway and lit a cigarette. Some things about Hollywood never changed. They just came up with new names for them. The place had been a run-down dump thirty years ago when it was called the El Rio. It was a run-down dump now. Bosch had never been there but he had grown up in Hollywood and remembered. He had stayed in enough places like it. With his mother. When she was still alive.

The Hideaway was a 1940s-era courtyard motel that during the day would be nicely shaded by a large banyan tree which stood in its center. At night, the motel's fourteen rooms receded into a darkness only the glow of red neon invaded. Harry noticed that the E in the sign announcing MONTHLY RATES was out.

When he was a boy and the Hideaway was the El Rio, the area was already in decay. But there wasn't as much neon and the buildings, if not the people, looked fresher, less grim. There had been a Streamline Moderne office building that looked like an ocean liner docked next to the motel. It had set sail a long time ago and another mini-mall was there now.

Looking at the Hideaway from his parked car, Harry knew it was a sorry place to stay the night. A sorrier place to die. He got out and headed over.

Yellow crime scene tape was strung across the mouth of the courtyard and was manned by uniformed officers. At one end of the tape bright lights from TV cameras focused on a group of men in suits. The one with the gleaming, shaven scalp was doing all the talking. As Bosch approached, he realized that the lights were blinding them. They could not see past the interviewers. He quickly showed his badge to one of the uniforms, signed his name on the Crime Scene Attendance Log the cop held on a clipboard and slipped under the tape.

The door to room 7 was open and light from inside spilled out. The sound of an electric harp also wafted from the room and that told Bosch that Art Donovan had caught the case. The crime scene tech always brought a portable radio with him. And it was always tuned to The Wave, a new-age music channel. Donovan said the music brought a soothing calm to a scene where people had killed or been killed.

Harry walked through the door, holding a handkerchief over his mouth and nose. It didn't help. The odor that was like no other assaulted him as soon as he passed the threshold. He saw Donovan on his knees dusting fingerprint powder onto the dials of the air-conditioner unit in the wall below the room's front, and only, window.

"Cheers," Donovan said. He was wearing a painter's mask to guard against the odor and the intake of the black powder. "In the bathroom."

Bosch took a look around, quickly, since it was likely he would be told to leave as soon as the suits discovered him. The room's queen-sized bed was made with a faded pink coverlet. There was a single chair with a newspaper on it. Bosch walked over and noted that it was the *Times*, dated six days earlier. There was a bureau and mirror combination to the side of the bed. On top of it was an ashtray with a single butt pressed into it after being half smoked. There was also a .38 Special in a nylon boot holster, a wallet and a badge case. These last three had been dusted with the black fingerprint powder. There was no note on the bureau—the place Harry would've expected it to be.

"No note," he said, more to himself than Donovan.

"Nope. Nothing in the bathroom, either. Have a look. That is, if you don't mind losing your Christmas dinner."

Harry looked down the short hallway that went to the rear off the left side of the bed. The bathroom door was on the right and he felt reluctance as he approached. He believed there wasn't a cop alive who hadn't thought at least once of turning his own hand cold.

He stopped at the threshold. The body sat on the dingy white floor tile, its back propped against the tub. The first thing to register on Bosch was the boots. Gray snakeskins with bulldog heels. Moore had worn them the night they had met for drinks. One boot was still on the right foot and he could see the manufacturer's symbol, an *S* like a snake, on the worn rubber heel. The left boot was off and stood upright next to the wall. The exposed foot, which was in a sock, had been wrapped in a plastic evidence bag. The sock had once been white, Bosch guessed. But now it was grayish and the limb was slightly bloated.

On the floor next to the door jamb was a twenty-gauge shotgun with side-by-side barrels. The stock was splintered along the bottom edge. A four-inch-long sliver of wood lay on the tile and had been circled with a blue crayon by Donovan or one of the detectives.

Bosch had no time to deliberate on these facts. He just tried to take it all in. He raised his eyes the length of the body. Moore was wearing jeans and a sweatshirt. His hands were dropped at his sides. His skin was gray wax. The fingers thick with putrefaction, the forearms bulging like Popeye's. Bosch saw a misshapen tattoo on the right arm, a devil's grinning face below a halo.

The body was slumped back against the tub and it almost appeared that Moore had rolled his head back as if to dip it into the tub, maybe to wash his hair. But Bosch realized it only looked that way because most of the head was simply not there. It had been destroyed by the force of the double-barrel blast. The light blue tiles that enclosed the tub area were awash in dried blood. The brown drip trails all went down into the tub. Some of the tiles were cracked where shotgun pellets had struck.

Bosch felt the presence of someone behind him. He turned into the stare of Assistant Chief Irvin Irving. Irving was wearing no mask and holding no rag to his mouth and nose.

"Evening, Chief."

Irving nodded and said, "What brings you here, Detective?"

Bosch had seen enough to be able to put together what had happened. He stepped away from the threshold, moved around Irving and walked toward the front door. Irving followed. They passed two men from the medical examiner's office who were wearing matching blue jumpsuits. Outside the room Harry threw his handkerchief into a trash can brought to the scene by the cops. He lit a cigarette and noticed that Irving was carrying a manila file in his hand.

"I picked it up on my scanner," Bosch said. "Thought I'd come out since I'm supposed to be on call tonight. It's my division, it's supposed to be my call."

"Yes, well, when it was established who was in the room, I decided to move the case to Robbery-Homicide Division immediately. Captain Grupa contacted me. I made the decision."

"So it's already been established that's Moore in there?"

"Not quite." He held up the manila file. "I ran by records and pulled his prints. They will be the final factor, of course. There is also the dental—if there is enough left. But all other appearances lead to that conclusion. Whoever's in there checked in under the name Rodrigo Moya, which was the alias Moore used in BANG. And there's a Mustang parked behind the motel that was rented under that name. At the moment, I don't think there is much doubt here among the collective investigative team."

Bosch nodded. He had dealt with Irving before, when the older man was a deputy chief in command of the Internal Affairs Division. Now he was an AC, one of the top three men in the department, and his purview had been extended to include IAD, narcotics intelligence and investigation, and all detective services. Harry momentarily debated whether he should risk pushing the point about not getting the first call.

"I should have been called," he said anyway. "It's my case. You took it away before I even had it."

"Well, Detective, it was mine to take and give away, wouldn't you agree? There is no need to get upset. Call it streamlining. You know Robbery-Homicide handles all officer deaths. You would have had to pass it to them eventually. This saves time. There is no ulterior motive here other than expediency. That's the body of an officer in there. We owe it to him and his family, no matter what the circumstances of his death are, to move quickly and professionally."

Bosch nodded again and looked around. He saw an RHD detective named Sheehan in a doorway below the MONTHLY RATE sign near the front of the motel. He was questioning a man of about sixty who was wearing a sleeveless T-shirt despite the evening chill and chewing a sodden cigar stump. The manager.

"Did you know him?" Irving asked.

"Moore? No, not really. I mean, yes, I knew him. We worked the same division, so we knew each other. He was on night shift mostly, working the streets. We didn't have much contact..."

Bosch did not know why in that moment he decided to lie. He wondered if Irving had read it in his voice. He changed the subject.

"So, it's suicide—is that what you told the reporters?"

"I did not tell the reporters a thing. I talked to them, yes. But I said nothing about the identity of the body in this room. And will not, until it is officially confirmed. You and I can stand here and say we are pretty sure that is Calexico Moore in there but I won't give that to them until we've done every test, dotted every *i* on the death certificate."

He slapped the manila file hard on his thigh.

"This is why I pulled his personnel file. To expedite. The prints will go with the body to the medical examiner." Irving looked back toward the door of the motel room. "But you were inside, Detective Bosch, you tell me."

Bosch thought a moment. Is this guy interested, or is he just pulling my chain? This was the first time he had dealt with Irving outside of the adversarial situation of an Internal Affairs investigation. He decided to take a chance.

"Looks like he sits down on the floor by the tub, takes off his boot and pulls both triggers with his toe. I mean, I assume it was both barrels, judging by the damage. He pulls the triggers with his toe, the recoil throws the shotgun into the door jamb, splintering off a piece of the stock. His head goes the other way. Onto the wall and into the tub. Suicide."

"There you go," Irving said. "Now I can tell Detective Sheehan that you concur. Just as if you had gotten the first call out. No reason for anybody to feel left out."

"That's not the point, Chief."

"What is the point, Detective? That you can't go along to get along? That you do not accept the command decisions of this department? I am losing my patience with you, Detective. Something I had hoped would never happen to me again."

Irving was standing too close to Bosch, his wintergreen breath puffing right in his face. It made Bosch feel pinned down by the man and he wondered if it was done on purpose. He stepped back and said, "But no note."

"No note yet. We still have some things to check."

Bosch wondered what. Moore's apartment and office would have been checked when he first turned up missing. Same with his wife's home. What was left? Could Moore have mailed a note to somebody? It would have arrived by now.

"When did it happen?"

"Hopefully, we'll get an idea from the autopsy tomorrow morning. But I am guessing he did it shortly after he checked in. Six days ago. In his first interview, the manager said Moore checked in six days ago and hadn't been seen outside the room since. This jibes with the condition of the room, the condition of the body, the date on the newspaper."

The autopsy was tomorrow morning. That told Bosch that Irving had this one greased. It usually took three days to get an autopsy done. And the Christmas holiday would back things up even further.

Irving seemed to know what he was thinking.

"The acting chief medical examiner has agreed to do it tomorrow morning. I explained there would be speculation in the media that would not be fair to the man's wife or the department. She agreed to cooperate. After all, the acting chief wants to become the permanent chief. She knows the value of cooperation."

Bosch didn't say anything.

"So we will know then. But nobody, the manager included, saw Sergeant Moore after he checked in six days ago. He left specific instructions that he was absolutely not to be disturbed. I think he went ahead and did it shortly after checking in."

"So why didn't they find him sooner?"

"He paid for a month in advance. He demanded no disturbances. A place like this, they don't offer daily maid service anyway. The manager thought he was a drunk who was either going to go on a binge or try to dry out. Either way, a place like this, the manager can't be choosey. A month, that's $600. He took the money.

"And they made good on their promise not to go to room seven until today, when the manager's wife noticed that Mr. Moya's car—the Mustang—had been broken into last night. That and, of course, they were curious. They knocked on his door to tell him but he didn't answer. They used a passkey. The smell told them what was happening as soon as they opened the door."

Irving said that Moore/Moya had set the air-conditioner on its highest and coldest level to slow decomposition and keep the odor contained in the room. Wet towels had been laid across the floor at the bottom of the front door to further seal the room.

"Nobody heard the shot?" Bosch asked.

"Not that we found. The manager's wife is nearly deaf and he says he didn't hear anything. They live in the last room on the other side. We've got stores on one side, an office building on the other. They all close at night. Alley behind. We are going through the registry and will try to track other guests that were here the first few days Moore was. But the manager says he never rented the rooms on either side of Moore's. He figured Moore might get loud if he was detoxing cold turkey.

"And, Detective, it is a busy street—bus stop right out front. It could have been that nobody heard a thing. Or if they heard it, didn't know what it was."

After some thought, Bosch said, "I don't get renting the place for a month. I mean, why? If the guy was going to off himself, why try to hide it for so long? Why not do it and let them find your body, end of story?"

"That's a tough one," Irving said. "Near as I can figure it, he wanted to cut his wife a break."

Bosch raised his eyebrows. He didn't get it.

"They were separated," Irving said. "Maybe he didn't want to put this on her during the holidays. So he tried to hold up the news a couple weeks, maybe a month."

That seemed pretty thin to Bosch but he had no better explanation at the moment. He could think of nothing else to ask at the moment. Irving changed the subject, signaling that Bosch's visit to the crime scene was over.

"So, Detective, how is the shoulder?"

"It's fine."

"I heard you went down to Mexico to polish your Spanish while you mended."

Bosch didn't reply. He wasn't interested in this banter. He wanted to tell Irving that he didn't buy the scene, even with all the evidence and explanations that had been gathered. But he couldn't say why, and until he could, he would be better off keeping quiet.

Irving was saying, "I have never thought that enough of our officers—the non-Latins, of course—make a good enough effort to learn the second language of this city. I want to see the whole depart—"

"Got a note," Donovan called from the room.

Irving broke away from Bosch without another word and headed to the door. Sheehan followed him into the room along with a suit Bosch recognized as an Internal Affairs detective named John Chastain. Harry hesitated a moment before following them in.

One of the ME techs was standing in the hallway near the bathroom door with the others gathered around him. Bosch wished he hadn't thrown away his handkerchief. He kept the cigarette in his mouth and breathed in deeply.

"Right rear pocket," the tech said. "There's putrefaction but you can make it out. It was folded over twice so the inside surface is pretty clean."

Irving backed out of the hallway holding a plastic evidence bag up and looking at the small piece of paper inside it. The others crowded around him. Except for Bosch.

The paper was gray like Moore's skin. Bosch thought he could see one line of blue writing on the paper. Irving looked over at him as if seeing him for the first time. "Bosch, you will have to go."

Harry wanted to ask what the note said but knew he would be rejected. He saw a satisfied smirk on Chastain's face.

At the yellow tape he stopped to light another cigarette. He heard the clicking of high heels and turned to see one of the reporters, a blonde he recognized from Channel 2, coming at him with a wireless microphone in her hand and a model's phoney smile on her face. She moved in on him in a well-practiced and quick maneuver. But before she could speak Harry said, "No comment. I'm not on the case."

"Can't you just—"

"No comment."

The smile dropped off her face as quick as a guillotine's blade. She turned away angrily. But within a moment her heels were clicking sharply again as she moved with her cameraman into position for the A-shot, the one her report would lead with. The body was coming out. The strobes flared and the six cameramen formed a gauntlet. The two medical examiner's men, pushing the covered body on a gurney, passed through it on the way to the waiting blue van. Harry noticed that a grim-faced Irving, walking stoically erect, trailed behind—but not far enough behind to be left out of the video frame. After all, any appearance on the nightly news was better than none, especially for a man with an eye on the chief's office.

After that, the crime scene began to break up. Everybody was leaving. The reporters, cops, everybody. Bosch ducked under the yellow tape and was looking around for Donovan or Sheehan when Irving came up on him.

"Detective, on second thought, there is something I need you to do that will help expedite matters. Detective Sheehan has to finish securing the scene here. But I want to beat the media to Moore's wife. Can you handle next-of-kin notification? Of course, nothing is definite but I want his wife to know what is happening."

Bosch had made such a show of indignation earlier, he couldn't back away now. He wanted part of the case; he got it.

"Give me the address," he said.

A few minutes later Irving was gone and the uniforms were pulling down the yellow tape. Bosch saw Donovan heading to his van, carrying the shotgun, which was wrapped in plastic, and several smaller evidence bags.

Harry used the van's bumper to tie his shoe while Donovan stowed the evidence bags in a wooden box that had once carried Napa Valley wine.

"What do you want, Harry? I just found out you weren't supposed to be here."

"That was before. This is now. I just got put on the case. I got next-of-kin duty."

"Some case to be put on."

"Yeah, well, you take what they give. What did he say?"

"Who?"

"Moore."

"Look, Harry, this is—"

"Look, Donnie, Irving gave me next of kin. I think that cuts me in. I just want to know what he said. I knew this guy, okay? It won't go anywhere else."

Donovan exhaled heavily, reached into the box and began sorting through the evidence bags.

"Really didn't say much at all. Nothing that profound."

He turned on a flashlight and put the beam on the bag with the note in it. Just one line.

I found out who I was

Three

THE ADDRESS IRVING HAD GIVEN HIM WAS IN CAN-
yon Country, nearly an hour's drive north of Hollywood. Bosch took
the Hollywood Freeway north, then connected with the Golden State
and took it through the dark cleft of the Santa Susana Mountains.
Traffic was sparse. Most people were inside their homes eating roasted
turkey and dressing, he guessed. Bosch thought of Cal Moore and
what he did and what he left behind.

I found out who I was.

Bosch had no clue to what the dead cop had meant by the one line
scratched on a small piece of paper and placed in the back pocket.
Harry's single experience with Moore was all he had to go on. And
what was that? A couple of hours drinking beer and whiskey with a
morose and cynical cop. There was no way to know what had happened in the meantime. To know how the shell that protected him
had corroded.

He thought back on his meeting with Moore. It had been only a few
weeks before and it had been business, but Moore's problems managed to come up. They met on a Tuesday night at the Catalina Bar
& Grill. Moore was working but the Catalina was just a half block
south of the Boulevard. Harry was waiting at the bar in the back
corner. They never charged cops the cover.

Moore slid onto the next stool and ordered a shot and a Henry's, the same as Bosch had on the bar in front of him. He was wearing jeans and a sweatshirt that hung loose over his belt. Standard undercover attire and he looked at home in it. The thighs of the jeans were worn gray. The sleeves of the sweatshirt were cut off and peeking from below the frayed fringe of the right arm was the face of a devil tattooed in blue ink. Moore was handsome in a rugged way, but he was at least three days past needing a shave and he had a look about him, an unsteadiness—like a hostage released after long captivity and torment. In the Catalina crowd he stood out like a garbage man at a wedding. Harry noticed that the narc hooked gray snakeskin boots on the side rungs of the stool. They were bulldoggers, the boots favored by rodeo ropers because the heels angled forward to give better traction when taking down a roped calf. Harry knew street narcs called them "dustbusters" because they served the same purpose when they were taking down a suspect high on angel dust.

They smoked and drank and small-talked at first, trying to establish connections and boundaries. Bosch noticed that the name Calexico truly represented Moore's mixed heritage. Dark complexioned, with hair black as ink, thin hips and wide shoulders, Moore's dark, ethnic image was contradicted by his eyes. They were the eyes of a California surfer, green like antifreeze. And there was not a trace of Mexico in his voice.

"There's a border town named Calexico. Right across from Mexicali. Ever been there?"

"I was born there. That's how come I got the name."

"I've never been."

"Don't worry, you haven't missed much. Just a border town like all the rest. I still go on down every now and then."

"Family?"

"Nah, not anymore."

Moore signaled the bartender for another round, then lit a cigarette off the one he had smoked down to the filter.

"I thought you had something to ask about," he said.

"Yeah, I do. I gotta case."

The drinks arrived and Moore threw his shot back in one smooth movement. He had ordered another before the bartender had finished writing on the tab.

Bosch began to outline his case. He had caught it a few weeks earlier and so far had gotten nowhere. The body of a thirty-year-old male, later identified through fingerprints as James Kappalanni of Oahu, Hawaii, was dumped beneath the Hollywood Freeway crossing over Gower Street. He had been strangled with an eighteen-inch length of baling wire with wooden dowels at the ends, the better to grip the wire with after it had been wrapped around somebody's neck. Very neat and efficient job. Kappalanni's face was the bluish gray color of an oyster. The blue Hawaiian, the acting chief medical examiner had called him when she did the autopsy. By then Bosch knew through NCIC and DOJ computer runs that in life he had also been known as Jimmy Kapps, and that he had a drug record that printed out about as long as the wire somebody had used to take his life.

"So it wasn't too big a surprise when the ME cut him open and found forty-two rubbers in his gut," Bosch said.

"What was in them?"

"This Hawaiian shit called glass. A derivative of ice, I am told. I remember when ice was a fad a few years back. Anyway, this Jimmy Kapps was a courier. He was carrying this glass inside his stomach, had probably just gotten off the plane from Honolulu when he walks into the baling wire.

"I hear this glass is expensive stuff and the market for it is extremely competitive. I guess I'm looking for some background, maybe shake an idea loose here. 'Cause I've got nothing on this. No ideas on who did Jimmy Kapps."

"Who told you about glass?"

"Major narcs downtown. Not much help."

"Nobody really knows shit, that's why. They tell you about black ice?"

"A little. That's the competition, they said. Comes from the Mexicans. That's about all they said."

Moore looked around for the bartender, who was down at the other end of the bar and seemed to be purposely ignoring them.

"It's all relatively new," he said. "Basically, black ice and glass are the same thing. Same results. Glass comes from Hawaii. And black ice comes from Mexico. The drug of the twenty-first century, I guess you'd call it. If I was a salesman I'd say it covers all the demographics. Basically, somebody took coke, heroin and PCP and rocked 'em all up together. A powerful little rock. It's supposed to do everything. It's got a crack high but the heroin also gives it legs. I'm talking about hours, not minutes. Then it's got just a pinch of dust, the PCP, to give it a kick toward the end of the ride. Man, once it really takes hold on the streets, they get a major market going, then, shit, forget about it, there'll be nothing but a bunch of zombies walking around."

Bosch said nothing. Much of this he already knew but Moore was going good and he didn't want to knock him off track with a question. He lit a cigarette and waited.

"Started in Hawaii," Moore said. "Oahu. They were making ice over there. Just plain ice, they called it. That's rocking up PCP and coke. Very profitable. Then it evolved. They added heroin. Good stuff, too. Asian white. Now they call it glass. I guess that was their motto or something; smooth as glass.

"But in this business there is no lock on anything. There is only price and profit."

He held up both hands to signify the importance of these two factors.

"The Hawaiians had a good thing but they had trouble getting it to the mainland. You got boats and you got planes and these can be regulated to a good degree. Or, at least, to some degree. I mean, they can be checked and watched. So they end up with couriers like this Kapps who swallow the shit and fly it over. But even that is harder than it seems. First of all, you got a limited quantity that you can move. What, forty-two balloons in this guy? What was that, about a hundred grams? That's not much for the trouble. Plus you got the DEA, they got people in the planes, airports. They're looking for people like Kapps. They call them 'rubber smugglers.' They've got a whole shakedown profile. You know, a list of what to look for. People sweating but with dry lips, licking their lips—the anti-diarrhetic does that. That Kaopectate shit. The rubber smugglers swig that shit like it's Pepsi. It gives them away.

"Anyway, what I am saying is that the Mexicans got it a whole helluva lot easier. Geography is on their side. They have boats and planes and they also have a two-thousand-mile border that is almost nonexistent as a form of control and interdiction. They say the feds stop one pound of coke for every ten that gets by them. Well, when it comes to black ice, they aren't even getting an ounce at the border. I know of not one single black ice bust at the border."

He paused to light a cigarette. Bosch saw a tremor in his hand as he held the match.

"What the Mexicans did was steal the recipe. They started replicating glass. Only they're using homegrown brown heroin, including the tar. That's the pasty shit at the bottom of the cooking barrel. Lot of impurities in it, turns it black. That's how they come up with calling it black ice. They make it cheaper, they move it cheaper and they sell it cheaper. They've 'bout put the Hawaiians out of the business. And it's their own fucking product."

Moore seemed to conclude there.

Harry asked, "Have you heard anything about the Mexicans taking down the Hawaiian couriers, maybe trying to corner the market that way?"

"Not up here, at least. See, you gotta remember, the Mexicans make the shit. But they ain't the ones necessarily selling it on the street. You're talking several levels removed when you get down to the street."

"But they still have to be calling the shots."

"True. That's true."

"So who put down Jimmy Kapps?"

"Got me, Bosch. This is the first I've heard about it."

"Your team ever make any arrests of black ice dealers? Shake anybody down?"

"A few, but you're talking about the lowest rungs on the ladder. White boys. Rock dealers on the Boulevard are usually white boys. It's easier for them to do business. Now, that doesn't mean it isn't Mexicans givin' it to them. It also doesn't mean it ain't South-Central gangs givin' it. So the arrests we've made probably wouldn't help you any."

He banged his empty beer mug on the bar until the bartender looked up and was signaled for another round. Moore seemed to be getting morose and Bosch hadn't gotten much help from him.

"I need to go further up the ladder. Can you get me anything? I don't have shit on this and it's three weeks old. I've got to come up with something or drop it and move on."

Moore was looking straight ahead at the bottles that lined the rear wall of the bar.

"Look, I'll see what I can do," he said. "But you gotta remember, we don't spend time on black ice. Coke and dust, some reefer, that's what we deal in day in and day out. Not the exotics. We're a numbers squad, man. But I've got a connection at DEA. I'll talk to him."

Bosch looked at his watch. It was near midnight and he wanted to go. He watched Moore light a cigarette though he still had one burning in the crowded ashtray. Harry still had a full beer and shot in front of him but stood up and began digging in his pockets for money.

"Thanks, man," he said. "See what you can do and let me know."

"Sure," Moore said. After a beat he said, "Hey, Bosch?"

"What?"

"I know about you. You know...what's been said around the station. I know you've been in the bucket. I wonder, did you ever come up against an IAD suit name of Chastain?"

Bosch thought a moment. John Chastain was one of the best. In IAD, complaints were classified at the end as sustained, unsustained or unfounded. He was known as "Sustained" Chastain.

"I've heard of him," he said. "He's a three, runs one of the tables."

"Yeah, I know he's a detective third grade. Shit, everybody knows that. What I mean is, did he…is he one of them that came after you?"

"No, it was always somebody else."

Moore nodded. He reached over and took the shot that had been in front of Bosch. He emptied it, then said, "Chastain, from what you've heard, do you think he is good at what he does? Or is he just another suit with a shine on his ass?"

"I guess it depends on what you mean by good. But, no, I don't think any of them are good. Job like that, they can't be. But give 'em the chance, any one of them will burn you down and bag your ashes."

Bosch was torn between wanting to ask what was going on and not wanting to step into it. Moore said nothing. He was giving Bosch the choice. Harry decided to keep out of it.

He said, "If they've got a hard-on for you, there isn't much you can do. Call the union and get a lawyer. Do what he says and don't give the suits anything you don't have to."

Moore nodded silently once more. Harry put down two twenty-dollar bills that he hoped would cover the tab and still leave something for the bartender. Then he walked out.

He never saw Moore again.

Bosch connected with the Antelope Valley Freeway and headed northeast. On the Sand Canyon overpass he looked across the free-way and saw a white TV van heading south. There was a large *9* painted on its side. It meant Moore's wife would already know by the time Bosch arrived. And Bosch felt a slight twinge of guilt at that, mixed with relief that he would not be the one breaking the news.

The thought made him realize that he did not know the widow's name. Irving had given him only an address, apparently assuming Bosch knew her name. As he turned off the freeway onto the Sierra Highway, he tried to recall the newspaper stories he had read during the week. They had carried her name.

But it didn't come to him. He remembered that she was a teacher—an English teacher, he thought—at a high school in the Valley. He remembered that the reports said they had no children. And he remembered that she had been separated a few months from her husband. But the name, her name, eluded him.

He turned on to Del Prado, watched the numbers painted on the curbs and then finally pulled to a stop in front of the house that had once been Cal Moore's home.

It was a common ranch-style home, the kind minted by the hundreds in the planned communities that fed the freeways to overflow each morning. It looked large, like maybe four bedrooms, and Bosch thought that was odd for a childless couple. Maybe there had been plans at one time.

The light above the front door was not on. No one was expected. No one was wanted. Still, in the moonlight and shadow, Bosch could see the front lawn and knew that the mower was at least a month past due. The tall grass surrounded the post of the white Ritenbaugh Realty sign that was planted near the sidewalk.

There were no cars in the driveway and the garage door was closed, its two windows dark empty sockets. A single dim light shone from behind the curtained picture window next to the front door. He wondered what she would be like and if she would feel guilt or anger. Or both.

He threw his cigarette into the street and then got out and stepped on it. Then he headed past the sad-looking For Sale sign to the door.

Four

THE MAT ON THE PORCH BELOW THE FRONT DOOR
said welcome but it was worn and nobody had bothered to shake the
dust off it in some time. Bosch noticed all of this because he kept his
head down after knocking. He knew that looking at anything would
be better than looking at this woman.

Her voice answered after his second knock.

"Go away. No comment."

Bosch had to smile, thinking how he had used that one himself
tonight.

"Hello, Mrs. Moore? I'm not a reporter. I'm with the L.A. police."

The door came open a few inches and her face was there, backlit
and hidden in shadow. Bosch could see the chain lock stretching
across the opening. Harry was ready with his badge case already out
and opened.

"Yes?"

"Mrs. Moore?"

"Yes?"

"I am Harry Bosch. Um, I'm a detective, LAPD. And I've been
sent out—could I come in? I need . . . to ask you a few questions and
inform you of some, uh, developments in—"

"You're late. I've had Channel 4 and 5 and 9 already out here.

When you knocked I figured you were somebody else. Two or seven. I can't think who else."

"Can I come in, Mrs. Moore?"

He put his badge wallet away. She closed the door and he heard the chain slide out of its track. The door came open and she signaled him in with her arm. He stepped into an entryway of rust-colored Mexican tile. There was a round mirror on the wall and he saw her in it, closing and locking the door. He saw she held tissue in one hand.

"Will this take long?" she asked.

He said no and she led him to the living room, where she took a seat on an overstuffed chair covered in brown leather. It looked very comfortable and it was next to the fireplace. She motioned him toward a couch that faced the fireplace. This was where the guests always sat. The fireplace had the glowing remnants of a dying fire. On the table next to where she sat he saw a box of tissues and a stack of papers. More like reports or maybe scripts; some were in plastic covers.

"Book reports," she said, having noticed his gaze. "I assigned books to my students with the reports due before the Christmas vacation. It was going to be my first Christmas alone and I guess I wanted to make sure I had something to keep me busy."

Bosch nodded. He looked around the rest of the room. In his job, he learned a lot about people from their rooms, the way they lived. Often the people could no longer tell him themselves. So he learned from his observations and believed that he was good at it.

The room in which they sat was spare. Not much furniture. It didn't look like a lot of entertaining of friends or family happened here. There was a large bookshelf at one end of the room that was filled by hardback novels and oversized art books. No TV. No sign of children. It was a place for quiet work or fireside talks.

But no more.

In the corner opposite the fireplace was a five-foot Christmas tree with white lights and red balls, a few homemade ornaments that looked as if they might have been passed down through generations. He liked the idea that she had put up the tree by herself. She had continued her life and its routines amidst the ruins of her marriage. She had put the tree up for herself. It made him feel her strength. She had a hard shell of hurt and maybe loneliness but there was a sense of strength, too. The tree said she was the kind of woman who would survive this, would make it through. On her own. He wished he could remember her name.

"Before you start," she said, "can I ask you something?"

The light from the reading lamp next to her chair was low wattage but he could clearly see the intensity of her brown eyes.

"Sure."

"Did you do that on purpose? Let the reporters come up here first so you wouldn't have to do the dirty work? That's what my husband used to call it. Telling families. He called it the dirty work and he said the detectives always tried to get out of it."

Bosch felt his face grow warm. There was a clock on the fireplace mantel that now seemed to be ticking very loudly in the silence. He finally managed to say, "I was told only a short time ago to come here. I had a little trouble finding it. I—"

He stopped. She knew.

"I'm sorry. I guess you're right. I took my time."

"It's okay. I shouldn't put you on the spot. It must be a terrible job."

Bosch wished he had a fedora like the ones the detectives in the old movies always had; that way he could hold it in his hands and fiddle with it and let his fingers trace its brim, give him something to do. He looked at her closely now and saw the quality of damaged beauty about her. Mid-thirties, he guessed, with brown hair and blonde highlights, she seemed agile, like a runner. Clearly defined jawline above the taut muscles of her neck. She had not used makeup to try to hide the lightly etched lines that curved under her eyes. She wore blue jeans and a baggy white sweatshirt that he thought might have been her husband's once. Bosch wondered how much of Calexico Moore she still carried in her heart.

Harry actually admired her for taking the shot at him about the dirty work. He knew he deserved it. In the three minutes he had known her he thought she reminded him of someone but he wasn't sure who. Someone from his past maybe. There was a quiet tenderness there beside her strength. He kept bringing his eyes back to hers. They were magnets.

"Anyway, I'm Detective Harry Bosch," he began again, hoping she might introduce herself.

"Yes, I've heard of you. I remember the newspaper articles. And I'm sure my husband spoke of you—I think it was when they sent you out to Hollywood Division. Couple years ago. He said before that one of the studios had paid you a lot of money to use your name and do a TV movie about a case. He said you bought one of those houses on stilts up in the hills."

Bosch nodded reluctantly and changed the subject.

"I don't know what the reporters told you, Mrs. Moore, but I have been sent out to tell you that it appears your husband has been found and he is dead. I am sorry to have had to tell you this. I—"

"I knew and you knew and every cop in town knew it would come to this. I didn't talk to the reporters. I didn't need to. I told them no comment. When that many of them come to your house on Christmas night, you know it's because of bad news."

He nodded and looked down at the imaginary hat in his hands.

"So, are you going to tell me? Was it an official suicide? Did he use a gun?"

Bosch nodded and said, "It looks like it but nothing is definite un—"

"Until the autopsy. I know, I know. I'm a cop's wife. Was, I mean. I know what you can say and can't say. You people can't even be straight with me. Until then there are always secrets to keep to yourselves."

He saw the hard edge enter her eyes, the anger.

"That's not true, Mrs. Moore. I'm just trying to soften the im—"

"Detective Bosch, if you want to tell me something, just tell me."

"Yes, Mrs. Moore, it was with a gun. If you want the details, I can give you the details. Your husband, if it was your husband, took his face off with a shotgun. Gone completely. So, we have to make sure it was him and we have to make sure he did it himself, before we can say anything for sure. We are not trying to keep secrets. We just don't have all the answers yet."

She leaned back in her chair, away from light. In the veil of shadows Bosch saw the look on her face. The hardness and anger in her eyes had softened. Her shoulders seemed to untighten. He felt ashamed.

"I'm sorry," he said. "I don't know why I told you that. I should have just—"

"That's okay. I guess I deserved it.... I apologize, too."

She looked at him then without anger in her eyes. He had broken through the shell. He could see that she needed to be with someone. The house was too big and too dark to be alone in right now. All the Christmas trees and book reports in the world couldn't change that. But there was more than that making Bosch want to stay. He found that he was instinctively attracted to her. For Bosch it had never been an attraction of an opposite but the reverse of that myth. He had always seen something of himself in the women who attracted him. Why it was this way, he never understood. It was just there. And now this woman whose name he didn't even know was there and he was being drawn to her. Maybe it was a reflection of himself and his own needs, but it was there and he had seen it. It hooked him and made him want to know what had etched the circles beneath such sharp eyes. Like himself, he knew, she carried her scars on the inside, buried deep, each one a mystery. She was like him. He knew.

"I'm sorry but I don't know your name. The deputy chief just gave me the address and said go."

She smiled at his predicament.

"It's Sylvia."

He nodded.

"Sylvia. Um, is that coffee I smell by any chance?"

"Yes. Would you like a cup?"

"That would be great, if it's not too much trouble."

"Not at all."

She got up and as she passed in front of him so did his doubts.

"Listen, I'm sorry. Maybe I should go. You have a lot to think about and I'm intruding here. I've—"

"Please stay. I could use the company."

She didn't wait for an answer. The fire made a popping sound as the flames found the last pocket of air. He watched her head toward the kitchen. He waited a beat, took another look around the room and stood up and headed toward the lighted doorway of the kitchen.

"Black is fine."

"Of course. You're a cop."

"You don't like them much, do you. Cops."

"Well, let's just say I don't have a very good record with them."

Her back was to him and she put two mugs on the counter and poured coffee from a glass pot. He leaned against the doorway next to the refrigerator. He was unsure what to say, whether to press on with business or not.

"You have a nice home."

"No. It's a nice house, not a home. We're selling it. I guess I should say I'm selling it now."

She still hadn't turned around.

"You know you can't blame yourself for whatever he did."

It was a meager offering and he knew it.

"Easier said than done."

"Yeah."

There was a long moment of silence then before Bosch decided to get on with it.

"There was a note."

She stopped what she was doing but still did not turn.

"'I found out who I was.' That's all he said."

She didn't say anything. One of the mugs was still empty.

"Does it mean anything to you?"

She finally turned to him. In the bright kitchen light, he could see the salty tracks that tears had left on her face. It made him feel inadequate, that he was nothing and could do nothing to help heal her.

"I don't know. My husband...he was caught on the past."

"What do you mean?"

"He was just—he was always going back. He liked the past better than the present or the hope of the future. He liked to go back to the time he was growing up. He liked...He couldn't let things go."

He watched tears slide into the grooves below her eyes. She turned back to the counter and finished pouring the coffee.

"What happened to him?" he asked.

"What happens to anybody?" For a while after that she didn't speak, then said, "I don't know. He wanted to go back. He had a need for something back there."

Everybody has a need for their past, Bosch thought. Sometimes it pulls harder on you than the future. She dried her eyes with tissue and then turned and gave him a mug. He sipped it before speaking.

"Once he told me he lived in a castle," she said. "That's what he called it, at least."

"In Calexico?" he asked.

"Yes, but it was for a short while. I don't know what happened. He never told me a lot about that part of his life. It was his father. At some point, he wasn't wanted anymore by his father. He and his mother had to leave Calexico—the castle, or whatever it was—and she took him back across the border with her. He liked to say he was from Calexico but he really grew up in Mexicali. I don't know if you've ever been there."

"Just to drive through. Never stopped."

"That's the general idea. Don't stop. But he grew up there."

She stopped and he waited her out. She was looking down at her coffee, an attractive woman who looked weary of this. She had not yet seen that this was a beginning for her as well as an end.

"It was something he never got over. The abandonment. He often went back there to Calexico. I didn't go but I know he did. Alone. I think he was watching his father. Maybe seeing what could have been. I don't know. He kept pictures from when he was growing up. Sometimes at night when he thought I was asleep, he'd take them out and look at them."

"Is he still alive, the father?"

She handed him a mug of coffee.

"I don't know. He rarely spoke of his father and when he did he said his father was dead. But I don't know if that was metaphorically dead or that he actually was dead. He was dead as far as Cal went. That was what mattered. It was a very private thing with Cal. He still felt the rejection, all these years later. I could not get him to talk about it. Or, when he would, he would just lie, say the old man meant nothing and that he didn't care. But he did. I could tell. After a while, after years, I have to say that I stopped trying to talk with him about it. And he would never bring it up. He'd just go down there—sometimes for a weekend, sometimes a day. He'd never talk about it when he came back."

"Do you have the photos?"

"No, he took them when he left. He'd never leave them."

Bosch sipped some coffee to give himself time to think.

"It seems," he began, "I don't know, it seems like . . . could this have had anything to do with . . ."

"I don't know. All I can tell you is that it had a lot to do with us. It was an obsession with him. It was more important to him than me. It's what ended it for us."

"What was he trying to find?"

"I don't know. In the last few years he shut me out. And I have to say that after a while I shut him out. That's how it ended."

Bosch nodded and looked away from her eyes. What else could he do? Sometimes his job took him too far inside people's lives and all he could do was stand there and nod. He was asking questions he felt guilty asking because he had no right to the answers. He was just the messenger boy here. He wasn't supposed to find out why somebody would hold a double-barrel shotgun up to his face and pull the triggers.

Still, the mystery of Cal Moore and the pain on her face wouldn't let him go. She was captivating in a way that went beyond her physical beauty. She was attractive, yes, but the hurt in her face, the tears and yet the strength in her eyes tugged at him. The thought that occurred to him was that she did not deserve this. How could Cal Moore have fucked up so badly?

He looked back at her.

"There was another thing he told me once. Uh, I've had some experience with IAD, uh, that's Internal—"

"I know what it is."

"Yes, well, he asked me for some advice. Asked me about if I knew somebody that was asking questions about him. Name of Chastain. Did Cal tell you about this? What it was about?"

"No, he didn't."

Her demeanor was changing. Bosch could actually see the anger welling up from inside again. Her eyes were very sharp. He had struck a nerve.

"But you knew about it, right?"

"Chastain came here once. He thought I would cooperate with whatever it was he was doing. He said I made a complaint about my husband, which was a lie. He wanted to go through the house and I told him to leave. I don't want to talk about this."

"When did Chastain come?"

"I don't know. Couple months ago."

"You warned Cal?"

She hesitated and then nodded.

Then Cal came to the Catalina and asked me for advice, Harry realized.

"You sure you don't know what it was about?"

"We were separated by then. We didn't talk. It was over between us. All I did was tell Cal that this man had come and that he had lied about who made the complaint. Cal said that was all they do. Lie. He said don't worry about it."

Harry finished his coffee but held the mug in his hand. She had known her husband had somehow fallen, had betrayed their future with his past, but she had stayed loyal. She had warned him about Chastain. Bosch couldn't fault her for that. He could only like her better.

"What are you doing here?" she asked.

"What?"

"If you are investigating my husband's death, I would assume you already know about IAD. You are either lying to me, too, or don't know. If that's the case, what are you doing here?"

He put the mug down on the counter. It gave him a few extra seconds.

"I was sent out by the assistant chief to tell you what was—"

"The dirty work."

"Right. I got stuck with the dirty work. But like I said, I sort of knew your husband and . . ."

"I don't think it's a mystery you can solve, Detective Bosch."

He nodded—the old standby.

"I teach English and Lit at Grant High in the Valley," she said. "I assign my students a lot of books written about L.A. so they can get a feel for the history and character of their community. Lord knows, few of them were born here. Anyway, one of the books I assign is *The Long Goodbye*. It's about a detective."

"I've read it."

"There is a line. I know it by heart. 'There is no trap so deadly as the trap you set for yourself.' Whenever I read that I think of my husband. And me."

She started to cry again. Silently, never taking her eyes off Bosch. This time he didn't nod. He saw the need in her eyes and crossed the room and put his hand on her shoulder. It felt awkward, but then she moved into him and leaned her head against his chest. He let her keep crying until she pulled away.

An hour later, Bosch was home. He picked up the half-filled glass of wine and the bottle that had been sitting on the table since dinner. He went out on the back porch and sat and drank and thought about things until early into the morning hours. The glow of the fire across the pass was gone. But now something burned within himself.

Calexico Moore had apparently answered a question that all people carry deep within themselves—that Harry Bosch, too, had longed to answer. *I found out who I was.*

And it had killed him. It was a thought that pushed a fist into Bosch's guts, into the most secret folds of his heart.

Five

THURSDAY, THE MORNING AFTER CHRISTMAS, WAS one of those days the postcard photographers pray for. There was no hint of smog in the sky. The fire in the hills had burned out and the smoke had long been blown over the hills by Pacific breezes. In its stead the Los Angeles basin basked under a blue sky and puffy cumulus clouds.

Bosch decided to take the long way down out of the hills, driving on Woodrow Wilson until it crossed Mulholland and then taking the winding route through Nichols Canyon. He loved the views of the hills covered with blue wisteria and violet ice plants, topped with aging million-dollar homes that gave the city its aura of fading glory. As he drove he thought of the night before and how it had made him feel to comfort Sylvia Moore. It made him feel like a cop in a Rockwell painting. Like he had made a difference.

Once he was out of the hills he took Genesee to Sunset and then cut over to Wilcox. He parked behind the station and walked past the fenced windows of the drunk tank into the detective bureau. The gloom in the squad room was thicker than cigarette smoke in a porno theater. The other detectives sat at their tables with their heads down, most talking quietly on the phone or with their faces buried in the paperwork that haunted their lives with its never-ceasing flow.

Harry sat down at the homicide table and looked across at Jerry Edgar, his some-of-the-time partner. There were no permanently assigned partners anymore. The bureau was shorthanded and there was a departmental hiring and promotion freeze because of budget cuts. They were down to five detectives on the homicide table. The bureau commander, Lieutenant Harvey "Ninety-eight" Pounds, managed this by working detectives solo except on key cases, dangerous assignments or when making arrests. Bosch liked working on his own, anyway, but most of the other detectives complained about it.

"What's going on?" Bosch asked Edgar. "Moore?"

Edgar nodded. They were alone at the table. Shelby Dunne and Karen Moshito usually came in after nine and Lucius Porter was lucky if he was sober enough to get in by ten.

"Little while ago Ninety-eight came out of the box and said they got the fingerprint match. It was Moore. He blew his own shit away."

They were silent for a few minutes after that. Harry scanned the paperwork on his desk but couldn't help thinking about Moore. He imagined Irving or Sheehan or maybe even Chastain calling Sylvia Moore to tell her the identification was confirmed. Harry could see his slim connection to the case disappearing like smoke. Without having to turn, he realized someone was standing behind him. He looked around to see Pounds looking down at him.

"Harry, c'mon in."

An invitation to the glass box. He looked at Edgar, who raised his eyes in a who-knows gesture. Harry got up and followed the lieutenant into his office at the head of the squad room. It was a small room with windows on three sides that enabled Pounds to look out on his charges but limit his actual contact with them. He didn't have to hear them or smell them or know them. The blinds that were often used to cut off his sight of them were open this morning.

"Sit down, Harry. I don't have to tell you not to smoke. Have a good Christmas?"

Bosch just looked at him. He was uncomfortable with this guy calling him Harry and asking him about Christmas. He hesitantly sat down.

"What's up?" he said.

"Let's not get hostile, Harry. I'm the one who should be hostile. I just heard you spent a good part of Christmas night at that dump motel, the Hideaway, where nobody in this world would want to be and where Robbery-Homicide happened to be conducting an investigation."

"I was on call," Bosch said. "And I should have been called out to the scene. I went by to see what was going on. Turned out, Irving needed me, anyway."

"That's fine, Harry, if you leave it at that. I have been told to tell you not to get any ideas about the Moore case."

"What's that supposed to mean?"

"Just what it sounds like it means."

"Look, if you—"

"Never mind, never mind." Pounds raised his hands in a calming gesture, then pinched the bridge of his nose, signifying the onset of a headache. He opened the center drawer of his desk and took out a small tin of aspirin. He took two without water.

"Enough said, okay?" Pounds said. "I'm not—I don't need to get into—"

Pounds made a choking sound and jumped up from his desk. He moved past Bosch and out of the box to the water fountain near the entrance to the bureau. Bosch didn't even watch him. He just sat in his chair. Pounds was back in a few moments and continued.

"Excuse me. Anyway, what I was saying was that I don't need an argument with you every time I bring you in here. I really think you have to work through this problem you have with dealing with the command structure of this department. You take it to extremes."

Bosch could still see chalky white aspirin caking at the corners of his mouth. Pounds cleared his throat again.

"I was just passing on an aside in your best—"

"Why doesn't Irving pass it on himself?"

"I didn't say—look, Bosch, forget it. Just forget it. You've been told and that's that. If you have any ideas about last night, about Moore, drop them. It's being handled."

"I am sure it is."

The warning delivered, Bosch stood up. He wanted to throw this guy through his glass wall but would settle for a cigarette out behind the drunk tank.

"Siddown," Pounds said. "That's not why I brought you in."

Bosch sat down again and quietly waited. He watched Pounds try to compose himself. He opened the drawer again and pulled out a wood ruler, which he absentmindedly manipulated in his hands while he began to talk.

"Harry, you know how many homicides we've caught in the division this year?"

The question came from left field. Harry wondered what Pounds was up to. He knew he had handled eleven cases himself, but he had been out of the rotation for six weeks during the summer while in Mexico recovering from the bullet wound. He figured the homicide squad for about seventy cases in the year. He said, "I have no idea."

"Well, I'm going to tell you," Pounds said. "Right now we are at sixty-six homicides for the year to date. And, of course, we've still got five days to go. Probably, we'll pick up another. I'm thinking, at least one. New Year's Eve is always trouble. We'll pro—"

"So what about it? I remember we had fifty-nine last year. Murder is going up. What else is new?"

"What is new is that the number of cases we have cleared is going down. It is less than half that number. Thirty-two out of sixty-six cases have been cleared. Now, a good number of those cases have been cleared by you. I have you with eleven cases. Seven have been cleared by arrest or other. We have warrants out on two others. Of the two you have open, one is idle pending developments and you are actively pursuing the James Kappalanni matter. Correct?"

Bosch nodded. He didn't like the way this was going but wasn't sure why.

"The problem is the overall record," Pounds said. "When taken in its entirety...well, it's a pitiful record of success."

Pounds slapped the ruler hard into his palm and shook his head. An idea was forming in Harry's mind about what this was about, but still there was a part missing. He wasn't sure exactly what Pounds was up to.

"Think of it," Pounds continued. "All those victims—and their families!—for whom justice eludes. And then, and then, think how badly the public's confidence in us, in this department, will erode when the *L.A. Times* trumpets across their Metro page that more than half the killers in Hollywood Division walk away from their crimes?"

"I don't think we have to worry about public confidence going down," Bosch said. "I don't think it can."

Pounds rubbed the bridge of his nose again and quietly said, "This is not the time for your unique cynical view of the job, Bosch. Don't bring your arrogance in here. I can take you off that table and put you on autos or maybe juvies any time I want to make the move. Get me? I'd gladly take the heat when you took a beef to the union."

"Then where's your homicide clearance rate going to be? What's it going to say in the Metro section then? Two thirds of the killers in Hollywood walk?"

Pounds put the ruler back in the drawer and closed it. Bosch thought there was a thin smile on his face and he began to believe he had just talked his way into a trap. Pounds then opened another drawer and brought a blue binder up onto the desk. It was the type used to keep records of a murder investigation but Bosch saw few pages inside it.

"Point well taken," Pounds said. "Which brings us to the point of this meeting. See, we're talking about statistics, Harry. We clear one more case and we're at the halfway mark. Instead of saying more than half get away, we can say half of the killers are caught. If we clear two more, we can say *more* than half are cleared. Get me?"

Pounds nodded when Bosch said nothing. He made a show of straightening the binder on his desk, then he looked directly at Bosch.

"Lucius Porter won't be back," he said. "Talked to him this morning. He is going stress-related. Said he is getting a doctor lined up."

Pounds reached into the drawer and pulled up another blue murder book. Then another. Bosch could see what was happening now.

"And I hope he has a good one lined up," Pounds was saying as he added the fifth and sixth binders to the pile. "Because last I checked this department doesn't consider cirrhosis of the liver a stress-related malady. Porter's a lush, simple as that. And it's not fair that he claim a stress disability and take early retirement because he can't handle his booze. We're going to bust him at the administrative hearing. I don't care if he has Mother Theresa as his lawyer. We'll bust him."

He tapped his finger on top of the pile of blue binders. "I've looked through these cases—he has eight open cases—and it's just pathetic. I've copied the chronologies and I'm going to verify them. I'll bet dollars to doughnuts they are replete with fraudulent entries. He was sitting on a stool somewhere, his head on the bar, when he says he was interviewing wits or doing the legwork."

Pounds shook his head sadly.

"You know, we lost our checks and balances when we stopped partnering our investigators. There was nobody to watch this guy. Now I'm sitting here with eight open investigations that were as slipshod as anything I've ever seen. For all I know, each one could've been cleared."

And whose idea was it to make detectives work solo, Bosch wanted to say but didn't. Instead, he said, "You ever hear the story about when Porter was in uniform about ten years back? He and his partner stopped one time to write up a citation for some shitbag they saw sitting on a curb drinking in public. Porter was driving. It was routine—just a misdee writeup—so he stayed behind the wheel. He's sitting there when the shitbag stands up and caps his partner in the face. Standing there, both hands on his cite book, takes it right between the eyes and Porter sat there watching."

Pounds looked exasperated.

"I know that story, Bosch," Pounds said. "They re-enact it for every class of recruits that goes through the academy. A lesson in what not to do, how not to fuck up. But it's ancient history. If he wanted a stress-out, he should've taken it then."

"That's the point, man. He didn't take it then when he could have. He tried to make it through. Maybe he tried for ten years and then he just went down in the flood of all the shit in the world. What do you want him to do? Take the same out Cal Moore took? You get a star in your file for saving the city the pension?"

Pounds did not speak for a few seconds, then said, "Very eloquent, Bosch, but in the long run it is none of your business what happens to Porter. I should not have brought it up. But I did so you would understand what I have to say now."

He went through his housekeeping trick of making sure all the corners were aligned on the stack of blue binders. Then he pushed the stack across the desk toward Bosch.

"You are taking Porter's caseload. I want you to shelve the Kappalanni matter for a few days. You're not getting anywhere at the moment. Put it down until after the first and dive into this.

"I want you to take Porter's eight open cases and study them. Do it quickly. I want you to look for the one you think you can do something with quickly and then hit it with everything you've got for the next five days—until New Year's Day. Work the weekend, I'll approve the overtime. If you need one of the others on the table to double up with you, no problem. But put somebody in jail, Harry. Go get me an arrest. I—we need to clear one more case to get to that halfway mark. The deadline is midnight, New Year's Eve."

Bosch just looked at him over the stack of binders. He had the full measure of this man now. Pounds wasn't a cop anymore. He was a bureaucrat. He was nothing. He saw crime, the spilling of blood, the suffering of humans, as statistical entries in a log. And at the end of the year the log told him how well he did. Not people. Not the voice from within. It was the kind of impersonal arrogance that poisoned much of the department and isolated it from the city, its people. No wonder Porter wanted out. No wonder Cal Moore pulled his own plug. Harry stood up and picked up the stack of binders and stared at Pounds with a look that said, I know you. Pounds turned his eyes away.

At the door, Bosch said, "You know, if you bust Porter down, he'll just get sent back here to the table. Then where will you be? Next year how many cases will there still be open?"

Pounds's eyebrows went up as he considered this.

"If you let him go, you'll get a replacement. A lot of sharp people on the other tables. Meehan over on the juvenile table is good. You bring him over to our table and I bet you'll see your stats go up. But if you go ahead and bust Porter and bring him back, we might be doing this again next year."

Pounds waited a moment, to make sure Bosch was done, before speaking.

"What is it with you, Bosch? When it comes to investigations Porter couldn't carry your lunch. Yet you're standing there trying to save his ass. What's the point?"

"There is no point, Lieutenant. I guess that's the point. Get me?"

He carried the binders to his spot at the table and dropped them on the floor next to his chair. Edgar looked at him. So did Dunne and Moshito, who had recently arrived.

"Don't ask," Harry said.

He sat down and looked at the pile at his feet and didn't want to have anything to do with it. What he wanted was a cigarette but there was no smoking in the squad room, at least while Pounds was around. He looked up a number in his Rolodex and dialed. The call was not picked up until the seventh ring.

"What now?"

"Lou?"

"Who is it?"

"Bosch."

"Oh, yeah, Harry. Sorry, I didn't know who was calling. What's going on? You hear I'm going for a stress-out?"

"Yeah. That's why I'm calling. I got your cases—Pounds gave 'em to me—and, uh, I want to try to turn one real quick, like by the end of the week. I was wondering if you had any idea—you think you might know which one I should hit? I'm starting from scratch."

There was a long silence on the phone.

"Harry, shit," he finally said and for the first time Bosch realized he might already be drunk. "Aw, damn. I didn't think that cocksucker would dump it all on you. I, uh, Harry . . . Harry, I didn't do too good on . . ."

"Hey, Lou. It's no biggee, you know? My decks were cleared. I'm just looking for a place to start. If you can't point me, that's okay. I'll just look through the stuff."

He waited and realized the others at the table had been listening to him and not even acting like they weren't.

"Fuck it," Porter said. "I, aw fuck it, I don't know, Harry. I—I haven't been on it, you know what I mean. I been kinda fallin' apart here. You hear about Moore? Shit, I saw the news last night. I . . ."

"Yeah, it's too bad. Listen, Lou, don't worry about it, okay? I'll look through the stuff. I got the murder books here and I'll look through 'em."

Nothing.

"Lou?"

"Okay, Harry. Give me a call back if you want. Maybe later I'll think of something. Right now I'm not too fucking good."

Bosch thought a few moments before saying anything else. In

his mind he pictured Porter on the other end of the line standing in total darkness. Alone.

"Listen," he said in a low voice. "You better...you have to watch out for Pounds on your application. He might ask the suits to check you out, you know what I mean, put a couple guys on you. You gotta stay out of the bars. He might try to bust your application. Understand?"

After a while Porter said he understood. Bosch hung up then and looked at the others at the table. The squad room always seemed loud until he had to make phone calls he didn't want anyone to hear. He got out a cigarette.

"Ninety-eight dumped Porter's whole caseload on you?" Edgar asked.

"That's right. That's me, the bureau garbage man."

"Yeah, then what's that make us, chopped liver?"

Bosch smiled. He could tell Edgar didn't know whether to be happy he avoided the assignment or mad because he was passed over.

"Well, Jed, if you want, I'll hustle back into the box and tell Ninety-eight that you're volunteering to split this up with me. I'm sure the pencil-pushing prick will—"

He stopped because Edgar had kicked him under the table. He turned in his seat and saw Pounds coming up from behind. His face was red. He had probably heard the last exchange.

"Bosch, you're not going to smoke that disgusting thing in here, are you?"

"No, Lieutenant, I was just on my way out back."

He pushed his chair back and walked out to the back parking lot to smoke. The back door of the drunk tank was unlocked and open. The Christmas-night drunks had already been loaded into the jail bus and hauled to arraignment court to make their pleas. A trustee in gray overalls was spraying the floor of the tank with a hose. Harry knew the concrete floor of the tank had been graded on a slight incline as an aid in this daily cleansing. He watched the dirty water slosh out the door and into the parking lot where it flowed to a sewer drain. There was vomit and blood in the water and the smell from the tank was terrible. But Harry stood his ground. This was his place.

When he was done he threw his cigarette butt into the water and watched the flow take it to the drain.

Six

IT FELT LIKE THE DETECTIVE BUREAU HAD BECOME A fishbowl and he was the only one in the water. He had to get away from the curious eyes that were watching him. Bosch picked up the stack of blue binders and walked out the back door into the parking lot. Then he quickly walked back into the station through the watch office door, went down a short hallway past the lockup and up a staircase to the second-floor storage room. It was called the Bridal Suite because of the cots in the back corner. An unofficial official cooping station. There was an old cafeteria table up there and a phone. And it was quiet. It was all he needed.

The room was empty today. Bosch put the stack of binders down and cleared a dented bumper marked with an evidence tag off the table. He leaned it against a stack of file boxes next to a broken surfboard that had also been tagged as evidence. Then he got down to work.

Harry stared at the foot-high stack of binders. Pounds said the division had sixty-six homicides so far in the year. Figuring the rotation and including Harry's two-month absence while recovering from the bullet wound, Porter had probably caught fourteen of the cases. With eight still open, that meant he had cleared six others. It wasn't a bad record, considering the transient nature of homicide in Hollywood. Nationwide, the vast majority of murder victims know their killer. They are the people they eat with, drink with, sleep with, live with. But Hollywood was different. There were no norms. There were only deviations, aberrations. Strangers killed strangers here. Reasons were not a requirement. The victims turned up in alleys, on freeway shoulders, along the brushy hillsides in Griffith Park, in bags dropped like garbage into restaurant Dumpsters. One of Harry's open files was the discovery of a body in parts—one on each of the fire escape landings of a six-story hotel on Gower. That one didn't raise too many eyebrows in the bureau. The joke going around was that it was a lucky thing that the victim hadn't stayed at the Holiday Inn. It was fifteen stories.

The bottom line was that in Hollywood a monster could move smoothly in the flow of humanity. Just one more car on the crowded freeway. And some would always be caught and some would always be untraceable, unless you counted the blood they left behind.

Porter had gone six and eight before punching out. It was a record that wouldn't get him any commendations but, still, it meant six more monsters were out of the flow. Bosch realized he could balance Porter's books if he could clear one of the eight open cases. The broken-down cop would at least go out with an even record.

Bosch didn't care about Pounds and his desire to clear one more case by midnight on New Year's Eve. He felt no allegiance to Pounds and believed the annual tabulating, charting and analyzing of lives sacrificed added up to nothing. He decided that if he was to do this job, he would do it for Porter. Fuck Pounds.

He pushed the binders to the back of the table so he would have room to work. He decided to quickly scan each murder book and separate them into two piles. One stack for possible quick turns, another for the cases he did not think he could do anything with in a short time.

He reviewed them in chronological order, starting with a Valentine's Day strangulation of a priest in a stall at a bathhouse on Santa Monica. By the time he was done two hours had passed and Harry had only two of the blue binders in his stack of possibilities. One was a month old. A woman was pulled from a bus stop bench on Las Palmas into the darkened entranceway of a closed Hollywood memorabilia store and raped and stabbed. The other was the eight-day-old discovery of the body of a man behind a twenty-four-hour diner on Sunset near the Directors Guild building. The victim had been beaten to death.

Bosch focused on these two because they were the most recent cases and experience had instilled in him a firm belief that cases become exponentially more difficult to clear with each day that passes. Whoever strangled the priest was as good as gold. Harry knew the percentages showed that the killer had gotten away.

Bosch also saw that the two most recent cases could quickly be cleared if he caught a break. If he could identify the man found behind the restaurant, then that information could lead to his family, friends and associates and most likely to a motive and maybe a killer. Or, if he could trace the stabbing victim's movement back to where she was before going to the bus stop, he might be able to learn where and how the killer saw her.

It was a toss-up and Bosch decided to read each case file thoroughly before deciding. But going with the percentages he decided to read the freshest case first. The body found behind the restaurant was the warmest trail.

On first glance, the murder book was notable for what it did not contain. Porter had not picked up a finished, typed copy of the autopsy protocol. So Bosch had to rely on the Investigator's Summary reports and Porter's own autopsy notes, which simply said the victim had been beaten to death with a "blunt object"—policespeak meaning just about anything.

The victim, estimated to be about fifty-five years old, was referred to as Juan Doe #67. This because he was believed to be Latin and was the sixty-seventh unidentified Latin man found dead in Los Angeles County during the year. There was no money on the body, no wallet and no belongings other than the clothing—all of it manufactured in Mexico. The only identification key was a tattoo on the upper left chest. It was a monocolor outline of what appeared to be a ghost. There was a Polaroid snapshot of it in the file. Bosch studied this for several moments, deciding the blue line drawing of a Casper-like ghost was very old. The ink was faded and blurred. Juan Doe #67 had gotten the tattoo as a young man.

The crime scene report Porter had filled out said the body had been found at 1:44 A.M. on December 18 by an off-duty police officer, identified only by his badge number, going in for an early breakfast or late dinner when he saw the body lying next to the Dumpster near the kitchen door of the Egg and I Diner.

R/O #1101 had recently reported code seven and parked behind the location with the intention of entering to eat. Victim was viewed on the eastern side of the Dumpster. Body was lying in a supine position, head to the north and feet to the south. Extensive injuries were readily noticeable and R/O notified the watch commander that a homicide call out was necessary. R/O saw no other individuals in the vicinity of the Dumpster before or after the body was located.

Bosch looked through the binder for a summary filed by the reporting officer but there was none. He next reviewed the other photos in the binder. These were of the body in place, before the techs had moved it to the morgue.

Bosch could see the victim's scalp had been rent open by one vicious blow. There were also wounds on the face and dried black blood on the neck and all over the once-white T-shirt the man was wearing. The dead man's hands lay open at his sides. In close-ups of the hands, Bosch saw two fingers on the right hand bent backward in compound fractures—classic defense wounds. Aside from the wounds, Bosch noted the rough and scarred hands and the ropey muscles that went up the arms. He had been a worker of some kind. What had he been doing in the alley behind the diner at one o'clock in the morning?

Next in the binder were witness statements taken from employees at the Egg and I. They were all men, which seemed wrong to Bosch because he had eaten at the Egg and I on several early mornings and remembered that there were always waitresses working the tables. Porter had apparently decided they were unimportant and concentrated only on the kitchen help. Each of the men interviewed said he did not recall seeing the victim in life or death.

Porter had scribbled a star on the top of one of the statements. It was from a fry cook who had reported to work at 1 A.M. and had walked right past the east side of the Dumpster and through the kitchen door. He had seen no body on the ground and was sure he would have seen one if there had been one to see when he made his entrance.

That had helped Porter set the timing of the slaying to sometime during the forty-four-minute window between the arrivals of the fry cook and the police officer who found the body.

Next in the file were printouts from LAPD, National Crime Index, California Department of Justice, and Immigration and Naturalization Service computer runs on the victim's fingerprints. All four were negative. No matches. Juan Doe #67 remained unidentified.

At the back of the binder were notes Porter had taken during the autopsy, which had not been conducted until Tuesday, Christmas Eve, because of the usual backlog of cases at the coroner's office. Bosch realized that it might have been Porter's last official duty to watch one more body be cut up. He didn't come back to work after the holiday.

Perhaps Porter knew he would not return, for his notes were sparse, just a single page with a few thoughts jotted down. Some of them Bosch could not read. Other notes he could understand but they were meaningless. But near the bottom of the page Porter had circled a notation that said, "TOD—12 to 6 P.M."

Bosch knew the notation meant that, based on the rate of decrease in liver temperature and other appearances of the body, the time of death was likely to have been between noon and 6 P.M., but no later than 6 P.M.

This did not make sense, Bosch thought at first. That put the time of death at least seven and a half hours before the discovery of the body. It also did not jibe with the fry cook not seeing any body by the Dumpster at 1 A.M.

These contradictions were the reason Porter had circled the notation. It meant Juan Doe #67 had not been killed behind the diner. It meant he was killed somewhere else, nearly half a day earlier, and then dumped behind the diner.

He took a notebook out of his pocket and began to make a list of people he wanted to talk to. First on the list was the doctor who had performed the autopsy; Harry needed to get the completed autopsy protocol. Then he noted Porter down for a more detailed interview. After that he wrote the fry cook's name on the list because Porter's notes only said the cook did not see a body on the ground while going into work. There was nothing about whether the cook saw anybody else or anything unusual in the alley. He also made a note to check with the waitresses who had been on duty that morning.

To complete his list, Bosch had to pick up the phone and call the watch commander's office.

"I want to talk to eleven-oh-one," Bosch said. "Can you look it up on the board there and tell me who that is?"

It was Kleinman again. He said, "Very funny, smart guy."

"What?" Bosch said, but at that moment it struck him. "Is it Cal Moore?"

"Was Cal Moore. Was."

Harry hung up the phone as several thoughts crowded into his brain at once. Juan Doe #67 had been found on the day before Moore checked into the Hideaway. He tried to piece out what this could mean. Moore stumbles onto a body in an alley early one morning. The next day he checks into a motel, turns up the air-conditioner and puts two barrels of double-ought buckshot into his face. The message he leaves behind is as simple as it is mysterious.

I found out who I was

Bosch lit a cigarette and crossed #1101 off his list, but he continued to center his thoughts on this latest piece of information. He felt impatient, bothered. He fidgeted in the chair, then stood up and began to walk in a circle around the table. He worked Porter into the framework this development provided and ran through it several times. Each time it was the same. Porter gets the call out on the Juan Doe #67 case. He obviously would have had to talk to Moore at the scene. The next day Moore disappears. The next week Moore is found dead, and then the next day Porter announces he is getting a doctor and is pulling the pin. Too many coincidences.

He picked up the phone and called the homicide table. Edgar answered and Harry asked him to reach across the table and check his Rolodex for Porter's home number. Edgar gave it to him and said, "Harry, where you at?"

"Why, Ninety-eight looking for me?"

"Nah. One of the guys from Moore's unit called a few minutes ago. Said he was looking for you."

"Yeah, why?"

"Hey, Harry, I'm only passing on the message, not doing your job for you."

"Okay, okay. Which one called?"

"Rickard. He just asked me to tell you they had something for you. I gave him your pager number 'cause I didn't know if you were coming back anytime soon. So, where you at?"

"Nowhere."

He hung up and dialed Porter's house. The phone rang ten times. Harry hung up and lit another cigarette. He didn't know what to think about all of this. Could Moore have simply stumbled onto the body as it said in the report? Could he have dumped it there? Bosch had no clues.

"Nowhere," he said aloud to the room full of storage boxes.

He picked up the phone again and dialed the medical examiner's office. He gave his name and asked to be connected to Dr. Corazón, the acting chief. Harry refused to say what the call was about to the operator. The phone was dead for nearly a minute before Corazón picked up.

"I'm in the middle of something here," she said.

"Merry Christmas to you, too."

"Sorry."

"It's the Moore cut?"

"Yes, but I can't talk about it. What do you need, Harry?"

"I just inherited a case and there's no autopsy in the file. I'm trying to find out who did it so I can get a copy."

"Harry, you don't need to ask for the acting chief to track that. You could ask any of the investigators I have sitting around here on their asses."

"Yeah, but they aren't as sweet to me as you."

"Okay, hurry up, what's the name?"

"Juan Doe #67. Date of death was the eighteenth. The cut was the twenty-fourth."

She said nothing and Bosch assumed she was checking a scheduling chart.

"Yeah," she said after a half minute. "The twenty-fourth. That was Salazar and he's gone now. Vacation. That was his last autopsy until next month. He went to Australia. It's summer there."

"Shit."

"Don't fret, Harry. I have the package right here. Sally expected Lou Porter would be by to pick it up today. But Lou never came. How'd you inherit it?"

"Lou pulled the pin."

"Jeez, that was kind of quick. What's his—hold on—"

She didn't wait for him to say he would. This time she was gone more than a minute. When she came back, her voice had a higher pitch to it.

"Harry, I really've got to go. Tell you what, wanna meet me after work? By then I'll've had some time to read through this and I'll tell you what we've got. I just remembered that there is something kind of interesting here. Salazar came to me for a referral approval."

"Referral to what?"

"An entomologist—a bug doctor—over at UCLA. Sally found bugs."

Bosch already knew that maggots would not have bred in a body dead twelve hours at the most. And Salazar would not have needed an entomologist to identify them anyway.

"Bugs," he said.

"Yeah. In the stomach content analysis and nasal swabs. But I don't have time at the moment to discuss this. I've got four impatient men in the autopsy suite waiting for me. And only one of 'em is dead."

"I guess that would make the live ones Irving, Sheehan and Chastain, the three musketeers."

She laughed and said, "You got it."

"Okay. When and where do you want to meet?"

He looked at his watch. It was almost three.

"Maybe around six?" she said. "That would give me time to finish here and look through this package on your Juan Doe."

"Should I come there?"

His pager began to chirp. He cut it off with a well-practiced move with his right hand to his belt.

"No, let's see," she said. "Can you meet me at the Red Wind? We can wait out the rush hour."

"I'll be there," Harry said.

After hanging up he checked the number on his pager, recognized it as a pay phone exchange and dialed it.

"Bosch?" a voice said.

"Right."

"Rickard. I worked with Cal Moore. The BANG unit?"

"Right."

"I got something for you."

Bosch didn't say anything. He felt the hairs on the top of his hands and forearms begin to tingle. He tried to place the name

Rickard with a face but couldn't. The narcs kept such odd hours and were a breed unto themselves. He didn't know who Rickard was.

"Or, I should say, Cal left something for you," Rickard spoke into the silence. "You wanna meet? I don't want this to go down in the station."

"Why not?"

"I've got my reasons. We can talk about that when I see you."

"Where's that gonna be?"

"You know a place on Sunset, the Egg and I? It's a diner. Decent food. The hypes don't hang out here."

"I know it."

"Good. We're in the last booth in the back, right before the kitchen door. The table with the only black guy in the place. That's me. There's parking in the back. In the alley."

"I know. Who's 'we'?"

"Cal's whole crew is here."

"That where you guys always hang out?"

"Yeah, before we hit the street. See ya soon."

Seven

THE RESTAURANT'S SIGN HAD BEEN CHANGED SINCE the last time he had been there. It was now the *All-American* Egg and I, which meant it had probably been sold to foreigners. Bosch got out of his Caprice and walked through the back alley, looking at the spot where Juan Doe #67 had been dumped. Right outside the backdoor of a diner frequented by the local narc crew. His thoughts on the implications of this were interrupted by the panhandlers in the alley who came up to him shaking their cups. Bosch ignored them but their presence served to remind him of another shortcoming in Porter's meager investigation. There had been nothing in the reports about vagrants in the alley being interviewed as possible witnesses. It would probably be impossible to track them down now.

Inside the restaurant, he saw four young men, one of them black, in a rear booth. They were sitting silently with their faces turned down to the empty coffee cups in front of them. Harry noticed a closed manila file on the table as he pulled a chair away from an empty table and sat at the end of the booth.

"I'm Bosch."

"Tom Rickard," the black one said. He put out his hand and then introduced the other three as Finks, Montirez and Fedaredo.

"We got tired of being around the office," Rickard said. "Cal used to like this place."

Bosch just nodded and looked down at the file. He saw the name written on the tab was Humberto Zorrillo. It meant nothing to him. Rickard slid the file across the table to him.

"What is it?" Harry asked, not yet touching it.

"Probably the last thing he worked on," Rickard said. "We were going to give it over to RHD but thought what the hell, he was working it up for you. And those boys down there at Parker are just trying to drag him through the shit. Ain't going to help with that."

"What do you mean?"

"I mean they can't let it be that the man killed himself. They hafta dissect his life and figure out exactly why he did this and why he done that. The man fucking killed himself. What else is there to say about it?"

"You don't want to know why?"

"I already know why, man. The job. It will get us all in the end. I mean, I know why."

Bosch just nodded again. The other three narcs still hadn't said anything.

"I'm just letting off steam," Rickard said. "Been one of those days. Longest fucking day of my life."

"Where was this?" Harry asked, pointing to the file. "Didn't RHD already go through his desk?"

"Yeah, they did. But that file wasn't in it. See, Cal left it in one of the BANG cars—one of those undercover pieces of shit we use. In the pocket behind the front seat. We never noticed it during the week he was missing because today was the first time any of us rode in the back of the car. We usually take two cars out on operations. But today we all jumped in one for a cruise on the Boulevard after we came in and heard the news. I saw it shoved down into the pocket. It's got a little note inside. Says to give it to you. We knew he was working on something for you 'cause of that night he peeled off early to go meet with you at the Catalina."

Bosch still hadn't opened the file. Just looking at it gave him an uneasy feeling.

"He told me that night at the Catalina that the shoeflies were on him. You guys know why?"

"No, man, we don't know what was going down. We just know they were around. Like flies on shit. IAD went through his desk before RHD. They took files, his phone book, even took the fucking typewriter off the desk. That was the only one we had. But what it was about, we don't know. The guy had a lot of years in and it burns my ass that they were gunning for him. That's what I meant before about the job doing him in. It'll get all of us."

"What about outside the job? His past. His wife said—"

"I don't want to hear about that shit. She's the one who put the suits on him. Made up some story when he walked out and dropped the dime on him. She just wanted to bring him down, you ask me."

"How do you know it was her?"

"Cal told us, man. Said the shoeflies might come around asking questions. Told us it came from her."

Bosch wondered who had been lying, Moore to his partners or Sylvia to himself. He thought about her for a moment and couldn't see it, couldn't see her dropping the dime. But he didn't press it with the four narcs. He finally reached down and picked up the file. Then he left.

He was too curious to wait. He knew that he should not even have the file. That he should pick up a phone and call Frankie Sheehan at RHD. But he unconsciously took a quick look around the car to make sure he was alone and began to read. There was a yellow Post-it note on the first page.

Give to Harry Bosch.

It was not signed or dated. It was stuck to a sheet of paper with five green Field Interview cards held to it with a paper clip. Harry detached the FI cards and shuffled through them. Five different names, all males. Each had been stopped by members of the BANG unit in October or

November. They were questioned and released. Each card held little more information than a description, home address, driver's license number, and date and location of the shakedown. The names meant nothing to Bosch.

He looked at the sheet the cards had been attached to. It was marked INTERNAL MEMO and had a subheading that said BANG Intelligence Report #144. It was dated November 1 and had a FILED stamp mark on it that was dated two days after that.

In the course of gathering intelligence on narcotics activities in Reporting District 12 officers Moore, Rickard, Finks, Fedaredo and Montirez have conducted numerous field interrogations of suspects believed to be involved in drug sales in the area of Hollywood Boulevard. In recent weeks it has come to these officers' attention the fact that individuals were involved in the sale of a drug known as "black ice" which is a narcotic combining heroin, cocaine and PCP in rock form. The demand for this drug remains low on the street at this time but its popularity is expected to increase.

Officers assigned to this unit believe several transient-type individuals are engaged in the street level sale of "black ice." Five suspects have been identified through investigation but no arrests have followed. The street sales network is believed to be directed by an individual whose identity is not known to officers at this time.

Informants and users of "black ice" have revealed that the predominant form of the drug sold at street level in the reporting zone comes from Mexico, rather than Hawaii where ice originated—refer to DEA advisory 502—and still is imported to the mainland in large quantities.

Reporting officers will contact DEA for intelligence on sources of this narcotic and will continue to monitor activities in RD12.

Sgt. C. V. Moore #1101

Bosch reread the report. It was a cover-your-ass paper. It said nothing and meant nothing. It had no value but could be produced to show a superior that you were aware of a problem and had been taking steps to attack it. Moore must have realized that black ice was becoming more than a rarity on the street and wanted to file a report to shield himself against future repercussions.

Next in the file was an arrest report dated November 9 of a man named Marvin Dance for possession of a controlled substance. The report said Dance was arrested by BANG officers on Ivar after they watched him make a delivery of black ice to a street dealer. BANG unit officers Rickard and Finks had set up on Dance on Ivar north of the Boulevard. The suspect was sitting in a parked car and the narcs watched as another man walked up and got in.

The report said Dance took something out of his mouth and handed it to the other man, who then got out of the car and walked on. The two officers split up and Finks followed the walker until he was out of Dance's sight, then stopped him and seized an eightball—eight individually wrapped grams of black ice in a balloon. Rickard kept a watch on Dance, who remained in the car waiting for the next dealer to come for the product. After Finks radioed that he had made his bust, Rickard moved in to take down Dance.

But Dance swallowed whatever else was in his mouth. While he sat cuffed on the sidewalk, Rickard searched the car and found no drugs. But in a crumpled McDonald's cup in the gutter by the car door, the narc found six more balloons, each containing an eightball.

Dance was arrested for sales and possession with intent to sell. The report said the suspect refused to talk to the arresting officers about the drugs other than to say the McDonald's cup was not his. He didn't ask for a lawyer but one arrived at the station within an hour and informed the officers that it would be unconstitutional for them to take his client to a hospital to have his stomach pumped or to search his client's feces when the time came for him to use the bathroom. Moore, who got involved in processing the arrest at the station, checked with the on-call DA and was told the lawyer was right.

Dance was released on $125,000 bail two hours after his arrest. Bosch thought this was curious. The report said time of arrest was 11:42 P.M. That meant that in two hours in the middle of the night, Dance had come up with a lawyer, bail bondsman and the ten percent cash—$12,500—needed to make bail.

And no charges were ever filed against Dance. The next page of the file was a rejection slip from the DA's office. The filing deputy who reviewed the case determined that there was insufficient evidence linking Dance to the McDonald's cup that was in the gutter three feet from his car.

So, no possession charge. Next, the sales charge was scuttled because the narcs saw no money change hands when Dance gave the eightball to the man who had gotten in the car. His name was Glenn Druzon. He was seventeen years old and had refused to testify that he had received the balloon from Dance. In fact, the rejection report said, he was ready to testify that he had the balloon with him before he got into the car with Dance. If called he would testify that he had tried to sell it to Dance but Dance was not interested.

The case against Dance was kicked. Druzon was charged with possession and later put on juvenile probation.

Bosch looked away from the reports and down the alley. He could see the circular copper-and-glass Directors Guild building rising at the end. He could just see the top of the Marlboro Man billboard that had been on Sunset for as long as he could remember. He lit a cigarette.

He looked at the DA reject form again. Clipped to it was a mug shot of the blond-haired Dance smirking at the lens. Bosch knew that what had happened was the routine way in which many, if not most, street cases go. The small fish, the bottom feeders, get hooked up. The bigger fish break the line and swim away. The cops knew that all they could do was disrupt things, never rid the streets of the problem. Take one dealer down and somebody takes his place. Or an attorney on retainer springs him and then a DA with a four-drawer caseload cuts him loose. It was one of the reasons why Bosch stayed in homicide. Sometimes he thought it was the only crime that really counted.

But even that was changing.

Harry took the mug shot and put it in his pocket, then closed the file for the time being. He was bothered by the Dance arrest. He wondered what connection Calexico Moore had seen between Dance and Jimmy Kapps that had prompted him to put it in the file for Bosch.

Bosch took a small notebook out of his inside coat pocket and began to make a chronological list. He wrote:

Nov. 9   Dance arrested
Nov. 13   Jimmy Kapps dead
Dec. 4   Moore, Bosch meet

Bosch closed the notebook. He knew he had to go back into the diner to ask Rickard a question. But first he reopened the file. There was only one page left, another unit intelligence report. This one was a summary of a briefing Moore had gotten from a DEA agent assigned to Los Angeles. This was dated December 11, meaning it had been put together by Moore a week after he and Bosch had met at the Catalina.

Harry tried to figure how this played with everything else and what, if anything, it meant. At their meeting Moore had withheld information, but afterward had gone to the DEA to request information. It was as if he were playing both sides of the fence. Or, possibly, Moore was trying to hotdog Bosch's case, trying to put it together on his own.

Bosch began reading the report slowly, unconsciously bending the top corners of the file with his fingers.

Information provided this date by DEA asst. special agent in charge Rene Corvo, Los Angeles bureau operations indicates origin of black ice is primarily Baja California. Target 44Q3 Humberto Zorrillo (11/11/54) believed operating a clandestine lab in the Mexicali zone that is producing Mexican ice for distribution in the U.S. Subject lives on a 6,000-acre bull ranch SW Mexicali. State Judicial Police has not moved against Zorrillo for political reasons. Mode of transport used by this operation is unknown. Air surveillance shows no airstrip on ranch property. It is DEA opinion based on experience that the operation uses vehicle routes through Calexico or possibly San Ysidro, however, no shipments intercepted at those crossings at this time. It is believed that subject enjoys support and cooperation of officers with the SJP. He is widely known and revered as a hero in the barrios of SW Mexicali. Subject's support is based in part on generous donations of jobs, med supplies, barrio dwellings and cook camps in the poor neighborhoods he grew up in. Some of the residents in SW neighborhoods refer to Zorrillo as El Papa de Mexicali. Additionally, Zorrillo's rancho remains under heavy guard 24-hours. El Papa—The Pope—is rarely seen outside of the rancho. Exception is weekly trips to observe bulls bred on the ranch at bullrings in Baja. SJP authorities advise at this time that their cooperation in any DEA action that focuses on Zorrillo would be impossible.

Sgt. C. V. Moore #1101

Bosch stared for a few moments at the file after closing it. He had a jumble of differing thoughts. He was a man who didn't believe in coincidences, and so he had to wonder about how Cal Moore's presence had come to throw a shadow across everything on his own plate. He looked at his watch and saw it would soon be time to get going to meet Teresa Corazón. But, finally, all the movement in his mind could not distract him from the thought that was pushing through. Frankie Sheehan at RHD should have the information in the Zorrillo file. Bosch had worked with Sheehan at RHD. He was a good man and a good investigator. If he was conducting a legitimate investigation, he should have the file. If he wasn't, then it didn't matter.

He got out of the car and headed back to the diner. This time he walked in through the kitchen door on the alley. The BANG crew was still there, the four young narcs sitting as quietly as if they were in the back room at a funeral home. Bosch's chair was still there, too. He sat down again.

"What's up?" Rickard said.

"You read this, right? Tell me about the Dance bust."

"What's to tell?" Rickard said. "We kick ass, the DA kicks the case. What's new? It's a different drug, man, but it's the same old thing."

"What made you set up on Dance? How'd you know he was making deliveries there?"

"Heard it around."

"Look, it's important. It involves Moore."

"How?"

"I can't tell you now. You have to trust me until I put a few things together. Just tell me who got the tip. That's what it was, right?"

Rickard seemed to weigh the choices he had.

"Yeah, it was a tip. It was my snitch."

"Who was it?"

"Look, man, I can't—"

"Jimmy Kapps. It was Jimmy Kapps, wasn't it?"

Rickard hesitated again and that confirmed it for Bosch. It angered him that he was finding this out almost by accident and only after a cop's death. But the picture was clearing. Kapps snitches off Dance as a means of knocking out some of the competition. Then he flies back to Hawaii, picks up a bellyful of balloons and comes back. But Dance isn't in lockup anymore and Jimmy Kapps gets taken down before he can sell even one of his balloons.

"Why the fuck didn't you come talk to me when you heard Kapps got put down? I've been trying to get a line on this and all the—"

"What're you talking about, Bosch? Moore met you that night on the Kapps thing. He..."

It became apparent to everybody at the table that Moore had not told Bosch everything he knew that night at the Catalina. The silence fell heavy on them. If they hadn't known it before, they knew it now. Moore had been up to something. Bosch finally spoke.

"Did Moore know your snitch was Kapps?"

Rickard hesitated once more, but then nodded.

Bosch stood up and slid the file across the table to a spot in front of Rickard.

"I don't want this. You call Frank Sheehan at RHD and tell him you just found it. It's up to you but I wouldn't say that you let me look at it first. And I won't, either."

Harry made a move to step away from the table but then stopped.

"One other thing. This guy Dance, any of you seen him around?"

"Not since the bust," Fedaredo said.

The other three shook their heads.

"If you can dig him up, let me know. You got my number."

Outside the diner's kitchen door Bosch looked again at the spot in the alley where Moore had found Juan Doe #67. Supposedly. He didn't know what to believe about Moore anymore. But he couldn't help but wonder what the connection was between the Juan Doe and Dance and Kapps, if there was a connection at all. He knew the key was to find out who the man with the worker's hands and muscles had been. Then he would find the killer.

Eight

AT PARKER CENTER, HARRY WALKED PAST THE MEMO-
rial sculpture in front and into the lobby where he had to badge the
officer at the front counter to get in. The department was too big
and impersonal. The cops at the counter would recognize no one
below the rank of commander.

The lobby was crowded with people coming and going. Some
were in uniform, some in suits, some with VISITOR stickers on
their shirts and the wide-eyed look of citizens venturing into the
maze for the first time. Harry had come to regard Parker Center as
a bureaucratic labyrinth that hindered rather than eased the job of
the cop on the street. It was eight floors with fiefdoms on every hallway on every floor. Each was jealously guarded by commanders and
deputy chiefs and assistant chiefs. And each group had its suspicions
about the others. Each was a society within the great society.

Bosch had been a master of the maze during his eight years in
Robbery-Homicide. And then he crashed and burned under the
weight of an Internal Affairs investigation into his shooting of an
unarmed suspect in a series of killings. Bosch had fired as the man
reached under a pillow in his killing pad for what Harry thought
was a gun. But there was no gun. Beneath the pillow was a toupee.
It was almost laughable, except for the man who took the bullet.
Other RHD investigators tied him to eleven killings. His body was

shipped in a cardboard box to a crematorium. Bosch was shipped out to Hollywood Division.

The elevator was crowded and smelled like stale breath. He got out on the fourth floor and walked into the Scientific Investigations Division offices. The secretary had already left. Harry leaned over the countertop and reached the button that buzzed open the half door. He walked through the Ballistics lab and into the squad room. Donovan was still there, sitting at his desk.

"How'd you get in here?"

"Let myself in."

"Harry, don't do that. You can't go around breaching security like that."

Bosch nodded his contrition.

"What do you want?" Donovan asked. "I don't have any of your cases."

"Sure you do."

"What one?"

"Cal Moore."

"Bullshit."

"Look, I've got a part of it, okay? I just have a few questions. You can answer them if you want. If you don't, that's fine, too."

"What've you got?"

"I'm running down some things that came up on a couple cases I'm working and they run right across Cal Moore's trail. And so I just...I just want to be sure about Moore. You know what I mean?"

"No, I don't know what you mean."

Bosch pulled a chair away from another desk and sat down. They were alone in the squad room but Bosch spoke low and slow, hoping to draw the SID tech in.

"Just for my own knowledge I need to be sure. What I am wondering is, can you tell me if all the stuff checked out."

"Checked out to what?"

"Come on, man. Was it him and was there anybody else in that room?"

There was a long silence and then Donovan cleared his throat. He finally said, "What do you mean, you're working cases that cross his trail?"

Fair enough question, Bosch thought. There was a small window of opportunity there.

"I got a dead drug dealer. I had asked Moore to do some checking on the case. Then, I got a dead body, a Juan Doe, in an alley off Sunset. Moore's the one who found the body. The next day he checks into that dump and does the number with the shotgun. Or so it looks. I just want some reassurances it's the way it looks. I heard they got an ID over at the morgue."

"So what makes you think these two cases are connected with Moore's thing?"

"I don't think anything right now. I'm just trying to eliminate possibilities. Maybe it's all coincidences. I don't know."

"Well," Donovan said. "I don't know what they got over at the ME's, but I got lifts in the room that belonged to him. Moore was in that room. I just got finished with it. Took me all day."

"How come?"

"The DOJ computer was down all morning. Couldn't get prints. I went up to personnel to get Moore's prints from his package and they told me Irving had already raided it. He took the prints out and took 'em over to the coroner. You know, you're not supposed to do that, but who's gonna tell him, get on his shit list. So I had to wait for the Justice computer to come back on line. Got his prints off of that after lunch and just finished with it a little while ago. That was Moore in the room."

"Where were the prints?"

"Hang on."

Donovan rolled back his chair to a set of file cabinets and unlocked a drawer with a key from his pocket. While he was leafing through the files, Bosch lit a cigarette. Donovan finally pulled out a file and then rolled his chair back to his desk.

"Put that shit out, Harry. I hate that shit."

Bosch dropped the cigarette to the linoleum, stepped on it and then kicked the butt under Donovan's desk. Donovan began reviewing some pages he had pulled from a file. Bosch could see that each one showed a top-view drawing of the motel room where Moore's body was found.

"Okay, then," Donovan said. "The prints in the room came back to Moore. All of them. I did the comp—"

"You said that."

"I'm getting to it, I'm getting to it. Let's see, we have a thumb—fourteen points—on the stock of the weapon. That, I guess, was the bell ringer, the fourteen."

Harry knew that only five matching points in a fingerprint comparison were needed for an identification to be accepted in court. A fourteen-point match of a print on a gun was almost as good as having a photo of the person holding the gun.

"Then, we . . . let's see . . . we had four three-pointers on the barrels of the weapon. I think these kind of got smudged when it kicked out of his hands. So we got nothing real clear there."

"What about the triggers?"

"Nope. Nothing there. He pulled the triggers with his toe and he was still wearing a sock, remember?"

"What about the rest of the place. I saw you dusting the air-conditioner."

"Yeah, but I didn't get anything there on the dial. We thought he turned the air up, you know, to control decomp. But the dial was clean. It's plastic with a rough surface, so I don't think it would have held anything for us."

"What else?"

Donovan looked back down at his charts.

"I got a lift off his badge—index and thumb, five and seven points respectively. The badge was on the bureau with the wallet. But nothing on the wallet. Only smears. On the gun on the bureau I only got a bunch of smears but a clear thumb on the cartridge.

"Then, let's see, I got the whole hand just about, a palm, thumb and three fingers on the left cabinet door under the bathroom sink. I figure he must've put his hand on it to steady himself when he was getting on the floor there. What a way to go, man."

"Yeah. That's it?"

"Yeah. Er, no. On the newspaper—there was a newspaper on the chair, I got a big match there. Thumb again and three fingers."

"And the shells?"

"Only smudges. Couldn't get anything on the shells."

"What about the note?"

"Nothing on it."

"Somebody check the handwriting?"

"Well, actually, it was printing. But Sheehan had it checked by somebody in suspicious documents. He said it matched. Few months back Moore moved out on his wife and took a place in Los Feliz called The Fountains. He filled out a change-of-address form. It was there in the personnel file Irving grabbed. Anyway, the change-of-address card was printed, too. There were a lot of commonalities with the note. You know, 'Found' and 'Fountains.'"

"What about the shotgun? Anybody trace the serial?"

"The number had been filed and acid-burned. No trace. You know, Harry, I shouldn't be saying so much. I think we should just..."

He didn't finish the sentence. He turned his chair back to the file cabinet and began to put his charts away.

"I'm almost done, man. What about a projectile pattern? Did you do one?"

Donovan closed and locked the file drawer and turned back around.

"Started to. Haven't finished. But you're talking side-by-side barrels, double-ought shells. That's an immediate spread pattern. I'd say he could have done it from six inches away and gotten that kind of damage. No mystery there."

Bosch nodded and looked at his watch, then stood up.

"One last thing."

"Might as well. I've already told you enough to put my ass in a permanent sling. You going to be careful with what I've told you?"

"'Course I am. Last thing. Outstanding prints. How many lifts you get that you haven't matched to Moore?"

"Not a one. I was wondering if anybody would care about that."

Bosch sat back down. This made no sense. Bosch knew that. A motel room was like a working girl. Every customer leaves a little something, his mark, behind. It didn't matter if the rooms were made up and reasonably cleaned between renters. There was always something, a telltale sign. Harry could not accept that every surface Donovan had checked had been clean except for those where Moore's prints were found.

"What do you mean nobody cared?"

"I mean nobody said shit. I told Sheehan and that IAD stiff that's been following him around. They acted like it didn't mean a thing to them. You know? It was like 'big deal, so there were no other prints.' I guess they never did a motel-room stiff before. Shit, I thought I'd be collecting prints in there last night 'til midnight. But all I got were the ones I just told you about. That was the goddamned cleanest motel room I've ever printed. I mean, I even put on the laser. Didn't see a thing but wipe marks where the room had been cleaned up. And if you ask me, Harry, that wasn't the kinda place the management cared too much about cleanliness."

"You told Sheehan this, right?"

"Yeah, I told him when I got done. I was thinking, you know, it being Christmas night that they were going to say I was full of shit and just trying to get home to the family. But I told 'em and they just said, fine, that'll be all, good night, Merry Christmas. I left. Fuck it."

Bosch thought about Sheehan and Chastain and Irving. Sheehan was a competent investigator. But with those two hovering over him, he could have made a mistake. They had gone into the motel room one hundred percent sure it was a suicide. Bosch would have done the same. They even found a note. After that they would have probably had to find a knife in Moore's back to change their minds. The lack of other prints in the room, no serial number on the shotgun. These were things that should've been enough to cut the percentage of their assuredness back to fifty-fifty. But they hadn't made a dent in their assumption. Harry began to wonder about the autopsy results, if they would back the suicide conclusion.

He stood up once more, thanked Donovan for the information and left.

He took the stairs down to the third floor and walked into the RHD suite. Most of the desks lined in three rows were empty, as it was after five o'clock. Sheehan's was among those that were deserted in the Homicide Special bullpen. A few of the detectives still there glanced up at him but then looked away. Bosch was of no interest to them. He was a symbol of what could happen, of how easily one could fall.

"Sheehan still around?" he asked the duty detective who sat at the front desk and handled the phone lines, incoming reports and all the other shitwork.

"Gone for the day," she said without looking up from a staff vacation schedule she was filling out. "Called from the ME's office a few minutes ago and said he was code seven until the A.M."

"There a desk I can use for a few minutes? I have to make some phone calls."

He hated to ask for such permission, having worked in this room for eight years.

"Just pick one," she said. She still didn't look up.

Bosch sat down at a desk that was reasonably clear of clutter. He called the Hollywood homicide table, hoping there would still be someone there. Karen Moshito answered and Bosch asked if he had any messages.

"Just one. Somebody named Sylvia. No last name given."

He took the number down, feeling his pulse quicken.

"Did you hear about Moore?" Moshito asked.

"You mean the ID? Yeah, I heard."

"No. The cut is screwed up. Radio news says the autopsy is inconclusive. I never heard of a shotgun in the face being inconclusive."

"When did this come out?"

"I just heard it on KFWB at five."

Bosch hung up and tried Porter's number once more. Again there was no answer and no tape recording picked up. Harry wondered if the broken-down cop was there and just not answering. He imagined Porter sitting with a bottle in the corner of a dark room, afraid to answer the door or the phone.

He looked at the number he had written down for Sylvia Moore. He wondered if she had heard about the autopsy. That was probably it. She picked up after three rings.

"Mrs. Moore?"

"It's Sylvia."

"This is Harry Bosch."

"I know."

She didn't say anything further.

"How are you holding up?"

"I think I'm okay. I...I called because I just want to thank you. For the way you were last night. With me."

"Oh, well, you didn't—it was..."

"You know that book I told you about last night?"

"*The Long Goodbye?*"

"There's another line in it I was thinking about. 'A white knight for me is as rare as a fat postman.' I guess nowadays there are a lot of fat postmen." She laughed very softly, almost like her crying. "But not too many white knights. You were last night."

Bosch didn't know what to say and just tried to envision her on the other end of the silence.

"That's very nice of you to say. But I don't know if I deserve it. Sometimes I don't think the things I have to do make me much of a knight."

They moved on to small talk for a few moments and then said good-bye. He hung up and sat still for a moment, staring at the phone and thinking about things said and unsaid. There was something there. A connection. Something more than her husband's death. More than just a case. There was a connection between them.

He turned the pages of the notebook back to the chronological chart he had made earlier.

Nov. 9 Dance arrested
Nov. 13 Jimmy Kapps dead
Dec. 4 Moore, Bosch meet

He now started to add other dates and facts, even some that did not seem to fit into the picture at the moment. But his overriding feeling was that his cases were linked and the link was Calexico Moore. He didn't stop to consider the chart as a whole until he was finished. Then he studied it, finding that it gave some context to the thoughts that had jumbled in his head in the last two days.

Nov. 1 BANG cya memo on black ice
Nov. 9 Rickard gets tip—from Jimmy Kapps
Nov. 9 Dance arrested, case kicked
Nov. 13 Jimmy Kapps dead
Dec. 4 Moore, Bosch meet—Moore holds back
Dec. 11 Moore receives DEA briefing
Dec. 18 Moore finds body—Juan Doe #67
Dec. 18 Porter assigned Juan Doe case
Dec. 19 Moore checks in, Hideaway—suicide?
Dec. 24 Juan Doe #67 autopsy—bugs?
Dec. 25 Moore's body found
Dec. 26 Porter pulls pin
Dec. 26 Moore autopsy—inconclusive?

But he couldn't study it too long without thinking of Sylvia Moore.

Nine

BOSCH TOOK LOS ANGELES STREET TO SECOND AND then up to the Red Wind. In front of St. Vibiana's he saw an entourage of bedraggled, homeless men leaving the church. They had spent the day sleeping in the pews and were now heading to the Union Street mission for dinner. As he passed the *Times* building he looked up at the clock and saw it was exactly six. He turned on KFWB for the news. The Moore autopsy was the second story, after a report on how the mayor had become the latest victim in a wave of kamikazi AIDS protests. He was hit with a balloon full of pig blood on the white stone steps of City Hall. A group called Cool AIDS took credit.

"In other news, an autopsy on the body of Police Sergeant Calexico Moore was inconclusive in confirming that the narcotics officer took his own life, according to the Los Angeles County coroner's office. Meanwhile, police have officially classified the death as suicide. The thirty-eight-year-old officer's body was found Christmas Day in a Hollywood motel room. He had been dead of a shotgun blast for about a week, authorities said. A suicide note was found at the scene but the contents have not been released. Moore will be buried Monday."

Bosch turned the radio off. The news report had obviously come from a press release. He wondered what was meant by the autopsy results being inconclusive. That was the only grain of real news in the whole report.

After parking at the curb in front of the Red Wind he went inside but did not see Teresa Corazón. He went into the restroom and splashed water on his face. He needed a shave. He dried himself with a paper towel and tried to smooth his mustache and curly hair with his hand. He loosened his tie, then stood there a long moment staring at his reflection. He saw the kind of man not many people approached unless they had to.

He got a package of cigarettes from the machine by the restroom door and looked around again but still didn't see her. He went to the bar and ordered an Anchor and then took it to an empty table by the front door. The Wind was becoming crowded with the after-work crowd. People in business suits and dresses. There were a lot of combinations of older men with younger women. Harry recognized several reporters from the *Times*. He began to think Teresa had picked a bad place to meet, if she intended to show up at all. With today's autopsy story, she might be noticed by the reporters. He drained the beer bottle and left the bar.

He was standing in the chilled evening air on the front sidewalk, looking down the street into the Second Street tunnel, when he heard a horn honk and a car pulled to a stop in front of him. The electric window glided down. It was Teresa.

"Harry, wait inside. I'll just find a place to park. Sorry I'm late."

Bosch leaned into the window.

"I don't know. Lot of reporters in there. I heard on the radio about the Moore autopsy. I don't know if you want to risk getting hassled."

He could see reasons for it and against it. Getting her name in the paper improved her chances of changing acting chief ME to permanent chief. But the wrong thing said or a misquote could just as easily change acting to interim or, worse yet, former.

"Where can we go?" she asked.

Harry opened the door and got in.

"Are you hungry? We can go down to Gorky's or the Pantry."

"Yeah. Is Gorky's still open? I want some soup."

It took them fifteen minutes to wend their way through eight blocks of downtown traffic and to find a parking space. Inside Gorky's they ordered mugs of home-brewed Russian beer and Teresa had the chicken-rice soup.

"Long day, huh?" he offered.

"Oh, yeah. No lunch. Was in the suite for five hours." Bosch needed to hear about the Moore autopsy but knew he could not just blurt out a question. He would have to make her want to tell it.

"How was Christmas? You and your husband get together?"

"Not even close. It just didn't work. He never could deal with what I do and now that I have a shot at chief ME, he resents it even more. He left Christmas Eve. I spent Christmas alone. I was going to call my lawyer today to tell her to resume filing but I was too busy."

"Should've called me. I spent Christmas with a coyote."

"Ahh. Is Timido still around?"

"Yeah, he still comes around every now and then. There was a fire across the pass. I think it spooked him."

"Yeah, I read about that. You were lucky."

Bosch nodded. He and Teresa Corazón had had an on-and-off relationship for four months, each meeting sparked with this kind of surface intimacy. But it was a relationship of convenience, firmly grounded on physical, not emotional, needs and never igniting into deep passion for either of them. She had separated earlier in the year from her husband, a UCLA Medical School professor, and had apparently singled Harry out for her affections. But Bosch knew he was a secondary diversion. Their liaisons were sporadic, usually weeks apart, and Harry was content to allow Teresa to initiate each one.

He watched her bring her head down to blow onto a spoonful of soup and then sip it. He saw slices of carrot floating in the bowl. She had brown ringlets that fell to her shoulders. She held some of the tresses back with her hand as she blew on another spoonful and then sipped. Her skin was a deep natural brown and there was an exotic, elliptical shape to her face accentuated by high cheekbones. She wore red lipstick on full lips and there was just a whisper of fine white peach fuzz on her cheeks. He knew she was in her mid-thirties but he had never asked exactly how old. Lastly, he noticed her fingernails. Unpolished and clipped short, so as not to puncture the rubber gloves that were the tools of her trade.

As he drank the heavy beer from its heavy stein, he wondered if this was the start of another liaison or whether she really had come to tell him of something significant in the autopsy results of Juan Doe #67.

"So now I need a date for New Year's Eve," she said, looking up from the soup. "What are you staring at?"

"Just watching you. You need a date, you got one. I read in the paper that Frank Morgan's playing at the Catalina."

"Who's he and what does he play?"

"You'll see. You'll like him."

"It was a dumb question anyway. If he's someone you like, then he plays the saxophone."

Harry smiled, more to himself than her. He was happy to know he had a date. Being alone on New Year's Eve bothered him more than Christmas, Thanksgiving, any of the other days. New Year's Eve was a night for jazz, and the saxophone could cut you in half if you were alone.

She smiled and said, "Harry, you're so easy when it comes to lonely women."

He thought of Sylvia Moore, remembering her sad smile. "So," Teresa said, seeming to sense that he was drifting away. "I bet you want to know about the bugs inside Juan Doe #67."

"Finish your soup first."

"Nope, that's okay. It doesn't bother me. I always get hungry, in fact, after a long day chopping up bodies."

She smiled. She said things like that often, as if daring him not to like what she did for a living. He knew she was still hooked by her husband. It didn't matter what she said. He understood.

"Well, I hope you don't miss the knives when they make you permanent chief. You'll be cutting budgets then."

"No, I'd be a hands-on chief. I'd handle the specials. Like today. But after today, I don't know if they'll ever make me permanent."

Harry sensed that now he was the one who had shaken a bad feeling loose and sent her traveling with it. Now might be the right time.

"You want to talk about it?"

"No. I mean I do, but I can't. I trust you, Harry, but I think I have to keep this close for the time being."

He nodded and let it go, but he intended to come back to it later and find out what had gone wrong on the Moore autopsy. He took his notebook out of his coat pocket and put it on the table.

"Okay, then, tell me about Juan Doe #67."

She pushed the soup bowl to the side of the table and pulled a leather briefcase onto her lap. She pulled out a thin manila file and opened it in front of her.

"Okay. This is a copy so you can keep it when I'm done explaining. I went over the notes and everything else Salazar had on this. I guess you know, cause of death was multiple blunt-force trauma to the head. Crushing blows to the frontal, parietal, sphenoid and supraorbital."

As she described these injuries she touched the top of her forehead, the back of her head, her left temple and rim of her left eye. She did not look up from the paperwork.

"Any one of these was fatal. There were other defensive wounds which you can look at later. Um, he extracted wood splinters from two of the head injuries. Looks like you are talking about something like a baseball bat, but not as wide, I think. Tremendous crushing blows, so I think we are talking about something with some leverage. Not a stick. Bigger. A pick handle, shovel, something like—possibly a pool cue. But most likely something unfinished. Like I said, Sally pulled splinters out of the wounds. I'm not sure a pool cue with a sanded and lacquered finish would leave splinters."

She studied the notes a moment.

"The other thing—I don't know if Porter told you this, but this body most likely was dumped in that location. Time of death is at least six hours before discovery. Judging by the traffic in that alley and to the rear door of the restaurant, that body could not have gone unnoticed there for six hours. It had to have been dumped."

"Yeah, that was in his notes."

"Good."

She started turning through the pages. Briefly looking at the autopsy photos and putting them to the side.

"Okay, here it is. Tox results aren't back yet but the colors of the blood and liver indicate there will be nothing there. I'm just guessing—or, rather, Sally is just guessing, so don't hold us to that."

Harry nodded. He hadn't taken any notes yet. He lit a cigarette and she didn't seem to mind. She had never protested before, though once when he was attending an autopsy she walked in from the adjoining suite and showed him a lung from a forty-year-old, three-pack-a-day man. It looked like an old black loafer that had been run over by a truck.

"But as you know is routine," she continued, "we took swabs and did the analysis on the stomach contents. First, in the earwax we found a kind of brown dust. We combed some of it out of the hair, and got some from the fingernails, too."

Bosch thought of tar heroin, an ingredient in black ice.

"Heroin?"

"Good guess, but no."

"Just brown dust."

Bosch was writing in his notebook now.

"Yeah, we put it on some slides and blew it up and as near as we can tell it's wheat. Wheat dust. It's—it apparently is pulverized wheat."

"Like cereal? He had cereal in his ears and hair?"

A waiter in a white shirt and black tie with a brush mustache and his best dour Russian look came to the table to ask if they wanted anything else. He looked at the stack of photos next to Teresa. On top was one of Juan Doe #67 naked on a stainless steel table. Teresa quickly covered it with the file and Harry ordered two more beers. The man walked slowly away from the table.

"You mean some kind of wheat cereal?" Bosch asked again. "Like the dust at the bottom of the box or something?"

"Not exactly. Keep that thought, though, and let me move on. It will all tie up."

He waved her on.

"On the nasal swabs and stomach content, two things came up that are very interesting. It's kind of why I like what I do, despite other people not liking it for me." She looked up from the file and smiled at him. "Anyway, in the stomach contents, Salazar identified coffee and masticated rice, chicken, bell pepper, various spices and pig intestine. To make a long story short, it was chorizo—Mexican sausage. The intestine used as sausage casing leads me to believe it was some kind of homemade sausage, not manufactured product. He had eaten this shortly before death. There had been almost no breakdown in the stomach yet. He may've even been eating when he was assaulted. I mean, the throat and mouth were clear but there was still debris in the teeth.

"And by the way, they were all original teeth. No dental work at all—ever. You getting the picture that this man was not from around here?"

Bosch nodded, remembering Porter's notes said all of Juan Doe #67's clothing was made in Mexico. He was writing in the notebook.

She said, "There was also this in the stomach."

She slid a Polaroid photograph across the table. It was of a pinkish insect with one wing missing and the other broken. It looked wet, as indeed it would be, considering where it had been found. It lay on a glass culture dish next to a dime. The dime was about ten times the size of the bug.

Harry noticed the waiter standing about ten feet away with two mugs of beer. The man held the mugs up and raised his eyebrows. Bosch signaled that it was safe to approach. The waiter put the glasses down, stole a glance at the bug photo and then moved quickly away. Harry slid the photo back to Teresa.

"So what is it?"

"*Trypetid*," she said, and she smiled.

"Shoot, I was about to guess that," he said.

She laughed at the lame joke.

"It's a fruit fly, Harry. Mediterranean variety. The little bug that lays big waste to the California citrus industry. Salazar came to me to send it out on referral because we had no idea what it was. I had an investigator take it over to UCLA to an entomologist Gary suggested. He identified it for us."

Gary, Bosch knew, was her estranged, soon to be ex-husband. He nodded at what she was telling him but was not seeing the significance of the find.

She said, "We go on to the nasal swabs. Okay, there was more wheat dust and then we found this."

She slid another photo across the table. This was also a photo of a culture dish with a dime in it. There was also a small pinkish-brown line near the dime. This was much smaller than the fly in the first photo, but Bosch could tell it was also some kind of insect.

"And this?" he asked.

"Same thing, my entomologist tells me. Only this is a youngun. This is a larva."

She folded her fingers together and pointed her elbows out. She smiled and waited.

"You love this, don't you?" he said. He drafted off a quarter of his beer. "Okay, you got me. What's it all mean?"

"Well, you have a basic understanding of the fruit fly right? It chews up the citrus crop, can bring the entire industry to its knees, umpty-ump millions lost, no orange juice in the morning, et cetera, et cetera, the decline of civilization as we know it. Right?"

He nodded and she went on, talking very quickly. "Okay, we seem to have an annual medfly infestation here. I'm sure you've seen the quarantine signs on the freeways or heard the helicopters spraying malathion at night."

"They make me dream of Vietnam," Harry said.

"You must have also seen or read about the movement against malathion spraying. Some people say it poisons people as well as these bugs. They want it stopped. So, what's a Department of Agriculture to do? Well, one thing is step up the other procedure they use to get these bugs.

"The USDA and state Medfly Eradication Project release billions of sterile medflies all across southern California. Millions every week. See, the idea is that when the ones that are already out there mate, they'll do it with sterile partners and eventually the infestation will die out because less and less are reproduced. It's mathematical, Harry. End of problem—if they can saturate the region with enough sterile flies."

She stopped there but Bosch still didn't get it.

"Geez, this is all really fantastic, Teresa. But does it get to a point eventually or are we just—"

"I'm getting there. I'm getting there. Just listen. You are a detective. Detectives are supposed to listen. You once told me that solving murders was getting people to talk and just listening to them. Well, I'm telling it."

He held his hands up. She went on.

"The flies released by the USDA are dyed when they are in the larval stage. Dyed pink, so they can keep track of them or quickly separate the sterile ones from the nonsterile ones when they check those little traps they have in orange trees all over the place. After the larvae are dyed pink, they are irradiated to make them sterile. Then they get released."

Harry nodded. It was beginning to sound interesting.

"My entomologist examined the two samples taken from Juan Doe #67 and this is what he found." She referred to some notes in the file. "The adult fly obtained from the deceased's stomach was both dyed and sterilized, female. Okay, nothing unusual about that. Like I said, they release something like three hundred million of these a week—billions over the year—and so it would seem probable that one might be accidentally swallowed by our man if he was anywhere in, say, southern California."

"That narrows it down," Bosch said. "What about the other sample?"

"The larva is different." She smiled again. "Dr. Braxton, that's the bug doctor, said the larval specimen was dyed pink as to USDA specifications. But it had not yet been irradiated—sterilized—when it went up our Juan Doe's nose."

She unfolded her hands and put them down at her sides. Her factual report was concluded. Now it was time to speculate and she was giving him the first shot.

"So inside his body he has two dyed flies; one sterilized and one not sterilized," Bosch said. "That would lead me to conclude that shortly before his death, our boy was at the location where these flies are sterilized. Millions of flies around. One or two could have gotten in his food. He could have breathed one in through the nose. Anything like that."

She nodded.

"What about the wheat dust? In the ears and hair."

"The wheat dust is the food, Harry. Braxton said that is the food used in the breeding process."

He said, "So I need to find where they make, where they breed, these sterile flies. They might have a line on Juan Doe. Sounds like he was a breeder or something."

She smiled and said, "Why don't you ask me where they breed them."

"Where do they do it, Teresa?"

"Well, the trick is to breed them where they are already a part of the natural insect population or environment and therefore not a problem in case some happen to slip out the door before getting their dose of radiation.

"And, so, the USDA contracts with breeders in only two places; Hawaii and Mexico. In Hawaii there are three breeding contractors on Oahu. In Mexico there is a breeder down near Zihuatanejo and the largest of all five is located near—"

"Mexicali."

"Harry! How did you know? Did you already know all of this and let me—"

"It was just a guess. It fits with something else I've been working on."

She looked at him oddly and for a moment he was sorry he had spoiled her fun. He drained his beer mug and looked around for the squeamish waiter.

Ten

SHE DROVE HIM BACK TO GET HIS CAR NEAR THE RED Wind and then followed him out of downtown and up to his home in the hills. She lived in a condo in Hancock Park, which was closer, but she said she had been spending too much time there lately and wanted a chance to see or hear the coyote. He knew her real reason was that it would be easier for her to extricate herself from his place than to ask him to leave hers.

Bosch didn't mind, though. The truth was, he felt uncomfortable at her place. It reminded him too much of what L.A. was coming to. It was a fifth-floor loft with a view of downtown in a historic residence building called the Warfield. The exterior of the building was still as beautiful as the day in 1911 it was completed by George Allan Hancock. Beaux Arts architecture with a blue-gray terracotta facade. George hadn't spared the oil money and from the street the Warfield, with its fleurs-de-lys and cartouches, showed it. But it was the interior—the current interior, that is—that Bosch found objectionable. The place had been bought a few years back by a Japanese firm and completely gutted, then retrofitted, renovated and revamped. The walls in each apartment were knocked down and each place was nothing but a long, sterile room with fake wood floors, stainless-steel counters and track lighting. Just a pretty shell, Bosch thought. He had a feeling George would've thought the same.

At Harry's house they talked while he lit the hibachi on the porch and put an orange roughy filet on the grill. He had bought it Christmas Eve and it was still fresh and large enough to split. Teresa told him the County Commission would probably informally decide before New Year's on a permanent chief medical examiner. He wished her good luck but privately wasn't sure he meant it. It was a political appointment and she would have to toe the line. Why get into that box? He changed the subject.

"So, if this guy, this Juan Doe, was down in Mexicali—near where they make these fruit flies—how do you think his body got all the way up here?"

"That's not my department," Teresa said.

She was at the railing, staring out over the Valley. There were a million lights glinting in the crisp, cool air. She was wearing his jacket over her shoulders. Harry glazed the fish with a pineapple barbecue sauce and then turned it over.

"It's warm over here by the fire," he said. He dawdled a bit over the filet and then said, "I think what it was is that maybe they didn't want anybody checking around that USDA contractor's business. You know? They didn't want that body connected to that place. So they take the guy's body far away."

"Yeah, but all the way to L.A.?"

"Maybe they were...well, I don't know. That is pretty far away."

They were both silent with their thoughts for a few moments. Bosch could hear and smell the pineapple sizzling as it dripped on the coals. He said, "How do you smuggle a dead body across the border?"

"Oh, I think they've smuggled larger things than that across, don't you?"

He nodded.

"Ever been down there, Harry, to Mexicali?"

"Just to drive through on my way to Bahia San Felipe, where I went fishing last summer. I never stopped. You?"

"Never."

"You know the name of the town just across the border? On our side?"

"Uh uh."

"Calexico."

"You're kidding? Is that where—"

"Yup."

The fish was done. He forked it onto a plate, put the cover on the grill and they went inside. He served it with Spanish rice he made with Pico Pico. He opened a bottle of red wine and poured two glasses. Blood of the gods. He didn't have any white. As he put everything on the table he saw a smile on her face.

"Thought I was a TV dinner guy, didn't you."

"Crossed my mind. This is very nice."

They clicked glasses and ate quietly. She complimented him on the meal but he knew the fish was a little too dry. They descended into small talk again. The whole time he was looking for the opening to ask her about the Moore autopsy. It didn't come until they were finished.

"What will you do now?" she asked after putting her napkin on the table.

"Guess I'll clear the table and see if—"

"No. You know what I mean. About the Juan Doe case."

"I'm not sure. I want to talk to Porter again. And I'll probably look up the USDA. I'd like to know more about how those flies get here from Mexico."

She nodded and said, "Let me know if you want to talk to the entomologist. I can arrange that."

He watched her as she once again got the far-off stare that had been intruding all night.

"What about you?" he asked. "What will you do now?"

"About what?"

"About the problems with the Moore autopsy."

"That obvious, huh?"

He got up and cleared the plates away. She didn't move from the table. He sat back down and emptied the bottle into the glasses. He decided he would have to give her something in order for her to feel comfortable giving him something in return.

"Listen to me, Teresa. I think you and I should talk about things. I think we have two investigations, probably three investigations, here, that may all be part of the same thing. Like different spokes on the same wheel."

She brought her eyes up, confused. "What cases? What are you talking about?"

"I know that all of what I'm about to say is outside your venue but I think you need to know it to help make your decision. I've been watching you all night and I can tell you have a problem and don't know what to do."

He hesitated, giving her a chance to stop him. She didn't. He told her about Marvin Dance's arrest and its relation to the Jimmy Kapps murder.

"When I found out Kapps had been bringing ice over from Hawaii, I went to Cal Moore to ask about black ice. You know, the competition. I wanted to know where it comes from, where you get it, who's selling it, anything that would help me get a picture of who might've put down Jimmy Kapps. Anyway, the point is I thought Moore shined me on, said he knew nothing, but today I find out he was putting together a file on black ice. He was gathering string on my case. He held stuff back from me, but at the same time was putting something together on this when he disappeared. I got the file today. There was a note. It said 'Give to Harry Bosch' on it."

"What was in it? The file."

"A lot. Including an intelligence report, says the main source of black ice is probably a ranch down in Mexicali."

She stared at him but said nothing.

"Which brings us to our Juan Doe. Porter bails out and the case comes to me today. I am reading through the file and I'll give you one guess who it was that found the body and then disappeared the next day."

"Shit," she said.

"Exactly. Cal Moore. What this means I don't know. But he is the reporting officer on the body. The next day he is in the wind. The next week he is found in a motel room, a supposed suicide. And then the next day—after the discovery of Moore has been in the papers and on TV—Porter calls up and says, 'Guess what, guys, I quit.' Does all of this sound aboveboard to you?"

She abruptly stood up and walked to the sliding door to the porch. She stared through the glass out across the pass.

"Those bastards," she said. "They just want to drop the whole thing. Because it might embarrass somebody."

Bosch walked up behind her.

"You have to tell somebody about it. Tell me."

"No. I can't. You tell me everything."

"I've told you. There isn't much else and it's all a jumble. The file didn't have much, other than that the DEA told Moore that black ice is coming up from Mexicali. That's how I guessed about the fruit fly contractor. And then there's Moore. He grew up in Calexico and Mexicali. You see? There are too many coincidences here that I don't think are coincidences."

She still faced the door and he was talking to her back, but he saw the reflection of her worried face in the glass. He could smell her perfume.

"The important thing about the file is that Moore didn't keep it in his office or his apartment. It was in a place where someone from IAD or RHD wouldn't find it. And when the guys on his crew found it, there was the note that said to give it to me. You understand?"

The confused look in the glass answered for her. She turned and moved into the living room, sitting on the cushioned chair and running her hands through her hair. Harry stayed standing and paced on the wood floor in front of her.

"Why would he write a note saying give the file to me? It wouldn't have been a note to himself. He already knew he was putting the file together for me. So, the note was for someone else. And what does that tell us? That he either knew when he wrote it that he was going to kill himself. Or he—"

"Knew he was going to be killed," she said.

Bosch nodded. "Or, at least, he knew he had gotten into something too deep. That he was in trouble. In danger."

"Jesus," she said.

Harry approached and handed her her wineglass. He bent down close to her face.

"You have to tell me about the autopsy. Something's wrong. I heard that bullshit press release they put out. Inconclusive. What is that shit? Since when can't you tell if a shotgun blast to the face killed somebody or not?

"So tell me, Teresa. We can figure out what to do."

She shrugged her shoulders and shook her head, but Harry knew she was going to tell.

"They told me because I wasn't a hundred percent—Harry, you can't reveal where you got this information. You can't."

"It won't get back to you. If I have to, I will use it to help us, but it won't get back to you. That's my promise."

"They told me not to discuss it with anyone because I couldn't be completely sure. The assistant chief, Irving, that arrogant prick knew just where to stick it in. Talking about the County Commission deciding soon about my position. Saying they would be looking for a chief ME who knew discretion. Saying what friends he had on the commission. I'd like to take a scalpel—"

"Never mind all of that. What was it you weren't one hundred percent sure about?"

She drained her wineglass. Then the story came out. She told him that the autopsy had proceeded as routine, other than the fact that in addition to the two case detectives observing it, Sheehan and Chastain from IAD, was assistant police chief Irving. She said a lab technician was also on hand to make the fingerprint comparisons.

"The decomposition was extensive," Teresa said. "I had to take the finger tips off and spray them with a chemical hardening agent. Collins, that's my lab tech, was able to take prints after that. He made the comparison right there because Irving had brought exemplars. It was a match. It was Moore."

"What about the teeth?"

"Dental was tough. There wasn't much left that hadn't been fragged. We made a comparison between a partial incisor found in the tub and some dental records Irving came up with. Moore had had a root canal and it was there. That was a match, too."

She said she began the autopsy after confirming the identity and immediately concluded the obvious: that damage from the double-barrel-shotgun blast was massive and fatal. Instantly. But it was while examining the material that had separated from the body that she began to question whether she could rule Moore's death a suicide.

"The force of the blast resulted in complete cranial displacement," she said. "And, of course, the autopsy protocol calls for examination of all vital organs, including the brain.

"Problem was the brain was mostly unmassed due to the wide projectile pattern. I believe I was told the pellets came from a double-barrel, side-by-side configuration. I could see that. The projectile pattern was very wide. Nevertheless, a large portion of the frontal lobe and corresponding skull fragment were left largely intact, though it had been separated.

"You know what I mean? The diagram said this had been charted in the bathtub. Is this . . . too much? I know you knew him."

"Not that well. Go on."

"So I examined this piece, not really expecting anything more than what I was seeing earlier. But I was wrong. There was hemorrhagic demarcation in the lobe along the skull lining."

She took a hit off his wineglass and breathed heavily, as if casting out a demon.

"And so, you see Harry, that was a big fucking problem."

"Tell me why."

"You sound like Irving. 'Tell me why. Tell me why.' Well, it should be obvious. For two reasons. First of all you don't have that much hemorrhage on instant death like that. There is not much bleeding in the brain lining when the brain has been literally disconnected from the body in a split second. But while there is some room for some debate on that—I'll give that to Irving—there is no debate whatsoever on the second reason. This hemorrhaging was clearly indicative of a contrecoup injury to the head. No doubt in my mind at all."

Harry quickly reviewed the physics he had learned over the ten years he had been watching autopsies. Contrecoup brain injury is damage that occurs to the side of the brain opposite the insult. The brain, in effect, was a Jell-O mold inside the skull. A jarring blow to the left side often did its worst damage to the right side because the force of impact pushed the Jell-O against the right side of the skull. Harry knew that for Moore to have the hemorrhage Teresa described to the front of the brain, he would have to be struck from behind. A shotgun blast to the face would not have done it.

"Is there any way...," he trailed off unclear of what he wanted to ask. He suddenly became aware of his body's pangs for a cigarette and smacked the end of a fresh pack on his palm.

"What happened?" he asked as he opened it.

"Well, when I started explaining, Irving got all uptight and kept asking, 'Are you sure? Is that a hundred percent accurate? Aren't we jumping the gun?' and on and on like that. I think it was pretty clear. He didn't want this to be anything other than a suicide. The minute I raised a doubt he started talking about jumping to conclusions and the need to move slowly. He said the department could be embarrassed by what an investigation could lead to if we did not proceed slowly and cautiously and correctly. Those were his words. Asshole."

"Let sleeping dogs lie," Bosch said.

"Right. So I just flat-out told them I was not going to rule it a suicide. And then... then they talked me out of ruling it a homicide. So that's where the inconclusive comes from. A compromise. For now. It makes me feel like I am guilty of something. Those bastards."

"They're just going to drop it," Bosch said.

He couldn't figure it out. The reluctance had to be because of the IAD investigation. Whatever Moore was into, Irving must believe it either led him to kill himself or got him killed. And either way Irving didn't want to open that box without knowing first what was in it. Maybe he never wanted to know. That told Bosch one thing. He was on his own. No matter what he came up with, turning it over to Irving and RHD would get it buried. So if Bosch went on with it, he was freelancing.

"Do they know that Moore was working on something for you?" Teresa asked.

"By now they do, but they probably didn't when they were with you. Probably won't make any difference."

"What about the Juan Doe case? About him finding the body."

"I don't know what they know on that."

"What will you do?"

"I don't know. I don't know anything. What will you do?"

She was silent for a long time, then she got up and walked to him. She leaned into him and kissed him on the lips. She whispered, "Let's forget about all of this for a while."

He conceded to her in their lovemaking, letting her lead and direct him, use his body the way she wanted. They had been together often enough so that they were comfortable and knew each other's ways. They were beyond the stages of curiosity or embarrassment. At the end, she was straddled over him as he leaned back, propped on pillows, against the headboard. Her head snapped back and her clipped nails dug painlessly into his chest. She made no sound at all.

In the darkness he looked up and saw the glint of silver dripping from her ears. He reached up and touched the earrings and then ran his hands down her throat, over her shoulders and breasts. Her skin was warm and damp. Her slow methodical motion drew him further into the void where everything else in the world could not go.

When they were both resting, she still huddled on top of him, a sense of guilt came over him. He thought of Sylvia Moore. A woman he had met only the night before, how could she intrude on this? But she had. He wondered where the guilt came from. Maybe it was for what was still ahead of them.

He thought he heard the short, high-pitched bark of the coyote in the distance behind the house. Teresa raised her head off his chest and then they heard the animal's lonesome baying.

"Timido," he heard her say quietly.

Harry felt the guilt pass over him again. He thought of Teresa. Had he tricked her into telling him? He didn't think so. Maybe, again, it was guilt over what he had not yet done. What he knew he would do with the information she had given.

She seemed to know his thoughts were away from her. Perhaps a change in his heartbeat, a slight tensing in his muscles.

"Nothing," she said.

"What?"

"You asked what I was going to do. Nothing. I'm not going to get involved in this bullshit any further. If they want to bury it, let them bury it."

Harry knew then that she would make a good permanent chief medical examiner for the county of Los Angeles.

He felt himself falling away from her in the dark.

Teresa rolled off him and sat on the edge of the bed, looking out the window at the three-quarter moon. They had left the curtain open. The coyote howled once more. Bosch thought he could hear a dog answering somewhere in the distance.

"Are you like him?" she asked.

"Who?"

"Timido. Alone out there in the dark world."

"Sometimes. Everybody is sometimes."

"Yes, but you like it, don't you?"

"Not always."

"Not always..."

He thought about what to say. The wrong word and she'd be gone.

"I'm sorry if I'm distant," he tried. "There's a lot of things..."

He didn't finish. There was no excuse.

"You do like living up here in this little, lonely house, with the coyote as your only friend, don't you?"

He didn't answer. The face of Sylvia Moore inexplicably came back into his mind. But this time he felt no guilt. He liked seeing her there.

"I have to go," Teresa said. "Long day tomorrow."

He watched her walk naked into the bathroom, picking her purse up off the night table as she went. He listened as the shower ran. He imagined her in there, cleaning all traces of him off and out of her and then splashing on the all-purpose perfume she always carried in her purse to cover up any smells left on her from her job.

He rolled to the side of the bed to the pile of his clothes on the floor and got out his phone book. He dialed while the water still ran. The voice that answered was dulled with sleep. It was near midnight.

"You don't know who this is and I never talked to you." There was silence while Harry's voice registered.

"Okay, okay. Got it. I understand."

"There's a problem on the Cal Moore autopsy."

"Shit, I know that, man. Inconclusive. You don't have to wake me up to—"

"No, you don't understand. You are confusing the autopsy with the press release on the autopsy. Two different things. Understand now?"

"Yeah...I think I do. So, what's the problem?"

"The assistant chief of police and the acting chief ME don't agree. One says suicide, the other homicide. Can't have both. I guess that's what you call inconclusive in a press release."

There was a low whistling sound in the phone.

"This is good. But why would the cops want to bury a homicide, especially one of their own? I mean, suicide makes the department look like shit as it is. Why bury a murder unless it means there's something—"

"Right," Bosch said and he hung up the phone.

A minute later the shower was turned off and Teresa came out, drying herself with a towel. She was totally unabashed about her nakedness with him and Harry found he missed that shyness. It had eventually left all the women he became involved with before they eventually left him.

He pulled on blue jeans and a T-shirt while she dressed. Neither spoke. She looked at him with a thin smile and then he walked her out to her car.

"So, we still have a date for New Year's Eve?" she asked after he opened the car door for her.

"Of course," he said, though he knew she would call with an excuse to cancel it.

She leaned up and kissed him on the lips, then slipped into the driver's seat.

"Good-bye, Teresa," he said but she had already closed the door.

It was midnight when he came back inside. The place smelled of her perfume. And his own guilt. He put Frank Morgan's *Mood Indigo* on the CD player and stood there in the living room without moving, just listening to the phrasing on the first solo, a song called "Lullaby." Bosch thought he knew nothing truer than the sound of a saxophone.

Eleven

SLEEP WAS NOT A POSSIBILITY. BOSCH KNEW THIS. HE stood on the porch looking down on the carpet of lights and let the chill air harden his skin and his resolve. For the first time in months he felt invigorated. He was in the hunt again. He let everything about the cases pass through his mind and made a mental list of people he had to see and things he had to do.

On top was Lucius Porter, the broken-down detective whose pullout was too timely, too coincidental to be coincidental. Harry realized he was becoming angry just thinking about Porter. And embarrassed. Embarrassed at having stuck his neck out for him with Pounds.

He went to his notebook and then dialed Porter's number one more time. He was not expecting an answer and he wasn't disappointed. Porter had at least been reliable in that respect. He checked the address he had written down earlier and headed out.

Driving down out of the hills he did not pass another car until he reached Cahuenga. He headed north and got on the Hollywood Freeway at Barham. The freeway was crowded but not so that traffic was slow. The cars moved northward at a steady clip, a sleekly moving ribbon of lights. Out over Studio City, Bosch could see a police helicopter circling, a shaft of white light cast downward on a crime scene somewhere. It almost seemed as if the beam was a leash that held the circling craft from flying high and away.

He loved the city most at night. The night hid many of the sorrows. It silenced the city yet brought deep undercurrents to the surface. It was in this dark slipstream that he believed he moved most freely. Behind the cover of shadows. Like a rider in a limousine, he looked out but no one looked in.

There was a random feel to the dark, the quirkiness of chance played out in the blue neon night. So many ways to live. And to die. You could be riding in the back of a studio's black limo, or just as easily the back of the coroner's blue van. The sound of applause was the same as the buzz of a bullet spinning past your ear in the dark. That randomness. That was L.A.

There was flash fire and flash flood, earthquake, mudslide. There was the drive-by shooter and the crack-stoked burglar. The drunk driver and the always curving road ahead. There were killer cops and cop killers. There was the husband of the woman you were sleeping with. And there was the woman. At any moment on any night there were people being raped, violated, maimed. Murdered and loved. There was always a baby at his mother's breast. And, sometimes, a baby alone in a Dumpster.

Somewhere.

Harry exited on Vanowen in North Hollywood and went east toward Burbank. Then he turned north again into a neighborhood of rundown apartments. Bosch could tell by the gang graffiti it was a mostly Latino neighborhood. He knew Porter had lived here for years. It was all he could afford after paying alimony and for his booze.

He turned into the Happy Valley Trailer Park and found Porter's double-wide at the end of Greenbriar Lane. The trailer was dark, not even a light on above the door, and there was no car under the aluminum-roofed carport. Bosch sat in his car smoking a cigarette and watching for a while. He heard mariachi music wafting into the neighborhood from one of the Mexican clubs over on Lankershim. Soon it was drowned out by a jet that lumbered by overhead on its way to Burbank Airport. He reached into the glove compartment for a leather pouch containing his flashlight and picks and got out.

After the third knock went unanswered, Harry opened the pouch. Breaking into Porter's place did not give him pause. Porter was a player in this game, not an innocent. To Bosch's mind, Porter had forfeited protection of his privacy when he had not been straight with him, when he hadn't mentioned that Moore had been the one who found Juan Doe #67's body. Now Bosch was going to find Porter and ask him about that.

He took out the miniature flashlight, turned it on and then held it in his mouth as he stooped down and worked a pick and tiny pressure wrench into the lock. It took him only a few minutes to push the pins and open the door.

A sour odor greeted Bosch when he entered. He recognized it as the smell of a drunk's sweat. He called Porter's name but got no answer.

He turned on the lights as he moved through the rooms. There were empty glasses on nearly every horizontal surface. The bed was unmade and the sheets were a dingy white. Amidst the glasses on the night table was an ashtray overloaded with butts. There was also a statue of a saint Bosch could not identify. In the bathroom off the bedroom, the bathtub was filthy, a toothbrush was on the floor and in the wastebasket there was an empty bottle of whiskey, a brand either so expensive or so cheap that Harry had never heard of it. But he suspected it was the latter.

In the kitchen, there was another empty bottle in the trash can. There were also dirty dishes piled on the counters and sink. He opened the refrigerator and saw only a jar of mustard and an egg carton. Porter's place was very much like its owner. It showed a marginal life, if it could be called that at all.

Back in the living room Bosch picked a framed photograph up off a table next to a yellow couch. It was a woman. Not too attractive, except to Porter maybe. An ex-wife he couldn't get over. Maybe. Harry put the photo back down and the phone rang.

He traced the noise to the bedroom. The phone was on the floor next to the bed. He picked up on the seventh ring, waited a moment and in a voice designed to appear jerked from sleep said, "Huh?"

"Porter?"

"Yeah."

The line went dead. It hadn't worked. But had Bosch recognized the voice? Pounds? No, not Pounds. Only one word spoken. But, still, the accent was there. Spanish, he thought. He filed it away in his mind and got up off the bed. Another plane crossed above and the trailer shuddered. He went back into the living room where he made a half-hearted search of a one-drawer desk, though he knew that no matter what he found it wouldn't solve the immediate problem: where was Porter?

Bosch turned all the lights off and relocked the front door as he left. He decided to start in North Hollywood and work his way south toward downtown. In every police division there was a handful of bars that carried a heavy clientele of cops. Then after two, when they closed, there were the all-night bottle clubs. Mostly they were dark pits where men came to drink hard and quietly, as if their lives depended on it. They were havens from the street, places to go to forget and forgive yourself. It was at one of these Bosch believed he would find Porter.

He began with a place on Kittridge called the Parrot. But the bartender, a one-time cop himself, said he hadn't seen Porter since Christmas Eve. Next, he went to the 502 on Lankershim and then Saint's on Cahuenga. They knew Porter in these places but he hadn't been at either tonight.

It went like that until two. By then, Bosch had worked his way down into Hollywood. He was sitting in his car in front of the Bullet, trying to think of nearby bottle-club locations, when his pager went off. He checked the number and didn't recognize it. He went back into the Bullet to use the pay phone. The lights in the bar came on after he dialed. Last call was over.

"Bosch?"

"Yeah."

"It's Rickard. Bad time?"

"Nah. I'm at the Bullet."

"Hell, man, then you're close by."

"For what? You got Dance?"

"Nah, not quite. I'm at a rave behind Cahuenga and south of the boulevard. Couldn't sleep so I thought I'd do some hunting. No Dance but I got my eye on one of his old salesmen. One of the ones that was on the shake cards in the file. Name's Kerwin Tyge."

Bosch thought a moment. He remembered the name. He was one of the juvies the BANG team had stopped and checked out, tried to scare off the street. His name was on one of the file cards in the ice file Moore had left behind.

"What's a rave?"

"An underground. They got a warehouse off this alley. A fly-by-night party. Digital music. They'll run all night, 'til about six. Next week it will be somewhere else."

"How'd you find it?"

"They're easy to find. The record stores on Melrose put out the phone numbers. You call the number, get on the list. Twenty bucks to get in. Get stoned and dance 'til dawn."

"He selling black ice?"

"Nah, he's selling sherms out front."

A sherm was a cigarette dipped in liquid PCP. Went for twenty bucks a dip and would leave its smoker dusted all night. Tyge apparently was no longer working for Dance.

"I figure we can make a righteous bust," Rickard said. "After that, we might squeeze Dance out of his ass. I think Dance has blown, but the kid might know where. It's up to you. I don't know how important Dance is to you."

"Where do you want me?" Bosch asked.

"Come west on the Boulevard and just when you pass Cahuenga come south at the very next alley. The one that comes down behind the porno shops. It's dark but you'll see the blue neon arrow. That's the place. I'm about a half block north in a red piece-of-shit Camaro. Nevada plates. I'll be waiting. Hafta figure out a scam or something to grab him with the shit."

"You know where the dip is?"

"Yeah. He's got it in a beer bottle in the gutter. Keeps going in and out. Brings his clients outside. I'll think of something by the time you get here."

Bosch hung up and went back out to the car. It took him fifteen minutes to get there because of all the cruisers on the Boulevard. In the alley he parked illegally behind the red Camaro. He could see Rickard sitting low in the driver's seat.

"Top of the morning to ya," the narc said when Bosch slipped into the Camaro's passenger seat.

"Same. Our boy still around?"

"Oh, yeah. Seems like he's having a good night, too. He's selling shermans like they're the last thing on earth. Too bad we gotta spoil his fun."

Bosch looked down the dark alley. In the intervals of blue light cast by a blinking neon arrow he could see a grouping of people in dark clothes in front of a door in the brick siding of the warehouse. Occasionally, the door would open and someone would go in or come out. He could hear the music when the door was open. Loud, techno-rock, a driving bass that seemed to shake the street. As his eyes adjusted, he saw that the people outside were drinking and smoking, cooling off after dancing. A few of them held blown-up balloons. They would lean on the hoods of the cars near the door, suck from the balloon and pass it on as if it were a joint.

"The balloons are full of nitrous oxide," Rickard said.

"Laughing gas?"

"Right. They sell it at these raves for five bucks a balloon. They can make a couple grand off one tank stolen from a hospital or dentist."

A girl fell off a car hood and her balloon of gas shot away into the dark. Others helped her up. Bosch could hear their shrieks of laughter.

"That legal?"

"It's a flopper. It's legal to possess—a lot of legit uses for it. But it's a misdee to consume recreationally. We don't even bother with it, though. Somebody wants to suck on it and fall down and split their head open, have at it, I say. Why should—there he is now."

The slight figure of a teenager walked through the warehouse door and over to the cars parked along the alley.

"Watch him go down," Rickard said.

The figure disappeared behind a car, dropping down.

"See, he's making a dip. Now he'll wait a few minutes 'til it dries a little and his customer comes out. Then he'll make the deal."

"Want to go get him?"

"No. We take him with just the one sherm, that's nothing. That's personal possession. They won't even keep him overnight in the drunk tank. We need him with his dip if we wanna squeeze him good."

"So what do we do?"

"You just get back in your car. I want you to go back around on Cahuenga and come up the alley the other way. I think you can get in closer. Park it and then try to work your way up to be my backup. I'll come down from this end. I got some old clothes in the trunk. Undercover shit. I got a plan."

Bosch then went back to the Caprice, turned it around and drove out of the alley. He drove around the block and came up from the south side. He found a spot in front of a Dumpster and stopped. When he saw the hunched-over figure of Rickard moving down the alley, Harry got out and started moving. They were closing in on the warehouse door from both sides. But while Bosch remained in the shadows, Rickard—now wearing a grease-stained sweatshirt and carrying a bag of laundry—was walking down the center of the alley, singing. Because of the noise from the warehouse Bosch wasn't sure but he thought it was Percy Sledge's "When a Man Loves a Woman," delivered in a drunken slur.

Rickard had the undivided attention of the people standing outside the warehouse door. A couple of the stoned girls cheered his singing. The distraction allowed Bosch to move within four cars of the door and about three cars from the spot where Tyge had his dip.

As he passed the spot, Rickard stopped his song in mid-chorus and acted as if he had just spotted a treasure. He ducked between the two parked cars and came up with the beer bottle in hand. He was about to place it in his bag when the boy moved quickly between the cars and grabbed the bottle. Rickard refused to let go and spun so that the boy's back was now to Bosch. Harry started moving.

"It's mine, man," Rickard yelled.

"I put it there, bro. Let it go before it spills."

"Go get your own, man. This here's mine."

"Let it go!"

"You sure it's yours?"

"It's mine!"

Bosch hit the boy forcefully from behind. He let go of the bottle and doubled over the trunk of the car. Bosch kept him pinned there, pushing his forearm against the boy's neck. The bottle stayed in Rickard's hand. None of it spilled.

"Well, if you say so, I guess it's yours," the narc said. "And I guess that makes you under arrest."

Bosch pulled his cuffs off his belt and hooked the boy up and then pulled him off the trunk. Some of the others were gathering around now.

"Fuck off, people," Rickard said loudly. "Go back inside and sniff your laughing gas. Go get deaf. This here don't concern you unless you want to go along with this boy to the shit can."

He bent down to Tyge's ear and said, "Right, *bro?*"

When nobody in the crowd moved, Rickard took a menacing step toward them and they scattered. A couple of the girls ran back into the warehouse. The music drowned out Rickard's laugh. He then turned around and grabbed Tyge by the arm.

"Let's go. Harry, let's take your wheels."

They drove in silence for a while toward the station on Wilcox. They hadn't discussed it earlier but Harry was going to let Rickard make the play. Rickard was riding in the back with the boy. In the mirror, Harry saw he had greasy, unkempt brown hair that fell to his shoulders. About five years earlier he should have had braces put on his teeth but one look at him and Bosch could tell he came from a home where things like that were not a consideration. He had a gold earring and an uninterested look on his face. But the teeth were what got to Bosch. Crooked and protruding, they more than anything else showed the desperation of his life.

"How old are you now, Kerwin?" Rickard said. "And don't bother lying. We got a file on you at the station. I can check."

"Eighteen. And you can wipe your ass with the file. I don't give a shit."

"Wooo!" Rickard yelped. "Eighteen. Looks like we got ourselves an A-dult here, Harry. No holding hands all the way to the juvie hall. We'll go put this kid in seven thousand, see how quick he starts keeping house with one of the heavies."

Seven thousand was what most cops and criminals called the county adult detention center, on account of the phone number for inmate information, 555-7000. The jail was downtown and it was four floors of noise and hate and violence sitting atop the county sheriff's headquarters. Somebody was stabbed there every day. Somebody raped every hour. And nothing was ever done about it. Nobody cared, unless you were the one getting raped or stabbed. The sheriff's deputies who ran the place called it an NHI detail. No Humans Involved. Bosch knew if they were going to squeeze this kid that Rickard had picked the right way to go.

"We got you bagged and tagged, Kerwin," Rickard said. "There's at least two ounces in here. Got you cold for possession with intent to sell, dude. You're gone."

"Fuck you."

The kid drew each word out with sarcasm. He was going to go down fighting. Bosch noticed that Rickard was holding the green beer bottle outside the window so the fumes wouldn't fill the car and give them headaches.

"That's not nice, Kerwin. Especially, when the man driving here is willing to do a deal.... Now if it was me, I'd just let you make your deals with the brothers in seven thousand. Couple days there and you'll be shaving your legs and walking 'round in pink underwear they dipped in the Hawaiian Punch."

"Fuck off pig. Just get me to a phone."

They were on Sunset, coming up to Wilcox. Almost there and Rickard hadn't even gotten around to what they wanted. It didn't look as if the kid was going to deal, no matter what they wanted.

"You'll get a phone when we feel like giving you a phone. You're tough now, white boy, but it don't last. Everybody gets broken down inside. You'll see. Unless you want to help us out. We just want to talk to your pal Dance."

Bosch turned onto Wilcox. The station was two blocks away. The kid said nothing and Rickard let the silence go for a block before giving another try.

"What do you say, kid? Give an address. I'll dump this shit right now. Don't be one of those fools who think seven thousand makes them the man. Like it's some fucking rite of passage. It ain't, kid. It's just the end of the line. That what you want?"

"I want you to die."

Bosch pulled into the driveway that led to the station's rear parking lot. They would have to process the arrest here first, book the evidence, then take the kid downtown. Harry knew they would have to go through with it. The kid wasn't talking. They had to show him that they weren't bluffing.

Twelve

BOSCH DIDN'T GET BACK TO HIS SEARCH FOR PORTER until four in the morning. By then he had had two cups of coffee in the station and was holding his third. He was back in the Caprice, alone and roaming the city.

Rickard had agreed to ferry Kerwin Tyge downtown. The kid had never talked. His shell of hardened rejection, cop hate and misguided pride never cracked. At the station, it had become a mission for Rickard to break the kid. He renewed the threats, the questions, with a zeal that Bosch found disturbing. He finally told Rickard that it was over. He told the narc to book the kid and they'd try again later. After stepping out of the interview room, the two decided to meet at seven thousand at 2 P.M. That would give the kid about a ten-hour taste of the big house, enough time to make a decision.

Now Bosch was cruising the bottle clubs, the after-hour joints where "members" brought their own bottles and were charged for the setups. The setups, of course, were a ripoff, and some clubs even charged a membership fee. But some people just couldn't drink at home alone. And some people didn't have much of a home.

At a stoplight on Sunset at Western, a blur passed the car on the right and a figure lunged over the passenger side of the hood. Bosch instinctively drew his left hand up to his belt and almost dropped his coffee but then realized the man had begun to rub a newspaper on the windshield. Half past four in the morning and a homeless man was cleaning his windshield. Badly. The man's efforts only smudged the glass. Bosch pulled a dollar out of his pocket and handed it out the window to the man when he came around to do the driver's side. He waved him away.

"Don't worry about it, partner," he said and the man silently walked away.

Bosch headed off, hitting bottle clubs in Echo Park near the police academy and then Chinatown. No sign of Porter. He crossed over the Hollywood Freeway into downtown, thinking of the kid as he passed the county lockup. He'd be on seven, the narco module, where the inhabitants were generally less hostile. He'd probably be okay.

He saw the big blue trucks pulling out of the garage on the Spring Street side of the *Times* building, heading off with another morning's cargo of news. He tried a couple of bottle clubs near Parker Center, then one near skid row. He was scratching bottom now, getting near the end of the line and running out of places to check.

The last place he stopped was Poe's, which was centrally located on Third Avenue near skid row, the *Los Angeles Times*, St. Vibiana's and the glass bank towers of the financial district, where alcoholics were manufactured wholesale. Poe's did a good business in the morning hours before downtown came alive with hustle and greed.

Poe's was on the first floor of a prewar brick walkup that had been tagged for demolition by the Community Redevelopment Agency. It had not been earthquake-proofed and retrofitting it would cost more than the building was worth. The CRA had bought it and was going to knock it down to put up condos that would draw live-in residents downtown. But the whole thing was on hold. Another city agency, the Office of Preservation, wanted the Poe building, as it was informally known, granted landmark status and was suing to stop the demolition. So far they had held up the plan four years. Poe's was still open. The four floors above it were abandoned.

Inside, the place was a black hole with a long, warped bar and no tables. Poe's wasn't a place to sit in a booth with friends. It was a place to drink alone. A place for executive suicides who needed courage, broken cops who couldn't cope with the loneliness they built into their lives, writers who could no longer write and priests who could no longer forgive even their own sins. It was a place to drink mean, as long as you still had the green. It cost you five bucks for a stool at the bar and a dollar for a glass of ice to go with your bottle of whiskey. A soda setup was three bucks but most of these people took their medicine straight up. It was cheaper that way and more to the point. It was said that Poe's was not named after the writer but for the general philosophy of its clientele: Piss on Everything.

Even though it was dark outside, stepping into Poe's was like walking into a cave. For a moment, Bosch was reminded of that first moment after dropping into a VC tunnel in Vietnam. He stood utterly still by the door until his eyes focused in the dim light and he saw the red leather padding on the bar. The place smelled worse than Porter's trailer. The bartender, in a wrinkled white shirt and unbuttoned black vest, stood to the right, backed by the rows of liquor bottles; each with the bottle owner's name attached on a piece of masking tape. A red stem of neon ran along the booze shelf, behind the bottles, and gave them an eerie glow.

From the darkness to Bosch's left, he heard, "Shit, Harry, whaddaya doing? You looking for me?"

He turned and there was Porter at the other end of the bar, sitting so he could see whoever came in before they could see him. Harry walked over. He saw a shot glass in front of Porter along with a half-filled water glass and a third-filled bottle of bourbon. There was a twenty and three ones fanned out on the bar as well and a package of Camels. Bosch felt anger rising in his throat as he approached and came up on Porter's back.

"Yeah, I'm looking for you."

"Whassup?"

Bosch knew he had to do what he had to do before any sympathy could crack through his anger. He yanked Porter's sport coat down over his shoulders so his arms were caught at his sides. A cigarette dropped out of his hand to the floor. Bosch reached around and pulled the gun out of his shoulder holster and put it on the bar.

"What're you still carrying for, Lou? You pulled the pin, remember? What, you scared of something?"

"Harry, what's going on? Why are you doing this?"

The bartender started walking down behind the bar to the aid of his club member but Bosch fixed him with a cold stare, held up his hand like a traffic cop and said, "Cool it. It's private."

"Damned right. It's a private club and you ain't a member."

"It's okay, Tommy," Porter spoke up. "I know him. I'll take care of it."

A couple of men who had been sitting a few stools from Porter got up and moved to the other end of the bar with their bottles and drinks. A couple of other drunks were already down there watching. But nobody left, not with booze still in their jars and it not quite being six o'clock yet. There would be no place else to go. Bars wouldn't open until seven and the hour or so until then could last a lifetime. No, they weren't going anywhere. This crew would sit there and watch a man murdered if they had to.

"Harry, c'mon," Porter said. "Cool it yourself. We can talk."

"Can we? Can we? Why didn't you talk when I called the other day? How about Moore? Did you have a talk with Cal Moore?"

"Look, Harry—"

Bosch spun him around off the stool and face first into the wood-paneled wall. He came easier than Harry had thought he would and hit the wall hard. His nose made a sound like an ice-cream cone hitting the sidewalk. Bosch leaned his back against Porter's back, pinning him face first against the wall.

"Don't 'Look, Harry' me, Porter. I stood up for you, man, 'cause I thought you were...I thought you were worth it. Now I know, Porter. I was wrong. You quit on the Juan Doe. I want to know why. I want to know what's going on."

Porter's voice was muffled by the wall and his own blood. He said, "Harry, shit, I think you broke my nose. I'm bleeding."

"Don't worry about it. What about Moore? I know he reported the body."

Porter made some kind of wet snorting sound but Bosch just pushed him harder. The man stunk of sour body odor, booze and cigarettes, and Bosch wondered how long he had been sitting in Poe's, watching the door.

"I'm calling the police now," the bartender yelled. He stood holding the phone out so Bosch would see it was a real threat, which of course it wasn't. The bartender knew if he dialed that phone every stool in the bar would be left spinning as the drunks filed out. There would be no one left to scam on the change or to leave quarters for his cup.

Using his body to keep Porter pinned to the wall, Bosch pulled out his badge wallet and held it up. "I am the police. Mind your own fucking business."

The bartender shook his head as if to say what is this fine business coming to, and put the phone back next to the cash register. The announcement that Bosch was a police officer resulted in about half the other customers jerking their drinks down and leaving. There were probably warrants out for everybody in the place, Bosch thought.

Porter was starting to mumble and Bosch thought he might be crying again, like on the phone Thursday morning.

"Harry, I—I didn't think I was doing...I had—"

Bosch bounced harder against his back and heard Porter's forehead hit the wall.

"Don't start that shit with me, Porter. You were takin' care of yourself. That's what you were doing. And—"

"I'm sick. I'm gonna be sick."

"—and right now, believe it or not, right now the only one that really cares about you is me. You fuck, you just tell me what you did. Just tell me what you did and we're square. It goes nowhere else. You go for your stress out and I never see your face again."

Bosch could hear his wet breathing against the wall. It was almost as if he could hear him thinking.

"You sure, Harry?"

"You don't have a choice. You don't start talking, you end up with no job, no pension."

"He, uh—I just...there's blood on my shirt. It's roon."

Bosch pushed harder against him.

"Okay, okay, okay. I'll tell ya, I'll tell...I just did him a favor, thas all, and he ended up deader'n shit. When I heard, I, uh, I couldn't come back in, see. I didn't know what happened. I mean, I mean, they—somebody could be looking for me. I got scared, Harry. I'm scared. I been sitting in bars since I talked to you yesterday. I stink like shit. And now all this blood. I need a napkin. I think they're after me."

Bosch took his weight off him but held one hand pressed against his back so he would not go anywhere. He reached back to the bar and took a handful of cocktail napkins off a stack near a bowl of matches. He held them over Porter's shoulder and the broken cop worked his hand loose from his jacket and took them. He turned his head away from the wall to press the napkins to his swelling nose. Harry saw tears on his face and looked away.

The door to the bar opened then and dawn's early gray light shot into the bar. A man stood there, apparently adjusting to the darkness of the bar as Bosch had done. Bosch saw he was dark complexioned with ink-black hair. Three tattooed tears dripped down his cheek from the corner of his left eye. Harry knew he was no banker or lawyer who needed a double-scotch breakfast to start the day. He was some kind of player, maybe finishing a night collecting for the Italians or Mexicans and needing something to smooth out the edges. The man's eyes finally fell on Bosch and Porter, then to Porter's gun, which was still on the bar. The man sized up the situation and calmly and wordlessly backed out through the door.

"Fucking great," the bartender yelled. "Would you get the hell out of here. I'm losing customers. The both of you, get the fuck out."

There was a sign that said Toilet and an arrow pointing down a darkened hallway to Bosch's left. He pushed Porter that way. They turned a corner and went into the men's room, which smelled worse than Porter. There was a mop in a bucket of gray water in the corner, but the cracked tile floor was dirtier than the water. He pushed Porter toward the sink.

"Clean yourself up," Bosch said. "What was the favor? You said you did something for Moore. Tell me about it."

Porter was looking at his blurred reflection in a piece of stainless steel that was probably put in when the management got tired of replacing broken mirrors.

"It won't stop bleeding, Harry. I think it's broke."

"Forget your nose. Tell me what you did."

"I, uh—look, all he did was tell me that he knew some people that would appreciate it if the stiff behind the restaurant didn't get ID'd for a while. Just string it out, he said, for a week or two. Christ, there was no ID on the body, anyway. He said I could do the computer runs on the prints cause he knew they wouldn't bring a match. He said just take my time with it and that these people, the ones he knew, would take care of me. He said I'd get a nice Christmas present. So, I, you know, I went through the motions last week. I wouldn't have gotten anywhere with it, anyway. You know, you saw the file. No ID, no wits, no nothing. The guy'd been dead at least six hours before he got dumped there."

"So what spooked you? What happened Christmas?"

Porter blew his nose into a bouquet of paper towels and this brought more tears to his eyes.

"Yeah, it's broke. I'm not getting any air through. I gotta go to a clinic, get it set. Anyway…well, nothing happened Christmas. That's the thing. I mean, Moore'd been missing for almost a week and I was getting pretty nervous about the whole thing. On Christmas Moore didn't come, nobody did. Then when I'm walking home from the Lucky my neighbor in the trailer next door says to me about how real sorry she was about that dead cop they found. I said thanks and went inside and put on the radio. I hear it's Moore and that scares me shitless, Harry. It did."

Porter soaked a handful of towels and began stroking his blood-stained shirt in a manner that Bosch thought made him look more pathetic than he was. Bosch saw his empty shoulder holster and remembered he had left the gun on the bar. He was reluctant to go back and get it while Porter was talking.

"See, I knew Moore wasn't no suicide. I don't care what they're putting out at Parker. I know he didn't do himself like that. He was into something. So, I decided, that was enough. I called the union and got a lawyer. I'm outta here, Harry. I'm gonna get cleaned up and go to Vegas, maybe get in with casino security. Millie's out there with my boy. I wanna be close by."

Right, Bosch thought. And always be looking over your shoulder. He said, "You're bleeding again. Wash your face. I'm going to get some coffee. I'm taking you out of here."

Bosch moved through the door but Porter stopped him.

"Harry, you going to take care of me on this?"

Bosch looked at his damaged face a long moment before saying, "Yeah, I'll do what I can."

He walked back out to the bar and signaled the bartender, who was standing all the way down at the other end smoking a cigarette. The man, about fifty, with faded blue tattoos webbing both fore-arms like extra veins, took his time coming over. By then Bosch had a ten-dollar bill on the bar.

"Give me a couple coffees to go. Black. Put a lot of sugar in one of them."

"'Bout time you got outta here." The bartender nodded at the ten-dollar bill. "And I'm taking out for the napkins, too. They're not for cops who go round beat'n' on people. That oughta 'bout cover it. You can just leave that on the bar."

He poured coffee that looked like it had been sitting in the glass pot since Christmas into foam cups. Bosch went to Porter's spot at the bar and gathered up the Smith thirty-eight and the twenty-three dollars. He moved back to his ten-dollar bill and lit a cigarette.

Not realizing Bosch was now watching, the bartender poured a gagging amount of sugar into both coffees. Bosch let it slide. After snapping plastic covers on the cups, the bartender brought them over to Bosch and tapped one of the tops, a smile on his face that would make a woman frigid.

"This is the one with no—hey, what is this shit?"

The ten Bosch had put down on the bar was now a one. Bosch blew smoke in the bartender's face as he took the coffees and said, "That's for the coffee. You can shove the napkins."

"Just get the fuck out of here," the bartender said. Then he turned and started walking down to the other end of the bar, where several of the patrons were impatiently holding their empty glasses up. They needed more ice to chill their plasma.

Bosch pushed the door to the restroom open with his foot but didn't see Porter. He pushed the door to the only stall open and he wasn't there either. Harry left the room and quickly pushed through the women's restroom door. No Porter. He followed the hallway around another corner and saw a door marked Exit. He saw drops of blood on the floor. Regretting his play with the bartender and wondering if he'd be able to track Porter by calling hospitals and clinics, he hit the door's push bar with his hip. It opened only an inch or so. There was something on the other side holding it closed.

Bosch put the coffees down on the floor and put his whole weight on the door. It slowly moved open as the blockage gave way. He squeezed through and saw a Dumpster had been shoved against the door. He was standing in an alley behind Poe's and the morning light, flowing down the alley from the east, was blinding.

There was an abandoned Toyota, its wheels, hood and one door gone, sitting dead in the alley. There were more Dumpsters and the wind was blowing trash around in a swirl. And there was no sign of Porter.

Thirteen

BOSCH SAT AT THE COUNTER AT THE ORIGINAL PAN-
try drinking coffee, picking at a plate of eggs and bacon, and waiting for a second wind to come. He hadn't bothered with trying to
follow Porter. He knew that there would be no chance. Knowing
Bosch wanted him, even a broken-down cop like Porter would know
enough to stay away from the likely places Harry would look. He
would stay in the wind.

Harry had his notebook out and opened to the chronological
chart he had constructed the day before. But he could not concentrate on it. He was too depressed. Depressed that Porter had run
from him, that he hadn't trusted him. Depressed that it seemed
clear that Moore's death was connected to the darkness that was
out there at the outer edge of every cop's vision. Moore had crossed
over. And it had killed him.

I found out who I was.

The note bothered him, too. If Moore wasn't a suicide, where did
it come from? It made him think about what Sylvia Moore had said
about the past, about how her husband had been snared in a trap he
had set for himself. He then thought of calling her to tell her what
he had learned but discarded the idea for the time being. He did not
have the answers to questions she would surely ask. Why was Calexico
Moore murdered? Who did it?

It was just after eight o'clock. Bosch left money on the counter and walked out. Outside two homeless men shook cups in front of him and he acted like they weren't even there. He drove over to Parker Center and got into the lot early enough to get a parking space. He first checked the Robbery-Homicide Division offices on the third floor but Sheehan wasn't in yet. Next he went up to the fourth to Fugitives, to pick up where Porter would have if he hadn't made his deal with Moore. Fugitives also handled missing-persons reports and Bosch always thought there was something symbiotic about that. Most missing persons were fugitives from something, some part of their lives.

A missing-persons detective named Capetillo asked Bosch what he needed and Harry asked to see the male Latin missings for the last ten days. Capetillo led him to his desk and told him to have a seat while he went to the files. Harry looked around and his eyes fell on a framed photo of the portly detective posed with a woman and two young girls. A family man. Taped to the wall above the desk was a bullfight poster advertising the lineup for a fight two years earlier at Tijuana's Bullring by the Sea. The names of the six matadors were listed down the right side. The entire left side of the poster was a reproduction of a painting of a matador turning with a charging bull, leading the horns away with the flowing red cape. The caption inscribed below the painting said "El Arte de la Muleta."

"The classic veronica."

Bosch turned. It was Capetillo and he was holding a thin file in one hand.

"Excuse me?" Bosch asked.

"The veronica. Do you know anything about the *corrida de toros*? The bullfights?"

"Never been."

"Magnificent. I go at least four times a year. Nothing compares to it. Football, basketball, nothing. The veronica is that move. He slyly leads the horns away. In Mexico the bullfight is called the brave festival, you know."

Bosch looked at the file in the detective's hand. Capetillo opened it and handed Bosch a thin stack of papers.

"That's all we have in the last ten days," Capetillo said. "Your Mexicans, Chicanos, a lot don't report their missings to police. A cultural thing. Most just don't trust the cops. Lot of times when people don't turn up, they just figure they went south. A lot of people are here illegally. They won't call the cops."

Bosch made it through the stack in five minutes. None of the reports fit the description of Juan Doe #67.

"What about telexes, inquiries from Mexico?"

"Now that's something different. We keep official correspondence separate. I could look. Why don't you tell me what you're pushing."

"I'm pushing a hunch. I have a body with no identification. I think the man may have come from down there, maybe Mexicali. This is a guess more than anything else."

"Hang tight," Capetillo said and he left the cubicle again.

Bosch studied the poster again, noticing how the matador's face betrayed no sign of indecision or fear, only concentration on the horns of death. The bullfighter's eyes were flat and dead like a shark's. Capetillo was back quickly.

"Nice hunch. I have three reports received in the last two weeks. They all concern men that sound like your guy but one more than the others. I think we got lucky."

He handed a single piece of paper to Bosch and said, "This one came from the consulate on Olvera Street yesterday."

It was a photocopy of a telex to the consulate by a State Judicial Police officer named Carlos Aguila. Bosch studied the letter, which was written in English.

Seeking information regarding the disappearance of Fernal Gutierrez-Llosa, 55, day laborer, Mexicali. Whereabouts unknown. Last sighting. 12/17—Mexicali.

Description. 5-foot-8, 145 pounds. Brown eyes, brown hair, some gray. Tattoo right upper chest (blue ink ghost symbol— City of Lost Souls barrio).

Contact: Carlos Aguila, 57-20-13, Mexicali, B.C.

Bosch reread the page. There wasn't much there but it was enough. Fernal Gutierrez-Llosa disappeared in Mexicali on the seventeenth and early the next morning the body of Juan Doe #67 was found in Los Angeles. Bosch looked quickly at the other two pages Capetillo had but they dealt with men who were too young to be Juan Doe #67. He went back to the first sheet. The tattoo was the clincher.

"I think this is it," he said. "Can I get a copy?"

"Of course. You want me to call down there? See if they can send some prints up?"

"Nah, not yet. I want to check a few other things out." Actually, he wanted to limit Capetillo's involvement to just the help he had given.

"There's one thing," Bosch said. "You know what this City of Lost Souls description means? This reference to the tattoo."

"Yeah. Basically, the tattoo is a barrio symbol. Fernal Gutierrez-Llosa resided in the barrio Ciudad de los Personas Perdidos—City of Lost Souls. Many of the barrio dwellers down there do this. Mark themselves. It's similar to graffiti up here. Only down there, they mark themselves and not the frigging walls as much. The police down there know what tattoos symbolize what barrios. It is fairly common in Mexicali. When you contact Aguila he can tell you. Maybe he can send you a photo, if you need it."

Bosch was silent for a moment as he pretended to reread the consulate paper. City of Lost Souls, he thought. A ghost. He tumbled this piece of information in his mind the way a boy who has found a baseball turns it in his hands to study the seams for wear. He was reminded of the tattoo on Moore's arm. The devil with a halo. Was that from a Mexicali barrio?

"You say the cops there keep track of these tattoos?"

"That's right. It's one of the few decent jobs they do."

"How d'you mean?"

"I mean, have you ever been down there? On a detail? It's third world, man. The police, uh, apparatus, I guess you'd call it, is very primitive by our standards. Fact, it would not surprise me if they have no fingerprints on this man to send you. I'm surprised they even sent anything to the consul here in the first place. This Aguila, he must've had a hunch like you."

Bosch took one last look at the poster on the wall, thanked Capetillo for his help and the copy of the consulate's telex and then left the office.

He got on an elevator to go down and saw Sheehan already on it. The car was crowded and Sheehan was at the back, behind the pile. They didn't talk until they got off on three.

"Hey, Frankie," Bosch said. "Didn't get a chance to talk to you Christmas night."

"What're you doing here, Harry?"

"I'm waiting for you. You must be running late, or do you check in on the fifth floor nowadays?"

That was a little poke at Sheehan. The IAD squads were on the fifth floor. It was also to let Sheehan know that Harry had an idea of what was going on with the Moore case. Since Sheehan was going down, he had come from either the fifth or sixth floors. That was either IAD or Irving's office. Or maybe both.

"Don't fuck with me, Bosch. Reason I haven't been in is I've been busy this morning, thanks to the games you like to play."

"What do you mean?"

"Don't worry about it. Look, I don't like you being seen with me in here, anyway. Irving gave me specific instructions about you. You are not in this investigation. You helped out the other night but it ended there."

They were in the hallway outside the RHD offices. Bosch didn't like the sound of Sheehan's tone. He had never known Frankie to bow his head to the brass like this.

"C'mon, Frankie, let's go get a cup. You can tell me what's bugging you."

"Nothing's bugging me, man. You forget, I worked with you. I know how you get your teeth on something and won't let go. Well, I'm telling you where things stand. You were there the night we found him. It ended there. Go back to Hollywood."

Bosch took a step toward him and lowered his voice. He said, "But we both know it didn't end there, Frankie. And it's not going to end there. So if you feel you gotta do it, go tell Irving I said it's so."

Sheehan stared at him for a few seconds and then Bosch saw the resolve fade away.

"Awright, Harry, c'mon in. I'm going to be kicking myself for this later."

They walked to Sheehan's desk and Bosch pulled a chair from another desk alongside it. Sheehan took off his coat and put it on a hanger on a rack next to the desk. After he sat down, adjusted his shoulder holster and folded his arms, he said:

"Know where I've been all morning? The ME's, trying to work out a deal to keep a lid on this a few hours. Seems overnight we sprang a leak and already this morning Irving's getting calls that we are sitting on a homicide of one of our own officers. You wouldn't know anything about this, would you?"

Harry said, "Only thing I know is I've been thinking about the scene out at the motel and the autopsy being inconclusive, like they say, and I'm not thinking suicide anymore."

"You're not thinking anything. You're not on it. Remember? And what about this?"

He opened a drawer and brought a file up. It was the Zorrillo file Rickard had shown him the day before.

"Don't bother telling me you haven't seen this before. Because then I might take it over to SID and have 'em run prints on it. I'd bet my wife's diaphragm I'd find yours."

"You'd lose, Frankie."

"Then I'd have more kids. But I wouldn't lose, Harry."

Bosch waited a beat for him to settle down.

"All this huffin' and puffin' at me tells me one thing: you don't see a suicide, either. So quit with the bullshit."

"You're right. I don't. But I got an assistant chief sitting on my ass and he's gotten the bright idea of sticking me with an IAD suit on this. So it's like I got both my feet in buckets of shit before I even start off."

"You saying they don't want this to go anywhere?"

"No, I am not saying that."

"What are they going to tell the *Times*?"

"Press conference this afternoon. Irving's going to give it to everybody. He'll say we are looking at the possibility—the *possibility*—of homicide. Fuck giving it to the *Times*. Who said it was the *Times* making the noise anyway?"

"Lucky, I guess."

"Yeah, be careful, Bosch. You slip like that with Irving and he'll fry your ass. He'd love to, with your record and all the history going back with you. I already have to figure out about this file. You told Irving you didn't know the guy and now we have a file that shows he was doing some digging for you."

Bosch realized he had forgotten to remove the Post-it tag Moore had placed on the file.

"Tell Irving whatever you want. Think I care?" Bosch looked down at the file. "What do you think?"

"About this file? I think nothing out loud."

"C'mon, Frankie, I ask Moore to look around on this dope killing and he ends up in a motel with his head in the tub in small pieces. It was a very smooth job, right down to not a single lift belonging to anybody else being found in that room."

"So what if it was smooth and there's no other prints? In my book some guys deserve what they got coming, you know?"

There was the break in Sheehan's defense. Whether intentional or not, he was telling Bosch that Moore had crossed.

"I need more than that," he said in a very low voice. "You got the weight on you but I don't. I'm a free agent and I'm going to put it together. Moore might've crossed, yeah, but nobody should've put him down on the tiles like that. We both know that. Besides, there are other bodies."

Harry could see this had grabbed Sheehan's attention.

"We can trade," Bosch said quietly.

Sheehan stood up and said, "Yeah, let's go get that coffee."

Five minutes later they were at a table in the second-floor cafeteria and Bosch was telling him about Jimmy Kapps and Juan Doe #67. He outlined the connections between Moore and Juan Doe, Juan Doe and Mexicali, Mexicali and Humberto Zorrillo, Zorrillo and black ice, black ice and Jimmy Kapps. On and on it went. Sheehan asked no questions and took no notes until Harry was done.

"So what do you think?" he asked then.

"I think what you think," Bosch said. "That Moore had crossed. Maybe he was fronting up here for Zorrillo, the ice man, and got so deep he couldn't get out. I don't know how it all ties up yet but I still have some ideas I am playing with. I'm thinking a number of things. Maybe he wanted out and the ice man whacked him. Maybe he was working that file, going to give me something, and they whacked him."

"Possibilities."

"There's also the possibility that word of the IAD investigation your partner Chastain was conducting got around, and they saw Moore as a danger and whacked him."

Sheehan hesitated. It was the moment of truth. If he discussed the IAD investigation he would be breaking enough departmental regs to get shipped permanently out of RHD. Like Harry.

"I could get busted for talking about that," Sheehan said. "Could end up like you, out there in the cesspool."

"It's all a cesspool, man. Doesn't matter if you're on the bottom or the top. You're still swimming in shit."

Sheehan took a sip of his coffee.

"IAD had taken a report, this was about two months ago, that Moore was some way involved in the traffic on the Boulevard. Possibly offering protection, possibly a deeper involvement. The source was not clear on that."

"Two months ago?" Bosch asked. "Didn't they get anything? I mean, Moore was still working the street all this time. Wasn't there enough to at least put him on a desk?"

"Look, you've got to remember that Irving put Chastain with me on this. But I'm not with Chastain. He doesn't do much talking to me. All he would tell me was the investigation was in its infancy when Moore disappeared. He had no proof substantiating or discrediting the claim."

"You know how hard he worked it?"

"I assume very hard. He's IAD. He's always looking for a badge to pull. And this looked like more than just departmental charges. This would have gone to the DA. So I assume he had a hard-on for it. He just didn't get anything. Moore must've been very good."

Not good enough, Bosch thought. Obviously.

"Who was the source?"

"You don't need that."

"You know I do. If I'm going to be a free agent on this I have to know what's what."

Sheehan hesitated but didn't make a good show of it.

"It was anonymous—a letter. But Chastain said it was the wife. That's what he figured. She turned him in."

"How's he so sure?"

"The details of the letter, whatever they were, Chastain said they would only be known by someone close to him. He told me it wasn't unusual. It often comes from the spouse. But he said that a lot of times it's bogus. A wife or husband will report something totally false, you know, if they are going through a divorce or something, just to fuck the other up with work. So, he spent a lot of time just seeing if that was the case here. 'Cause Moore and his wife were splitting up. He said she never admitted it but he was sure she sent it. He just never got very far with substantiating what was in it."

Bosch thought of Sylvia. He was sure they were wrong. "Did you talk to the wife, tell her the ID was confirmed?"

"No, Irving did that last night."

"He tell her about the autopsy, 'bout it not being suicide?"

"I don't know about that. See, I don't get to sit down with Irving like you with me here and ask him everything that comes into my head."

Bosch was wearing out his welcome.

"Just a few more, Frankie. Did Chastain focus on black ice?"

"No. When we got this file of yours yesterday, he about shit his pants. I got the feeling he was hearing about all that side of it for the first time. I kind of enjoyed that, Harry. If there was anything to enjoy about any of this."

"Well, now, you can tell him all the rest I told you."

"No chance. This conversation didn't take place. I gotta try to pull it all together like it was my own before I hand anything over to him."

Bosch was thinking quickly. What else was there to ask?

"What about the note? That's the part that doesn't fit now. If it was no suicide then where's this note come from?"

"Yeah, that's the problem. That's why we gave the coroner such a hard time. Far as we can guess, he either had it all along in his back pocket or whoever did him made him write it. I don't know."

"Yeah." Bosch thought a moment. "Would you write a note like that if somebody was about to put you down on the floor?"

"I don't know, man. People do things you'd never expect when they've got the gun on them. They always've got hope that things might turn out all right. That's the way I see it."

Bosch nodded. But he didn't know if he agreed or not.

"I gotta go," Sheehan said. "Let me know what comes up."

Bosch nodded and Sheehan left him there with two cups of coffee on the table. A few moments later Sheehan was back.

"You know, I never told you, it was too bad about what happened with you. We could use you back here, Harry. I've always thought that."

Bosch looked up at him.

"Yeah, Frankie. Thanks."

Fourteen

THE MEDFLY ERADICATION PROJECT CENTER WAS AT the edge of East L.A., on San Fernando Road not far from County-USC Med Center, which housed the morgue. Bosch was tempted to drop by to see Teresa but he figured he should give her time to cool. He also figured that decision was cowardly but he didn't change it. He just kept driving.

The project center was a former county psychiatric ward which had been abandoned to that cause years earlier when Supreme Court rulings made it virtually impossible for the government—in the form of the police—to take the mentally ill off the streets and hold them for observation and public safety. The San Fernando Road ward was closed as the county consolidated its psych centers.

It had been used since for a variety of purposes, including a set for a slasher movie about a haunted nuthouse and even a temporary morgue when an earthquake damaged the facility at County-USC a few years back. Bodies had been stored in two refrigerated trucks in the parking lot. Because of the emergency situation, county administrators had to get the first trucks they could get their hands on. Painted on the side of one of them had been the words "Live Maine Lobsters!" Bosch remembered reading about it in the "Only in L.A." column in the *Times*.

There was a check-in post at the entry manned by a state police officer. Bosch rolled down the window, badged him and asked who the head medfly eradicator was. He was directed to a parking space and an entrance to the administration suite.

The door to the suite still said No Unescorted Patients on it. Bosch went through and down a hallway, nodding to and passing another state officer. He came to a secretary's desk where he identified himself again to the woman sitting there and asked to see the entomologist in charge. She made a quick phone call to someone and then escorted Harry into a nearby office, introducing him to a man named Roland Edson. The secretary hovered near the door with a shocked look on her face until Edson finally told her that would be all.

When they were alone in the office, Edson said, "I kill flies for a living, not people, Detective. Is this a serious visit?"

Edson laughed hard and Bosch forced a smile to be polite. Edson was a small man in a short-sleeved white shirt and pale green tie. His bald scalp had been freckled by the sun and was scarred by misjudgments. He wore thick, rimless glasses that magnified his eyes and made him somewhat resemble his quarry. Behind his back his subordinates probably called him "The Fly."

Bosch explained that he was working a homicide case and could not tell Edson a lot of the background because the investigation was of a highly confidential nature. He warned him that other investigators might be back with more questions. He asked for some general information about the breeding and transport of sterile fruit flies into the state, hoping that the appeal for expert advice would get the bureaucrat to open up.

Edson responded by giving him much of the same information Teresa Corazón had already provided, but Bosch acted as if it was all new to him and took notes.

"Here's the specimen here, Detective," Edson said, holding up a paperweight. It was a glass block in which a fruit fly had been perpetually cast, like a prehistoric ant caught in amber.

Bosch nodded and steered the interview specifically toward Mexicali. The entomologist said the breeding contractor there was a company called EnviroBreed. He said EnviroBreed shipped an average of thirty million flies to the eradication center each week.

"How do they get here?" Bosch asked.

"In the pupal stage, of course."

"Of course. But my question is how?"

"This is the stage in which the insect is nonfeeding, immobile. It is what we call the transformation stage between larva and imago—adult. This works out quite well because it is an ideal point for transport. They come in incubators, if you will. Environment boxes, we call them. And then, of course, shortly after they get here metamorphosis is completed and they are ready to be released as adults."

"So when they get here, they have already been dyed and irradiated?"

"That is correct. I said that."

"And they are in the pupal stage, not larva?"

"Larvae is the plural, Detective, but, yes, that is essentially correct. I said that, also."

Bosch was beginning to think Edson was essentially an officious prick. He was sure they definitely called him The Fly around here.

"Okay," Harry said. "So what if, here in L.A., I found a larvae, I mean a larva, that was dyed but not irradiated? Is that possible?"

Edson was silent a moment. He didn't want to speak too soon and be wrong. Bosch was getting the idea that he was the type of guy who watched "Jeopardy" on the tube each night and barked out the answers ahead of the contestants even if he was alone.

"Well, Detective, any given scenario is possible. I would, however, say the example you just gave is highly unlikely. As I said, our suppliers send the pupae packages through an irradiation machine before they are shipped here. In these packages we often find larvae mixed with the pupae because it would generally be impossible to completely separate the two. But these larvae samplings have been through the same irradiation as the pupae. So, no, I don't see it."

"So if I had a person who on their body carried a single pupa that had been dyed but not irradiated, that person would not have come from here, right?"

"Yes, that would be my answer."

"Would?"

"Yes, Detective, that *is* my answer."

"Then where would this person have come from?"

Edson gave it some thought first. He used the eraser end of a pencil he had been fiddling with to press his glasses up on the bridge of his nose.

"I take it this person is dead, you having introduced yourself as a homicide detective and obviously being unable to ask the person this question yourself."

"You should be on 'Jeopardy,' Mr. Edson."

"It's Doctor. Anyway, I couldn't begin to guess where the person would have picked up this specimen you speak of."

"He could have been from one of the breeders you mentioned, down in Mexico or over in Hawaii, couldn't he?"

"Yes, that's a possibility. One of them."

"And what's another?"

"Well, Mr. Bosch, you saw the security we have around here. Frankly, there are some people who are not happy with what we are doing. Some extremists believe nature should take its course. If the medfly comes to southern California, who are we to try to eradicate it? Some people believe we have no business being in this business. There have been threats from some groups. Anonymous, but nevertheless, threats to breed nonsterile medflies and release them, causing a massive infestation. Now, if I were going to do that, I might dye them to obfuscate my opponent."

Edson was pleased with himself on that one. But Bosch didn't buy it. It did not fit with the facts. But he nodded, indicating to Edson that he would give it some consideration and thought. Then he said, "Tell me, how do these deliveries from the breeders get here? For example, how do they get here from the place down in Mexicali you deal with?"

Edson said that at the breeding facility thousands of pupae were packed into plastic tubes resembling six-foot-long sausages. The tubes were then strung in cartons complete with incubators and humidifiers. The environment boxes were sealed at the EnviroBreed lab under the scrutiny of a USDA inspector and then trucked across the border and north to Los Angeles. The deliveries from Enviro-Breed came two to three times a week, depending on availability of supply.

"The cartons are not inspected at the border?" Bosch asked.

"They are inspected but not opened. It could endanger the product if the cartons were opened. Each carton contains a carefully controlled environment, you understand. But as I said, the cartons are sealed under the eye of government inspectors, and each carton is reinspected upon the breaking of such seals at the eradication center to make sure there has been no tampering. Um, at the border, the Border Patrol checks the seal numbers and cartons against the driver's bill of lading and our separate notification of transport crossing. It's very thorough, Detective Bosch. The system was all hashed out at the highest levels."

Bosch said nothing for a while. He wasn't going to debate the security of the system, but he wondered who designed it at the highest levels, the scientists or the Border Patrol.

"If I was to go down there, to Mexicali, could you get me into EnviroBreed?"

"Impossible," Edson said quickly. "You have to remember these are private contractors. We get all our bred flies from privately owned facilities. Though we have a state USDA inspector at each facility and state entomologists, such as myself, make routine visits, we cannot order them to open their doors to an inquiry by police or anyone, for that matter, without showing notice of an infraction of our contract.

"In other words, Detective Bosch, tell me what they did and I will tell you if I can get you in there."

Bosch didn't answer. He wanted to tell Edson as little as possible. He changed the subject.

"These environment boxes that the bug tubes come in, how big are they?" he asked.

"Oh, they're a pretty decent size. We generally use a forklift when unloading deliveries."

"Can you show me one?"

Edson looked at his watch and said, "I suppose that is possible. I don't know what has come in, if anything."

Bosch stood up to force the issue. Edson finally did, too. He led Harry out of the office and down another hallway past more offices and labs that had once been the holding pens for the insane, the addicted and the abandoned. Harry recalled that once while a patrolman he had walked down this same hallway escorting a woman he had arrested on Mount Lee, where she was climbing the steel frame behind the first *O* of the Hollywood sign. She had a nylon cord with her, already tied into a noose at one end. A few years later he read in the newspaper that after getting out of Patton State Hospital she had gone back to the sign and done the job he had interrupted.

"Must be tough," Edson said. "Working homicides."

Bosch said what he always said when people said that to him.

"Sometimes it's not so bad. At least the victims I deal with are out of their misery."

Edson didn't say anything else. The hall ended at a heavy steel door, which he pushed open. They walked out onto a loading dock that was inside a large hangarlike building. About thirty feet away, there were a half dozen or so workers, all Latinos, placing white plastic boxes on wheeled dollies and then pulling them through a set of double doors on the other side of the unloading area. Bosch noted that each of the boxes was just about the size of a coffin.

The boxes were first being removed from a white van with a mini-forklift. On the side of the van the word "EnviroBreed" was painted in blue. The driver's door was open and a white man stood watching the work. Another white man with a clipboard was at the end of the truck, bending down to check numbers on the seals of each of the boxes and then making notes on the clipboard.

"We're in luck," Edson said. "A delivery in process. The environment boxes are taken into our lab where the M&M process, that's what we call metamorphosis around here, is completed."

Edson pointed through the open garage doors to a row of six orange pickup trucks parked outside in the lot.

"The mature flies are placed in covered buckets and we use our fleet to take them to the attack areas. They are released by hand. Right now the attack zone is about one hundred square miles. We are dropping fifty million sterile flies a week. More if we can get them. Ultimately, the steriles will overwhelm the wild fly population and breed it out of existence."

There was a note of triumph in the entomologist's voice. "Would you like to speak with the EnviroBreed driver?" Edson said. "I am sure he would be ha—"

"No," Bosch said. "I just wanted to see how it is done. I'd appreciate it, Doctor, if you kept my visit confidential."

As he said this, Bosch noticed the EnviroBreed driver was looking right at him. The man's face was deeply lined and tanned and his hair was white. He wore a straw plantation hat and smoked a brown cigarette. Bosch returned the stare, knowing full well that he had been made. He thought he saw a slight smile on the driver's face, then the man finally broke away his stare and went back to watching the unloading process.

"Then is there anything else I can do for you, Detective?" Edson said.

"No, Doc. Thanks for your cooperation."

"I'm sure you know your way out."

Edson turned and went back in through the steel door. Harry put a cigarette in his mouth but left it unlit. He waved a nattering of flies, probably pink medflies, he thought, away from his face, went down the loading-dock stairs and walked out through the garage door.

Driving back toward downtown, Bosch decided to get it over with and face Teresa. He pulled into the County-USC parking lot and spent ten minutes looking for a spot big enough to put the Caprice in. He finally found one in the back where the lot is on a rise over-looking the old railroad yard. He sat in the car for a few moments thinking about what to say and smoking and looking down at all the rusted boxcars and iron tracks. He saw a group of *cholos* in their oversized white T-shirts and baggy pants making their way through the yard. The one carrying a spray can dropped back from the others and along one of the old boxcars sprayed a scrip. It was in Spanish but Bosch understood it. It was the gang's imprimatur, its philosophy.

LAUGH NOW CRY LATER

He watched them until they had moved behind another line of box-cars. He got out and went into the morgue through the rear door, where the deliveries are made. A security guard nodded after seeing his badge.

Today was a good day inside. The smell of disinfectant had the upper hand over the odor of death. Harry walked past the doors to refrigeration rooms one and two and then through a door to a set of stairs that led up to the second-floor administration offices.

Bosch asked the secretary in the chief medical examiner's office if Dr. Corazón could see him. The woman, whose pale skin and pinkish hair made her resemble some of the clients around the place, spoke quietly on the phone and then told him to go in. Teresa was standing behind her desk, looking out the window. She had the same view Bosch had of the railroad yard and may have even seen him coming. But from the second floor, she also had a view that spanned the area from the towers of downtown to Mt. Washington. Bosch noticed how clear the towers were in the distance. It was a good day outside as well.

"I'm not talking to you," Teresa announced without turning around.

"C'mon."

"I'm not."

"Then why'd you let me in?"

"To tell you I am not talking to you and that I am very angry and that you have probably compromised my position as chief medical examiner."

"C'mon, Teresa. I hear you have a press conference later today. It will work out."

He couldn't think of anything else to say. She turned around and leaned back against the windowsill. She looked at him with eyes that could've carved his name on a tombstone. He could smell her perfume all the way across the room.

"And, of course, I have you to thank for that."

"Not me. I heard Irving called the press con—"

"Don't fuck with me, Harry. We both know what you did with what I told you. And we both know that little shit Irving automatically thinks I did it. I now have to consider myself seriously fucked as far as the permanent job goes. Take a good look around the office, Harry. Last time you'll ever see me here."

Bosch had always noticed how many of the professional women he encountered, mostly cops and lawyers, turned profane when arguing. He wondered if they felt it might put them on the same level as the men they were battling.

"It will work out," he said.

"What are you talking about? All he has to do is tell a few commissioners that I leaked information from a confidential, uncompleted investigation to the press and that will eliminate me completely from consideration."

"Listen, he can't be sure it was you and he'll probably think it was me. Bremmer, the *Times* guy who stirred this all up, we go back some. Irving will know. So quit worrying about it. I came to see if you want to have lunch or something."

Wrong move. He saw her face turn red with pure anger.

"Lunch or something? Are you kidding? Are you—you just told me we are the two likely suspects on this leak and you want me to sit with you in a restaurant? Do you know what could—"

"Hey, Teresa, have a nice press conference," Bosch cut in. He turned around and headed to the door.

On the way into downtown, his pager went off and Bosch noticed the number was Ninety-eight's direct line. He must be worried about his statistics, Harry thought. He decided to ignore the page. He also turned the Motorola radio in the car off.

He stopped at a *mariscos* truck parked on Alvarado and ordered two shrimp tacos. They were served on corn tortillas, Baja style, and Bosch savored the heavy cilantro in the salsa.

A few yards from the truck stood a man reciting scripture verses from memory. On top of his head was a cup of water that nestled comfortably in his seventies-style Afro and did not spill. He reached up for the cup and took a drink from time to time but never stopped bouncing from book to book of the New Testament. Before each quote, he gave his listeners the chapter and verse numbers as a reference. At his feet was a glass fishbowl half full of coins. When he was done eating, Bosch ordered a Coke to go and then dropped the change into the fishbowl. He got a "God bless you" back.

Fifteen

THE HALL OF JUSTICE TOOK UP AN ENTIRE BLOCK across from the criminal courts building. The first six floors housed the sheriff's department and the top four the county jail. Anyone could tell this from the outside. Not just because of the bars behind the windows, but because the top four floors looked like an abandoned, burned-out shell. As if all the hate and anger held in those un-air-conditioned cells had turned to fire and smoke and stained the windows and concrete balustrades forever black.

It was a turn-of-the-century building and its stone-block construction gave it an ominous fortresslike appearance. It was one of the only buildings in downtown that still had human elevator operators. An old black woman sat on a padded stool in the corner of each of the wood-paneled cubicles and pulled the doors open and worked the wheel that leveled the elevator with each floor it stopped at.

"Seven thousand," Bosch said to the operator as he stepped on. It had been some time since he had been in the Hall and he could not remember her name. But he knew she had been working the elevators here since before Harry was a cop. All of the operators had. She opened the door on the sixth floor where Bosch saw Rickard as soon as he stepped out. The narc was standing at the glass window at the check-in counter, putting his badge case into a slide drawer.

"Here you go," Bosch said and quickly put his badge in the drawer.

"He's with me," Rickard said into the microphone.

The deputy behind the glass exchanged the badges for two visitor clearance badges and slid them out. Bosch and Rickard clipped them to their shirts. Bosch noticed they were cleared to visit the High Power block on the tenth floor. High Power was where the most dangerous criminal suspects were placed while awaiting trial or to be shipped out to state prisons following guilty verdicts.

They began walking down a hall to the jail elevator. "You got the kid in High Power?" Bosch asked.

"Yeah. I know a guy. Told him one day, that's all we needed. The kid's going to be shitless. He's going to tell you everything he knows about Dance."

They took the security elevator up, this one operated by a deputy. Bosch figured it had to be the worst job in law enforcement. When the door opened on ten they were met by another deputy, who checked their badges and had them sign in. Then they moved through two sets of sliding steel doors to an attorneys' visiting area, which consisted of a long table with benches running down both sides of it. There was also a foot-high divider running lengthwise down the table. At the far end of the table a female attorney sat on one side, leaning toward the divider and whispering to a client, who cupped his ears with his hands to hear better. The muscles on the inmate's arms bulged and stretched the sleeves of his shirt. He was a monster.

On the wall behind them was a sign that read NO TOUCHING, KISSING, REACHING ACROSS THE DIVIDER. There was also another deputy at the far end, leaning against the wall, his own massive arms folded, and watching the lawyer and her client.

As they waited for the deputies to bring out Tyge, Bosch became aware of the noise. Through the barred door behind the visiting table he could hear a hundred voices competing and echoing in a metallic din. There were steel doors banging somewhere and occasionally an unintelligible shout.

A deputy walked up to the barred door and said, "It'll be a few minutes, fellas. We have to get him out of medical."

The deputy was gone before either of them could ask what happened. Bosch didn't even know the kid but felt his stomach tighten. He looked over at Rickard and saw he was smiling.

"We'll see how things have changed now," the narc cop said.

Bosch didn't understand the delight Rickard seemed to take in this. For Bosch, it was the low end of the job, dealing with desperate people and using desperate tactics. He was here because he had to be. It was his case. But he didn't get it with Rickard.

"So, how come you're doing this? What do you want?"

Rickard looked over at him.

"What do I want? I want to know what's going on. I think you're the only one that might know. So if I can help out, I'll help out. If it costs this kid his asshole, then that's the cost. But what I want to know from you is what is happening here. What did Cal do and what's going to be done about it?"

Bosch leaned back and tried to think for a few moments about what to say. He heard the monster at the end of the table start to raise his voice, something about not accepting the offer. The deputy took a step toward him, dropping his arms to his sides. The inmate went quiet. The deputy's sleeves were rolled up tight to reveal his impressive biceps. On his bulging left forearm Bosch could see the "CL" tattoo, almost like a brand on his white skin. Harry knew that, publicly, deputies who had the tattoo claimed the letters stood for Club Lynwood, after the sheriff's station in the gang-infested L.A. suburb. But he knew the letters also stood for *chango luchador*, monkey fighter. The deputy was a gang member himself, albeit one sanctioned to carry weapons and paid by the county.

Bosch looked away. He wished he could light a cigarette but the county had passed a no-smoking code, even in the jail. It had nearly caused an inmate riot.

"Look," he said to Rickard, "I don't know what to tell you about Moore. I'm working on it but I'm not, you know what I mean?

Thing is, it runs across two cases I do have. So, it's unavoidable. If this kid can give me Dance, then it's a help. I could look at Dance for my two cases, maybe even Moore's. But I don't know that. I do know, and they will go public with this today, that Moore looks like a homicide. What they won't go public with is that he crossed. That's why IAD was sniffing around. He crossed."

"Can't be," Rickard said, but there was no conviction in it. "I'd've known."

"You can't know people that well, man. Everybody's got a private room."

"So what's Parker Center going to do?"

"I don't know. I don't think they know what to do. I think they wanted to let it go as suicide. But the ME started making waves, so they'll call it homicide. But I don't think they are going to put the dirty laundry basket out there on Spring Street for every reporter in town to pick through."

"Well, they better get their shit together. I'm not going to stand by. I don't care if he crossed, man. I've seen him do things. He was a good cop. I've seen him go into a gallery and take out four dealers without a backup. I've seen him step between a pimp and his property and take the punch meant for her, pop his teeth right onto the sidewalk. I been with him when he blew nine stoplights trying to get a wretched old hype to the hospital before he went out on a heroin overdose.

"Those aren't things a cop on the pad does. So what I'm saying is that if he crossed, then I think he was trying to cross back and that's why somebody did him."

He stopped then and Bosch didn't interrupt the silence. They both knew that once you cross, you can never come back. Bosch could hear footsteps coming toward the bars.

Rickard said, "They better show me something down there at Parker, not let this thing go. Or I'll show them something."

Bosch wanted to say something but the deputy was at the door with Tyge. He looked like he had aged ten years in the last ten hours. Now he had a distance in his eyes that reminded Bosch of men he had seen and known in Vietnam. There was also a bruise high on his left cheek bone.

The door was slid open by means of unseen electronics and the boy/man walked to the bench after the deputy pointed the way. He sat down tentatively and seemed purposely to keep his eyes away from Rickard.

"How's it hanging, Kerwin?" Rickard asked.

Now the boy looked at Rickard and his eyes made Bosch's stomach knot. He remembered the first night he had spent in McLaren Youth Hall as a boy. The pure fear and screaming loneliness. And there he had been surrounded by kids, most of them nonviolent. This boy had been surrounded for the last twelve hours by wild animals. Bosch felt ashamed to be part of this but said nothing. It was Rickard's show.

"Look, my man, I know you're probably having a not-so-fun time in there. That's why we came by t'see if you changed your mind any about what we discussed last night."

Rickard was speaking very low so the monster at the end would not hear.

When the boy said nothing, gave no indication that he even heard, Rickard pressed on.

"Kerwin, you want out of here? Here's your man. Mr. Harry Bosch. He'll let me drop the whole thing, even though it was a righteous bust, if you talk to us about this cat Dance. Here, look-it here."

Rickard unfolded a piece of white paper from his shirt pocket. It was a standard case-filing form from the district attorney's office.

"Man, I have forty-eight hours to file a case on you. 'Cause of the weekend, that puts it over 'til Monday. This here is the paperwork about you. I haven't done nothing with it 'cause I wanted to check with you one more time to see if you wanted to help yourself out.

If you don't, then I'll go file it and this will be your home for the next—probably you're looking at a year with good time."

Rickard waited and nothing happened.

"A year. What do you think you'll be like after a year back in there, Kerwin?"

The boy looked down for a moment and then the tears rolled down his cheeks.

"Go to hell," he managed to say in a strangled voice. Bosch already was there. He would remember this one for a long time. He realized that he was clenching his teeth and tried to relax his jaw. He couldn't.

Rickard leaned forward to say something to the boy but Bosch put his hand on his shoulder to stop him.

"Fuck it," Bosch said. "Cut him loose."

"What?"

"We're dropping it."

"The fuck you talking about?"

The boy looked over at Bosch, an expression of skepticism on his face. But it was no act with Bosch. He felt sick at what they had done.

"Look," Rickard said. "We got two ounces of PCP off this asshole. He's mine. If he don't want to help out, then too fucking bad. He goes back into the zoo."

"No, he doesn't." And then Bosch leaned close to Rickard so the deputy behind the boy could not hear. "No, he doesn't, Rickard. We're taking him out. Now do it, or I'm going to fuck you up."

"What did you say?"

"I'll go to the fifth floor with it. This boy should've never been up here with that charge. That's on you, Rickard. I'll make the complaint. Your connection in here will get burned too. You want that? Just because you couldn't get this kid to talk?"

"You think IAD's going to give a shit about a little punk pusher?"

"No. But they'll give a shit about bagging you. They'll love you. You'll come out walking slower than this boy."

Harry leaned back away from him. Nobody said anything for a few moments and Bosch could see Rickard thinking it through, trying to decide if it was a bluff.

"A guy like you, going to IAD. I can't see it."

"That's the risk you take."

Rickard looked down at the paper in his hand and then slowly crumpled it.

"Okay, my man, but you better put me on the list."

"What list?"

"The one you got of people you have to watch your back with."

Bosch stood up and so did Rickard.

"We're cutting him loose," Rickard said to the guard.

Bosch pointed to the boy and said, "I want an escort with this man until he is out of there, got it?"

The deputy nodded. The boy said nothing.

It took an hour to get him out. After Rickard signed the appropriate papers and they got their badges back, they waited wordlessly by the glass window on the seventh floor.

Bosch was disgusted with himself. He had lost sight of the art. Solving cases was simply getting people to talk to you. Not forcing them to talk. He had forgotten that this time.

"You can go if you want," he said to Rickard.

"As soon as he walks out that door and you've got him, I'm gone. Want nothing to do with him. But I want to see him leave with you, Bosch. In case any of this comes back on me."

"Yeah, that's smart."

"Yes, it is."

"But you still've got a lot to learn, Rickard. Everything isn't black and white. Not everybody has to be ground into the sidewalk. You take a kid like that and—"

"Spare me the lesson, Bosch. I might have a lot to learn but it won't be from you. You're a class A fuckup. Think the only thing you could teach me is how to climb down the ladder. No thanks."

"Sure," Bosch said and walked to the other side of the room where there was a bench. He sat down and fifteen minutes later the boy came out. He walked between Rickard and Bosch to the elevator. Outside the Hall of Justice, Rickard headed off to his car after simply saying to Bosch, "Fuck you."

"Right," Bosch said.

He stood on the sidewalk, lit a cigarette and offered one to the boy. He declined.

"I'm not telling you anything," the boy said.

"I know. That's cool. You want me to take you anywhere? A real doctor? A lift back to Hollywood?"

"Hollywood's fine."

They walked to Bosch's car, which was parked two blocks away at Parker Center and he took Third Street toward Hollywood. They were halfway there before either one spoke.

"You have a place? Where do you want me to drop you?"

"Anywhere."

"No place?"

"No."

"Family?"

"Nope."

"What will you do?"

"Whatever."

Harry turned north on Western. They were silent for another fifteen minutes or so, until Bosch pulled to a stop in front of the Hideaway.

"What's this?"

"Sit tight. I'll only be a minute."

Inside the office, the manager tried to rent Bosch room seven but Harry flipped him his badge and told him try again. The manager, who was still wearing a dingy sleeveless T-shirt, gave him the key to room thirteen. He went back to the car and got in and gave the boy the key. He also took out his wallet.

"You've got a room in there for a week," Bosch said. "For what it's worth, which you probably don't think is much, my advice is that you think about things and then get as far away from this town as you can. There are better places to live than this."

The boy looked at the key in his hand. Bosch then handed him all the money he had, which was only $43.

"What, you give me a room and money and you think I'm going to talk to you? I've seen TV, man. The whole thing was a hoax, you and that guy."

"Don't misunderstand, kid. I'm doing this because it's something that I need to do. It doesn't mean I think what you do for a living is okay. I don't. If I ever see you out on the street again I'm going to come down on you. It's a pretty fucking desperate chance but it's a chance just the same. Do with it what you want. You can go. It's no hoax."

The boy opened the car door and got out. He looked back in at Bosch.

"Then why're you doing it?"

"I don't know. I guess 'cause you told him to go to hell. I should've said that and I didn't. I gotta go."

The boy looked at him a moment before speaking.

"You know, man, Dance's gone. I don't know why you're all worried about him."

"Look, kid, I didn't do—"

"I know."

Harry just looked at him.

"He left, man. Left town. He said our source split and so he went down to see if he could get the thing going again. You know, he wants to step up and be the source, now."

"Down?"

"He said Mexico, but that's all I know. He's gone. That's why I was doing sherms."

The boy closed the door and disappeared into the courtyard of the motel. Bosch sat there thinking and Rickard's question came back to him. Where would the boy be in a year? Then he thought of himself staying in rundown motels so many years ago. Bosch had made it through. Had survived. There was always the chance. He restarted the car and pulled out.

Sixteen

TALKING TO THE KID SEALED IT. BOSCH KNEW HE WAS going to Mexico. All the spokes on the wheel pointed to the hub. The hub was Mexicali. But, then he'd known that all along.

He drove to the station on Wilcox, trying to determine a strategy. He knew he would have to contact Aguila, the State Judicial Police officer who had sent the letter identifying Juan Doe #67 to the consulate. He would also have to contact the DEA, which had provided the intelligence report to Moore. He would have to get the trip cleared by Pounds, but he knew that might end it right there. He would have to work around that.

In the bureau, the homicide table was empty. It was after four on a Friday, and a holiday week as well. With no new cases; the detectives would clear out as soon as possible to go home to families and lives outside the copshop. Harry could see Pounds in his glass booth; his head was down and he was writing on a piece of paper, using his ruler to keep his sentences on a straight line.

Bosch sat down and checked through a pile of pink message slips at his spot. Nothing needing an immediate return. There were two from Bremmer at the *Times* but he had left the name Jon Marcus— a code they had once worked out so it would not become known that the reporter was calling for Bosch. There were a couple from DAs who were prosecuting cases Harry had worked and needed information or the location of evidence. There was a message that Teresa had called but he looked at the time on the note and saw that he had seen her since then. He guessed that she had called to tell him she wasn't talking to him.

There was no message from Porter and no message from Sylvia Moore. He took out the copy of the inquiry from Mexicali that the missing-persons detective, Capetillo, had given him and dialed the number Carlos Aguila had provided. The number was a general exchange for the SJP office. His Spanish was unconfident despite his recent refresher, and it took Bosch five minutes of explanations before he was connected to the investigations unit and asked once again for Aguila. He didn't get him. Instead, he got a captain who spoke English and explained that Aguila was not in the office but would return later and would also be working Saturday. Bosch knew that the cops in Mexico worked six-day weeks.

"Can I be of help?" the captain asked.

Bosch explained that he was investigating a homicide and was answering the inquiry Aguila had sent to the consulate in Los Angeles. The description was similar to the body he had. The captain explained that he was familiar with the case, that he had taken the report before handing the case to Aguila. Bosch asked whether there were fingerprints available to confirm the identification but the captain said there were none. Chalk one up for Capetillo, Bosch thought.

"Perhaps you have a photograph from your morgue of this man that you could send to us," the captain said. "We could make identification from the family of Mr. Gutierrez-Llosa."

"Yes. I have photos. The letter said Gutierrez-Llosa was a laborer?"

"Yes. He found day work at the circle where employers come to find workers. Beneath the statue of Benito Juarez."

"Do you know if he worked at a place, a business called Enviro-Breed? It does business with the state of California."

There was a long silence before the Mexican replied.

"I am sorry. I do not know of his work history. I have taken notes and will discuss this with Investigator Aguila upon his return. If you send the photographs we will act promptly on securing positive identification. I will personally expedite this matter and contact you."

Now Bosch let silence fill the phone connection. "Captain, I didn't get your name."

"Gustavo Grena, director of investigations, Mexicali."

"Captain Grena, please tell Aguila that he will have the photos tomorrow."

"That soon?"

"Yes. Tell him I'm bringing them down myself."

"Investigator Bosch, this is not necessary. I believe—"

"Don't worry, Captain Grena," Bosch cut him off. "Tell him I will be there by early afternoon, no later."

"As you wish."

Bosch thanked him and hung up. He looked up and saw Pounds staring at him through the glass in his office. The lieutenant raised his thumb and his eyebrows in an inquiring, pleading way. Bosch looked away.

A laborer, Bosch thought. Fernal Gutierrez-Llosa was a day laborer who got jobs at the circle, whatever that was. How did a day laborer fit? Perhaps he was a mule who brought black ice across the border. And perhaps he had not been a part of the smuggling operation at all. Perhaps he had done nothing to warrant his death other than to be somewhere he should not have been, seen something he should not have seen.

What Bosch had were just parts of the whole. What he needed was the glue that would correctly hold them together. When he had first received his gold shield he had a partner on the robbery table in Van Nuys who told him that facts weren't the most important part of an investigation, the glue was. He said the glue was made of instinct, imagination, sometimes guesswork and most times just plain luck.

Two nights earlier Bosch had looked at the facts that lay inside a run-down motel room and from them extrapolated a cop's suicide. He now knew he'd been wrong. He considered the facts again, along with everything else he had collected, and this time he saw a cop's murder as one of several connected murders. If Mexicali was the hub of the wheel with so many spokes, then Moore was the bolt that held the wheel on.

He took out his notebook and looked up the name of the DEA agent who was listed on the intelligence report Moore had put in the Zorrillo file. He then got the DEA's local number out of his Rolodex and dialed it. The man who answered asked who was calling when Bosch asked for Corvo.

"Tell him it's the ghost of Calexico Moore."

One minute later a voice said, "Who's this?"

"Corvo?"

"Look, you want to talk, give me an ID. Otherwise I hang up."

Bosch identified himself.

"What's with the ruse, man?"

"Never mind. I want to meet."

"You haven't given me a reason yet."

"You want a reason? Okay. Tomorrow morning, I'm going to Mexicali. I'm going after Zorrillo. I could use some help from somebody who knows his shit. I thought you might want to talk first. Being that you were Cal Moore's source."

"Who says I even knew the guy?"

"You took my call, didn't you? You also were passing DEA intelligence to him. He told me."

"Bosch, I spent seven years under. You trying to bluff me? Uh-uh. Try some of the eightball dealers on Hollywood Boulevard. They might buy your line."

"Look, man, at seven o'clock I'll be at the Code Seven, in the back bar. After that, I'll be heading south. It's your choice. If I see you, I see you."

"And if I decide to show up, how will I know you?"

"Don't worry. I'll know you. You'll be the guy who still thinks he's undercover."

When he hung up, Harry looked up and saw Pounds hovering near the homicide table, standing there reading the latest CAP report, another sore subject for the division's statisticians. Crimes Against Persons, meaning all crimes of violence, were growing at a rate faster than the overall crime rate. That meant not only was crime going up but the criminals were becoming meaner, more prone to violence. Bosch noticed the white dust on the upper part of the lieutenant's pants. It was there often and was cause for great comical debate and derision in the squad room. Some of the dicks said he was probably blowing coke up his nose and was just sloppy about it. This was especially humorous because Pounds was one of the department's born-agains. Others said the mystery dust was from sugar donuts that he secretly scarfed down in the glass booth after closing the blinds so no one would see. Bosch, though, figured it out once he identified the odor that was always about Pounds. Harry believed the lieutenant had the habit of putting baby powder on in the morning before he put on his shirt and tie—but after putting on his pants.

Pounds looked away from his report and said in a phoney matter-of-fact voice, "So how's it looking? Getting anywhere with the cases?"

Bosch smiled reassuringly and nodded but said nothing. He'd make Pounds work for it.

"Well, what's up?"

"Oh, some things. Have you heard from Porter today?"

"Porter? No, why? Forget about him, Bosch. He's a mutt. He can't help you. What have you got? You haven't filed any updates. I just went through the box. Nothing from you there."

"I've been busy, Lieutenant. I got something going on Jimmy Kapps and I got an ID and possible death scene on Porter's last case. The one dumped in the alley off Sunset last week. I'm close to knowing who and why. Maybe tomorrow on both of them. I'm going to work through the weekend if that's okay with you."

"Excellent. By all means, take the time you need. I'll fill the over-time authorization out today."

"Thanks."

"But why juggle the cases? Why don't you pick the one you think is easier to complete? We need to clear a case."

"I think the cases are related, that's why."

"Are you—" Then Pounds held up his hand, signaling Bosch not to speak. "Better come into my office for this."

After sitting down behind his glass-topped desk, Pounds immediately picked up his ruler and began manipulating it in his hand.

"Okay, Harry, what's going on?"

Bosch was going to wing it. He tried to make his voice sound as though he had hard evidence to back everything he was saying. Truth was it was all a lot of speculation and not a lot of glue. He sat down in the chair in front of the lieutenant's desk. He could smell the baby powder on the other man.

"Jimmy Kapps was a payback. Found out yesterday that he set up a bust on a competitor named Dance. He was putting black ice out on the street. Jimmy apparently didn't like that 'cause he's trying to make Hawaiian ice the growth market. So he snitched Dance off to the BANG guys. Only after Dance got taken down, the DA kicked the case. A bad bust. He walked. Four days later Kapps gets the whack."

"Okay, okay," Pounds said. "Sounds good. Dance is your suspect then?"

"Until I come up with something better. He's in the wind."

"Okay, now how does this tie in with the Juan Doe case?"

"The DEA says the black ice that Dance was putting out comes from Mexicali. I got a tentative ID from the state police down there. Looks like our Juan Doe was a guy named Gutierrez-Llosa. He was from Mexicali."

"A mule?"

"Possibly. Couple things don't fit with that. The state police down there carried him as a day laborer."

"Maybe he went for the big money. A lot of them do."

"Maybe."

"And you think he got whacked back, a payback for Kapps?"

"Maybe."

Pounds nodded. So far so good, Bosch thought. They were both silent for a few moments. Pounds finally cleared his throat.

"That's quite a lot of work for two days, Harry. Very good. Now where do you go from here?"

"I want to go after Dance and get the Juan Doe ID confirmed..." He trailed off. He wasn't sure how much to give Pounds. He knew he was going to keep his trip to Mexicali out of it.

"You said Dance is in the wind."

"I'm told that by a source. I'm not sure. I plan to go looking this weekend."

"Fine."

Bosch decided to open the door a little further. "There's more to it, if you want to hear it. It's about Cal Moore."

Pounds put the ruler down on the desk, folded his arms and leaned back. His posture signaled caution. They were stepping into an area where careers could be permanently damaged.

"Aren't we getting on thin ice, here? The Moore case is not ours."

"And I don't want it, Lieutenant, I've got these two. But it keeps coming up. If you don't want to know, fine. I can deal with it."

"No, no, I want you to tell me. I just don't like this kind of...uh, entanglement. That's all."

"Yeah, entanglement is a good word. Anyway, like I said, it was the BANG crew that made the Dance bust. Moore wasn't there until after it went down, but it was his crew.

"After that, you have Moore finding the body on the Juan Doe case."

"Cal Moore found the body?" Pounds said. "I didn't see that in Porter's book."

"He's in there by badge number. Anyway, he was the one that found the body dumped there. So you've got his presence around both of these cases. Then, the day after he finds Juan Doe in the alley he checks into that motel and gets his brains splattered in the bathtub. I suppose you've heard RHD now says it was no suicide."

Pounds nodded. But he had a paralyzed look on his face. He had thought he was going to get a summary of a couple of case investigations. Not this.

"Somebody whacked him, too," Bosch continued. "So now you have three cases. You have Kapps, then Juan Doe, then Moore. And you have Dance in the wind."

Bosch knew he had said enough. He could now sit back and watch Pounds's mind go to work. He knew that the lieutenant knew that he should probably pick up the phone and call Irving to ask for assistance or at least direction. But Pounds knew that a call like that would result in RHD taking jurisdiction over the Kapps and Juan Doe cases. And the RHD dicks would take their sweet-ass time about it. Pounds wouldn't see any of the cases closed out for weeks. "What about Porter? What's he say about all of this?"

Bosch had been doing his best to keep Porter clear. He didn't know why. Porter had fallen and had lied, but somewhere inside Bosch still felt something. Maybe it was that last question. *Harry, you going to take care of me on this?*

"I haven't found Porter," Bosch lied. "No answer on his phone. But I don't think he'd had much time to put all of this together."

Pounds shook his head disdainfully.

"Of course not. He probably was on a drunk."

Bosch didn't say anything. It was in Pounds's court now "Listen, Harry, you're not...you're being straight with me here, right? I can't afford to have you running around like a loose cannon. I've got it all, right?"

Bosch knew that what he meant was he wanted to know how badly he could be fucked if this went to shit.

Bosch said, "You know what I know. There are two cases, probably three, including Moore, out there to be cleared. You want 'em cleared in six, eight weeks, then I'll write up the paper and you can ship it to Parker Center. If you want to get them cleared by the first like you said, then let me have the four days."

Pounds was staring off somewhere above Bosch's head and using the ruler to scratch himself behind the ear. He was making a decision.

"Okay," he finally said. "Take the weekend and see what you can do. We'll see where things stand Monday. We might have to call in RHD then. Meantime, I want to hear from you tomorrow and Sunday. I want to know your movements, what's happening, what progress has been made."

"You got it," Bosch said. He stood up and turned to leave. He noticed that above the door was a small crucifix. He wondered if that had been what Pounds had been staring at. Most said he was a political born-again. There were a lot in the department. They all joined a church up in the Valley because one of the assistant chiefs was a lay preacher there. Bosch guessed they all went there Sunday mornings and gathered around him, told him what a great guy he was.

"I'll talk to you tomorrow, then," Pounds said from behind.

"Right. Tomorrow."

A short while after that, Pounds locked his office and went home. Bosch hung around the office alone, drinking coffee and smoking and waiting for the six o'clock news. There was a small black-and-white television on top of the file cabinet behind the autos table. He turned it on and played with the rabbit ears until he got a reasonably clear picture. A couple of the uniforms walked down from the watch office to watch.

Cal Moore had finally made the top of the news. Channel 2 led with a report on the press conference at Parker Center in which Assistant Chief Irvin Irving revealed new developments. The tape showed Irving at a cluster of microphones. Teresa stood behind him. Irving credited her with finding new evidence during the autopsy that pointed to homicide. Irving said a full-scale homicide investigation was underway. The report ended with a photograph of Moore and a voiceover from the reporter.

"Investigators now have the task, and they say the personal obligation, to dig deep into the life of Sergeant Calexico Moore to determine what it was that led him to the beat-up motel room where someone executed him. Sources tell me the investigators do not have much to start with, but they do start with a debt of thanks to the acting chief medical examiner, who discovered a murder that had been written off...as a cop's lonely suicide."

The camera zoomed in closer on Moore's face here and the reporter ended it, "And so, the mystery begins..."

Bosch turned the TV off after the report. The uniforms went back down the hall and he went back to his spot at the homicide table and sat down. The picture they had shown of Moore had been taken a few years back, Harry guessed. His face was younger, the eyes clearer. There was no portent of a hidden life.

Thinking about it brought to mind the other photographs, the ones Sylvia Moore had said her husband had collected over his life and looked at from time to time. What else had he saved from the past? Bosch didn't have one photo of his mother. He hadn't known his father until the old man was on his deathbed. What baggage did Cal Moore carry with him?

It was time for him to head for the Code 7. But before heading out to the car, Harry walked down the hall to the watch office. He picked up the clipboard that hung on the wall next to the wanted flyers and carried the station's duty roster clipped to it. He doubted that it would have been updated in the last week and he was correct. He found Moore's name and address in Los Feliz on the page listing sergeants. He copied the address into his notebook and then headed out.

Seventeen

BOSCH DRAGGED DEEPLY ON A CIGARETTE AND THEN dropped the butt into the gutter. He hesitated before pulling the Billy club that was the door handle of the Code 7. He stared across First Street to the grass square that flanked City Hall and was called Freedom Park. Beneath the sodium lights he saw the bodies of homeless men and women sprawled asleep in the grass around the war memorial. They looked like casualties on a battlefield, the unburied dead.

He went inside, walked through the front restaurant and then parted the black curtains that hid the entrance to the bar like a judge's robes. The place was crowded with lawyers and cops and blue with cigarette smoke. They had all come to wait out the rush hour and either gotten too comfortable or too drunk. Harry went down to the end of the bar where the stools were empty and ordered a beer and a shot. It was seven on the dot according to the Miller clock over the bar. He scanned the room in the mirror behind the bar but saw nobody he could assume was the DEA agent Corvo. He lit another cigarette and decided he would give it until eight.

The moment he decided that he looked back in the mirror and saw a short, dark man with a full black beard split the curtain and hesitate as his eyes focused in the dim bar. He wore blue jeans and a pullover shirt. Bosch saw the pager on his belt and the bulge the gun made under his shirt. The man looked around until their eyes met in the mirror and Harry nodded once. Corvo came over and took the stool next to him.

"So you made me," Corvo said.

"And you made me. I guess we both need to go back to the academy. You want a beer?"

"Look, Bosch, before you start getting friendly on me, I gotta tell you I don't know about this. I don't know what this is about. I haven't decided whether to talk to you."

Harry took his cigarette from the ashtray and looked at Corvo in the mirror.

"I haven't decided if Certs is a breath mint or a candy."

Corvo slid back off his stool.

"Have a good one."

"C'mon Corvo, have a beer, why don't you? Relax, man."

"I checked you out before I came over. The line on you is that you're just another head case. You're on the fast track to nowhere. RHD to Hollywood, the next stop probably riding shotgun in a Wells Fargo truck."

"No, the next stop is Mexicali. And I can go down there blind, maybe walk in on whatever you got going with Zorrillo, or you can help me and yourself by telling me what's what."

"What's what is that you aren't going to do anything down there. I leave here I pick up the phone and your trip is over."

"I leave here and I'm gone, on my way. Too late to stop. Have a seat. If I've been an asshole, I'm sorry. It's the way I am sometimes. But I need you guys and you guys need me."

Corvo still didn't sit down.

"Bosch, what are you gonna do? Go down to the ranch, put the pope over your shoulder and carry him back up here? That it?"

"Something like that."

"Shit."

"Actually, I don't know what I'm going to do. I'm just going to play it as it comes. Maybe I never see the pope, maybe I do. You want to risk it?"

Corvo slid back onto the stool and signaled the bartender. He ordered the same as Bosch. In the mirror Bosch noticed a long, thick scar cutting through the right side of Corvo's beard. If he had grown the beard to cover the purplish-pink slug on his cheek, it hadn't worked. Then again, maybe he didn't want it to. Most DEA agents Bosch knew or had worked with had a macho swagger about them. A scar couldn't hurt. It was a life of bluffing and bluster. Scars were worn like badges of courage. But Bosch wondered if the guy could do much undercover work with such a recognizable physical anomaly.

After the bartender put down the drinks, Corvo threw back the shot like a man used to it.

"So," he said. "What are you really going down there for? And why should I trust you the least bit?"

Bosch thought about it for a few moments. "Because I can give you Zorrillo."

"Shit."

Bosch didn't say anything. He had to give Corvo his due, had to let him run out his string. After he was done posturing they would get down to business. Bosch thought at the moment that the one thing the movies and TV shows didn't get wrong or overexaggerate was the relationship of jealousy and distrust that existed between local and federal cops. One side always thought it was better, wiser, more qualified. Usually, the side that thought that was wrong.

"Okay," Corvo said. "I'll bite. What have you got?"

"Before I get into it. I have one question. Who are you, man? I mean, you're up here in L.A. Why are you the one in Moore's files? How come you're the expert on Zorrillo?"

"That's about ten questions. The basic answer to all of them is I'm a control agent on an investigation in Mexicali that is being jointly worked by Mexico City and L.A. offices. We are equidistant;

we are splitting the case. I'm not telling you anything else until I know you're worth talking to. Talk."

Bosch told him about Jimmy Kapps, Juan Doe and the ties between their deaths and Dance and Moore and the Zorrillo operation. Lastly, he said that he had information that Dance had gone to Mexico, probably Mexicali, after Moore was murdered.

Corvo drained his beer glass and said, "Tell me something, because it's a big fucking hole in your scenario. How come you think this Juan Doe was whacked out down there? And then, how come his body was taken all the way up here? Doesn't make sense to me."

"The autopsy puts his death six to eight hours before Moore found it, or said he found it up here. There were things about the autopsy that tie it to Mexicali, to a specific location in Mexicali. I think they wanted to get it out of Mexicali to make sure it was not connected to that location. It got sent to L.A. because there was already a truck heading this way. It was convenient."

"You're talking jigsaws, Bosch. What location are we talking about?"

"We aren't talking. That's the problem. I'm talking. You haven't said shit. But I'm here to trade. I know your record. You guys haven't taken down one of Zorrillo's shipments. I can give you Zorrillo's pipeline. What can you give me?"

Corvo laughed and shot a peace sign at the bartender. He brought two more beers.

"Know something? I like you. Believe it or not. I did check you out but I do like what I know of you. But something tells me you don't have shit worth trading for."

"You ever check out a place down there called EnviroBreed?"

Corvo looked down at the beer placed in front of him and seemed to be composing his thoughts. Bosch had to prompt him.

"Yes or no?"

"EnviroBreed is a plant down there. They make these sterile fruit flies to set loose around here. It's a government contractor. They have to breed the bugs down there 'cause—"

"I know all of that. How come you know?"

"The only reason is that I was involved in setting plans on our operation down there. We wanted a ground Observation Point on the target's ranch. We went into the industrial parks that border the ranch to look for candidates. EnviroBreed was obvious. American-managed. It was a government contractor. We went to see if we could set up an OP, maybe on the roof or an office or something. The ranch property starts just across the street."

"But they said no."

"No, actually, they said yes. We said no."

"How come?"

"Radiation. Bugs—they got those damned flies buzzing all over the goddamn place. But most of all the view was obscured. We went up on the roof and we could see the ranch all right but the barn and stables—the whole bull-breeding facility—was in line between EnviroBreed and the main ranch facilities. We couldn't use the place. We told the guy there, thanks but no thanks."

"What was your cover? Or did you just come out and say DEA?"

"Nah, we cooked something up. Said we were from the National Weather Service on a project tracking desert and mountain wind systems. Some bullshit like that. The guy bought it."

"Right."

Corvo wiped his mouth with the back of his hand.

"So, how does EnviroBreed figure into it from this end?"

"My Juan Doe. He had those bugs you were talking about in his body. I think he was probably killed there."

Corvo turned so he was looking directly at Bosch. Harry continued to watch him in the mirror behind the bar. "Okay, Bosch, let's say you've got my attention. Go ahead and spin the tale."

Bosch said he believed that EnviroBreed, which he didn't even know was across from Zorrillo's ranch until Corvo told him, was part of the black ice pipeline. He told Corvo the rest of his theory: that Fernal Gutierrez-Llosa was a day laborer who either hired on as a mule and didn't make the grade or had worked at the bug breeding plant and seen something he should not have seen or done something he should not have done. Either way, he was beaten to death, his body put in one of the white environment boxes and taken with a shipment of fruit flies to Los Angeles. His body was then dumped in Hollywood and reported by Moore, who probably handled everything on this end.

"They had to get the body out of there because they couldn't bring an investigation into the plant. There is something there. At least, something that was worth killing an old man for."

Corvo had his arm up on the bar and his face in the palm of his hand. He said, "What did he see?"

"I don't know. I do know that EnviroBreed has a deal with the feds not to have their shipments across the border bothered with. Opening those boxes could damage the goods."

"Who have you told this to?"

"Nobody."

"Nobody? You have told no one about EnviroBreed?"

"I've made some inquiries. I haven't told anyone the story I just told you."

"Who have you made inquiries with? You called the SJP?"

"Yeah. They put out a letter to the consulate on the old man. That's how I put it together. I still have to make a formal ID of the body when I'm down there."

"Yeah, but did you bring up EnviroBreed?"

"I asked if they ever heard of him working at EnviroBreed."

Corvo spun back toward the bar with an exasperated sigh.

"Who did you talk to there?"

"A captain named Grena."

"I don't know him. But you've probably spoiled your lead. You just don't go to the locals with this sort of thing. They pick up the phone, tell Zorrillo what you just said and then pick up a bonus at the end of the month."

"Maybe it's spoiled, maybe it isn't. Grena brushed me off and may think that's it. At least I didn't go walking into the bug place and ask to set up a weather station."

Neither spoke. Each one thinking about what the other had said so far.

"I'm going to get down on this right away," Corvo said after a while. "You have to promise me you won't go fucking around with it when you get down there."

"I'm not promising anything. And so far I've done all the giving here. You haven't said shit."

"What do you want to know?"

"About Zorrillo."

"All you really gotta know is that we've wanted his ass for a long time."

This time Bosch signaled for two more beers. He lit a cigarette and saw the smoke blur his reflection in the mirror.

"Only thing you have to know about Zorrillo is that he is one smart fucker and, like I said, it wouldn't surprise me in the least if he already knows you're coming. Fuckin' SJP. We only deal with the *federales*. Even them you can trust about as much as an ex-wife."

Bosch nodded meaningfully, just hoping Corvo would continue.

"If he doesn't know now, he'll know before you get there. So you've got to watch your ass. And the best way of doing that is not to go. With you, I know, that isn't an option. The second best way is to skip the SJP altogether. You can't trust 'em. The pope has people inside there. Okay?"

Bosch nodded at him in the mirror. He decided to stop nodding all the time.

"Now, I know everything I just said went in your ears and out your asshole," Corvo said. "So what I'm willing to do is put you with a guy down there, work it from there. Name's Ramos. You go down, say your howdy-dos with the local SJPs, act like everything is nice, and then hook up with Ramos."

"If this EnviroBreed thing pans out and you make a move on Zorrillo, I want to be there."

"You will. Just hang with Ramos. Okay?"

Bosch thought it over a few moments and said, "Yeah. Now tell me about Zorrillo. You keep going off on other shit."

"Zorrillo's been around a long time. We've got intelligence on him going back to the seventies at least. A career doper. One of the bounces on the trampoline, I'd guess you'd call him."

Bosch had heard the term before but was confident Corvo would get around to explaining it anyway.

"Black ice is just his latest thing. He was a *marijuanito* when he was a kid. Pulled out of the barrio by someone like himself today. He took backpacks of grass over the fence when he was twelve, made the truck runs when he was older and just worked his way up. By the eighties, when we had most of our efforts concentrated on Florida, the Colombians contracted with the Mexicans. They flew cocaine to Mexico and the Mexicans took it across the border, using the same old pot trails. Mexicali across to Calexico was one of them. They called the route the Trampoline. The shit bounces from Colombia to Mexico and then up to the states.

"And Zorrillo became a rich man. From the barrio to that nice big ranch with his own personal *guardia* and half the cops in Baja on his payroll. And the cycle started over. He pulled most his people out of the slums. He never forgot the barrio and it never forgot him. A lot of loyalty. That's when he got the name El Papa. So once we shifted our resources a little bit to address the cocaine situation in Mexico, the pope moved on to heroin. He had tar labs in the nearby barrios. Always had volunteers to mule it across. For one trip he'd pay one of those poor suckers down there more than they'd make in five years doing anything else."

Bosch thought of the temptation, that much money for what amounted to so little risk. Even those who were caught spent little time in jail.

"It was a natural transition to go from tar heroin to black ice. Zorrillo's an entrepreneur. Obviously, this is a drug that is in its infancy as far as awareness in the drug culture goes. But we think he is the country's main supplier. We've got black ice showing up all over the place. New York, Seattle, Chicago, all your large cities. Whatever operation you stumbled over in L.A., that was just a drop in the bucket. One of many. We think he's still running straight heroin with his barrio mules but the ice is his growth product. It's the future and he knows it. He's shifting more and more of his operation into it and he's going to drive Hawaiians out. His overhead is so low, his stuff is selling twenty bucks a cap below the going rate for Hawaiian ice, or glass, or whatever they call it this week. And Zorrillo's stuff is better. He's putting the Hawaiians out of business on the mainland. Then when the demand for this thing really starts to escalate—conceivably as fast as crack did in the mid-eighties—he'll bump the price and have a virtual monopoly until the others catch up with him.

"Zorrillo's kinda like one of those fishing boats with the ten-mile net behind it. He's circling around and he's going to pull that sucker closed on all the fish."

"An entrepreneur," Bosch said, just to be saying something.

"Yeah, that's what I'd call him. You remember a couple years ago the Border Patrol found the tunnel in Arizona? Went from a warehouse on one side of the border to a warehouse on the other? In Nogales? Well, we think that he was an investor in that. One of them at least. It was probably his idea."

"But the bottom line is you've never touched him."

"Nope. Whenever we'd get close, somebody'd end up dead. I guess you'd say he's a violent sort of entrepreneur."

Bosch envisioned Moore's body in the dingy motel bathroom. Had he been planning to make a move, to go against Zorrillo?

"Zorrillo's tied in with the *eMe*," Corvo said. "Word is he can have anybody anywhere whacked out. Supposedly back in the seventies there was all kinds of slaughter going on for control of the pot trails. Zorrillo emerged on top. It was like a gang war, barrio against barrio. He has since united all of them but back then, his was the dominant clan. Saints and Sinners. A lot of the *eMe* came out of that."

The *eMe* was the Mexican Mafia, a Latino gang with control over inmates in most of Mexico's and California's prisons. Bosch knew little about them and had had few cases that involved members. He did know that allegiance to the group was strictly enforced. Infractions were punishable by death.

"How do you know all of that?" he asked.

"Informants over the years. The ones that lived to talk about it. We've got a whole history on our friend the pope. I even know he's got a velvet painting of Elvis in his office at the ranch."

"Did his barrio have a sign?"

"What do you mean, a sign?"

"A symbol."

"It's the devil. With a halo."

Bosch emptied his beer and looked around the bar. He saw a deputy district attorney he knew was part of a team that rubber-stamped investigations of police shootings. He was sitting alone at a table with a martini. There were a few cops Bosch recognized huddled at other tables. They all were smoking, dinosaurs all. Harry wanted to leave, to go somewhere he could think about this information. The devil with a halo. Moore had it tattooed on his arm. He had come from the same place as Zorrillo. Harry could feel his adrenaline kicking up a notch.

"How will I get together with Ramos down there?"

"He'll come to you. Where're you staying?"

"I don't know."

"Stay at the De Anza, in Calexico. It's safer on our side of the border. Water's better for you, too."

"Okay. I'll be there."

"Another thing is, you can't take a weapon across. I mean, it's easy enough to do. You flash your badge at the crossing and nobody's going to check your trunk. But if something happens down there, the first thing that will be checked is whether you checked your gun in at the police station in Calexico."

He nodded meaningfully at Bosch.

"They have a gun locker at Calexico PD where they check weapons for crossing cops. They keep a log, you get a receipt. Professional courtesy. So check a weapon. Don't take it across and then think you can say you left it up here at home. Check it in down there. Get it on the log. Then you don't have a problem. *Comprende?* It's like having an alibi for your gun in case something happens."

Bosch nodded. He knew what Corvo was telling him.

Corvo took out his wallet and gave Bosch a business card. "Call anytime and if I'm not in the office they will locate me. Just tell the operator it's you. I'll leave your name and word that you are to be put through."

Corvo's speech pattern had changed. He was talking faster. Bosch guessed this was because he was excited about the EnviroBreed tip. The DEA agent was anxious to get on it. Harry studied him in the mirror. The scar on his cheek seemed darker now, as if it had changed color with his mood. Corvo looked at him in the mirror.

"Knife fight," he said, fingering the scar. "Zihuatanejo. I was under, working a case. Carrying my piece in my boot. Guy got me here before I could get to the boot. Down there they don't have hospitals for shit. They did a bad job on it and I ended up with this. I couldn't go under anymore. Too recognizable."

Bosch could tell he liked telling the story. He was stoked with bravado as he told it. It was probably the one time he had come close to his own end. Bosch knew what Corvo was waiting for him to ask. He asked anyway.

"And the guy who did it? What did he get?"

"A state burial. I put him down once I got to my piece."

Corvo had found a way to make killing a man who brought a knife to a gunfight sound heroic. At least to his own ears. He probably told the story a lot, every time he caught someone new looking at the scar. Bosch nodded respectfully and slipped off his stool and put money on the bar.

"Remember our deal. You don't move on Zorrillo without me. Make sure you tell Ramos."

"Oh, we've got a deal," Corvo said. "But I'm not guaranteeing it will happen when you're down there. We aren't going to rush anything. Besides, we've lost Zorrillo. Temporarily, I'm sure."

"What are you talking about, you've lost him?"

"I mean we haven't had a bona fide sighting in about ten days or so. We think he's there on the ranch, though. He's just laying low, changing his routine."

"Routine?"

"The pope is a man who likes to be seen. He likes to taunt us. Usually, he rides the ranch in a Jeep, hunting coyotes, shooting his Uzi, admiring his bulls. There is one bull in particular, a champion that once killed a matador. El Temblar, he is called. Zorrillo often goes out to watch this bull. It's like him, I guess. Very proud.

"Anyway, Zorrillo has not been seen on the ranch or the Plaza de Toros, which was his Sunday custom. He hasn't been seen cruising the barrios, reminding himself of where he came from. He's a well-known figure in them all. He gets off on this pope of Mexicali shit."

Bosch tried to imagine Zorrillo's life. A celebrity in a town that celebrated nothing. He lit a cigarette. He wanted to get out of there.

"So when was the last bona fide?"

"If he is still there, he hasn't come out of the compound since December fifteenth. That was a Sunday. He was at the plaza watching his bulls. That's the last bona fide. After that, we have some informants who move that up to the eighteenth. They say they saw him at the compound, dicking around outside. But that's it. He's either split or he is laying low, like I said."

"Maybe because he ordered a cop blown away."

Corvo nodded.

Bosch left alone after that. Corvo said he was going to use the pay phone. Harry stepped out of the bar, felt the brisk night air and took the last drag on his cigarette. He saw movement in the darkness of the park across the street. Then one of the crazies moved into the cone of light beneath a streetlight. It was a black man, high-stepping and making jerking movements with his arms. He made a crisp turn and began moving back into the darkness. He was a trombone player in a marching band in a world somewhere else.

Eighteen

THE APARTMENT BUILDING WHERE CAL MOORE HAD lived was a three-story affair that stuck out on Franklin about the same way cabs do at the airport. It was one of the many stuccoed, post–World War II jobs that lined the streets in that area. It was called The Fountains but they had been filled in with dirt and made into planters. It was about a block from the mansion that was head-quarters for the Church of Scientology and the complex's white neon sign threw an eerie glow down to where Bosch was standing on the curb. It was near ten o'clock, so he wasn't worried about anyone offering him a personality test. He stood there smoking and studying the apartment building for a half hour before finally decid-ing to go ahead with the break-in.

It was a security building but it really wasn't. Bosch slipped the lock on the front gate with a butter knife he kept with his picks in the glove compartment of the Caprice. The next door, the one lead-ing to the lobby, he didn't have to worry about. It needed to be oiled and showed this by not snapping all the way closed. Bosch went through the door, checked a listing of tenants and found Moore's name listed next to number seven, on the third floor.

Moore's place was at the end of a hallway that split the center of the floor. At the door, Harry saw the police evidence sticker had been placed across the jamb. He cut it with the small penknife attached to his key chain and then knelt down to look at the lock. There were two other apartments on the hallway. He heard no TV sound or talking coming from either. The lighting in the hall was good, so he didn't need the flashlight. Moore had a standard pin tumbler dead bolt on the door. Using a curved tension hook and sawtooth comb, he turned the lock in less than two minutes.

With his handkerchief-wrapped hand on the knob ready to open the door, he wondered again how prudent he was in coming here. If Irving or Pounds found out, he'd be back on the street in blue before the first of the year. He looked down the hall behind him once more and opened the door. He had to go in. Nobody else seemed to care what had happened to Cal Moore and that was fine. But Bosch did care for some reason. He thought maybe he would find that reason here.

Once inside the apartment, he closed and relocked the door. He stood there, a couple of feet inside, letting his eyes adjust. The place smelled musty and was dark, except for the bluish-white glow of the Scientology light that leaked through the sheer curtains over the living room window. Bosch walked into the room and switched on a lamp on an end table next to an old misshapen sofa. The light revealed that the place had come furnished in the same decor it had maybe twenty years ago. The navy blue carpet was worn flat as Astroturf in pathways from the couch to the kitchen and to the hallway that went off to the right.

He moved farther in and took quick glances in the kitchen and the bedroom and the bathroom. He was struck by the emptiness of the place. There was nothing personal here. No pictures on the walls, no notes on the refrigerator, no jacket hung over the back of a chair. There wasn't even a dish in the sink. Moore had lived here but it was almost as if he hadn't existed.

He didn't know what he was looking for, so he started in the kitchen. He opened cabinets and drawers. He found a box of cereal, a can of coffee and a three-quarters-empty bottle of Early Times. In another cabinet he found an unopened bottle of sweet rum with a

Mexican label. Inside the bottle was a stalk of sugar cane. There was some silverware and cooking tools in the drawers, several books of matches from Hollywood area bars like Ports and the Bullet.

The freezer was empty, except for two trays of ice. On the top shelf in the refrigerator section below there was a jar of mustard, a half-finished package of now-rancid bologna and a lone can of Budweiser, its plastic six-pack collar still choking it. On the lower shelf on the door was a two-pound bag of Domino sugar.

Harry studied the sugar. It was unopened. Then he thought, What the hell, I've come this far. He took it out and opened it and slowly poured it into the sink. It looked like sugar to him. It tasted like sugar to him. There was nothing else in the bag. He turned on the hot water and watched as the white mound was washed down the drain.

He left the bag on the counter and went into the bathroom. There was a toothbrush in the holder, shaving equipment behind the mirror. Nothing else.

In the bedroom Bosch first went into the walk-in closet. An assortment of clothes was on hangers and more filled a plastic laundry basket on the floor. On the shelf there was a green plaid suitcase and a white box with the word "Snakes" printed on it. Bosch first dumped the basket over and checked the pockets of the dirty shirts and pants. They were empty. He picked through the hanging clothes until he reached the back of the closet and found Moore's dress uniform wrapped in plastic. Once you left patrol, there was really only one reason to save it. To be buried in. Bosch thought saving it was a bad omen, a lack of confidence. As required by the department, he kept one uniform, to be worn in time of civil crisis such as a major earthquake or riot. But he had dumped his dress blues ten years ago.

He brought down the suitcase; it was empty and smelled musty. It had not been used for some time. He pulled down the boot box but could tell it was empty before he opened it. There was some tissue paper inside it.

Bosch put it back up on the shelf, remembering how he had seen

Moore's one boot standing upright on the tile in the bathroom at the Hideaway. He wondered if Moore's killer had had difficulty pulling it off to complete the suicide scene. Or had he ordered Moore to take it off first? Probably not. The blow to the back of the head that Teresa found meant Moore probably hadn't known what hit him. Bosch envisioned the killer, his identity cloaked in shadow, coming up from behind and swinging the stock of the shotgun against the back of Moore's head. Moore goes down. The killer pulls off the boot, drags him into the bathroom, props him against the tub and pulls both triggers. Wipe off the triggers, press the dead man's thumb against the stock and rub his hands on the barrels to make convincing smears. Then set the boot upright on the tile. Add the splinter from the stock and the scene was set. Suicide.

The queen-sized bed was unmade. On the night table were a couple of dollars in change and a small framed photograph of Moore and his wife. Bosch bent over and studied it without touching it. Sylvia was smiling and appeared to be sitting in a restaurant, or perhaps at a banquet table at a wedding. She was beautiful in the picture and her husband was looking at her as if he knew it.

"You fucked up, Cal," Harry said to no one.

He moved to the bureau, which was so old and scarred by cigarettes and knife-cut initials that the Salvation Army might even reject it. In the top drawer were a comb and a cherrywood picture frame lying face down. Bosch picked up the frame and saw that it was empty. He considered this for a few moments. The frame had a floral design carved into it. It would have been expensive and obviously did not come with the apartment. Moore had brought it with him. Why was it empty? He would have liked to be able to ask Sheehan if he or anybody else had taken a photograph from the apartment as part of the investigation. But he couldn't without revealing he had been here.

The next drawer contained underwear and socks and a stack of folded T-shirts, nothing else. There were more clothes in the third drawer, all having been neatly folded at a laundry. Beneath a stack of shirts was a skin magazine which announced on the cover that nude photos of a leading Hollywood actress were provided inside. Bosch leafed through the magazine, more out of curiosity than belief there would be a clue inside. He was sure the magazine had been pawed over by every dick and blue suit who had been in the apartment during the investigation into Moore's disappearance.

He put the magazine back after seeing that the photos of the actress were dark, grainy shots in which it could just barely be determined that she was barebreasted. He assumed they were from an early movie, made before she had enough clout to control the exploitation of her body. He imagined the disappointment of the men who bought the magazine only to discover those shots were the payoff on the cover's lurid promise. He imagined the actress's anger and embarrassment. And he wondered what they did for Cal Moore. A vision of Sylvia Moore flashed in his head. He shoved the magazine under the shirts and closed the drawer.

The last drawer of the bureau contained two things, a folded pair of faded blue jeans and a white paper bag that was crumpled and soft with age and contained a thick stack of photographs. It was what he had come for. Bosch instinctively knew this when he picked the bag up. He took it out of the bedroom, hitting the switch turning off the ceiling light as he went through the door.

Sitting on the couch next to the light, he lit a cigarette and pulled the stack of photos from the bag. Immediately he recognized that most of them were faded and old. These photographs somehow seemed more private and invasive than even those in the skin mag. They were pictures that documented Cal Moore's unhappy history.

The photos seemed to be in some kind of chronological order. Bosch could tell this because they moved from faded black and white to color. Other benchmarks, like clothing and cars, also seemed to prove this.

The first photo was a black-and-white shot of a young Latina in what looked like a white nurse's uniform. She was dark and lovely and wore a girlish smile and a look of mild surprise as she stood next to a swimming pool, her arms behind her back. Bosch saw the edge of a round object behind her and then realized she was holding a serving tray behind her back. She had not wanted to be photographed with the tray. She wasn't a nurse. She was a maid. A servant.

There were other photographs of her in the stack, extending over several years. Age was kind to her but it still exacted its toll. She retained an exotic beauty but worry lines formed and her eyes lost some of their warmth. In some of the photographs Bosch leafed through, she held a baby, then she posed with a little boy. Bosch looked closely and even with the print being black and white he could see that the boy with dark hair and complexion had light-colored eyes. Green eyes, Bosch thought. It was Calexico Moore and his mother.

In one of the photos the woman and the small boy stood in front of a large white house with a Spanish-tile roof. It looked like a Mediterranean villa. Rising behind the mother and boy, but unclear because of the focus, was a tower. Two darkly blurred windows, like empty eyes, were near the top. Bosch thought about what Moore had said to his wife about growing up in a castle. This was it.

In another of the photos the boy stood rigidly next to a man, an Anglo with blond hair and darkly tanned skin. They stood next to the sleek form of a late-fifties Thunderbird. The man held one hand on the hood and one on the boy's head. They were his possessions, the photo seemed to say. The man squinted into the camera.

But Bosch could see his eyes. They were the same green eyes of his son. The man's hair was thinning on top and by comparing photos of the boy with his mother taken at about the same time, Bosch guessed that Moore's father had been at least fifteen years older than his mother. The photo of the father and son was worn around the edges from handling. Much more worn than any of the others in the stack.

The next grouping of photos changed the venue. They were pictures from what was probably Mexicali. There were fewer photos to document a longer period of time. The boy was growing by leaps and the backgrounds of the photos had a third-world quality to them. They were shot in the barrio. More often than not there were crowds of people in the background, all Mexicans, all having that slight look of desperation and hope Bosch had seen in the ghettos of L.A.

And now there was another boy. He was the same age or slightly older. He seemed stronger, tougher. He was in many of the same frames with Cal. A brother maybe, Bosch thought.

It was in this grouping of photos that the mother began to show clearly the advance of age. The girl who hid the servant's tray was gone. A mother used to the harshness of life had replaced her. The photos now took on a haunting quality. It bothered Harry to study them because he believed that he understood the hold the pictures had on Moore.

The last black-and-white photo showed the two boys, shirtless and sitting back to back on a picnic table, laughing at a joke preserved forever in time. Calexico was a young teenager with a guileless smile on his face. The other boy, maybe a year or two older, looked like trouble. He had a hard, sullen look in his eyes. In the picture Cal had his right arm cocked and was making a muscle for the photographer.

Bosch saw the tattoo was already there. The devil with a halo. Saints and Sinners.

In the photos after that, the other boy never appeared again. These were color shots taken in Los Angeles. Bosch recognized City Hall shooting up in the background of one of them and the fountain in Echo Park in another. Moore and his mother had come to the United States. Whoever the other boy was, he had been left behind.

Toward the end of the stack, the mother dropped out of the photos as well. Harry wondered if that meant she was dead. The final two pictures were of Moore as an adult. The first was his graduation from the police academy. There was a shot of a class of newly sworn officers gathered on the grass outside what was later renamed the Daryl F. Gates Auditorium. They were throwing their hats into the air. Bosch picked Moore out of the crowd. He had his arm around the shoulder of another probee and there was genuine joy in his face.

And the last photo was of Moore in dress uniform pulling a young Sylvia close in a smiling cheek-to-cheek embrace. Her skin was smoother then, her eyes brighter and her hair longer and fuller. But she was still very much the same as now, still a beautiful woman.

He pushed the photographs back into the bag and put it on the couch next to him. He looked at the bag and was curious why the photos had never been mounted in an album or put on display. They were just glimpses of a lifetime kept in a bag and ready to go.

But he knew the reason. At his home he had stacks of his own pictures that he would never mount in a book, that he felt the need to hold when he looked at them. They were more than pictures of another time. They were parts of a life, a life that could not go forward without knowing and understanding what was behind.

Bosch reached up to the lamp and turned it off. He smoked another cigarette, the glow of its tip floating in the dark. He thought about Mexico and Calexico Moore.

"You fucked up," he whispered again.

He had told himself he had to come here to get a feel for Moore. That was how he had sold it to himself. But sitting there in the dark he knew there was more to it. He knew he had come because he wanted to understand a life's course that could not be explained. The only one with all the answers to all of the questions was Cal Moore. And he was gone.

He looked at the white neon glow on the curtains across the room and they looked like ghosts to him. It made him think of the worn photo of the father and son, fading to white. He thought of his own father, a man he never knew and did not meet until he was on his death bed. By then it had been too late for Bosch to change his own life's course.

He heard a key hit the dead bolt on the other side of the front door. He was up, with his gun out, moving quickly across the room to the hallway. He went into the bedroom first but then went back into the hall and into the bathroom because it afforded a better view of the living room. He dropped his cigarette into the toilet and heard it hiss as it died.

He heard the front door open and then a few seconds of silence. Then a light went on in the living room and he stepped back into the dark recesses of his hiding spot. In the medicine cabinet mirror he saw Sylvia Moore standing in the middle of the living room looking around as if it was her first time in the apartment. Her eyes fell on the white bag on the couch and she picked it up. Bosch watched her as she looked through the photographs. She lingered over the last one. It was the one of her. She held her hand to her cheek as if charting the changes of time.

When she was done, she put the photographs back in the bag and placed it back on the couch. She then started for the hallway and Bosch moved further back, silently stepping into the bathtub. Now a light came from the bedroom and he heard the closet door open. Hangers scraping on the bar. Bosch holstered his gun and then stepped out of the tub and the bathroom and into the hallway.

"Mrs. Moore? Sylvia?" he called from the hall, unsure how to get her attention without scaring her.

"Who's that?" came the high-pitched, frightened reply.

"It's me, Detective Bosch. It's okay."

She came out of the bedroom closet then, the fright wide in her eyes. She carried the hanger with her dead husband's dress uniform on it.

"Jesus, you scared me. What are you doing here?"

"I was going to ask you the same thing."

She held the uniform up in front of her as if Bosch had walked in on her while she was undressed. She took one step back toward the bedroom door.

"You followed me?" she said. "What's going on?"

"No, I didn't follow you. I was already here."

"In the dark?"

"Yes. I was thinking. When I heard somebody opening the door

I went into the bathroom. Then when I saw it was you, I didn't know how to come out without scaring you. Sorry. You scared me. I scared you."

She nodded once, seeming to accept his explanation. She was wearing a light blue denim shirt and unbleached blue jeans. Her hair was tied behind her head and she wore earrings made of a pinkish crystal. Her left ear had a second earring. It was a silver crescent moon with a star hooked on its bottom point. She put on a polite smile. Bosch became aware that he had not shaved in a day.

"Did you think it was the killer?" she said when he said nothing else. "Kind of like coming back to the scene of the crime?"

"Maybe. Something like that... Actually, no, I don't know what I thought. This isn't the scene of the crime, anyway."

He nodded toward the uniform she carried.

"I have to take this by McEvoy Brothers tomorrow."

She must have read the frown on his face.

"It's a closed-casket service. Obviously. But I think he would've liked it this way, wearing the dress blues. Mr. McEvoy asked me if I had it."

Harry nodded. They were still in the hallway. He backed out into the living room and she followed.

"What do you hear from the department? How are they going to handle it? The funeral, I mean."

"Who knows? But as of now, they are saying he went down in the line of duty."

"So he's going to get the show."

"I think so."

A hero's farewell, Bosch thought. The department wasn't into self-flagellation. It wasn't going to announce to the world that a bad cop was put down by the bad people he had done bad things for. Not unless it had to. And not when it could throw a hero's funeral at the media and then sit back and watch sympathetic stories on seven different channels that night. The department needed all the sympathy it could get.

He also realized that a line-of-duty death meant the widow would get full pension rights. If Sylvia Moore wore a black dress, dabbed at her eyes with a tissue at appropriate times and kept her mouth shut, she'd get her husband's paycheck for the rest of her life. Not a bad deal. Either way. If Sylvia was the one who tipped IAD, she now stood to lose the pension if she pressed it or went public. The department could claim Cal had been killed because of his extracurricular activities. No pension. Bosch was sure this didn't have to be explained to her.

"So when's the funeral?" he asked.

"It's Monday at one. At the San Fernando Mission Chapel. The burial is at Oakwood, up in Chatsworth."

Well, Bosch thought, if they are going to put on the show, that's the place to do it. A couple hundred motorcycle cops coming in in procession on curving Valley Circle Boulevard always made a good front-page photo.

"Mrs. Moore, why did you come here at"—he looked at his watch; it was 10:45—"so late to get your husband's dress blues?"

"Call me Sylvia."

"Sure."

"To tell you the truth, I don't know why now. I haven't been sleeping—I mean at all—since it...since he was found. I don't know. I just felt like taking a drive. I just got the key to the place today, anyway."

"Who gave it to you?"

"Assistant Chief Irving. He came by, said they were through with the apartment and if there was anything I wanted I could take it. Trouble is, there isn't. I had hoped I'd never see this place. Then the man at the funeral home called and said he needed the dress uniform if I had it. Here I am."

Bosch picked the bag of photographs up off the couch and held it out to her.

"What about these? Do you want them?"

"I don't think so."

"Ever see them before?"

"I think some of them. At least, some of them seemed familiar. Some of them I know I never saw."

"Why do you think that is? A man keeps photographs his whole life and never shows some of them to his wife?"

"I don't know."

"Strange." He opened the bag and while he was looking through the photos said, "What happened to his mother, do you know?"

"She died. Before I knew him. Had a tumor in her head. He was about twenty, he said."

"What about his father?"

"He told me he was dead. But I told you, I don't know if that was true. Because he never said how or when. When I asked, he said he didn't want to talk about it. We never did."

Bosch held up the photo of the two boys on the picnic table.

"Who's this?"

She stepped close to him and looked at the photo. He studied her face. He saw flecks of green in her brown eyes. There was a light scent of perfume.

"I don't know who it is. A friend, I guess."

"He didn't have a brother?"

"Not one he ever told me about. He told me when we got married, he said I was his only family. He said . . . said he was alone except for me."

Now Bosch looked at the photo.

"Kinda looks like him to me."

She didn't say anything.

"What about the tattoo?"

"What about it?"

"He ever tell you where he got it, what it means?"

"He told me he got it in the village he grew up in. He was a boy. Actually, it was a barrio. I guess. They called it Saints and Sinners.

That's what the tattoo means. Saints and Sinners. He said that was because the people that lived there didn't know which they were, which they would be."

He thought of the note found in Cal Moore's back pocket. *I found out who I was.* He wondered if she realized the significance of this in terms of the place he grew up. Where each young boy had to find out who he was. A saint or a sinner.

Sylvia interrupted his thoughts.

"You know, you didn't really say why you were already here. Sitting in the dark thinking. You had to come here to do that?"

"I came to look around, I guess. I was trying to shake something loose, get a feel for your husband. That sound stupid?"

"Not to me."

"Good."

"And did you? Did you shake something loose?"

"I don't know yet. Sometimes it takes a little while."

"You know, I asked Irving about you. He said you weren't on the case. He said you only came out the other night because the other detectives had their hands full with the reporters and...and the body."

Like a schoolboy, Bosch felt a tingling of excitement. She had asked about him. It didn't matter that now she knew he was free-lancing on the case, she had made inquiries about him.

"Well," he said, "that's true, to a degree. Technically, I am not on the case. But I have other cases that are believed to be tied in with the death of your husband."

Her eyes never left his. He could see she wanted to ask what cases but she was a cop's wife. She knew the rules. In that moment he was sure she did not deserve what she had been handed. None of it.

He said, "It really wasn't you, was it? The tip to IAD. The letter."

She shook her head no.

"But they won't believe you. They think you started the whole thing."

"I didn't."

"What did Irving say? When he gave you the key to this place."

"Told me that if I wanted the money, the pension, I should let it go. Not get any ideas. As if I did. As if I cared anymore. I don't. I knew that Cal went wrong. I don't know what he did, I just knew he did it. A wife knows without being told. And that as much as anything else ended it between us. But I didn't send any letter like that. I was a cop's wife to the end. I told Irving and the guy who came before him that they had it wrong. But they didn't care. They just wanted Cal."

"You told me before it was Chastain who came?"

"It was him."

"What exactly did he want? You said something about he wanted to look inside the house."

"He held up the letter and said he knew I wrote it. He said I might as well tell him everything. Well, I told him I didn't write it and I told him to get out. But at first he wouldn't leave."

"What did he say he wanted, specifically?"

"He—I don't really remember it all. He wanted bank account statements and he wanted to know what properties we had. He thought I was sitting there waiting for him to come so I could give him my husband. He said he wanted the typewriter and I told him we didn't even have one. I pushed him out and closed the door."

He nodded and tried to compute these facts into those he already had. It was too much of a whirlwind.

"You don't remember anything about what the letter said?"

"I didn't really get the chance to read it. He didn't show it to me to read because he thought—and he and the others still believe—that it came from me. So I only read a little before he put it back in his briefcase. It said something about Cal being a front for a Mexican. It said he was giving protection. It said something along the lines that he had made a Faustian pact. You know what that is, right? A deal with the devil."

Bosch nodded. He was reminded that she was a teacher. He also realized that they had been standing in the living room for at least ten minutes. But he made no move to sit down. He feared that any sudden movement would break the spell, send her out the door and away from him.

"Well," she said, "I don't know if I would have gotten so allegorical if I had written it, but essentially that letter was correct. I mean, I didn't know what he had done but I knew something happened. I could see it was killing him inside.

"Once—this was before he left—I finally asked him what was happening and he just said he had made a mistake and he would try to correct it himself. He wouldn't talk about it with me. He shut me out."

She sat down on the edge of an upholstered chair, holding the dress blues on her lap. The chair was an awful green color and there were cigarette burns on its right arm. Bosch sat down on the couch next to the bag of photos.

She said, "Irving and Chastain. They don't believe me. They just nod their heads when I tell them. They say the letter had too many intimate details. It had to be me. Meanwhile, I guess somebody is happy out there. Their little letter brought him down."

Bosch thought of Kapps and wondered if he could have known enough details about Moore to have written the letter. He had set up Dance. Maybe he had tried to set up Moore first. It seemed unlikely. Maybe the letter had come from Dance because he wanted to move up the ladder and Moore was in the way.

Harry thought of the coffee can he had seen in the kitchen cabinet and wondered if he should ask her if she wanted some. He didn't want the time with her to end. He wanted to smoke but didn't want to risk having her ask him not to.

"Do you want any coffee? There is some in the kitchen I could make."

She looked toward the kitchen as if its location or cleanliness had a role in her answer. Then she said no, she wasn't planning to stay that long.

"I am going to Mexico tomorrow," Bosch said.

"Mexicali?"

"Yes."

"It's the other cases?"

"Yes."

Then he told her about them. About black ice and Jimmy Kapps and Juan Doe #67. And he told her of the ties to both her husband and Mexicali. It was there he hoped to unravel the whirlwind.

He finished the story by saying, "As you can tell, people like Irving, they want this to go by. They don't really care who killed Cal because he had crossed. They write him off like a bad debt. They are not going to pursue it because they don't want it to blow up in their faces. You understand what I'm saying?"

"I was a cop's wife, remember?"

"Right. So you know. The thing about this is I care. Your husband was putting a file together for me. A file on black ice. It makes me think like maybe he was trying to do something good. He might have been trying to do the impossible. To cross back. It might've been what got him killed. And if it is, then I'm not letting it go by."

They were quiet a long time after that. Her face looked pained but her eyes remained sharp and dry. She pulled the suit up higher on her lap. Bosch could hear a police helicopter circling somewhere in the distance. It wouldn't be L.A. without police helicopters and spotlights circling at night.

"Black ice," she said after a while in a whispery voice.

"What about it?"

"It's funny, that's all." She was quiet a few moments and seemed to look around the room, realizing this was the place her husband had come to after leaving her. "Black ice. I grew up in the Bay Area—San Francisco mostly—and that was something we always were told to watch out for. But, you know, it was the other black ice we were told about."

She looked at him then and must have read his confusion. "In the winter, on those days when it really gets cold after a rain. When the rain freezes on the road, that's black ice. It's there on the road, on the black asphalt, but you can't see it. I remember my father teaching me to drive and he was always saying, 'Watch out for the black ice, girl. You don't see the danger until you are in it. Then it's too late. You're sliding out of control.'"

She smiled at the memory and said, "Anyway, that was the black ice I knew. At least while I was growing up. Just like Coke used to be a soda. The meaning of things can change on you."

He just looked at her. He wanted to hold her again, touch the softness of her cheek with his own.

"Didn't your father ever tell you to watch out for the black ice?" she asked.

"I didn't know him. I sorta taught myself to drive."

She nodded and didn't say anything but didn't look away. "It took me about three cars to learn. By the time I finally got it down, nobody would dare lend me a car. Nobody ever told me about the black ice, either."

"Well, I did."

"Thank you."

"Are you hung up on the past, too, Harry?"

He didn't answer.

"I guess we all are. What's that saying? Through studying the past we learn our future. Something like that. You seem to me to be a man still studying, maybe."

Her eyes seemed to look into him. They were eyes with great knowledge. And he realized that for all of his desires the other night, she did not need to be held or healed of pain. In fact, she was the healer. How could Cal Moore have run from this?

He changed the subject, not knowing why, only that he must push the attention away from himself.

"There's a picture frame in the bedroom. Carved cherrywood. But no picture. You remember it?"

"I'll have to look."

She stood, leaving her husband's suit on the chair, and moved into the bedroom. She looked at the frame in the top drawer of the bureau a long time before saying she didn't recognize it. She didn't look at Bosch until after she said this.

They stood there next to the bed looking at each other in silence. Bosch finally raised his hand, then hesitated. She took a step closer to him and that was the sign that his touch was wanted. He caressed her cheek, the way she had done it herself when she had studied the photograph earlier and thought she was alone. Then he dropped his hand down the side of her throat and around to the back of her neck.

They stared at each other. Then she came closer and brought her mouth up to his. Her hand came to his neck and pulled him to her and they kissed. She held him and pressed herself against him in a way that revealed her need. He saw her eyes were closed now and at that moment Bosch realized she was his reflection in a mirror of hunger and loneliness.

They made love on her husband's unmade bed, neither of them paying mind to where they were or what this would mean the next day or week or year. Bosch kept his eyes closed, wanting to concentrate on other senses—her smell and taste and touch.

Afterward, he pulled himself back, so that his head lay on her chest between her freckled breasts. She had her hands in his hair and was drawing her fingers through the curls. He could hear her heart beating in rhythm with his.

Nineteen

IT WAS AFTER ONE A.M. BY THE TIME BOSCH TURNED the Caprice onto Woodrow Wilson and began the long, winding ascent to his house. He saw the spotlights tracing eights on the low-lying clouds over Universal City. On the road he had to navigate his way around cars double-parked outside holiday parties and a discarded Christmas tree, a few strands of lonely tinsel still clinging to its branches, that had blown into his path. On the seat next to him were the lone Budweiser from Cal Moore's refrigerator and Lucius Porter's gun.

All his life he believed he was slumming toward something good. That there was meaning. In the youth shelter, the foster homes, the Army and Vietnam, and now the department, he always carried the feeling that he was struggling toward some kind of resolution and knowledge of purpose. That there was something good in him or about him. It was the waiting that was so hard. The waiting often left a hollow feeling in his soul. And he believed people could see this, that they knew when they looked at him that he was empty. He had learned to fill that hollowness with isolation and work. Sometimes drink and the sound of the jazz saxophone. But never people. He never let anyone in all the way.

And now he thought he had seen Sylvia Moore's eyes. Her true eyes, and he had to wonder if she was the one who could fill him.

"I want to see you," he had said when they separated outside The Fountains.

"Yes" was all she said. She touched his cheek with her hand and got into her car.

Now Bosch thought about what that one word and the accompanying touch could mean. He was happy. And that was something new.

As he rounded the last curve, slowing for a car with its brights on to pass, he thought of the way she had looked at the picture frame for so long before saying she did not recognize it. Had she lied? What were the chances that Cal Moore would have bought such an expensive frame after moving into a dump like that? Not good, was the answer.

By the time he pulled the Caprice into the carport, he was full of confusing feelings. What had been in the picture? What difference did it make that she had held that back? If she did. Still sitting in the car, he opened the beer and drank it down quickly, some of it spilling onto his neck. He would sleep tonight, he knew.

Inside, he went to the kitchen, put Porter's gun in a cabinet and checked the phone machine. There were no messages. No call from Porter saying why he had run. No call from Pounds asking how it was going. No call from Irving saying he knew what Bosch was up to.

After two nights with little sleep, Bosch looked forward to his bed as he did on few other nights. It was most often this way, part of a routine he kept. Nights of fleeting rest or nightmares followed by a single night when exhaustion finally drove him down hard into a dark sleep.

As he gathered the covers and pillows about him, he noticed there was still the trace of Teresa Corazón's powdery perfume on them. He closed his eyes and thought about her for a moment. But soon her image was pushed out of his mind by Sylvia Moore's face. Not the photo from the bag or the night stand, but the real face. Weary but strong, her eyes focused on Bosch's own.

The dream was like others Harry had had. He was in the dark place. A cavernous blackness enveloped him and his breath echoed in the dark. He sensed, or rather, he knew in the way he had knowledge of place in all his dreams that the darkness ended ahead and he must go there. But this time he was not alone. That was what was different. He was with Sylvia, and they huddled in the black, their sweat stinging their eyes. Harry held her and she held him. And they did not speak.

They broke from each other's embrace and began to move through the darkness. There was dim light ahead and Harry headed that way. His left hand was extended in front of him, his Smith & Wesson in its grasp. His right hand was behind him, holding hers and leading her along. And as they came into the light Calexico Moore was waiting there with the shotgun. He was not hidden, but he stood partially silhouetted by the light that poured into the passage. His green eyes were in shadow. And he smiled. Then he raised the shotgun.

"Who fucked up?" he said.

The roar was deafening in the blackness. Bosch saw Moore's hands fly loose from the shotgun and up away from his body like tethered birds trying to take flight. He back-stepped wildly into the darkness and was gone. Not fallen, but disappeared. Gone. Only the light at the end of the passage remained in his wake. In one hand Harry still gripped Sylvia's hand. In the other, the smoking gun.

He opened his eyes then.

Bosch sat up on the bed. He saw pale light leaking around the edges of the curtains on the windows facing east. The dream had seemed so short, but he realized because of the light he had slept until morning. He held his wrist up to the light and checked his watch. He had no alarm clock because he never needed one. It was six o'clock. He rubbed his face in his palms and tried to reconstruct the dream. This was unusual for him. A counselor at the sleep dysfunction lab at the VA had once told him to write down what he remembered from his dreams. It was an exercise, she said, to try to inform the conscious mind what the subconscious side was saying. For months he kept a notebook and pen by the bed and dutifully recorded his morning memories. But Bosch had found it did him no good. No matter how well he understood the source of his nightmares, he could not eliminate them from his sleep. He had dropped out of the sleep deprivation counseling program years ago.

Now, he could not recapture the dream. Sylvia's face disappeared in the mist. Harry realized he had been sweating heavily. He got up and pulled the bed sheets off and dumped them in a basket in the closet. He went to the kitchen and started a pot of coffee. He showered, shaved and dressed in blue jeans, a green corduroy shirt and a black sport coat. Driving clothes. He went back to the kitchen and filled his Thermos with black coffee.

The first thing he took out to the car was his gun. He removed the rug that lined the trunk and then lifted out the spare tire and the jack that were stowed beneath it. He placed the Smith & Wesson, which he had taken from his holster and wrapped in an oilcloth, in the wheel well and put the spare tire back on top of it. He put the rug back in place and laid the jack down along the rear of the trunk. Next he put his briefcase in and a duffel bag containing a few days' changes of clothes. It all looked passable, though he doubted anyone would even look.

He went back inside and got his other gun out of the hallway closet. It was a forty-four with grips and safety configured for a right-handed shooter. The cylinder also opened on the left side. Bosch couldn't use it because he was left-handed. But he had kept it for six years because it had been given to him as a gift by a man whose daughter had been raped and murdered. Bosch had winged the killer during a brief shootout during his capture near the Sepulveda Dam in Van Nuys. He lived and was now serving life without parole. But that hadn't been enough for the father. After the trial he gave Bosch the gun and Bosch accepted it because not to take it would have been to disavow the man's pain. His message to Harry was clear: next time do the job right. Shoot to kill. Harry took the gun. And he could have taken it to a gunsmith and had it reconfig-ured for left-hand use, but to do that would be to acknowledge the father had been right. Harry wasn't sure he was ready to do that.

The gun had sat on a shelf in the closet for six years. Now he took it down, checked its action to make sure it was still operable, and loaded it. He put it in his holster and was ready to go.

On his way out, he grabbed his Thermos in the kitchen and bent over the phone machine to record a new message.

"It's Bosch. I will be in Mexico for the weekend. If you want to leave a message, hang on. If it's important and you want to try to reach me, I'll be at the De Anza Hotel in Calexico."

It was still before seven as he headed down the hill. He took the Hollywood Freeway until it skirted around downtown, the office towers opaque behind the early morning mixture of fog and smog. He took the transition road to the San Bernardino Freeway and headed east, out of the city. It was 250 miles to the border town of Calexico and its sister city Mexicali, just on the other side of the fence. Harry would be there before noon. He poured himself a cup of coffee without spilling any and began to enjoy the drive.

The smog from L.A. didn't clear until Bosch was past the Yucaipa turnoff in Riverside County. After that the sky turned as blue as the oceans on the maps he had next to him on the seat. It was a windless day. As he passed the windmill farm near Palm Springs the blades of the hundreds of electric generators stood motionless in the morn-ing desert mist. It was eerie, like a cemetery, and Harry's eyes didn't linger.

Bosch drove through the plush desert communities of Palm Springs and Rancho Mirage without stopping, passing streets named after golfing presidents and celebrities. As he passed Bob Hope Drive, Bosch recalled the time he saw the comedian in Viet-nam. He had just come in from thirteen days of clearing Charlie's tunnels in the Cu Chi province and thought the evening of watch-ing Hope was hilarious. Years later he had seen a clip of the same show on a television retrospective on the comedian. This time, the performance made him feel sad. After Rancho Mirage, he caught Route 86 and was heading directly south.

The open road always presented a quiet thrill to Bosch. The feeling of going someplace new coupled with the unknown. He believed he did some of his best thinking while driving the open road. He now reviewed his search of Moore's apartment and tried to look for hidden meanings or messages. The ragged furniture, the empty suitcase, the lonely skin mag, the empty frame. Moore left behind a puzzling presence. He thought of the bag of photos again. Sylvia had changed her mind and taken it. Bosch wished he had borrowed the photo of the two boys, and the one of the father and son.

Bosch had no photographs of his own father. He had told Sylvia that he hadn't known him, but that had been only partially true. He had grown up not knowing and not, at least outwardly, caring who he was. But when he returned from the war he came back with a sense of urgency to know about his origins. It led him to seek out his father after twenty years of not even knowing his name.

Harry had been raised in a series of youth shelters and foster homes after authorities took him from his mother's custody. In the dormitories at McClaren or San Fernando or the other halls, he was comforted by his mother's steady visits, except during the times she was in jail. She told him they couldn't send him to a foster home without her consent. She had a good lawyer, she said, trying to get him back.

On the day the housemother at McClaren told him the visits were over because his mother was dead, he took the news unlike most boys of eleven. Outwardly, he showed nothing. He nodded that he understood and then walked away. But that day during the swimming period, he dove to the bottom of the deep end and screamed so loud and long that he was sure the noise was breaking through the surface and would draw the attention of the lifeguard. After each breath on top, he would go back down. He screamed and cried until he was so exhausted he could only cling to the pool's ladder, its cold steel tubes the arms that comforted him. Somehow he wished he could have been there. That was all. He somehow wanted to have protected her.

He was termed ATA after that. Available to Adopt. He began to move through a procession of foster homes where he was made to feel as though he was on tryout. When expectations were not met, it was on to the next house and the next pair of judges. He was once sent back to McClaren because of his habit of eating with his mouth open. And once before he was sent to a home in the Valley, the Choosers, as they were called by the ATAs, took Harry and several other thirteen-year-olds out to the rec field to throw a baseball around. Harry was the one chosen. He soon realized it was not because he exhibited the sterling virtues of boyhood. It was because the man had been looking for a lefthander. His plan was to develop a pitcher and lefthanders were the premium. After two months of daily workouts, pitching lessons and oral education on pitching strategies, Harry ran away from the home. It was six weeks before the cops later picked him up on Hollywood Boulevard. He was sent back to McClaren to await the next set of Choosers. You always had to stand up straight and smile when the Choosers came through the dorm.

He began his search for his father at the county recorder's office. The 1950 birth records of Hieronymus Bosch at Queen of Angels Hospital listed his mother as Margerie Philips Lowe and his father's name as his own; Hieronymus Bosch. But Harry, of course, knew this was not the case. His mother had once told him he was the namesake of an artist whose work she admired. She said the painter's five-hundred-year-old paintings were apt portraits of present L.A., a nightmarish landscape of predators and victims. She told him she would tell him his true father's name when the time was right. She was found dead in an alley off Hollywood Boulevard before that time came.

Harry hired a lawyer to petition the presiding judge of the juvenile dependency court to allow him to examine his own custody records. The request was granted and Bosch spent several days in the county Hall of Records archive. The voluminous documents given to him chronicled the unsuccessful lengths his mother had gone to keep custody of him. Bosch found it spiritually reassuring, but nowhere in the files was the name of the father. Bosch was at a dead end but wrote down the name of the lawyer who had filed all the papers in his mother's quest. J. Michael Haller. In writing it down, Bosch realized he knew the name. Mickey Haller had been one of L.A.'s premier criminal defense attorneys. He had handled one of the Manson girls. In the late fifties he had won an acquittal for the so-called Highwayman, a highway patrol officer accused of raping seven women he had stopped for speeding on lonely stretches of the Golden State. What was J. Michael Haller doing on a child custody case?

On nothing more than a hunch, Bosch went to the Criminal Courts Building and ordered all of his mother's cases from archives. In sorting through them, he found that in addition to the custody battle Haller had represented Margerie P. Lowe on six loitering arrests between 1948 and 1961. That was well into Haller's time as a top trial lawyer.

In his gut, Harry knew then.

The receptionist in the five-name law office on the top floor of a Pershing Square tower told Bosch that Haller had retired recently because of a medical condition. The phone book didn't list his residence but the roll of registered voters did. Haller was a Democrat and he lived on Canon Drive in Beverly Hills. Bosch would always remember the rosebushes that lined the walkway to his father's mansion. They were perfect roses.

The maid who answered the door said Mr. Haller was not seeing visitors. Bosch told the woman to tell Mr. Haller it was Margerie Lowe's son come to pay his respects. Ten minutes later he was led past members of the lawyer's family. All of them standing in the hallway with strange looks on their faces. The old man had told them to leave his room and send Bosch in alone. Standing at the bedside, Harry figured him for maybe ninety pounds now, and he didn't need to ask what was wrong because he could tell cancer was eating away at him from the inside out.

"I guess I know why you've come," he rasped.

"I just wanted to...I don't know."

He stood there in silence for quite a time, watching how it wore the man out just to keep his eyes open. There was a tube from a box on the bedside that ran under the covers. The box beeped every once in a while as it pumped painkilling morphine into the dying man's blood. The old man studied him silently.

"I don't want anything from you," Bosch finally said. "I don't know, I think I just wanted to let you know I made it by okay. I'm all right. In case you ever worried."

"You have been to the war?"

"Yes. I'm done with that."

"My son—my other son, he...I kept him away from that.... What will you do now?"

"I don't know."

After some more silence the old man seemed to nod. He said, "You are called Harry. Your mother told me that. She told me a lot about you.... But I could never.... Do you understand? Different times. And after it went by so long, I couldn't.... I couldn't reverse things."

Bosch just nodded. He hadn't come to cause the man any more pain. More silence passed and he heard the labored breathing.

"Harry Haller," the old man whispered then, a broken smile on the thin, peeling lips burned by chemotherapy. "That could have been you. Did you ever read Hesse?"

Bosch didn't understand but nodded again. There was a beep sound. He watched for a minute until the dosage seemed to take some effect. The old man's eyes closed and he sighed.

"I better get going," Harry said. "You take care."

He touched the man's frail, bluish hand. It gripped his fingers tightly, almost desperately, and then let go. As he stepped to the door, he heard the old man's rasp.

"I'm sorry, what did you say?"

"I said I did. I did worry about you."

There was a tear running down the side of the old man's face, into his white hair. Bosch nodded again and two weeks later he stood on a hill above the Good Shepherd section at Forest Lawn and watched them put the father he never knew in the ground. During the ceremony, he saw a grouping that he suspected was his half brother and three half sisters. The half brother, probably born a few years ahead of Bosch, was watching Harry during the ceremony. At the end, Bosch turned and walked away.

Near ten o'clock Bosch stopped at a roadside diner called El Oasis Verde and ate huevos rancheros. His table was at a window that looked out at the blue-white sheath called the Salton Sea and then farther east to the Chocolate Mountains. Bosch silently reveled in the beauty and the openness of the scene. When he was done, and the waitress had refilled his Thermos, he walked out into the dirt parking lot and leaned against the fender of the Caprice to breathe the cool, clean air and look again.

The half brother was now a top defense lawyer and Harry was a cop. There was a strange congruence to that that Bosch found acceptable. They had never spoken and probably never would.

He continued south as 86 ran along the flats between the Salton Sea and the Santa Rosa Mountains. It was agricultural land that steadily dropped below sea level. The Imperial Valley. Much of it was cut in huge squares by irrigation ditches and his drive was accompanied by the smell of fertilizer and fresh vegetables. Flatbed trucks, loaded with crates of lettuce or spinach or cilantro, occasionally pulled off the farm roads in front of him and slowed him down. But Harry didn't mind and waited patiently to pass.

Near a town called Vallecito, Bosch pulled to the side of the road to watch a squad of low-flying aircraft come screaming over a mountain that rose to the southwest. They crossed 86 and flew out over the Salton. Bosch knew nothing about identifying war aircraft in the modern era. These jets had evolved into faster and sleeker machines than those he remembered from Vietnam. But they had flown low enough for him to clearly see that beneath each craft's wings hung the hardware of war. He watched the three jets bank and come about in a tight triangle pattern and retrace their path back to the mountain. After they crossed above him, Harry looked down at his maps and found blocks marked off to the southwest as closed to the public. It was the U.S. Naval Gunnery Range at Superstition Mountain. The map said it was a live bombing area. Keep out.

Bosch felt a dull vibration rock the car slightly and then the following rumble. He looked up from the map and thought he could make out the plume of smoke beginning to rise from the base of Superstition. Then he felt and heard another bomb hit. Then another.

As the jets, the silvery skin of each reflecting a diamond of sunlight, passed overhead again to begin another run, Bosch pulled back onto the road behind a flatbed truck with two teenagers in the back. They were Mexican fieldworkers with weary eyes that seemed already knowledgeable about the long, hard life ahead of them. They were about the same age as the two boys on the picnic table in the photo that had been in the white bag. They stared at Bosch with indifference.

In a few moments it was clear to pass the slow-moving truck. Bosch heard other explosions from Superstition Mountain as he moved away. He went on to pass more farms and mom-and-pop restaurants. He passed a sugar mill where a line painted at the top of its huge silo marked sea level.

The summer after he had talked to his father Bosch had picked up the books by Hesse. He was curious about what the old man had meant. He found it in the second book he read. Harry Haller was a character in it. A disillusioned loner, a man of no real identity, Harry Haller was the steppenwolf.

That August Bosch joined the cops.

He believed he felt the land rising. The farmland gave way to brown brush and there were dust devils rising in the open land. His ears popped as he ascended. And he knew the border was nearing long before he passed the green sign that told him Calexico was twenty miles away.

Twenty

CALEXICO WAS LIKE MOST BORDER TOWNS: DUSTY and built low to the ground, its main street a garish collision of neon and plastic signage, the inevitable golden arches being the recognizable if not comforting icon amid the drive-through Mexican auto insurance offices and souvenir shops.

In town, Route 86 connected with 111 and dropped straight down to the border crossroad. Traffic was backed up about five blocks from the exhaust-stained concrete auto terminal manned by the Mexican *federales*. It looked like the five o'clock lineup at the Broadway entrance to the 101 in L.A. Before he got caught up in it, Bosch turned east on Fifth Street. He passed the De Anza Hotel and drove two blocks to the police station. It was a one-story concrete-block affair that was painted the same yellow as the tablets lawyers used. From the signs out front, Bosch learned it was also Town Hall. It was also the town fire station. It was also the historical society. He found a parking space in front.

As he opened the door of the dirty Caprice he heard singing from the park across the street. On a picnic bench five Mexican men sat drinking Budweisers. A sixth man, wearing a black cowboy shirt with white embroidery and a straw Stetson, stood facing them, playing a guitar and singing in Spanish. The song was sung slowly and Harry had no trouble translating.

I don't know how to love you
I don't even know how to embrace you
Because what never leaves me
Is this pain that hurts me so

The singer's plaintive voice carried strongly across the park and Bosch thought the song was beautiful. He leaned against his car and smoked until the singer was done.

The kisses that you gave me my love
Are the ones that are killing me
But my tears are now drying
With my pistol and my heart
And here as always I spend my life
With the pistol and the heart

At the song's end, the men at the picnic table gave the singer a cheer and a toast.

Inside the glass door marked Police was a sour-smelling room no larger than the back of a pickup truck. On the left was a Coke machine, straight ahead was a door with an electronic bolt, and on the right was a thick glass window with a slide tray beneath it. A uniformed officer sat behind the glass. Behind him, a woman sat at a radio-dispatch console. On the other side of the console was a wall of square-foot-sized lockers.

"You can't smoke in there, sir," the uniform said.

He wore mirrored sunglasses and was overweight. The plate over his breast pocket said his name was Gruber. Bosch stepped back to the door and flicked the butt out into the parking lot.

"You know, it's a hundred-dollar fine for littering in Calexico, sir," Gruber said.

Harry held up his open badge and I.D. wallet.

"You can bill me," he said. "I need to check a gun."

Gruber smiled curtly, revealing his receding, purplish gums.

"I chew tobacco myself. Then you don't have that problem."

"I can tell."

Gruber frowned and had to think about that a moment before saying, "Well, let's have it. Man says he wants to check a gun has to turn the gun in to be checked."

He turned back to the dispatcher to see if she thought that he now had the upper hand. She showed no response. Bosch noticed the strain Gruber's gut was putting on the buttons of his uniform. He pulled the forty-four out of his holster and put it in the slide tray.

"Foe-dee foe," Gruber announced and he lifted the gun out and examined it. "You want to keep it in the holster?"

Bosch hadn't thought about that. He needed the holster. Otherwise he'd have to jam the Smith in his waistband and he'd probably lose it if he ended up having to do any running.

"Nah," he said. "Just checking the gun."

Gruber winked and took it over to the lockers, opened one up and put the gun inside. After he closed it, he locked it, took the key out and came back to the window.

"Let me see the I.D. again. I have to write up a receipt."

Bosch dropped his badge wallet into the tray and watched as Gruber slowly wrote out a receipt in duplicate. It seemed that the officer had to look from the I.D. card to what he was writing every two letters.

"How'd you get a name like that?"

"You can just write Harry for short."

"It's no problem. I can write it. Just don't ask me to say it. Looks like it rhymes with anonymous."

He finished and put the receipts into the tray and told Harry to sign them both. Harry used his own pen.

"Lookee there, a lefty signing for a right-handed gun," Gruber said. "Somethin' you don't see 'round here too often."

He winked at Bosch again. Bosch just looked at him.

"Just talking is all," Gruber said.

Harry dropped one of the receipts into the tray and Gruber exchanged it for the locker key. It was numbered.

"Don't lose it now," Gruber said.

As he walked back to the Caprice he saw that the men were still at the picnic table in the park but there was no more singing. He got into the Caprice and put the locker key in the ashtray. He never used it for smoking. He noticed an old man with white hair unlocking the door below the historical society sign. Bosch backed out and headed over to the De Anza.

It was a three-story, Spanish-style building with a satellite dish on the roof. Bosch parked in the brick drive up in front. His plan was to check in, drop his bags in his room, wash his face and then make the border crossing into Mexicali. The man behind the front desk wore a white shirt and brown bow tie to match his brown vest. He could not have been much older than twenty. A plastic tag on the vest identified him as Miguel, assistant front desk manager.

Bosch said he wanted a room, filled out a registration card and handed it back. Miguel said, "Oh, yes, Mr. Bosch, we have messages for you."

He turned to a basket file and pulled out three pink message forms. Two were from Pounds, one from Irving. Bosch looked at the times and noticed all three calls had come in during the last two hours. First Pounds, then Irving, then Pounds again.

"Wait a minute," he said to Miguel. "Is there a phone?"

"Around the corner, sir, to your right."

Bosch stood there with the phone in his hand wondering what to do. Something was up, or both of them wouldn't have tried to reach him. Something had made one or both of them call his house and they heard the taped message. What could have happened? Using his PacBell card he called the Hollywood homicide table, hoping someone was in and that he might learn what was going on. Jerry Edgar answered the call on the first ring.

"Jed, what's up? I've got phone calls from the weight coming out my ass."

There was a long silence. Too long.

"Jed?"

"Harry, where you at?"

"I'm down south, man."

"Where down south?"

"What is it, Jed?"

"Wherever you're at, Pounds is trying to recall you. He said if anybody talks to you, t'tell you to get your ass back here. He said—"

"Why? What's going on?"

"It's Porter, man. They found him this morning up at Sunshine Canyon. Somebody wrapped a wire 'round his neck so tight that it was the size of a watchband."

"Jesus." Bosch pulled out his cigarettes. "Jesus."

"Yeah."

"What was he doing up there? Sunshine, that's the landfill up in Foothill Division, right?"

"Shit, Harry, he was dumped there."

Of course. Bosch should have realized that. Of course. He wasn't thinking right.

"Right. Right. What happened?"

"What happened was that they found his body out there this morning. A rag picker come across it. He was covered in garbage and shit. But RHD traced some of the stuff. They got receipts from some restaurants. They got the name of the hauler the restaurants use and they've got it traced to a particular truck and a particular route. It's a downtown run. Was made yesterday morning. Hollywood's working it with them. I'm fixing to go start canvassing on the route. We'll find the Dumpster he came from and go from there."

Bosch thought of the Dumpster behind Poe's. Porter hadn't run out on him. He had probably been garroted and dragged out while Bosch was having his say with the bartender. Then he remembered the man with the tattooed tears. How had he missed it? He had probably stood ten feet from Porter's killer.

"I didn't go out to the scene but I hear he'd been worked over before they did him," Edgar said. "His face was busted up. Nose broke, stuff like that. A lot of blood, I hear. Man, what a pitiful way to go."

It wouldn't be long before they came into Poe's with photos of Porter. The bartender would remember the face and would gladly describe Bosch as the man who had come in, said he was a cop, and attacked Porter. Bosch wondered if he should tell Edgar now and save a lot of legwork. A survival instinct flared inside him and he decided to say nothing about Poe's.

"Why do Pounds and Irving want me?"

"Don't know. All I know is first Moore gets it, then Porter. Think maybe they're closing ranks or something. I think they want everybody in where it's nice and safe. Word going 'round here is that those two cases are one. Word is those boys had some kinda deal going. Irving's already doubled them up. He's running a joint op on both of them. Moore and Porter."

Bosch didn't say anything. He was trying to think. This put a new spin on everything.

"Listen to me, Jed. You haven't heard from me. We didn't talk. Understand?"

Edgar hesitated before saying, "You sure you want to play it that way?"

"Yeah. For now. I'll be talking to you."

"Watch your back."

Watch out for the black ice, Bosch thought as he hung up and stood there for a minute, leaning against the wall. Porter. How had this happened? He instinctively moved his arm against his hip but felt no reassurance. The holster was empty.

He had a choice now: go forward to Mexicali or go back to L.A. He knew if he went back it would mean the end of his involvement in the case. Irving would cut him out like a bad spot on a banana.

Therefore, he realized, he actually had no choice. He had to go on. Bosch pulled a twenty-dollar bill out of his pocket and went back to the front desk. He slid the bill across to Miguel.

"Yes, sir?"

"I'd like to cancel my room, Miguel."

"No problem. There is no charge. You never got the room."

"No, that's for you, Miguel. I have a slight problem. I don't want anybody to know I was here. Understand?"

Miguel was young but he was wise. He told Bosch his request was no problem. He pulled the bill off the counter and tucked it into a pocket inside his vest. Harry then slid the phone messages across.

"If they call again, I never showed up to get these, right?"

"That's right, sir."

In a few minutes he was in line for the crossing at the border. He noticed how the U.S. Customs and Border Patrol building where incoming traffic was handled dwarfed its Mexican counterpart. The message was clear; leaving this country was not a difficulty; coming in, though, was another matter entirely. When it was Bosch's turn at the gate he held his badge wallet open and out the window. When the Mexican officer took it, Harry then handed him the Calexico P.D. receipt.

"Your business?" the officer asked. He wore a faded uniform that had been Army green once. His hat was sweat-stained along the band.

"Official. I have a meeting at the Plaza Justicia."

"Ah. You know the way?"

Bosch held up one of the maps from the seat and nodded. The officer then looked at the pink receipt.

"You are unarmed?" he said as he read the paper. "You leave your forty-four behind, huh?"

"That's what it says."

The officer smiled and Bosch thought he could see disbelief in his eyes. The officer nodded and waved his car on. The Caprice immediately became engulfed in a torrent of automobiles that were moving on a wide avenue with no painted lines denoting lanes. At times there were six rows of moving vehicles and sometimes there were four or five. The cars made the transitions smoothly. Harry heard no horns and the traffic flowed quickly. He had gone nearly a mile before a red light halted traffic and he was able to consult his maps for the first time.

He determined he was on Calzado Lopez Mateos, which eventually led to the justice center in the southern part of the city. The light changed and the traffic began moving again. Bosch relaxed a little and looked around as he drove, careful to keep an eye on the changing lane configuration. The boulevard was lined with old shops and industrial businesses. Their pastel-painted facades had been darkened by exhaust fumes from the passing river of metal and it was all quite depressing to Bosch. Several large Chevrolet school buses with multicolor paint jobs moved on the road but they weren't enough to bring much cheer to the scene. The boulevard curved hard to the south and then rounded a circular intersection with a monument at its center, a golden man upon a rearing stallion. He noticed several men, most of them wearing straw cowboy hats, standing in the circle or leaning against the base of the monument. They stared into the sea of traffic. Day laborers waiting for work. Bosch checked the map and saw that the spot was called Benito Juarez Circle.

In another minute Bosch came upon a complex of three large buildings with groupings of antennas and satellite dishes on top of each. A sign near the roadway announced AYUNTAMIENTO DE MEXICALI.

He pulled into a parking lot. There were no parking meters or attendant's booth. He found a spot and parked. While he sat in the car, studying the complex, he couldn't help but feel as though he were running from something, or someone. The death of Porter shook him. He had been right there. It made him wonder how he had escaped and why the killer had not tried to take him as well. One obvious explanation was that the killer did not want to risk taking on two targets at once. But another explanation was that the killer was simply following orders, a hired assassin instructed to take down Porter. Bosch had the feeling that if that were so, the order had come from here in Mexicali.

Each of the three buildings in the complex fronted one side of a triangular plaza. They were of modern design with brown-and-pink sandstone facades. All the windows on the third floor of one of the buildings were covered from the inside with newspaper. To block the setting sun, Bosch assumed. It gave the building a shabby look. Above the main entranceway to this building chrome letters said POLICIA JUDICIAL DEL ESTADO DE BAJA CALIFORNIA. He got out of the car with his Juan Doe #67 file, locked the car door, and headed that way.

Walking through the plaza, Bosch saw several dozen people and many vendors selling food and crafts, but mostly food. On the front steps of the police building several young girls approached him with hands out, trying to sell him chewing gum or wristbands made of colorful threads. He said no thanks. As he opened the door to the lobby a short woman balancing a tray on her shoulder that contained six pies almost collided with him.

Inside, the waiting room contained four rows of plastic chairs that faced a counter on which a uniformed officer leaned. Almost every chair was taken and every person watched the uniform intently. He was wearing mirrored glasses and reading a newspaper.

Bosch approached him and told him in Spanish that he had an appointment with Investigator Carlos Aguila. He opened his badge case and placed it on the counter. The man behind it did not seem impressed. But he slowly reached under the counter and brought up a phone. It was an old rotary job, much older than the building they were in, and it seemed to take him an hour to dial the number.

After a moment, the desk officer began speaking rapid-fire Spanish into the phone. Harry could make out only a few words. Captain. Gringo. Yes. LAPD. Investigator. He also thought he heard the desk man say Charlie Chan. The desk officer listened for a few moments and then hung up. Without looking at Bosch he jerked his thumb toward the door behind him and went back to his newspaper. Harry walked around the counter and through the door into a hallway that extended both right and left with many doors each way.

He stepped back into the waiting room, tapped the desk officer on the shoulder and asked which way.

"To the end, last door," the officer said in English and pointed to the hallway to the left.

Bosch followed the directions and came to a large room where several men milled around standing and others sat on couches. There were bicycles leaning on the walls where there was not a couch. There was a lone desk, at which a young woman sat typing while a man apparently dictated to her. Harry noticed the man had a Barretta 9mm wedged in the waistband of his double-knit pants. He then noticed that some of the other men wore guns in holsters or also in their waistbands. This was the detective bureau. The chatter in the room stopped when Bosch walked in. He asked the man closest to him for Carlos Aguila. This caused another man to call through a doorway at the back of the room. Again, it was too fast but Bosch heard the word Chan and tried to think what it meant in Spanish. The man who had yelled then jerked his thumb toward the door and Bosch went that way. He heard quiet laughter behind him but didn't turn around.

The door led to a small office with a single desk. Behind it a man with gray hair and tired eyes sat smoking a cigarette. A Mexican newspaper, a glass ashtray and a telephone were the only items on the desk. A man with mirrored aviator glasses—what else was new?—sat in a chair against the far wall and studied Bosch. Unless he was sleeping.

"*Buenos dias,*" the older man said. In English he said, "I am Captain Gustavo Grena and you are Detective Harry Bosch. We spoke yesterday."

Bosch reached across the desk and shook his hand. Grena then indicated the man in the mirrors.

"And Investigator Aguila is who you have come to see. What have you brought from your investigation in Los Angeles?"

Aguila, the officer who had sent the inquiry to the Los Angeles consulate, was a small man with dark hair and light skin. His forehead and nose were burned red by the sun but Bosch could see his white chest through the open collar of his shirt. He wore jeans and black leather boots. He nodded to Bosch but made no effort to shake his hand.

There was no chair to sit down on so Harry walked up close to the desk and placed the file down. He opened it and took out morgue Polaroids of Juan Doe #67's face and the chest tattoo. He handed them to Grena, who studied them a moment and then put them down.

"You also look for a man, then? The killer, perhaps?" Grena asked.

"There is a possibility that he was killed here and his body taken to Los Angeles. If that is so, then your department should look for the killer, perhaps."

Grena put a puzzled look on his face.

"I don't understand," he said. "Why? Why would this happen? I am sure you must be mistaken, Detective Bosch."

Bosch shook his shoulders. He wasn't going to press it. Yet.

"Well, I'd like to at least get the identification confirmed and then go from there."

"Very well," Grena said. "I leave you with Investigator Aguila. But I have to inform you, the business you mentioned on the phone yesterday, EnviroBreed, I have personally interviewed the manager and he has assured me that your Juan Doe did not work there. I have saved you that much time."

Grena nodded as if to say his efforts were no inconvenience at all. Think nothing of it.

"How can they be sure when we don't have the ID yet?"

Grena dragged on his cigarette to give him time to think about that one. He said, "I provided the name Fernal Gutierrez-Llosa to him. No such employee at any time. This is an American contractor, we must be careful.... You see, we do not wish to step on the toes of the international trade."

Grena stood up, dropped his cigarette in the ash tray and nod-ded to Aguila. Then he left the office. Bosch looked at the mirrored glasses and wondered if Aguila had understood a word of what had just been said.

"Don't worry about the Spanish," Aguila said after Grena was gone. "I speak your language."

Twenty-One

BOSCH INSISTED THAT HE DRIVE, SAYING HE DID NOT want to leave the Caprice—it wasn't his, he explained—in the parking lot. What he didn't explain was that he wanted to be near his gun, which was still in the trunk. On their way through the plaza, they waved away the children with their hands out.

In the car, Bosch said, "How're we going to make the ID without prints?"

Aguila picked the file up off the seat.

"His friends and wife will look at the photos."

"We going to his house? I can lift prints, take 'em back to L.A. to have someone take a look. It would confirm it."

"It is not a house, Detective Bosch. It is a shack."

Bosch nodded and started the car. Aguila directed him farther south to Boulevard Lazaro Cardenas on which they headed west for a short while before turning south again on Avenida Canto Rodado.

"We go to the barrio," Aguila said. "It is known as Ciudad de los Personas Perdidos. City of Lost Souls."

"That's what the tattoo means, right? The ghost? Lost Souls?"

"Yes, that is correct."

Bosch thought a moment before asking, "How far is it from Lost Souls barrio to Saints and Sinners?"

"It is also in the southwest sector. Not far from Lost Souls. I will show it to you if you wish."

"Yeah, maybe."

"Is there a reason you ask?"

Bosch thought of Corvo's admonition not to trust the local police.

"Just curious," he said. "It's another case."

He immediately felt guilty at not being truthful with Aguila. He was a cop and Bosch felt he deserved the benefit of the doubt. But not according to Corvo. They drove in silence for a while after that. They were moving away from the city and the comfort of buildings and traffic. The commercial businesses and the shops and restaurants gave way to more shacks and cardboard shanties. Harry saw a refrigerator box near the side of the road that was somebody's home. The people they passed, sitting on rusted engine blocks, oil drums, stared at the car with hollow eyes. Bosch tried to keep his eyes on the dusty road.

"They called you Charlie Chan back there, how come?"

He asked primarily because he was nervous and thought conversation might distract him from his uneasiness and the unpleasantness of the journey they were making.

"Yes," Aguila said. "It is because I am Chinese."

Bosch turned and looked at him. From the side, he could look behind the mirrors and see the slight rounding of the eyes. It was there.

"Partly, I should say. One of my grandfathers. There is a large Chinese-Mexican community in Mexicali, Detective Bosch."

"Oh."

"Mexicali was created around 1900 by the Colorado River Land Company. They owned a huge stretch of land on both sides of the border, and they needed cheap labor to pick their cotton, their vegetables," Aguila said. "They established Mexicali. Across the border from Calexico. Like mirror images, I suppose, at least according to plan. They brought in ten thousand Chinese, all men, and they had a town. A company town."

Bosch nodded. He had never heard the story but found it interesting. He had seen many Chinese restaurants and signs on his drive through the city but did not recall seeing many Asians.

"They all stayed—the Chinese?" he asked.

"Most of them, yes. But like I said, ten thousand Chinamen. No women. The company wouldn't allow it. Thought it would take away from the work. Later, some women came. But most of the time the men married into Mexican families. The blood was mixed. But as you probably have seen, much of the culture was preserved. We will enjoy some Chinese food at siesta, okay?"

"Sure, okay."

"Police work has largely remained the domain of the traditional Mexicans. There are not many like me in the State Judicial Police. For this reason I am called Charlie Chan. I am considered an outsider by the others."

"I think I know how you feel."

"You will reach a point, Detective Bosch, where you will be able to trust me. I am comfortable waiting to discuss this other case you mentioned."

Bosch nodded and felt embarrassed and tried to concentrate on his driving. Soon Aguila directed him onto a narrow, unpaved road that cut through the heart of a barrio. There were flat-roofed concrete-block buildings with blankets hung in open doorways. Additions to these buildings were constructed of plywood and sheets of aluminum. There was trash and other debris scattered about. Haggard, gaunt-looking men milled around and stared at the Caprice with California plates as it went by.

"Pull to the building with the painted star," Aguila instructed.

Bosch saw the star. It was hand-painted on the block wall of one of the sad structures. Above the star was painted Personas Perdidos. Scrawled beneath it were the words Honorable Alcalde y Sheriff.

Bosch parked the Caprice in front of the hovel and waited for instructions.

"He is neither a mayor or sheriff if that's what you may be thinking," Aguila said. "Arnolfo Munoz de la Cruz is simply what you would call a peacekeeper here. To a place of disorder he brings order. Or tries. He is the sheriff of the City of Lost Souls. He brought the missing man to our attention. This is where Fernal Gutierrez-Llosa lived."

Bosch got out, carrying the Juan Doe file with him. As he walked around the front of the car, he again rubbed his hand against his jacket, where it hung over his holster. It was a subconscious move he made every time he got out of the car and was on the job. But this time, when the comforting feel of the gun beneath was not there, he became acutely aware that he was an unarmed stranger in a strange land. He could not retrieve his Smith from the trunk while in the presence of Aguila. At least not until he knew him better.

Aguila rang a clay bell that hung near the doorway of the structure. There was no door, just a blanket that was draped over a wood slat hammered across the top of the passage. A voice inside called, "Abierto," and they went inside.

Munoz was a small man, deeply tanned and with gray hair tied in a knot behind his head. He wore no shirt, which exposed the sheriff's star tattooed on the right side of his chest, the ghost on the left. He looked at Aguila and then at Bosch, staring curiously at him. Aguila introduced Bosch and told Munoz why they had come. He spoke slowly enough so that Bosch could understand. Aguila told the old man that he needed to take a look at some photographs. This confused Munoz—until Bosch slipped the morgue shots out of the file and he saw that the photographs were of a dead man.

"Is it Fernal Gutierrez-Llosa?" Aguila inquired after the man had studied the photographs long enough.

"It is him."

Munoz now looked away. Bosch looked around for the first time.

The one-room shack was very much like a large prison cell. Just the necessities. A bed. A box of clothes. A towel hung over the back of an old chair. A candle and a mug with a toothbrush in it on top of a cardboard box next to the bed. It had a squalid smell and he felt embarrassed that he had intruded.

"Where was his place?" he asked Aguila in English. Aguila looked at Munoz and said, "I am sorry for the loss of your friend, Mr. Munoz. It will be my duty to inform his wife. Do you know if she is here?"

Munoz nodded and said the woman was at her dwelling.

"Would you like to come with us to help?"

Munoz nodded again, picked a white shirt up off the bed and put it on. Then he went to the door, parted the curtain over the opening and held it for them.

Bosch first went to the trunk of the Caprice and got the print kit from his briefcase. Then they walked farther down the dusty street until they came to a plywood shack with a canvas canopy in front of it. Aguila touched Bosch on the elbow.

"Señor Munoz and I will deal with the woman. We will bring her out here. You go in and collect the fingerprints you need and do whatever else you need to do."

Munoz called out the name Marita and a few moments later a small woman peeked through the white plastic shower curtain hung across the doorway. When she saw Munoz and Aguila she came out. Bosch could tell by her face that she already knew the news that the men were there to deliver. Women were always that way. Harry thought of the first night he had seen Sylvia Moore. She knew. They all knew. Bosch handed the file to Aguila, in case the woman demanded to see the photos, and ducked into the room the woman and the Juan Doe had shared.

It was a room with spare furnishings. No surprise there. A queen-sized mattress lay on top of a wooden pallet. There was a single chair on one side of it and on the other a bureau had been made out of a wood and cardboard shipping crate. A few articles of clothing hung inside the box. The back wall of the room was a large piece of uncut aluminum with the Tecate beer trademark printed on it. Wood-slat shelves went across this, holding coffee cans, a cigar box and other small items.

Bosch could hear the woman crying quietly outside the shack and Munoz trying to console her. He looked around the room quickly, trying to decide which was a likely spot to lift prints. He was unsure if he even needed to do this. The woman's tears seemed to confirm the identity.

He walked to the shelves and used a fingernail to flip open the cigar box. It contained a dirty comb, a few pesos and a set of dominoes.

"Carlos?" he called out.

Aguila stuck his head in past the shower curtain.

"Ask if she has handled this box lately. It looks like it was her husband's stuff. If it's his, I'll try some lifts on it."

He heard the questioning in Spanish outside and the woman said she did not touch the box ever because it was her husband's. Using his nails Harry put the box on top of the makeshift bureau. He opened the print kit and took out a small spray bottle, a vial of black powder, a sable-hair brush, a wide roll of clear tape and a stack of 3 x 5 cards. He laid all of these out on the bed and set to work.

He picked up the spray bottle and pumped four sprays of ninhydrin mist over the box. After the mist settled, he took out a cigarette, lit it and then moved the still-burning match along the edge of the box about two inches from the surface. The heat brought up the ridges of several fingerprints in the ninhydrin. Bosch bent over the table and studied them, looking for complete examples. There were two. He uncapped the vial of black powder and lightly brushed some onto the prints, clearly defining the ridges and bifurcations. He then unrolled a short length of tape, held it down on one of the prints and lifted it. He pressed the tape against a white 3 x 5 card. He did it again with the other print. He had two good prints to take back with him.

Aguila came into the room then.

"Did you get a print?"

"A couple. Hopefully they are his and not hers. Doesn't seem to matter much. Sounded like she made an ID, too. She look at the pictures?"

Aguila nodded and said, "She insisted. Did you search the room?"

"For what?"

"I do not know."

"I looked around. Not much here."

"Did you take fingerprints from the coffee cans?"

Bosch looked at the shelves. There were three old Maxwell House cans. He said, "Nah, I figured her prints are on them. I don't want to have to print her to clear her for comparisons. It's not worth putting her through that."

Aguila nodded but then looked puzzled.

"Why would a poor man and his wife have three cans of coffee?"

It was a good point. Bosch went to the shelves and took down one can. It rattled and when he opened it he found a handful of pesos inside the can. The next one he pulled down was about a third full of coffee. The last one was the lightest. Inside he found papers, a baptismal certificate for Gutierrez-Llosa and a marriage license. The couple had been married thirty-two years. It depressed him to think about it. There was also a Polaroid photo of Gutierrez-Llosa and Bosch could see it was Juan Doe #67. Identity confirmed. And there was a Polaroid of his wife. And lastly, there was a stack of check stubs held together in a rubber band. Bosch looked through these, finding them all for small amounts of money from several businesses— the financial records of a day laborer. The businesses that didn't pay their day laborers in cash paid with checks. The last two in the stack were receipts for sixteen dollars each for checks issued by Enviro-Breed Inc. Bosch put the check stubs into his pocket and told Aguila he was ready to go.

While Aguila expressed condolences again to the new widow,

Bosch went to the trunk of the car to put away the fingerprint kit and the cards with the lifts he had taken. He looked over the trunk lid and saw Aguila still standing with Munoz and the woman. Harry quickly lifted up the rug on the right side of the trunk, pulled up the spare tire and grabbed his Smith. He put the gun in his holster and slid it around on his waist so that the gun would be on his back. It was under his jacket but an eye looking for such things could see it. However, Bosch was no longer worried about Aguila. He got in the car and waited. Aguila got in a few moments later.

Bosch watched the widow and the sheriff in the rear view mirror as they drove away.

"What will happen with her now?" he asked Aguila.

"You don't want to know, Detective Bosch. Her life was difficult before. Now, her hardships will only multiply. I believe she cries for herself as much as her lost husband. And rightly so."

Bosch drove in silence until they were out of Lost Souls and back on the main road.

"That was clever, what you did back there," he said after a while. "With the coffee cans."

Aguila didn't say anything. He didn't have to. Bosch knew he had been in there before and had seen the EnviroBreed stubs. Grena was scamming and Aguila didn't like it or approve of it or maybe he was just unhappy because he hadn't been cut in on the deal. Whatever the reason, he was pointing Bosch in the right direction. Aguila wanted Bosch to find the stubs. He wanted Bosch to know Grena was a liar.

"Did you go to EnviroBreed, check it out on your own?"

"No," Aguila said. "This would be reported to my captain. I could not go there after he had made the appropriate inquiry. Enviro-Breed is involved in international business. It holds contracts with government agencies in the United States. You must understand, it is a..."

"Delicate situation?"

"Yes, this is true."

"I'm familiar with those. I understand. You can't buck Grena but I can. Where is EnviroBreed?"

"Not far from here. To the southwest, where the land is mostly flat until it rises into the Sierra de los Cucapah. There are many industrial concerns there and large ranches."

"And how close is it between EnviroBreed and the ranch owned by the pope?"

"The pope?"

"Zorrillo. The pope of Mexicali. I thought you wanted to know about the other case I'm working."

They drove a little bit in silence. Bosch looked over and saw that Aguila's face had clouded. Even with the mirrors, Bosch could see this. His mention of Zorrillo probably confirmed a suspicion the Mexican detective had held since Grena had tried to derail the investigation. Bosch already knew from Corvo that EnviroBreed was just across the highway from the ranch. His question was merely one more test of Aguila.

It was a while before Aguila finally answered.

"The ranch and EnviroBreed are very close, I'm afraid."

"Good. Show me."

Twenty-Two

"LET ME ASK YOU A QUESTION," BOSCH SAID. "HOW come you sent that inquiry to the consul's office? I mean, you don't have missing persons down here. Somebody turns up missing, they crossed the border but you don't send out inquiries. What made you think this was different?"

They were heading toward the range of mountains that rose high above a layer of light brown smog from the city. They were going southwest on Avenida Val Verde and were moving through an area where ranch lands extended to the west and industrial parks lined the roadway to the east.

"The woman convinced me," Aguila said. "She came to the plaza with the sheriff and made the report. Grena gave me the investigation and her words convinced me that Gutierrez-Llosa would not cross the border willingly without her. So I went to the circle."

Aguila said the circle below the golden statue of Benito Juarez on Calzado Lopez Mateos was where men went to wait for work. Other day laborers interviewed at the circle said the EnviroBreed vans came two or three times a week to hire workers. The men who had worked at the bug-breeding plant had described it as difficult work. They made food paste for the breeding process and loaded heavy incubation cartons into the vans. Flies constantly flew in their mouths and eyes. Many who had worked there said they never went back, choosing to wait for other employers to stop at the circle.

But not Gutierrez-Llosa. Others at the circle had reported seeing him get into the EnviroBreed van. Compared to the other laborers, he was an old man. He did not have much choice in employers.

Aguila said that when he learned the product made at Enviro-Breed was shipped across the border, he sent out missing-person notices to consulates in southern California. Among his theories was that the old man had been killed in an accident at the plant and his body hidden to avoid an inquiry that could halt production. Aguila believed this was a common occurrence in the industrial sectors of the city.

"A death investigation, even accidental death, can be very expensive," Aguila said.

"La mordida."

"Yes, the bite."

Aguila explained that his investigation stopped when he discussed his findings with Grena. The captain said he would handle the EnviroBreed inquiry and later reported it to be a dead end. And that was where it stood until Bosch called with news of the body.

"Sounds like Grena got his bite."

Aguila did not answer this. They began to pass a ranch protected by a chain metal fence topped with razor wire. Bosch looked through it to the Sierra de los Cucapah and saw nothing in the vast expanse between the road and mountains. But soon they passed a break in the fence, an entrance to the ranch where there was a pickup truck parked lengthwise across the roadway. Two men were sitting in the cab and they looked at Bosch and he looked at them as he drove by.

"That's it, isn't it?" he said. "That's Zorrillo's ranch."

"Yes. The entrance."

"Zorrillo's name never came up before you heard it from me?"

"Not until you said it."

Aguila offered no other comment. In a minute they were coming up to some buildings inside the ranch's fence line but close to the road. Bosch could see a concrete barnlike structure with a garage door that was closed. There were corrals on either side of it and in these he saw a half dozen bulls in single pens. He saw no one around.

"He breeds bulls for the ring," Aguila said.

"I heard that. Lot of money in that around here, huh?"

"All from the seed of one prized bull. El Temblar. A very famous animal in Mexicali. The bull that killed Meson, the famous torero. He lives here now and roams the ranch at his will, taking the heifers as he wishes. A champion animal."

"The Tremble?" he said.

"Yes. It is said that man and earth tremble when the beast charges. That is the legend. The death of Meson a decade ago is very well known. A story recalled each Sunday at the plaza."

"And the Tremble just runs around in there loose? Like a watch-dog or something. A bulldog."

"Sometimes people stand at the fence waiting for a glimpse of the great animal. The bulls his seed produces are considered the most game in all of Baja. Pull over here."

Bosch turned onto the shoulder. He noticed Aguila was looking across the street at a line of warehouses and businesses. Some had signs on them. Most in English. They were companies that used cheap Mexican labor and paid low taxes to make products for the United States. There were furniture manufacturers, tile makers, circuit board factories.

"See the Mexitec Furniture building?" Aguila said. "The second structure down, with no sign, that is EnviroBreed."

It was a white building, and Aguila was right. No sign or other indication of what went on there. It was surrounded by a ten-foot fence topped with razor wire. Signs on the fence warned in two languages that it was electrified and there were dogs inside of it. Bosch didn't see any dogs and decided they were probably only put in the yard at night. He did see two cameras on the front corners of the building and several cars parked inside the compound. He saw no

EnviroBreed vans but the two garage doors at the front of the building were closed.

Bosch had to press a button, state his business and hold his badge up to a remote camera before the fence gate automatically rolled open. He parked next to a maroon Lincoln with California tags and they walked across the dusty unpaved lot to the door marked Office. He brushed his hand against the back of his hip and felt the gun under his jacket. A small measure of comfort. The door was opened as he reached for the doorknob and a man wearing a Stetson to shade his acne-scarred and sun-hardened face stepped out lighting a cigarette. He was an Anglo and Bosch thought he might have been the van driver he had seen at the eradication center in L.A.

"Last door on the left," the man said. "He's waiting."

"Who's he?"

"Him."

The man in the Stetson smiled and Bosch thought his face might crack. Bosch and Aguila stepped through the door into a wood-paneled hallway. It went straight back with a small reception desk on the left followed by three doors. At the end of the hall there was a fourth door. A young Mexican woman sat at the reception desk and stared at them silently. Bosch nodded and they headed back. The first door they passed was closed and letters on it said USDA. The next two doors had no letters. The one at the end of the hall had a sign that said:

·DANGER—RADIATION

NO UNAUTHORIZED ADMITTANCE

Harry saw a hook next to the door that had goggles and breathing masks hanging on it. He opened the last door on the left and they stepped into a small anteroom with a secretary's desk but no secretary.

"In here, please," a voice said from the next room.

Bosch and Aguila stepped into a large office that was weighted in the center by a huge steel desk. A man in a light blue guayabera shirt sat behind it. He was writing something in a ledger book and there was a Styrofoam cup of steaming coffee on the desk. Enough light came through the jalousie window behind him so that he didn't need a desk light. He looked about fifty years old, with gray hair that showed streaks of old black dye. He also was a gringo.

The man said nothing and continued writing. Bosch looked around and saw the four-picture closed-circuit television console on a low shelf against the wall next to the desk. He saw the black-and-white images from the gate and front corners. The fourth image was very dark and was an interior look at what Harry assumed was the cargo-loading room. He saw a white van with its rear doors open, two or three men loading large white boxes into it.

"Yes?" the man said. He still hadn't looked up.

"Quite a lot of security for flies."

Now he looked up. "Excuse me?"

"Didn't know they were so valuable."

"What can I do for you?" He threw his pen down on the desk to signal that the wheels of international commerce were grinding to a halt because of Bosch.

"Harry Bosch, Los Angeles po—"

"You said that at the gate. What can I do for you?"

"I am here to talk about one of your employees."

"Name?" He picked up the pen again and went back to work on the ledger.

"You know something? I would think that if a cop had come three hundred miles, crossed the border, just to ask you a few questions, then it might rate a little interest. But not with you. That bothers me."

The pen went down harder this time and bounced off the desk into the trash can next to it.

"Officer, I don't care whether it bothers you or not. I have a shipment of perishable material I must get on the road by four o'clock.

I can't afford to show the interest you seem to think you rate. Now, if you want to give me the employee's name—that is, if he was an employee—I will answer what I can."

"What do you mean 'was an employee'?"

"What?"

"You said, 'was,' just then."

"So?"

"So, what's it mean?"

"You said—you're the one who came in here with these questions. I—"

"And your name is?"

"What?"

"What is your name?"

The man stopped, thoroughly confused, and drank from the cup. He said, "You know, mister, you have no authority here."

"You said, 'even if the guy was an employee,' and I never said anything about 'was.' Makes me think, you already know we are talking about an individual that was. Who is dead now."

"I just assumed, okay. A cop comes all the way down from L.A., I just assumed we were talking about a dead guy. Don't try to put words—you can't come in here with that badge that isn't worth the tin it's made of once you cross that border and start pushing me. I don't have—"

"You want some authority? This is Carlos Aguila of the State Judicial Police here. You can consider that he is asking the same questions as me."

Aguila nodded but said nothing.

"That's not the point," the man behind the desk said. "The point is this typical bullshit American imperialism you bring with you. I find it very distasteful. My name is Charles Ely. I am proprietor of EnviroBreed. I do not know anything about the man you said worked here."

"I didn't tell you his name."

"It doesn't matter. You understand now? You made a mistake. You played this game wrong."

Bosch took the morgue photo of Gutierrez-Llosa out of his pocket and slid it across the desk. Ely did not touch the photo but looked down at it. He showed no reaction that Bosch could see. Then Bosch put down the pay stubs. Same thing. No reaction.

"Name is Fernal Gutierrez-Llosa," Bosch said. "A day laborer. I need to know when he worked here last, what he was doing."

Ely retrieved his pen from the trash can and flicked the photo back toward Bosch with it.

"Afraid I can't help. Day laborers we don't carry records on. We pay them with 'pay to bearer' checks at the end of each day. Different people all the time. I wouldn't know this man from Adam. And I believe we already answered questions about this man. From the SJP. A Captain Grena. I guess I will have to call him now to see why that wasn't sufficient."

Bosch wanted to ask whether he meant the payoff Ely had given Grena or the information wasn't sufficient. But he held back because it would come back on Aguila. Instead he said, "You do that, Mr. Ely. Meantime, somebody else around here might remember this man. I am going to take a look around."

Ely became immediately agitated. "No, sir, you are not going to have free range of this facility. Portions of this building are used to irradiate material and are considered dangerous and off limits to all but certified personnel. Other areas are subject to USDA monitoring and quarantine and we cannot allow anyone access. Again, you have no authority here."

"Who owns EnviroBreed, Ely?" Bosch asked.

Ely seemed startled by the change in subject.

"Who?" he sputtered.

"Who is the man, Ely?"

"I don't have to answer that. You have no—"

"The man across the street? Is the pope the man?"

Ely stood up and pointed at the door.

"I don't know what you are talking about but you're leaving. And I will be contacting both the SJP and the American and Mexican authorities. We will see if this is how they want police from Los Angeles to operate on foreign soil."

Bosch and Aguila moved back into the hall and closed the door. Harry stood there for a moment and listened for the sound of a telephone or steps. He heard nothing and then turned to the door at the end of the hall. He tried it but it was locked.

In front of the door marked USDA, he leaned his head forward and listened but heard nothing. He opened the door without knocking and a man with bureaucrat written all over him looked up from behind a small wooden desk. The room was about a quarter the size of Ely's suite. The man wore a short-sleeved white shirt with a thin blue tie. He had close-cropped gray hair, a mustache that looked like the end of a toothbrush and small, dead eyes that looked out from behind bifocals that squeezed against his pudgy pink temples. The plastic ink guard in his pocket had his name printed on the flap: Jerry Dinsmore. He had a half-eaten bean burrito on his desk, sitting on oil-stained paper.

"Can I help you?" he said with a mouthful.

Bosch and Aguila moved into the room.

Bosch showed him his ID and let him have a good look at it. Then he put the morgue photo on the desk, next to the burrito. Dinsmore looked at it and folded up the paper around his half-finished meal and put it in a drawer.

"Recognize him?" Bosch said. "Just a routine check. Infectious disease alert. Guy took it with him up to L.A. and croaked. We are retracing him so we can get anybody who had contact inoculated. We still got plenty of time. We hope."

Dinsmore was chewing his food much slower now. He looked down at the Polaroid and then up over his glasses at Bosch.

"Was he one of the men who worked around here?"

"We think so. We are checking with all the regular employees.

We thought you might recognize him. It depends on how close you got as far as whether you need to be quarantined."

"Well, I never get close to the laborers. I'm in the clear. But what is the disease that you are talking about? I don't see why LAPD is—this man looks like he was beaten."

"I'm sorry, Mr. Dinsmore, that's confidential until we determine if you are at risk. If you are, well, then we have to put our cards on the table. Now, how do you mean you never get close to the laborers? Are you not the inspection officer for this facility?"

Bosch expected Ely to burst in any moment.

"I am the inspector but I am only interested in the finished product. I inspect samples directly from the travel cases. Then I seal the cases. This is done in the shipping room. You have to remember, this is a private facility and consequently I do not have free reign of the breeding or sterilization labs. Therefore, I do not interface with the workers."

"You just said, 'samples.' So that means you don't look in all of the boxes."

"Wrong. I don't look in all of the larvae cylinders in each of the transport cases, but I do inspect and seal the cases. I don't see what this has to do with this man. He didn't—"

"I don't see it, either. Never mind. You're in the clear."

Dinsmore's small eyes widened slightly. Bosch winked at him to further confuse him. He wondered if Dinsmore was part of what was going on here or whether, like a mole, he was in the dark. He told him to go back to his burrito and then he and Aguila stepped back into the hall. Just at that moment the door at the end of the hall opened and through it stepped Ely. He pulled a breathing mask and goggles off his face and charged down the hall, coffee slopping over the sides of the Styrofoam cup.

"I want you two out of here unless you have a court order."

He was right up to Bosch now and anger was etching red lines on his face. It was the act he might have used to intimidate others but Bosch was not impressed. He looked down into the shorter man's coffee cup and smiled as a small piece of the puzzle slipped into place. The stomach contents of Juan Doe #67 had included coffee. That was how he had swallowed the medfly which had brought Bosch here. Ely followed his eyes down and saw the medfly floating on the surface of the hot liquid.

"Fuckin' flies," he said.

"You know," Bosch said, "I'll probably get that court order."

He couldn't think of anything else to say and didn't want to leave Ely with the satisfaction of throwing him out. He and Aguila headed for the exit.

"Don't count on it," Ely said. "This is Mexico. You aren't jackshit here."

Twenty-Three

BOSCH STOOD AT THE WINDOW OF HIS THIRD-FLOOR room in the Hotel Colorado on Calzado Justo Sierra and looked out at what he could see of Mexicali. To his left the view was obscured by the other wing of the hotel. But looking out to the right he saw the streets were clogged with cars and the colorful buses he had seen earlier. He could hear a mariachi band playing somewhere. There was the smell of frying grease in the air from a nearby restaurant. And the sky above the ramshackle city was purple and red in the day's dying light. In the distance he could see the buildings of the justice center and, near them to the right, the rounded shape of a stadium. Plaza de los Toros.

He had called Corvo in Los Angeles two hours earlier, left his number and location, and was waiting for a call back from his man in Mexicali, Ramos. He walked away from the window and looked at the phone. He knew it was time to make the rest of the calls but he hesitated. He grabbed a beer out of the tin ice bucket on the bureau and opened it. He drank a quarter of it and sat on the bed next to the phone.

There were three messages on the phone tape at his home, all of them from Pounds saying the same thing. "Call me."

But he didn't. Instead, he called the homicide table first. It was

Saturday night but the chances were it would still be all hands on deck because of Porter. Jerry Edgar answered.

"What's the situation?"

"Shit, man, you gotta come in." He was speaking in a very low voice. "Everybody's looking for you. RHD's got the lead on this thing so I don't know exactly what's happening. I'm just one of the gofers. But, I think, uh . . . I don't know, man."

"What? Say it."

"It's like they think you either did Porter or you might be next. It's hard to gauge what the fuck they're doing or thinking."

"Who's there?"

"Everybody. This is the command post. Irving's in there in the box with Ninety-eight now."

Bosch knew he couldn't let it go on much further. He had to call in. He might have already damaged himself beyond repair.

"Okay," he said. "I'm going to call them. I have to make one other call first. Thanks."

Bosch hung up and dialed another number, hoping he had remembered it correctly and that she would be home. It was near seven and he thought maybe she had gone out for dinner, but then she picked up on the sixth ring.

"It's Bosch. A bad time?"

"What do you want?" Teresa said. "Where are you? Everybody's looking for you, you know."

"I heard. But I'm outta town. I was just calling 'cause I heard they found my friend Lucius Porter."

"Yeah, they did. Sorry. I just got back from the cut."

"Yeah, I figured you'd do it."

And then silence before she said, "Harry, why do I get the feeling you want—that you aren't calling just because he was your friend?"

"Well . . ."

"Oh, shit, here we go again, right?"

"No. I just wanted to know how he got it is all. He was a friend. I worked with him. Never mind."

"I don't know why I let you do this to me. Shit. Mexican necktie, Harry. There, you happy? Got all you need now?"

"Garrote?"

"Yes. Steel baling wire, wrapped at the ends around two wooden pegs. I'm sure you've seen it before. Do I get to read this in the *Times* tomorrow, too?"

He was silent until he was sure she was done. He looked from the bed to the open window and saw the daylight was now completely gone. The sky was a deep red wine. He thought of the man at Poe's. Three tears.

"Did you do a compar—"

"Comparison to the Jimmy Kapps case? Yes. We're way ahead of you, but it won't be done for a few days."

"How come?"

"Because it takes that long to do wood-fiber testing between the dowel pegs and alloy-content analysis on the baling wire. We did do a cut analysis on the wire, though. It looks very good."

"Meaning?"

"Meaning it looks like the wire on the garrote used to kill Porter was cut from the same length of wire used to kill Kapps. The ends match. It's not one hundred percent because similar pliers will leave similar cut tracings. So we are doing the metal-alloy comparison. We'll know in a few days."

She seemed so matter-of-fact about it all. He was surprised she was still angry with him. The television reports of the night before seemed to be in her favor. He didn't know what to say. He had gone from being at ease in bed with her to being nervous on the phone with her.

"Thanks, Teresa," he finally said. "I'll see you."

"Harry?" she said before he could hang up.

"Yeah?"

"When you get back, I don't think you should call me again. I think we should keep it professional. If we see each other in the suite, then that's fine. But let's leave it there."

He didn't say anything.

"Okay?"

"Sure."

They hung up. Bosch sat without moving for several minutes. Finally, he picked the phone up again and dialed the direct line into the glass box. Pounds picked up immediately.

"It's Bosch."

"Where are you?"

"Mexicali. You left messages?"

"I called the hotel on your tape. They said you never checked in."

"I decided to stay on the other side of the border."

"Never mind the bullshit. Porter is dead."

"What!" Bosch tried his best to make it seem real. "What happened? I just saw him yesterday. He—"

"Never mind the bullshit, Bosch. What are you doing down there?"

"You told me to go where the case followed. It led here."

"I never told you to go to Mexico." He was yelling. "I want you back here ten minutes ago. This does not look good for you. We have a bartender that so help me Christ is ready to put your dick in the dirt on this. He—hang on."

"Bosch," a new voice on the line said. "Assistant Chief Irving here. What is your location?"

"I'm in Mexicali."

"I want you in my office at oh eight hundred tomorrow."

Bosch didn't hesitate. He knew he could not show any weakness.

"Can't do that, Chief. I have some unfinished business here that'll probably take me through tomorrow at least."

"We are talking about a fellow officer's murder here, Detective. I don't know if you realize this, but you could be in danger yourself."

"I know what I am doing. It's a fellow officer's murder that brings me here. Remember? Or doesn't Moore matter?"

Irving ignored that.

"You are refusing my direct order to return?"

"Look, Chief, I don't care what some bartender is telling you, you know I wasn't the doer."

"I never said that. But your conversation already reveals that you know more about this than you should if you were not involved."

"All I'm saying is that the answers to a lot of questions—about Moore, Porter and the rest—are down here. It's all down here. I'm staying."

"Detective Bosch, I was wrong about you. I gave you a lot of rope this time because I thought I detected a change in you. I see now that I was wrong. You fooled me again. You—"

"Chief, I am doing my—"

"Don't interrupt me! You may be unwilling to follow my explicit commands to return but don't you interrupt me. I am telling you that you don't want to return, fine. Don't. But you might as well never return, Bosch. Think about that. What you had before won't be waiting when you get back."

After Irving hung up Bosch picked a second bottle of Tecate from the bucket and lit a cigarette at the window. He didn't care about Irving's threats. Not that much, at least. He'd probably draw a suspension, maybe five days max. He could handle that. But Irving wouldn't move Bosch. Where could he send him? There weren't very many places lower than Hollywood. Instead, Bosch thought about Porter. He had been able to put it off, put it out of his mind. But now he had to think about Porter. Strangled with baling wire, left in a Dumpster. Poor bastard. But something in Bosch refused to let him grant the dead cop sympathy. Nothing about it touched his heart the way he thought it would, or should. It was a pitiful end of life. But he felt no pity. Porter had made fatal mistakes. Bosch promised himself that he would not and that he would go on.

He tried to focus on Zorrillo. Harry was sure that it was the pope who was manipulating things, who had sent the assassin to clean up the loose ends. If it was likely the same man had killed both Kapps and Porter, it was then easy to add Moore in as a victim as well. And possibly even Fernal Gutierrez-Llosa. The man with three tears. Did that leave Dance off the hook? Bosch doubted it. It might have taken Dance to lure Moore to the Hideaway. His thoughts reassured him that he was doing the right thing staying. The answers were here, not in L.A.

He went to his briefcase on the bureau and took out the mug shot of Dance that had been in the file Moore had put together. He looked at the practiced sulk of a young man who still had a boyish face and bleached blond hair. Now he wanted to move up the ladder and had come south of the border to make his case. Bosch realized that if Dance was in Mexicali he would not blend in easily. He'd have to have help.

The knock on the door startled him. Bosch quietly put down the bottle and took the gun off the night table. Through the peephole he saw a man of about thirty with dark hair and a thick mustache. He was not the room service waiter who had brought the beer.

"*Si?*"

"Bosch. It's Ramos."

Bosch opened the door on the chain and asked for some identification.

"Are you kidding? I don't carry ID around here. Let me in. Corvo sent me."

"How do I know?"

"Because you called L.A. Operations two hours ago and left your address. I tell you, I really get fucking paranoid having to explain all of this while standing out in the hallway."

Bosch closed the door, flipped off the chain and reopened it. He kept the gun in his hand but down at his side. Ramos walked past him into the room. He walked up to the window and looked out, then he walked away and began pacing near the bed. He said, "Smells like shit out there. Somebody cooking tortillas or some shit. Got any more brew? And by the way, the *federales* catch you with that piece and you might have trouble trying to get back across. How come you didn't stay in Calexico like Corvo told you to, man?"

If he had been anyone other than a cop, Bosch would have figured he was coked to the eyelids. But he decided it was probably something else, something he didn't know about yet, that made Ramos seem wired. Bosch picked up the phone and ordered a six-pack from room service, never taking his eyes off the man in his room. After he hung up, he put the gun in his waistband and sat down in the chair by the window.

"I didn't want to deal with the lines at the border," he said in answer to one of Ramos's many questions.

"You didn't want to put your trust in Corvo is what you mean. I don't blame you. Not that I don't trust him. I do. But I can see the need to want to go your own way. They got better food over here, anyway. But Calexico, there's a wild little town. It's one of those places, you never know what kind of shit is going down. You hit that place the wrong way and you go into a slide, man. I like it better over here myself. Did you eat?"

For a moment, Bosch thought about what Sylvia Moore had said about the black ice. Ramos was still pacing the room and Bosch noticed he had two electronic pagers on his belt. The agent was hyped on something. Bosch was sure of it.

"I already ate," Bosch said and moved his chair near the window because the room had taken on the tang of the agent's body odor.

"I know the best Chinese food in two countries. We could pop over for—"

"Hey! Ramos, sit down. You're making me nervous. Just sit down and tell me what's going on."

Ramos looked around himself as if seeing the room for the first time. He dragged a chair away from the wall near the door and straddled it backward in the middle of the room.

"What's going on, man, is that we are not too impressed with the shit you pulled at EnviroBreed today."

Bosch was surprised the DEA knew so much so fast but tried not to show it.

"That was not cool at all," Ramos was saying. "So I came here to tell you to quit the one-man show. Corvo told me that was your bag, but I didn't expect to see it so soon."

"What's the problem?" Bosch said. "It was my lead. From what Corvo said, you people didn't know shit about that place. I went in there to shake 'em up a little bit. That's all."

"These people don't shake, Bosch. That's what I am saying. Now look, enough said. I just wanted to say my little piece and to see what you have going besides the bug place. What I'm asking is, what are you doing here?"

Before Bosch could answer there was a loud knock on the door and the DEA agent jumped up off the chair, coming down in a crouched position.

"It's room service," Bosch said. "What's wrong with you?"

"Always get this way before we jam."

Bosch got up looking curiously at the DEA agent and went to the door. Through the peephole he saw the same man who had delivered the first two beers. He opened the door, paid for the delivery and gave Ramos a bottle from the new bucket.

Ramos chugged half the bottle before sitting back down. Bosch took a beer back to his seat.

"What do you mean by 'before we jam'?"

"Well," Ramos said after another swallow. "The stuff you gave Corvo was good info. But then you canceled that out by cowboying it over there today. You nearly fucked things up."

"You said that. What did you find out?"

"EnviroBreed. We ran down the info and it's a direct hit. We traced ownership through a bunch of blinds to a Gilberto Ornelas. That's a known alias for a guy named Fernando Ibarra, one of Zorrillo's lieutenants. We are working with the *federales* on getting search approvals. They are cooperating on this one. This new attorney general they got down here is clean and mean. He's working with us. So it's going to be a major jam, if we get the approval."

"When will you know?"

"Any time. One last piece has to fall."

"What's that?"

"If he's moving black ice across the border in EnviroBreed shipments, then how is he getting it from the ranch to the bug house? See, we've been watching the ranch and would've seen it. And we're pretty sure it's not manufactured at EnviroBreed. Too small, too many people around, too close to the road, et cetera, et cetera. All our intelligence says it's made on the ranch. Underground, in a bunker. We got aerials that show the heat patterns from the ventilation. Anyway, the question is then, how's he get it across the street to EnviroBreed?"

Bosch thought about what Corvo had said at the Code 7. That Zorrillo was suspected of helping to finance the tunnel that went under the border at Nogales.

"He doesn't take it across the street. He takes it under."

"Exactly," Ramos said. "We are working our informants on it right now. We get it confirmed, we get our approval from the attorney general and we go in. We hit the ranch and EnviroBreed simultaneously. Joint operation. The AG sends the federal militia. We send CLET."

Bosch hated all the acronyms law enforcement agencies cling to but asked what CLET was anyway.

"Clandestine Laboratory Enforcement Team. These guys are fuckin' ninjas."

Bosch thought this information over. He didn't understand why it was happening so quickly. Ramos was leaving something out. There had to be new intelligence on Zorrillo.

"You've seen him, haven't you? Zorrillo. Or somebody has."

"You got it. And that other little white squirrel you came down looking for. Dance."

"Where? When?"

"We have a CI inside the fence who saw the both of them outside the main compound shooting at targets this morning. And then we—"

"How close was he? The informant."

"Close enough. Not close enough to say 'Howdy do, Mr. Pope' but close enough to make the ID."

Ramos cackled loudly and got up to get another beer. He threw a bottle to Bosch, who wasn't yet done with his first.

"Where had he been?" Bosch asked.

"Christ, who knows? Only thing I care about is that he is back and he is going to be there when the CLETs come through the door. And by the way, you better not bring that gun with you or the *federales* will hook you up, too. They are giving a special weapons privilege to the CLETs but that is it. The AG is going to sign it—God, I hope this guy never gets bought off or assassinated. Anyway, like I'm saying, if they want you to have a gun, they'll give you something from their own armory."

"And how am I going to know when it goes down?"

Ramos was still standing. He jerked his head back and poured down half the bottle of beer. His odor had totally filled the room. Bosch held his bottle up near his mouth and nose so he'd smell the beer instead of the DEA agent. "We'll let you know," Ramos said. "Take this and wait." He tossed Bosch one of the pagers off his belt.

"You put that on and I'll give you a buzz when we are ready to rock. It will be soon. At least before New Year's, I'm hoping. We gotta move on this. There is no telling how long the target is going to stay in place this time."

He finished the beer and put the bottle on the table. He didn't pick up another. The meeting was done.

"What about my partner?" Bosch asked.

"Who, the Mex? Forget it. He's state. You can't tell him about this, Bosch. The pope has the SJP and the other locals wired. It's a given. Don't trust anybody over there, don't tell anybody over there. Just wear the pager like I said and wait for the beep. Go to the bullfights. Hang by the pool or something. Hell, man, look at yourself. You could use the color."

"I know Aguila better than I know you."

"Did you know he works for a man who is a regular guest of Zorrillo's at the bullfights each Sunday?"

"No," Bosch said. He thought of Grena.

"Did you know that to become a detective in the SJP, the promotion is bought for an average of two thousand dollars, not based on any skill in investigative technique?"

"No."

"I know you didn't. But that's the way it is here. You've got to understand that. Trust no one. You may be working with the last honest cop in Mexicali, but why bet your life on it?"

Bosch nodded and said, "One more thing, I want to come in tomorrow and check your mug books. You have Zorrillo's people?"

"Most of them. What do you want?"

"I'm looking for a guy with three tattooed tears. He's Zorrillo's hit man. He hit another cop yesterday in L.A."

"Jesus! Okay, in the morning, call me at this number. We'll set it up. If you make an ID we'll get the word to the AG. It'll help us get the search approval."

He gave Bosch a card with a phone number on it, nothing else. Then he was gone. Harry put the chain back on the lock.

Twenty-Four

BOSCH SAT ON THE BED WITH HIS BEER, THINKING about the reappearance of Zorrillo. He wondered where he had been and why he had left the safety of his ranch in the first place. Harry poked at the idea that maybe Zorrillo had been in L.A. and that it had taken his presence there to lure Moore to the motel room where he was put down on the bathroom floor. Maybe Zorrillo was the only one Moore would have gone there for.

The sharp sound of squealing brakes and crashing metal shot through the window. Before he even got up he heard voices arguing in the street below. The words grew harsher until they were threats being yelled so fast Bosch could not understand them. He went to the window and saw two men standing chests out beside two cars. One had rear-ended the other.

As he turned away he detected a small flash of blue light to his left. Before he had time to look, the bottle in his hand shattered and beer and glass exploded in all directions. He instinctively took a step back and launched himself over the bed and down onto the floor. He braced himself for more shots but none came. His heartbeat rapidly increased and he felt the familiar rush of mental clarity that comes only in situations of life and death. He crawled along the floor to the table and pulled the lamp plug out of the wall, dropping the room in darkness. As he reached up to the table for his gun, he heard the two cars speeding away in the street. A beautiful setup, he thought, but they missed.

He moved beneath the window opening and then stood up while pressing his back to the wall. All the while he was realizing how stupid he had been to literally pose in the window. He looked through the opening into the darkness where he believed he had seen the muzzle flash. There was no one there. Several of the windows of the other rooms were open and it was impossible to pinpoint where the shot had come from. Bosch looked back into his room and saw the headboard of the bed splintered at the spot where the bullet had impacted. By imagining a line from the impact point through the position he had held the bottle and then out the window, he focused on an open, but dark window on the fifth floor of the other wing. He saw no movement there other than the curtain swaying gently with the breeze. Finally, he put his gun in his waistband and left the room, his clothes smelling of beer and with small slivers of glass imbedded in his shirt and pricking his skin. He knew he had at least two slight glass cuts. One on his neck and one on his right hand, which had been holding the bottle. He held his cut hand to his neck wound as he walked.

He had judged that the open window belonged to the fourth room on the fifth floor. He now had his gun out and pointed in front of him as he moved slowly down the fifth-floor hallway. He was debating whether he should kick the door open but found the decision academic. A cool breeze from the open window flowed out through the open door of room 504.

The room was dark and Bosch knew he would be silhouetted by the lighted hallway. So he hit the room's entrance-light switch as he moved quickly through the doorway. He covered the room with his Smith and found it empty. The smell of burned gunpowder hung in the air. Harry looked out the window and followed the imaginary line down to his own third-floor room's window. It had been an easy shot. It was then that he heard the screeching of tires and saw the taillights of a large sedan pull out of the hotel parking lot and then speed away.

Bosch put the gun in his waistband and pulled his shirt out over it. He looked quickly around the room to see if the shooter had left anything behind him. The glint of copper from the fold of the bedspread where it was tucked beneath the pillows caught his eye. He pulled the bedspread out straight and lying there was a shell casing that had been ejected from a thirty-two rifle. He got an envelope out of the desk drawer and scooped the shell inside it.

As he left room 504 and walked down the hallway, no one looked out a door, no house detectives came running and no approaching sirens blared in the distance. No one had heard a thing, except maybe a bottle breaking. Bosch knew that the thirty-two fired at him had had a silencer screwed to the end of its barrel. Whoever it had been, he had taken his time and waited for the one shot. But he had missed. Had that been intentional? He decided it wasn't, to make a shot that close but intend to miss was too chancy. He had simply been lucky. His turn from the window at the last moment had probably saved his life.

Bosch headed back to his room to dig the slug out of the wall, bandage his wounds and check out. Along the way he started running when he realized he had to warn Aguila.

Back in his room, he quickly dug through his wallet for the piece of paper on which Aguila had written his address and phone number. Aguila picked up almost immediately. *"Bueno."*

"It's Bosch. Someone just took a shot at me."

"Yes. Where? Are you injured?"

"I am okay. In my room. They shot through the window. I'm calling to warn you."

"Yes?"

"We were together today, Carlos. I don't know if it's just me or the both of us. Are you okay?"

"Yes, I am."

Bosch realized he didn't know if Aguila had a family or was alone. In fact, he realized, he knew the man's ancestry but little else.

"What will you do?" Aguila asked.

"I don't know. I'm leaving here..."

"Come here, then."

"Okay, yes...No. Can you come here? I won't be here but I want you to come and find out whatever you can about the person who rented room 504. That's where the shot came from. You can get the information easier than me."

"I am leaving now."

"We'll meet at your place. I have something to do first."

A moon like the smile of the Cheshire cat hung over the top of the ugly silhouette of the industrial park on Val Verde. It was ten o'clock. Bosch sat in his car in front of the Mexitec furniture factory. He was about two hundred yards from EnviroBreed and he was waiting for the last car to leave the bug plant. It was a maroon Lincoln that he suspected was Ely's. On the seat next to him was a bag containing the items he had bought earlier. The smell of the roasted pork was filling the car and he rolled down the window.

As he watched the EnviroBreed lot, he was still breathing hard and the adrenaline continued to course through his arteries like amphetamine. He was sweating, though the evening air was quite cool. He thought of Moore and Porter and the others. Not me, he thought. Not me.

At 10:15 he saw the door to EnviroBreed open and a man came out, accompanied by the blur of two black figures. Ely. Dogs. The dark shapes bobbed up and down at his waist as he walked. Ely then scattered something in the lot but the dogs stayed by his side. He then slapped his hip and yelled, "Chow!" and the dogs scattered and chased each other to varying points in the lot where they fought over whatever it was Ely had thrown.

Ely got in the Lincoln. After a few moments Bosch saw the taillights flare and the car backed away from its space at the front of the lot. Bosch watched as the headlights traced a circle in the lot and then led the car to the gate. The gate slowly rolled open and the car slipped through. Then the driver hesitated on the fringe of the roadway, though it was clear to pull out. He waited until the gate had trundled closed, the dogs safely inside the fenced compound, and then pulled away. Bosch slipped down in his seat, even though the Lincoln had headed the other way, north toward the border.

Bosch waited a few minutes and watched. Nothing moved anywhere. No cars. No people. He didn't expect there to be any DEA surveillance because they would pull back when planning a raid, so as not to tip their hand. He hoped they would, at least. He got out with the bag, his flashlight and his lock picks. Then he leaned back into the car and pulled out the rubber floor mats, which he rolled up and put under his arm.

Bosch's take on EnviroBreed's security measures, from when he had been there during the day, was that they were strictly aimed at deterring entry, not sounding an alert once security had been breached. Dogs and cameras, a twelve-foot fence topped with electrified razor wire. But inside the plant Bosch had seen no tape on the windows in Ely's office, no electric eyes, not even an alarm key pad inside the front door.

This was because an alarm brought police. The breeders wanted to keep people out of the bug plant, but not if it drew the attention of authorities. It didn't matter if those authorities could be easily corrupted and paid to look the other way. It was just good business not to involve them. So, no alarms. This, of course, did not mean an alert would not be sent somewhere else—such as the ranch across the street—if a break-in occurred. But that was the risk Bosch was taking.

Bosch cut down the side of the Mexitec factory to an alley that ran behind the buildings that fronted Val Verde. He walked to the rear of EnviroBreed and waited for the dogs.

They came around quickly but silently. They were sleek black Dobermans and they moved right up to the fence. One made a low, guttural sound and the other followed suit. Bosch walked along the fence line, looking up at the razor wire. The dogs walked along with him, saliva dripping from their lagging tongues. Bosch saw the pen they were caged in during the day in the back. There was a wheelbarrow leaning up against the rear wall of the building and nothing else.

Except the dogs. Bosch crouched to the ground in the alley and opened up the bag. First he took out and opened the plastic bottle of Sueño Mas. Then he opened the wrapped paper bundle of roast pork he had bought at the Chinese takeout near the hotel. The meat was almost cold now. He took a chunk about the size of a baby's fist and pressed three of the extra-strength sleeping pills into it. He squeezed it in his hand and then lofted it over the fence. The dogs raced to it and one took a position over it but did not touch it. Bosch repeated the process and threw another piece over. The other dog stood over it.

They sniffed at the pork and looked at Bosch, sniffed some more. They looked around to see if their master might be nearby to help with a decision. Finding no help, they looked at each other. One dog finally picked his chunk up in its teeth and then dropped it. They both looked at Bosch and he yelled "Chow!"

The dogs did nothing. Bosch yelled the command a few more times but nothing changed. Then he noticed they were watching his right hand. He understood. He slapped his hand on his hip and issued the command again. The dogs ate the pork.

Bosch quickly made two more drug-laden snacks and threw them over the fence. They were eaten quickly. Bosch started pacing alongside the fence in the alley. The dogs stayed with him. He went back and forth twice, hoping the exercise would hurry their digestion. Harry ignored them for a while and looked up at the spiral of thin steel that ran along the top of the fence. He studied the glint it gave off in the moonlight. He also saw the electrical circuits spaced every twelve feet along the top and thought he heard a soft buzzing sound. The wire would tear a climber up and fry him before he got one leg over. But he was going to try.

He had to duck behind a Dumpster in the alley when he saw lights and a car came slowly down the alley. When it got closer he saw that it was a police car. He froze with momentary fear of how he would explain himself. He realized he had left the rolled car mats in the alley by the fence. The car slowed even more as it went by the EnviroBreed fence. The driver made a kissing sound at the dogs who still stood by the fence. The car moved on and Bosch came out of hiding.

The Dobermans stood on their side of the fence watching him for nearly an hour before one dropped into a sitting position and the other quickly did the same. The leader then worked its front paws forward until it was lying down. The follower did likewise. Bosch watched as their heads, almost in unison, bowed and then dropped onto their outstretched front legs. He saw urine forming in a puddle next to one of them. Both dogs kept their eyes open. When he took the last chunk of pork out of the wrapper and tossed it over the fence, he saw one of the dogs strain to raise his head and follow the arc of the falling food. But then the head dropped back down. Neither dog went for the offering. Bosch laced his fingers in the fence in front of the dogs and shook it, the steel making a whining sound, but the animals paid little attention.

It was time. Bosch crumpled the grease-stained paper and threw it in the Dumpster. He took a pair of work gloves out of the bag and put them on. Then he unfurled the front floor mat and held it by one end in his left hand. He took a high grip on the fence with his right, raised his right foot as high as he could and pointed his shoe into one of the diamond-shaped openings in the fence. He took a deep breath and in one move pulled himself up the fence, using his left hand and arm to swing the rubber mat up and over the top, so that it hung down over the spiral of razor wire like a saddle. He repeated the maneuver with the rear mat. They hung there side by side, their weight pressing the spiral of razor wire down.

It took him less than a minute to get to the top and gingerly swing one leg over the saddle and then pull the other over. The electric buzz was louder on top and he carefully moved his hand grips until he was able to drop down next to the still forms of the dogs. He took the small penlight from his pick set and put it on the dogs. Their eyes were open and dilated, their breathing heavy. He stood a moment watching their bodies rise and fall on the same beat, then he moved the light around on the ground until he found the uneaten piece of pork. He threw it over the fence, down the alley. Then, gripping the dogs by the collars, he dragged their bodies into their pen and latched the gate. The dogs were no longer a threat.

Bosch ran quietly up the side of the building and looked around the corner to make sure the parking lot was still empty. Then he came back down the side to the window of Ely's office.

He studied the window, double-checking to be sure he was correct about there being no alarm. He ran the light along all four sides of the louvered window and saw no wires, no vibration tape, no sign of an alarm. He opened the blade on his knife and pried back one of the metal strips that held the bottom pane of glass in place. He carefully slid the pane out of the window and leaned it against the wall. He moved the light through the opening and swung its beam around inside. The room was empty. He saw Ely's desk and other furnishings. The panel of four video tubes was black. The cameras were off.

After taking five glass sections out of the window and stacking them neatly against the outside wall, there was enough room for him to hoist himself up and crawl into the office.

The top of the desk was clear of paperwork and other clutter. The glass paperweight took the beam from the penlight and shot prism colors around the room. Bosch tried the drawers of the desk but found them locked. He opened them with a hook pick but found nothing of interest. There was a ledger in one drawer but it seemed to pertain to incoming breeding supplies.

He directed the light into the wastebasket on the floor inside the desk well and saw several crumpled pieces of paper. He emptied the basket on the floor. He reopened each piece of trash and then recrumpled it and dropped it back into the basket as he determined it was meaningless.

But not all of it was trash. He found one piece of crumpled paper that had several scribbles on it, including one that said:

Colorado 504

What to do with this? he thought. The paper was evidence of the effort to kill Bosch. But Bosch had discovered it during an illegal search. It was worthless unless found later during a legitimate search. The question was, when would that be? If Bosch left the crumpled paper in the trash can, there was a good chance the can would be emptied and the evidence lost.

He crumpled the paper back up and then took a long piece of tape off the dispenser on the desk. He attached one piece to the paper ball, which he then put in the trash can, pressing the other end of the tape down on the bottom of the can. Now, he hoped, if the can was emptied the crumpled paper would remain attached and inside the can. And maybe the person who emptied the can wouldn't notice.

He moved out of the office into the hall. By the lab door he took goggles and a breathing mask off the hook and put them on. The door had a common three-pin lock and he picked it quickly.

The doorway opened into blackness. He waited a beat and then moved into it. There was a cloying, sickly sweet smell to the place. It was humid. He moved the flashlight beam around what looked like the shipping room. He heard a fly buzzing in his ear and another insect was nattering around his masked face. He waved them off and moved farther through the room.

At the other end of the room, he passed through a set of double doors and into a room where the humidity was oppressive. It was lit by red bulbs that were spaced above rows of fiberglass bug bins. The warm air surrounded him. He felt a squadron of flies bumping and buzzing around his mask and forehead. Again, he waved them away. He moved to one of the bins and put his light into it. There was a brownish-pink mass of insect larvae moving like a slow-motion sea under the light.

He then cast the light about the room and saw a rack containing several tools and a small, stationary cement mixer that he guessed was what the day laborers used to mix the food paste for the bugs. Several shovels, rakes and brooms hung on pegs in a row at the back of the room. There were pallets containing large bags of pulverized wheat and sugar, and smaller bags of yeast. The markings on the bags were all in Spanish. He guessed this could be called the kitchen.

He played the light over the tools and noticed that one of the shovels stood out because it had a new handle. The wood was clean and light, while all of the other tools had handles that had darkened over time with dirt and human sweat.

Looking at the new handle Bosch knew that Fernal Gutierrez-Llosa had been killed here, beaten so hard with a shovel that it broke or became so blood-stained it had to be replaced. What had he seen that required his death? What had the simple day laborer done? Bosch swung the light around again until it came upon another set of doors at the far side of the room. On these a sign said:

DANGER! RADIATION! KEEP OUT!
PELIGRO! RADIACION!

He used his picks once again to open the door. He flashed the light around and saw no other doors. This was the terminus of the building. It was the largest of the three rooms in the complex and was divided in two by a partition with a small window in it. A sign on the partition said in English only:

PROTECTION MUST BE WORN

Bosch stepped around the partition and saw that this space was largely taken up by a large boxlike machine. Attached was a conveyor belt that carried trays into one side of the machine and then out the other side, where the trays would be dumped into bins like the ones he saw in the other room. There were more warning signs on the machine. This was where the larvae were sterilized by radiation.

He moved around to the other side of the room and saw large steel worktables with cabinets overhead. These were not locked and inside he saw boxes of supplies: plastic gloves and the sausagelike casings the larvae were shipped in, batteries and heat sensors. This was the room where the larvae were packed into casings and placed in the environment boxes. The end of the line. There was nothing else here that seemed significant.

Bosch stepped backward toward the door. He turned the flash off and there was only the small red glow from the surveillance camera mounted in the corner near the ceiling. What have I missed, he asked himself. What is left?

He put the light back on and walked back around the partition to the radiation machine. All of the signs in the building were designed to keep people away from this spot. This would be where the secret was. He focused on the floor-to-ceiling stacks of the wide steel trays used for moving larvae. He put his shoulder against one of the stacks and began to slide it on the floor. Beneath was only concrete. He tried the next stack and looked down and saw the edge of a trapdoor.

The tunnel.

But at that moment it hit him. The red light on the surveillance camera. The video panel in Ely's office had been off. And earlier, when Bosch had visited, he had noticed that the only interior view Ely had on video was of the shipping room.

It meant someone else was watching this room. He looked at his watch, trying to estimate how long he had been in the room. Two minutes? Three minutes? If they were coming from the ranch, he had little time. He looked down at the outline of the door in the floor and then up at the red eye in the darkness.

But he couldn't take the chance that no one was watching. He quickly pushed the stack back over the door in the floor and moved out of the third room. He retraced his path through the complex, hooking the mask and goggles on the peg by Ely's office. Then he went through the office and out the window. He quickly put the glass panes back in place, bending the metal strips back with his fingers.

The dogs were still lying in the same spot, their bodies pumping with each breath. Bosch hesitated but then decided to drag them out in case the monitor at the end of the camera's cable line was not being watched and he hadn't been seen. He grabbed them by the collars and dragged them out of the pen. He heard one try to growl but it sounded more like a whine. The other did likewise.

He hit the fence on the run, climbed it quickly but then forced himself to go slow over the floor mats. When he was at the top he thought he heard the sound of an engine above the sound of the electric buzz. As he was about to drop over, he jerked the mats up off the razor wire and dropped down with them into the alley.

He checked his pockets to make sure he had not dropped the picks or flashlight. Or his keys. His gun was still in its holster. He had everything. There was the sound of a vehicle now, maybe more than one. He definitely had been seen. As he ran down the alley toward Mexitec, he heard someone shouting *"Pedro y Pablo! Pedro y Pablo!"* The dogs, he realized. Peter and Paul were the dogs.

He crawled into his car and sat crouched in the front seat watching EnviroBreed. There were two cars in the front lot and three men that he could see. They were holding guns and standing beneath the spotlight over the front door. Then a fourth man came around the corner, speaking in Spanish. He had found the dogs. Something about the man looked familiar but it was too dark and Bosch was too far away to be able to see any tattoo tears. They opened the door and, like cops with their guns up, they went inside the building. That was Bosch's cue. He started the Caprice and pulled out onto the road. As he sped away he realized he was once again shaking with the release of tension, the high of a good scare. Sweat was running down out of his hair and drying in the cool night air on his neck.

He lit a cigarette and threw the match out the window. He laughed nervously into the wind.

Twenty-Five

ON SUNDAY MORNING BOSCH CALLED THE NUMBER Ramos had given him from a pay phone at a restaurant called Casa de Mandarin in downtown Mexicali. He gave his name and number, hung up and lit a cigarette. Two minutes later the phone rang and it was Ramos.

"*Qué pasa, amigo?*"

"Nothing. I want to look at the mugs you got, remember?"

"Right. Right. Tell you what. I'll pick you up on my way in. Give me a half hour."

"I checked out."

"Leaving, are you?"

"No, I just checked out. I usually do that when somebody tries to kill me."

"What?"

"Somebody with a rifle, Ramos. I'll tell you about it. Anyway, I'm in the wind at the moment. You want to pick me up, I'm at the Mandarin in downtown."

"Half hour. I want to hear about this."

They hung up and Bosch went back to his table, where Aguila was still finishing breakfast. They had both ordered scrambled eggs with salsa and chopped cilantro, fried dumplings on the side. The food was very good and Bosch had eaten quickly. He always did after a sleepless night.

The night before, after he drove laughing from EnviroBreed, they had met at Aguila's small house near the airport and the Mexican detective reported on his findings at the hotel. The desk clerk could offer little description of the man who rented 504 other than to say he had three tears tattooed on his cheek below the left eye.

Aguila had not asked where Bosch had been, seeming to know that an answer would not be given. Instead, he offered Harry the couch in his sparsely furnished house. Harry accepted but didn't sleep. He just spent the night watching the window and thinking about things until bluish gray light pushed through the thin white curtains.

Much of the time Lucius Porter had been in his thoughts. He envisioned the detective's body on the cold steel table, naked and waxy, Teresa Corazón opening him up with the shears. He thought of the pinprick-sized blood hemorrhages she would find in the corneas of his eyes, the confirmation of strangulation. And he thought of the times he had been in the suite with Porter, watching others be cut up and the gutters on the table filling with their debris. Now it was Lucius on the table, a piece of wood under his neck, propping his head back into position for the bone saw. Just before dawn Harry's thoughts became confused with fatigue and in his mind he suddenly saw it was himself on the steel table, Teresa nearby, readying her equipment for the cut.

He had sat up then and reached for his cigarettes. And he made a vow to himself that it would never be himself on that table. Not that way.

"Drug enforcement?" Aguila asked as he pushed his plate away.

"Huh?"

Aguila nodded to the pager on his belt. He had just noticed it.

"Yeah. They wanted me to wear it."

Bosch believed he had to trust this man and that he had earned that trust. He didn't care what Ramos had said. Or Corvo. All his life Bosch had lived and worked in society's institutions. But he hoped he had escaped institutional thinking, that he made his own decisions. He would tell Aguila what was happening when the time was right.

"I'm going over there this morning, look at some mugs and stuff. Let's get together later."

Aguila agreed and said he would go to the Justice Plaza to complete paperwork on the confirmation of Fernal Gutierrez-Llosa's death. Bosch wanted to tell him about the shovel with the new handle he had seen in EnviroBreed but thought better of it. He planned to tell only one person about the break-in.

Bosch drank coffee and Aguila drank tea for a while without speaking. Bosch finally asked, "Have you ever seen Zorrillo? In person?"

"At a distance, yes."

"Where was that? The bullfights?"

"Yes, at the Plaza de los Toros. El Papa often attends to see his bulls. But he has a box in the shade reserved each week for him. I have afforded only seats on the sun side of the arena. This is the reason for the distance from which I have viewed him."

"He pulls for the bulls, huh?"

"Excuse me?"

"He goes to see his bulls win? Not the fighters?"

"No. He goes to see that his bulls die honorably."

Bosch wasn't sure what that meant but let it go.

"I want to go today. Can we get in? I want to sit in a box near the pope's."

"I don't know. These are expensive. Sometimes they cannot sell them. Even so, they keep them locked..."

"How much?"

"You would need at least two hundred dollars American, I'm afraid. It is very expensive."

Bosch took out his wallet and counted out $210. He left a ten on the table for the breakfast and pushed the rest across the faded green tablecloth to Aguila. It occurred to him it was more money than Aguila made in a six-day week on the job. He wished he had not been so quick to make a decision that would have taken Aguila hours of careful consideration.

"Get us a box near the pope."

"You must understand, there will be many men with him. He will be—"

"I just want a look at him, is all. Just get us the box."

They left the restaurant then and Aguila said he would walk to the Justice Plaza, a couple blocks away. After he left, Harry stood in front of the restaurant waiting for Ramos. He looked at his watch and saw it was eight o'clock. He was supposed to be in Irving's office at Parker Center. He wondered if the assistant chief had initiated disciplinary action against him yet. Bosch would probably be put on a desk as soon as he got back into town.

Unless...unless he brought back the whole package in his back pocket. That was the only way he would have any leverage with Irving. He knew he had to come out of Mexico with everything tied together.

It dawned on him that it was stupid to be standing like a target on the sidewalk in front of the restaurant. He stepped back inside and watched for Ramos through the front door. The waitress approached him and bowed effusively several times and walked away. It must've been the three-dollar tip, he thought.

It took Ramos nearly an hour to get there. Bosch decided he didn't want to be without a car so he told the agent he would follow him. They drove north on Lopez Mateos. At the circle around the statue of Juarez they went east, into a neighborhood of unmarked warehouses. They went down an alley and parked behind a building that had been tagged dozens of times with graffiti. Ramos looked furtively around after he got out of the beat-up Chevy Camaro with Mexican plates he was driving.

"Welcome to our humble federal office," he said.

Inside, it was Sunday morning quiet. No one else was there. Ramos put on the overhead lights and Bosch saw several rows of desks and file cabinets. Toward the back were two weapons-storage lockers and a two-ton Cincinnati safe for storing evidence.

"Okay, let me see what we got while you tell me about last night. You are sure somebody tried to do you, right?"

"Only way to be surer was if I got hit."

The Band-Aid Bosch had used on his neck was covered by his collar. There was another on his right palm, which also was not very noticeable.

Bosch told Ramos about the hotel shooting, leaving out no detail, including that he had recovered a shell from room 504.

"What about the slug? Recoverable?"

"I assume it's still in the headboard. I didn't hang around long enough to check."

"No, I bet you went running to warn your pal, the Mexican. Bosch, I am telling you to wise up. He may be a good guy but you don't know him. He mighta been the one that set the whole thing up."

"Actually, Ramos, I did warn him. But then I left and did what you wanted me to do."

"What're you talking about?"

"EnviroBreed. I went in last night."

"What? Are you crazy, Bosch? I didn't tell you to—"

"C'mon, man, don't fuck with me. You told me all that shit last night so I would know what was needed to get the search okayed. Don't bullshit me. We're alone here. I know that's what you wanted and I got it. Put me down as a CI."

Ramos was pacing in front of the file cabinets. He was making a good show of it.

"Look, Bosch, I have to clear any confidential informant I use with my supe. So that's not going to fly. I can't—"

"Make it fly."

"Bosch, I—"

"Do you want to know what I found there or should we just drop it?"

That quieted the DEA agent for a few moments.

"Do you have your ninjas, the—what did you call them, the clits, in town yet?"

"CLETs, Bosch. And, yeah, they came in last night."

"Good. You're going to have to get going. I was seen."

Bosch watched the agent's face grow dark. He shook his head and dropped down into a chair.

"Fuck! How do you know?"

"There was a camera. I didn't see it until it was too late. I got out of there but some people came looking. I wasn't identifiable. I was wearing a mask. But, still, they know somebody was inside."

"Okay, Bosch, you aren't leaving me many options. What did you see?"

There it was. Ramos was acknowledging the illegal search. He was sanctioning it. Bosch would not have it come back on him now. He told the agent about the trapdoor hidden beneath the stack of bug trays in the radiation room.

"You didn't open it?"

"Didn't have time. But I wouldn't have done it anyway. I worked tunnels in Vietnam. Every trapdoor was just that, a trap. The people that came after I got out of there came by car, not through the tunnel. That tells you right there that there might be a rig in the tunnel."

He then told Ramos that his application for a search warrant or approval or whatever they called them in Mexico should include requests to seize all tools and debris from trash cans.

"Why?"

"Because the stuff you will find will help me make one of the murder cases I came down here for. There is also evidence of a conspiracy to murder a law enforcement officer—me."

Ramos nodded and didn't ask for further explanation. He wasn't interested. He got up and went to a file cabinet and pulled out two large black binders.

Bosch sat down at an empty desk and Ramos put the binders down in front of him.

"These are KOs—known operatives—associated with Humberto Zorrillo. We have some bio info on some of them. Others, it's just surveillance stuff. We might not even have a name."

Bosch opened the first binder and looked at the picture on top. It was a fuzzy eight-by-ten blow-up of a surveillance shot. Ramos said it was Zorrillo and Bosch had guessed as much. Dark hair, beard, intense stare through dark eyes. Bosch had seen the face before. Younger, no beard, a smile instead of the long, empty gaze. It was the grown-up face of the boy who had been in the pictures with Calexico Moore.

"What do you know about him?" Bosch asked Ramos. "You know anything about his family?"

"None that we know of. Not that we looked real hard. We don't give a shit where he came from, just what he's doing now and where he's going."

Bosch turned the plastic page and began looking at the mugs and surveillance shots. Ramos went back to his desk, rolled a piece of paper into a typewriter and began typing.

"I'm working up a CI statement here. I'll get it by somehow."

About two-thirds through the first book Bosch found the man with three tears. There were several photos of him—mugs and surveillance—from all angles and over several years. Bosch saw his face change as the tears were added from a smiling wiseass to a hardened con. The brief biographical data said his name was Osvaldo Arpis Rafaelillo and that he was born in 1952. They said his three stays in the *penitenciaro* were for murder as a juvenile, murder as an adult and drug possession. He had spent half his life in prisons. The data described him as a lifelong associate of Zorrillo's.

"Here, I got him," Bosch said.

Ramos came over. He recognized the man also.

"You're saying he was up in L.A. whacking out cops?"

"Yeah. At least one. I think he might have done the job on the first one, too. I think he also took down a courier for the competition. A Hawaiian named Jimmy Kapps. He and one of the cops were strangled the same way."

"Mexican necktie, right?"

"Right."

"And the laborer? The one you think got it at the bug house?"

"He could've done them all. I don't know."

"This guy goes way back. Arpis. Yeah, he just got out of the *penta* a year or so ago. He's a stone-cold killer, Bosch. One of the pope's main men. An enforcer. In fact, people 'round here call him 'Alvin Karpis,' you know, after that killer with the machine gun in the thirties? The Ma Barker gang? Arpis was put away for a couple hits but they say that doesn't do him service. He's really down for more than you can count."

Bosch stared at the photos and said, "That's all you got on him? This stuff here?"

"There's more around someplace but that's all you have to know. Most of it is just he said/she said informant stuff. The main story about Al Karpis is that when Zorrillo first made his move to the top, this guy was a one-man front line doing the heavy stuff. Every time Zorrillo had a piece of work to do, he'd turn to his buddy Arpis from the barrio. He'd get the job done. And like I said, they only bagged him a couple times. He probably paid his way out of the rest."

Bosch began writing some of the information from the bio in a notebook. Ramos kept talking.

"Those two, they came from a barrio south of here. Some—"

"Saints and Sinners."

"Yeah, Saints and Sinners. Some of the local cops, the ones I trust about as far as I can throw 'em, said Arpis had a real taste for killing. In the barrio they had a saying. *Quien eres?* Means who are you? It was a challenge. It meant what side are you on, you know? Are you with us or against us? Saint or Sinner? And when Zorrillo rose to power, he had Arpis taking out the people that were against them. The locals said that after they whacked somebody, they'd spread the word around the barrio. *El descubrio quien era.* Means—"

"He found out who he was."

"Right. It was good PR, made the natives fall in behind him. Supposedly they really got into it. Got to the point they were leaving messages with the body. You know? They'd kill a guy and write out 'He found out who he was,' or whatever and leave it pinned to his shirt."

Bosch said nothing and wrote nothing. Another piece of the puzzle dropped into place.

"Sometimes you still see it on graffiti around the barrio," Ramos said. "It's part of the folklore surrounding Zorrillo. It's part of what makes him the pope."

Harry finally closed his notebook and stood up.

"I got what I need."

"All right. Be careful out there, Bosch. Nothing that says they won't try again, especially if Arpis is on the job. You just want to hang out here today? It's safe."

"Nah, I'll be okay." He nodded and took a step toward the door. He touched the pager on his belt. "I will get a call?"

"Yeah, you're in. Corvo's coming down for the show so I gotta make sure you're there. Where you gonna be later today?"

"I don't know. I think I'm going to make like a tourist. Go to the historical society, take in a bullfight."

"Just be cool. You'll get a call."

"I better."

He walked out to the Caprice thinking only about the note that had been found in Cal Moore's back pocket.

I found out who I was.

Twenty-Six

IT TOOK BOSCH THIRTY MINUTES TO GET ACROSS THE border. The line of cars extended nearly half a mile back from the drab brown Border Patrol port of entry. While waiting and measuring his progress in one or two car-length movements, he ran out of change and one-dollar bills as an army of peasants came to his window holding up their palms or selling cheap bric-a-brac and food. Many of them washed the windshield unbidden with their dirty rags and then held up their hands for coins. Each progressive washing smeared the glass more until Bosch had to put on the wipers and use the car's own spray. When he finally made it to the checkpoint, the BP inspector in mirrored shades just waved him through after seeing his badge. He said, "Hose up here on the right if you want to wash the shit off your windshield."

A few minutes later he pulled into one of the parking spaces in front of the Calexico Town Hall. Bosch parked and looked out across the park while smoking a cigarette. There were no troubadours today. The park was almost empty. He got out and headed toward the door marked Calexico Historical Society, not sure what he was looking for. He had the afternoon to spend and all he knew was that he believed there was a deeper line running through Cal Moore's death—from his decision to cross to the note in his back pocket to the photo of him with Zorrillo so many years ago. Bosch wanted to find out what happened to the house he had called a castle and the man he had posed with, the one with the hair white as a sheet.

The glass door was locked and Bosch saw that the society didn't open until one on Sundays. He looked at his watch and saw he still had fifteen minutes to wait. He cupped his hands to the glass and looked in and saw no one inside the tiny space that included two desks, a wall of books and a couple of glass display cases.

He stepped away from the door and thought about using the time to get something to eat. He decided it was too early. Instead, he walked down to the police station and got a Coke from the machine in the mini-lobby. He nodded at the officer behind the glass window. It wasn't Gruber today.

While he stood leaning against the front wall, drinking the soda and watching the park, Harry saw an old man with a latticework of thin white hair on the sides of his head unlock the door to the historical society. He was a few minutes early, but Bosch headed down the walk and followed him in.

"Open?" he said.

"Might as well be," the old man said. "I'm here. Anything in particular I can help you with?"

Bosch walked into the center of the room and explained he was unsure what he wanted.

"I'm sort of tracing the background of a friend and I believe his father was a historical figure. In Calexico, I mean. I want to find their house if it's still standing, find out what I can about the old man."

"What's this fellow's name?"

"I don't know. Actually, I just know his last name was Moore."

"Hell, boy, that name don't much narrow it down. Moore's one of the big names around here. Big family. Brothers, cousins all over the place. Tell you what, let me—"

"You have pictures? You know, books with photos of the Moores? I've seen pictures of the father. I could pick—"

"Yeah, that's what I'm saying, let me set you up here with a couple things. We'll find your Moore. I'm kinda curious now myself. What're you doing this for your friend for, anyway?"

"Trying to trace the family tree. Put it all together for him."

A few minutes later the old man had him sitting at the other desk with three books in front of him. They were leather-bound and smelled of dust. They were the size of yearbooks and they wove photographic and written history together on every page. Randomly opening one of the books, he looked at a black-and-white photo of the De Anza Hotel under construction.

Then he started them in order. The first was called *Calexico and Mexicali: Seventy-five Years on the Border* and as he scanned the words and photos on the pages, Bosch picked up a brief history of the two towns and the men who built them. The story was the same one Aguila had told him, but from the white man's perspective. The volume he read described the horrible poverty in Taipei, China, and told how the men facing it gladly came to Baja California to seek their fortunes. It didn't say anything about cheap labor.

In the 1920s and 1930s Calexico was a boomtown, a company town, with the Colorado River Land Company's managers the lords of all they surveyed. The book said many of these men built opulent homes and estates on bluffs rising on the outskirts of town. As Bosch read he repeatedly saw the names of three Moore brothers. Anderson, Cecil and Morgan. There were other Moores listed as well, but the brothers were always described in terms of importance and had high-level titles in the company.

While leafing through a chapter called "A Dirt Road Town Paves Its Streets in Gold," Bosch saw the man he was interested in. He was Cecil Moore. There, amidst the description of the riches the cotton brought to Calexico, was a photograph of a man with prematurely white hair standing in front of a Mediterranean-style home the size of a school. It was the man in the photo Moore had kept in the crumpled white bag. And rising like a steeple on the left-hand side of the home was a tower with two arched windows side by side at its uppermost point. The tower gave the house the appearance of a Spanish castle. It was Cal Moore's childhood home.

"This is the man and this is the place," Bosch said, taking the book over to the old man.

"Cecil Moore," the man said.

"Is he still around?"

"No, none of those brothers are. He was the last to go, though. Last year about this time, went in his sleep, Cecil did. I think you're mistaken though."

"Why's that?"

"Cecil had no children."

Bosch nodded.

"Maybe you're right. What about this place. That gone, too?"

"You're not working on any family tree, are you now?"

"No. I'm a cop. I came from L.A. I'm tracing down a story somebody told me about this man. Will you help me?"

The old man looked at him and Bosch regretted not being truthful with him in the first place.

"I don't know what it's got to do with Los Angeles but go ahead, what else you want to know?"

"Is this place with the tower still there?"

"Yes, Castillo de los Ojos is still there. Castle of the Eyes. Gets its name from those two windows up in the tower. When they were lit at night, it was said that they were eyes that looked out on all of Calexico."

"Where is it?"

"It's on a road called Coyote Trail west of town. You take 98 out there past Pinto Wash to an area called Crucifixion Thorn. Turn onto Anza Road—like the hotel here in town. That'll take you to Coyote Trail. The castle's at the end of the road. You can't miss it."

"Who lives there now?"

"I don't think anyone does. He left it to the city, you know. But the city couldn't handle the upkeep on a place like that. They sold it—I believe the man came down from Los Angeles, matter of fact. But as far as I know he never moved in. It's a pity. I was hoping to have maybe made a museum out of it."

Bosch thanked him and left to head out to Crucifixion Thorn. He had no idea whether Castillo de los Ojos was anything more than a dead rich man's estate with no bearing on his case. But he had nothing else going and his impulse was to keep moving forward.

State road 98 was a two-lane blacktop that stretched west from Calexico town proper, running alongside the border, into farmland delineated into a huge grid by irrigation ditches. As he drove, he smelled green pepper and cilantro. And he realized after running alongside a field planted in cotton that this wide expanse was all once the Company's huge acreage.

Ahead, the land rose into hills and he could see Calexico Moore's boyhood home long before he was near. Castillo de los Ojos. The two arched windows were dark and hollow eyes against the peach-colored stone face of the tower rising from a promontory on the horizon.

Bosch crossed a bridge over a dry bed that he assumed was Pinto Wash, though there was no sign on the road. Glancing down into the dusty bed as he passed, Harry saw a lime-green Chevy Blazer parked below. He caught just a glimpse of a man behind the wheel with binoculars held to his eyes. Border Patrol. The driver was using the bed's low spot as a blind from which he could watch the border for crossers.

The wash marked the end of the farmland. Almost immediately the earth began to rise into brown-brush hills. There was a turnout in the road by a stand of eucalyptus and oak trees that were still in the windless morning. This time there was a sign marking the location:

CRUCIFIXION THORN NATURAL AREA

DANGER ABANDONED MINES

Bosch remembered seeing a reference in the books at the historical society to the turn-of-the-century gold mines that pockmarked the border zone. Fortunes had been found and lost by speculators. The hills had been heavy with bandits. Then the Company came and brought order.

He lit a cigarette and studied the tower, which was much closer now and rose from behind a walled compound. The stillness of the scene and the tower windows, like soulless eyes, somehow seemed morbid. The tower was not alone on the hill, though. He could see the barrel-tile roofs of other homes. But something about the tower rising singularly above them with its empty glass eyes seemed lonely. Dead.

Anza Road came up in another half mile. He turned north and the single-lane road curved and bumped and rose along the circumference of the hill. To his right he could look down on the farmland basin extending below. He turned left onto a road marked Coyote Trail and was soon passing large haciendas on sprawling estates. He could see only the second floors of most of them because of the walls that surrounded almost every property.

Coyote Trail ended in a circle that went around an ancient oak tree with branches that would shade the turnaround in the summer. Castillo de los Ojos was here at the end of the road.

From the street, an eight-foot-high stone wall eclipsed all but the tower. Only through a black wrought-iron gate was there a fuller view. Bosch pulled onto the driveway and up to the gate. Heavy steel chain and lock kept it closed. He got out, looked through the bars and saw that the parking circle in front of the house was empty. The curtains inside every front window were pulled closed.

On the wall next to the gate were a mailbox and an intercom. He pushed the ringer but got no response. He wasn't sure what he would have said if someone had answered. He opened the mailbox and found that empty, too.

Bosch left his car where it was and walked back down Coyote Trail to the nearest house. This was one of the few without a wall.

But there was a white picket fence and an intercom at the gate. And this time when he rang the buzzer, he got a response.

"Yes?" a woman's voice asked.

"Yes, ma'am, police. I was wondering if I can ask a few questions about your neighbor's house."

"Which neighbor?"

The voice was very old.

"The castle."

"Nobody lives there. Mr. Moore died some time ago."

"I know that, ma'am. I was wondering if I could come in and talk to you a moment. I have identification."

There was a delay before he heard a curt "Very well" over the speaker and the gate lock buzzed.

The woman insisted that he hold his ID up to a small window set in the door. He saw her in there, white-haired and decrepit, straining to see it from a wheelchair. She finally opened up.

"Why do they send a Los Angeles police officer?"

"Ma'am, I'm working on a Los Angeles case. It involves a man who used to live in the castle. As a boy, long ago."

She looked up at him through squinting eyes, as if she was trying to see past a memory.

"Are you talking about Calexico Moore?"

"Yes. You knew him?"

"Is he hurt?"

Bosch hesitated, then said, "I'm afraid he's dead."

"Up there in Los Angeles?"

"Yes. He was a police officer. I think it had something to do with his life down here. That's why I came out here. I don't really know what to ask…He didn't live here long. But you remember him, yes?"

"He didn't live here long but that doesn't mean I never saw him again. Quite the contrary. I saw him regularly over the years. He'd ride his bicycle or he'd drive a car and come and sit out there on the road and just watch that place. One time I had Marta bring him out a sandwich and a lemonade."

He assumed Marta was the maid. These estates came with them.

"He'd just watch and remember, I guess," the old woman was saying. "Terrible thing that Cecil did to him. He's probably paying for it now, that Cecil."

"What do you mean, 'terrible'?"

"Sending the boy and his mother away like that. I don't think he ever spoke to that boy or the woman again after that. But I'd see the boy and I'd see him as a man, come out here to look at the place. People 'round here say that's why Cecil put that wall up. Did that twenty years ago. They say it's because he got tired of seeing Calexico in the street. That was Cecil's way of doing things. You don't like what you see out your window, you put up a wall. But I'd still see young Cal from time to time. One time I took a cold drink out to him myself. I wasn't in this chair then. He was sitting in a car, and I asked him, 'Why do you come out here all the time?' and he just said, 'Aunt Mary, I like to remember.' That's what he said."

"Aunt Mary?"

"Yes. I thought that was why you came here. My Anderson and Cecil were brothers, God rest their souls."

Bosch nodded and waited a respectful five seconds before speaking.

"The man at the museum in town said Cecil had no children."

"'Course he said that. Cecil kept it a secret from the public. Big secret. He didn't want the company name blemished."

"Calexico's mother was the maid?"

"Yes, she—it sounds like you know all of this already."

"Just a few parts. What happened? Why did he send her and the boy away?"

She hesitated before answering, as if to compose a story that was more than thirty years old.

"After she became pregnant, she lived there—he made her—and

she had the baby there. Afterward, four or five years, he discovered she had lied to him. One day he had some of his men follow her across when she went to Mexicali to visit her mother. There was no mother. Just a husband and another son, this one older than Calexico. That was when he sent them away. His own blood he sent away."

Bosch thought about this for a long moment. The woman was staring off at the past.

"When was the last time you saw Calexico?"

"Oh, let me see, must have been years now. He eventually stopped coming around."

"Do you think he knew of his father's death?"

"He wasn't at the funeral, not that I blame him."

"I was told Cecil Moore left the property to the city."

"Yes, he died alone and he left everything to the city, not a thing to Calexico or any of the ex-wives and mistresses. Cecil Moore was a mean man, even in death. Of course the city couldn't do anything with that place. Too big and expensive to keep up. Calexico isn't a boomtown like it once was and can't keep a place like that. There was a thought that it would be used as a historical museum. But you couldn't fill a closet with the history of this town. Never mind the museum. The city sold the place. I heard, for more than a million. Maybe they'll operate in the black for a few years."

"Who bought it?"

"I don't know. But they never moved in. They got a caretaker comes around. I saw lights on over there last week. But, nope, nobody's ever moved in as far as I know. It must be an investment. In what I don't know. We're sitting out here in the middle of nowhere."

"One last question. Was there ever anybody else with Moore when he would watch the place?"

"Always alone. That poor boy was always out there alone."

On the way back into town Bosch thought about Moore's lonely vigils outside the house of his father. He wondered if his longings were for the house and its memories or the father who had sent him away. Or both.

Bosch's mind touched his memory of his brief meeting with his own father. A sick old man on his death bed. Bosch had forgiven him for every second he had been robbed. He knew he had to or he would face the rest of his life wasting his pain on it.

Twenty-Seven

THE LINE OF TRAFFIC TO GO BACK INTO MEXICO WAS longer and slower than the day before. Bosch figured this was because of the bullfight, which drew people from the entire region. It was a Sunday evening tradition as popular here as Raiders football was in L.A.

Bosch was two cars from the Mexican border officer when he realized he still had the Smith in its holster on his back. It was too late to do anything about it. When he got to the man, he simply said, "Bullfight," and was waved on through.

The sky was clear over Mexicali and the air cool. It looked like it would be perfect weather. Harry felt the tingle of anticipation in his throat. It was for two things: seeing the ritual of the fight and maybe seeing Zorrillo, the man whose name and lore had surrounded his last three days so thoroughly that Bosch found himself buying into his myth. He just wanted to see the pope in his own element. With his bulls. With his people.

Bosch took a pair of surveillance binoculars out of the glove compartment after parking at the Justice Plaza. The arena was only three blocks away and he figured they'd walk. After showing ID to the front-desk officer and being approved to go back, he found Aguila sitting behind the lone desk in the investigators' squadroom. He had several handwritten reports in front of him.

"Did you get the tickets?"

"Yes, I have them. We have a box on the sun side. This will not be a problem because the boxes get little sun."

"Is it close to the pope?"

"Almost directly across—if he is there today."

"Yeah, if. We'll see. You done?"

"Yes, I have completed the reports on the Fernal Gutierrez-Llosa investigation. Until a suspect is charged."

"Which will probably never happen down here."

"This is correct. . . . I believe we should go now."

Bosch held up the binoculars.

"I'm ready."

"You will be so close you will not need those."

"These aren't for looking at bulls."

As they walked toward the arena they moved into a steady stream of people heading the same way. Many of them carried little square pillows on which they would sit in the arena. They passed several young children holding armfuls of pillows and selling them for a dollar each.

After entering the gate, Bosch and Aguila descended a set of concrete stairs to an underground level where Aguila presented their box tickets to an usher. They were then led through a catacomblike passageway that curved as it followed the circumference of the ring. There were small wooden doors marked with numbers on their left.

The usher opened a door with the number seven on it and they went into a room no larger than a jail cell. Its floor, walls and ceiling were all unpainted concrete. The vaulted ceiling sloped downward from the back to a six-foot-wide opening that looked out into the ring. They were directly on the outer ring where matadors, toreros and other players in the fights stood and waited. Bosch could smell the dirt ring, its horse and bull odors, its blood. There were six steel chairs folded and leaning against the rear wall. They opened two and sat down after Aguila thanked the usher and closed and locked the door.

"This is like a pillbox," Bosch said as he looked through the window slot into the boxes across the ring. He did not see Zorrillo.

"What is a pillbox?"

"Never mind," Bosch said, realizing he had never been in one, either. "It's like a jail cell."

"Perhaps," Aguila said.

Bosch realized he had insulted him. These were the best seats in the house.

"Carlos, this is great. We'll see everything from here."

It was also loud in the concrete box and in addition to the smells from the ring there was the pervasive odor of spilled beer. The little room seemed to reverberate with a thousand steps as the stadium above them filled. A band played from seats high up in the stadium. Bosch looked out into the ring and saw the toreros being introduced. He felt the growing excitement of the crowd and the echo in the room grew louder with the cheers as the matadors bowed.

"I can smoke in here, right?" Bosch asked.

"Yes," Aguila said as he stood. *"Cervesa?"*

"I like that Tecate if they have it."

"Of course. Lock the door. I will knock."

Aguila nodded and left the room. Harry locked the door and wondered if he was doing it to protect himself or simply to keep uninvited observers out of the box. He realized once he was alone that he did not feel protected in the fortresslike surroundings. It was not like a pillbox after all.

He held the binoculars up and viewed the openings into the other boxes across the ring. Most of these were still empty and he did not see anyone among those already in place who he believed was Zorrillo. But he noticed that many of these boxes were customized. He could see shelves of liquor bottles or tapestries on the back walls, padded chairs. These were the shaded boxes of the regulars. Soon Aguila knocked and Bosch let him in with the beers. And the spectacle began.

The first two fights were uneventful and uninspired. Aguila

called them sloppy. The matadors were heartily booed by those in the arena when their final sword thrusts into each bull's neck failed to kill and each fight became a prolonged, bloody display that had little resemblance to art or a test of bravery.

In the third fight, the arena came alive and the noise thundered in the box where Bosch and Aguila sat when a bull black as pitch—except for the whitish Z branded on its back—charged violently into the side of one of the picadors' horses. The tremendous power of the beast pushed the horse's padded skirt up to the rider's thigh. The horseman drove his iron-pointed lance down into the bull's back and leaned his weight on it. But this seemed only to enrage the beast further. The animal found new strength and made another violent lunge into the horse. The confrontation was only thirty feet from Bosch, but still he lifted the binoculars for a closer look. In what was like a slow-motion tableau captured in the scope of the binoculars' frame, he saw the horse rear against its master's rein and the picador topple off into the dust. The bull continued its charge, its horns impaling the padded skirt and the horse went over on top of the picador.

The crowd became even louder, cheering wildly, as the banderilleros flooded the ring, waving capes and drawing the bull's attention from the fallen horse and rider. Others helped the picador to his feet and he limped to the ring gate. He then shrugged their hands away, refusing any further help. His face was slick with sweat and red with embarrassment and the cheers of the arena had a jeering quality. With the binoculars, Bosch felt as though he was standing next to the man. A pillow came down from the stands and glanced off the man's shoulder. He did not look up, for to do that would be to invite more.

The bull had won this crowd and in a few minutes they respectfully cheered its death. A matador's sword deeply imbedded in its neck, the animal's front legs buckled and its huge weight collapsed. A torero, a man who was older than all the other players, quickly moved in with a short dagger and stabbed it into the base of the bull's skull. Instant death after the prolonged torment. Bosch watched the man wipe the blade on the dead animal's black coat and then walk away, replacing the dagger in a sheath strapped to his vest.

Three mules in harness were brought into the ring, a rope was looped around the black bull's horns and the body was dragged around in a circle and then out. Bosch saw a red rose fall from above and hit the dead beast as it made a flattened path in the ring's dirt floor.

Harry studied the man with the dagger. Applying the coup de grace seemed to be his only role in each fight. Bosch couldn't decide if his job was administering mercy or more cruelty. The man was older; his black hair was streaked with gray and his face had a worn, impassive look. He had soulless eyes in a face of worn brown stone. Bosch thought of the man with three tear drops on his face. Arpis. What look did he have when he choked the life out of Porter, when he held the shotgun up to Moore's face and pulled the trigger?

"The bull was very brave and beautiful," Aguila said. He had said little through the first three fights other than to pronounce the skills of the matadors as expert or sloppy, good or bad.

"I guess Zorrillo would have been very proud," Bosch said, "if he had been here."

It was true, Zorrillo had not come. Bosch had found himself checking the empty box Aguila had pointed out but it had remained empty. Now, with one fight to go, it seemed unlikely that the man who bred the bulls for this day's fights would arrive.

"Do you wish to leave, Harry?"

"No. I want to watch."

"Good, then. This match will be the finest and most artful. Silvestri is Mexicali's greatest matador. Another *cervesa*?"

"Yeah. I'll get this one. What do you—"

"No. It is my duty, a small means of repaying."

"Whatever," Bosch said.

"Lock the door."

He did. Then he looked at his ticket, on which the names of the bullfighters were printed. Cristobal Silvestri. Aguila had said he was the most artful and bravest fighter he had ever seen. A cheer went up from the crowd as the bull, another huge black monster, charged into the ring to confront his killers. The toreros began moving about him with green and blue capes opening like flowers. Bosch was struck by the ritual and pageantry of the bullfights, even the sloppy ones. It was not a sport, he was sure of this. But it was something. A test. A test of skills and, yes, bravery, resolve. He believed that if he had the opportunity he would want to go often to this arena to be a witness.

There was a knock on the door and Bosch got up to let Aguila in. But when he opened the door there were two men waiting. One he did not recognize. The other he did but it took him a few moments to place him. It was Grena, the captain of investigations. From what little he could see past their two figures, there was no sign of Aguila.

"Señor Bosch, may we come in?"

Bosch stepped back but only Grena entered. The other man turned his back as if to guard the doorway. Grena closed and locked it.

"So we won't be disturbed, yes?" he said as he scanned the room. He did this at length, as if it were the size of a basketball court and needed careful study in determining there was no one else present.

"It is my custom to come for the last fight, Señor Bosch. Particularly, you see, when Silvestri is in the ring. A great champion. I hope you will enjoy this."

Bosch nodded and casually looked out into the ring. The bull was still lively and moving about the ring while the toreros sidestepped and waited for it to slow. "Carlos Aguila? He has gone?"

"*Cervesa*. But you probably already know that, Captain. So why don't you tell me what's up?"

"What is 'up'? How do you mean?"

"I mean what do you want, Captain. What are you doing here?"

"Ah, *si*, you want to watch our little pageant and do not wish to be bothered by business. Get to the point, is the way it is said, I believe."

"Yeah, that works."

There was a cheer and both men looked out into the ring. Silvestri had entered and was stalking the bull. He wore a white-and-gold suit of lights and he walked in a regal manner, his back straight and his head canted downward, as he sternly studied his adversary. The bull was still game as it charged about the ring, whipping the blue and yellow banderillas stuck in its neck from side to side.

Bosch pulled his attention back to Grena. The police captain was wearing a black jacket of soft leather, its right cuff barely covering his Rolex.

"My point is I want to know what you are doing, Señor Bosch. You don't come down here for bullfights. So why are you here? I am told identification of Señor Gutierrez-Llosa has been made. Why do you stay? Why do you bother Carlos Aguila with your time?"

Bosch was not going to tell this man anything but he did not want to endanger Aguila. Bosch would be leaving eventually, but not Aguila.

"I am leaving in the morning. My work is completed."

"Then you should leave tonight, eh? An early start?"

"Maybe."

Grena nodded.

"You see, I have had an inquiry from a Lieutenant Pounds of the LAPD. He is very anxious at your return. He asked me to tell you this personally. Why is that?"

Bosch looked at him and shook his head.

"I don't know. You would have to ask him."

There was a long silence during which Grena's attention was drawn to the ring again. Bosch looked that way, too, just in time to see Silvestri leading the charging bull past him with his cape.

Grena looked at him for a long time and then smiled, probably the way Ted Bundy had smiled at the girls on campus.

"You know the art of the cape?"

Bosch didn't answer and the two just stared at each other. A thin smile continued to play across the captain's dark face. *"Et ante de la muleta,"* Grena finally said. "It is deception. It is the art of survival. The matador uses the cape to fool death, to make death go where he is not. But he must be brave. He must risk himself over the horns of death. The closer death comes, the braver he becomes. Never for a moment can he show fear. Never show fear. To do so is to lose. It is to die. This is the art, my friend."

He nodded and Bosch just stared at him.

Grena smiled broadly now and turned to the door. He opened it and the other man was still there. As he turned to reclose the door he looked at Bosch and said, "Have a good trip, Detective Harry Bosch. Tonight, eh?"

Bosch said nothing and the door was closed. He sat there for a moment but his attention was drawn by the cheers to the ring. Silvestri had dropped to one knee in the center of the ring and had lured the bull to a charge. He remained stoically fixed in position until the beast was on him. He then moved the cape away from his body in a smooth flow. The bull rushed by within inches and Silvestri was untouched. It was beautiful and the cheers rose from the stadium. The unlocked door to the box opened and Aguila stepped in.

"Grena, what did he want?"

Bosch didn't answer. He held the binoculars up and checked Zorrillo's box. The pope wasn't there but now Grena was, staring back at him with the same thin smile on his lips.

Silvestri felled the bull with a single thrust of his sword, the blade diving deep between its shoulders and slicing through the heart. Instant death. Bosch looked over at the man with the dagger and thought he saw a trace of disappointment on his hardened face. His work wasn't needed.

The cheering for Silvestri's expert kill was deafening. And it did not let up as the matador made a circuit around the ring, his arms up to receive the applause. Roses, pillows, women's high-heeled shoes showered down into the ring. The bullfighter beamed in the adulation. The noise was so loud that it was quite some time before Bosch realized that the pager on his belt was sounding its call to him.

Twenty-Eight

AT NINE O'CLOCK BOSCH AND AGUILA TURNED OFF Avenida Cristobal Colon onto a perimeter road that skirted Rodolfo Sanchez Taboada Aeropuerto Internacional. The roadway passed several old Quonset-hut hangars and then a larger grouping of newer structures. On one of these was a sign that said Aero Carga. The huge bay doors had been spread a few feet and the opening was lit from the inside. It was their destination, a DEA front. Bosch pulled into the lot in front and parked near several other cars. He noticed that most of them had California plates.

As soon as he stepped out of the Caprice he was approached by four DEA types in blue plastic windbreakers. He showed his ID and evidently passed muster after one of them consulted a clipboard.

"And you?" the clipboard man said to Aguila.

"He's with me," Bosch said.

"We have you down as a solo entry, Detective Bosch. Now we have a problem."

"I guess I forgot to RSVP that I'd bring a date," Bosch said.

"It's not very funny, Detective Bosch."

"Of course not. But he's my partner. He stays with me."

Clipboard had a distressed look on his face. He was an Anglo with a ruddy complexion and hair that had been bleached almost white by the sun. He looked as though he had been watching the border a long time. He turned to look back at the hangar, as if hoping for direction on how to handle this. On the back of his windbreaker Bosch saw the large yellow *DEA* letters.

"Better get Ramos," Bosch said. "If my partner goes, I go. Then where's the integrity of the operation's security?"

He looked over at Aguila, who was standing stiffly with the three other agents around him like bouncers ready to toss somebody out of a nightclub on the Sunset Strip.

"Think about it," Bosch continued. "Anybody who's come this far has to go the distance. Otherwise, you got someone outside the circle. Out there and unaccounted for. Go ask Ramos."

Clipboard hesitated again, then told everybody to stay cool and took a radio from the pocket of his jacket. He radioed to someone called Staff Leader that there was a problem in the lot. Then everybody stood around for a few moments in silence. Bosch looked over at Aguila and when their eyes met he winked. Then he saw Ramos and Corvo, the agent from L.A., walking briskly toward them.

"What's this shit, Bosch," Ramos started before he got to the car. "Do you know what you've done? You've compromised the whole fucking operation. I gave explicit instru—"

"He's my partner on this, Ramos. He knows what I know. We are together on this. If he's out, then so am I. And when we leave, I go across the border. To L.A. I don't know where he goes. How will that hold with your theory on who can be trusted?"

In the light from the hangar, Bosch could see the pulse beating in an artery on Ramos's neck.

"See," Bosch said, "if you let him leave, you are trusting him. So, if you trust him, you might as well let him stay."

"Fuck you, Bosch."

Corvo put his hand on Ramos's arm and stepped forward.

"Bosch, if he fucks up or this operation in any way becomes compromised, I will make it known. You know what I mean? It'll be known in L.A. that you brought this guy in."

He made a signal across the car to the others and they stepped away from Aguila. The moonlight reflected on Corvo's face and Bosch saw the scar that split his beard on the right side. He wondered how many times the DEA agent would be telling the story of the knife fight tonight.

"And another thing," Ramos threw in. "He goes in naked. We only have one more vest. That's for your ass, Bosch. So if he gets hit, it's on you."

"Right," Bosch said. "I get it. No matter what goes wrong, it's my ass. I got it. I also have a vest in my trunk. He can use yours. I like my own."

"Briefing's at twenty-two hundred," Ramos said as he walked back toward the hangar.

Corvo followed and Bosch and Aguila fell in behind him. The other agents brought up the rear. Inside the cavernous hangar Bosch saw there were three black helicopters sitting side by side in the bay area. There were several men, most in black jumpsuits, milling about and drinking coffee from white cups. Two of the helicopters were wide-bodied personnel transport craft. Bosch recognized them. They were UH-1Ns. Hueys. The distinctive whop-whop of their rotors would forever be the sound of Vietnam to him. The third craft was smaller and sleeker. It looked like a craft manufactured for commercial use, like a news or police chopper, but it had been converted into a gunship. Bosch recognized the gun turret mounted on the right side of the copter's body. Beneath the cockpit another mount held an array of equipment, including a spotlight and night-vision sensor. The men in the black jumpsuits were stripping the white numbers and letters off the tail sections of the craft. They were preparing for a total blackout, a night assault. Bosch noticed Corvo come up next to him.

"We call it the Lynx," he said, nodding to the smallest of the three craft. "Mostly use 'em in Central and South America ops, but we snagged this one on its way down. It's for night work. You've got total night vision set up—infrared, heat-pattern displays. It will be the in-air command post tonight."

Bosch just nodded. He was not as impressed with the hardware as Corvo was. The DEA supervisor seemed more animated than during their meeting at the Code 7. His dark eyes were darting around the hangar, taking it all in. Bosch realized that he probably missed fieldwork. He was stuck in L.A. while guys like Ramos got to play the war games.

"And that's where you're going to be, you and your partner," Corvo said, nodding at the Lynx. "With me. Nice and safe. Observers."

"You in charge of this show, or is Ramos?"

"I'm in charge."

"Hope so." Then, looking at the war chopper, Bosch said, "Tell me something, Corvo, we want Zorrillo alive, right?"

"That's right."

"Okay, then, when we get him, what's the plan? He's a Mexican citizen. You can't take him over the border. You just going to give him to the Mexicans? He'll be running the penitentiary they put him in within a month. That is, if they put him in a pen."

It was a problem every cop in southern California had come up against. Mexico refused to extradite its citizens to the United States for crimes committed there. But it would prosecute them at home. The problem was that it was well known that the country's biggest drug dealers turned penitentiary stays into hotel visits. Women, drugs, alcohol and other comforts could be had as long as the money was paid. One story was that a convicted drug lord had actually taken over the warden's office and residence at a prison in Juarez. He had paid the warden $100,000 for the privilege, about four times what the warden made in a year. Now the warden was an inmate at the prison.

"I know what you're saying," Corvo said. "But don't worry about it. We got a plan for that. Only things you have to worry about are your own ass and your partner's. You better watch him good. And you better get some coffee. It's going to be a long night."

Bosch rejoined Aguila, who was standing at the workbench where the coffee had been set up. They nodded at some of the agents who were milling about the bench but the gestures were rarely returned. They were the invited uninvited. From where they stood, they could see into a suite of offices off the aircraft bays. There were several Mexicans in green uniforms sitting at desks and tables, drinking coffee and waiting.

"Militia," Aguila said. "From Mexico City. Is there no one in Mexicali that the DEA trusts?"

"Well, after tonight, they'll trust you."

Bosch lit a cigarette to go with the coffee and took an expansive look around the hangar.

"What do you think?" he said to Aguila.

"I think the pope of Mexicali is going to have a wake-up call tonight."

"Looks that way."

They moved away from the coffee bench to let others have at it and leaned against a nearby counter to watch the raid equipment being prepared. Bosch looked over toward the back of the hangar and saw Ramos standing with a group of men wearing bulky black jumpsuits. Harry walked over and saw that the men were wearing Nomex fire retardant suits beneath the jumpsuits. Some of them were smearing bootblack around their eyes and then pulling on black ski masks. The CLET squad. They couldn't wait to get in the air, to get going. Bosch could almost smell their adrenaline.

There were twelve of them. They were reaching into black trunks and laying out the equipment they would need for the night's mission. Bosch saw Kevlar helmets and vests, sound-disorientation grenades. Holstered already on one man's hip was a 9mm P-226 with an extended magazine. That would just be for backup, he guessed. He could see the barrel of a long gun protruding from one of the trunks. Ramos noticed him then and reached into the trunk and brought the weapon over. There was a strange leer spreading on his face.

"Check this shit out," Ramos said. "Colt only makes 'em for

the DEA, man. The RO636. It's a suppressed version of the standard nine submachine. Uses one-forty-seven-grain subsonic hollow points. You know what one of them will do? It'll go through three bodies before it even thinks about slowing down.

"It's got a suppressed silencer. Means no muzzle flash. These guys are always jumping labs. You get ether fumes and the muzzle flash could set it off. Boom—you land about two blocks away. But not with these. No muzzle flash. It's beautiful. I wish I was going in with one of these tonight."

Ramos was holding and ogling the weapon like a mother with her first baby.

"You were in Vietnam, weren't you, Bosch?" Ramos asked.

Bosch just nodded.

"I could tell. Something about you. I always can tell." Ramos handed the gun back to its owner. There was still an odd smile on his face. "I was too young for Nam and too old for Iraq. Ain't that a pisser?"

The raid briefing did not start until nearly ten-thirty. Ramos and Corvo gathered all the agents, the militia officers and Bosch and Aguila in front of a large bulletin board on which a blowup of an aerial photo of Zorrillo's ranch had been tacked. Bosch could see that the ranch contained vast areas of open, unused land. The pope had found security in space. To the west of his property were the Cucapah Mountains, a natural boundary, while in the other directions he had created a buffer zone of thousands of acres of scrubland. Ramos and Corvo stood on either side of the bulletin board and Ramos conducted the meeting. By using a yardstick as a pointer he delineated the boundaries of the ranch and identified what he called the population center—a large, walled compound that included a hacienda, ranch house and adjoining bunker-type building. He then circled the breeding corrals and barn located about a mile from the population center along the perimeter of the ranch that fronted Val Verde

Highway. He also pointed out the EnviroBreed compound across the highway.

Next, Ramos tacked up another blowup, this one detailing about a quarter of the ranch—ranging from the population center to the breeding center/EnviroBreed compound area. This shot was close enough that tiny figures could be seen on the roofs of the bunker building. In the scrubland behind the buildings there were black figures against the light brown and green earth. The bulls. Bosch wondered which one of them was El Temblar. He could hear one of the militia officers translating the meeting for a group of the guardsmen gathered around him.

"Okay, these photos are about thirty hours old," Ramos said. "We had NASA do a fly-over in a U-thirty-four. We also had them shoot heat resonance strips and that's where this gets good. The reds you see are the hot spots."

He tacked a new blowup next to the other. This was a computer-generated graphic that had red squares—the buildings—against a sea of blues and greens. There were small dots of red outside the square and Bosch assumed these were the bulls.

"These photos were taken at the same second yesterday," Ramos said. "By jumping back and forth between the graphic and the live shot we can pinpoint certain anomalies. These squares become the buildings and most of these smaller red blotches become the bulls."

He used the yardstick to refer back and forth between the two blowups. Bosch realized that there were more red spots on the graphic than there were bulls on the photo.

"Now these marks do not correspond with animals on the photo," Ramos said. "What they do correspond with is the feed boxes."

With Corvo's help they pinned up two more enlargements. These were the closest shots so far. Bosch could clearly make out the tin roof of a small shed. There was a black steer standing near it. In the corresponding graphic, both the steer and the shed were bright red.

"These basically are little shelters to keep rain off the hay and feed for the livestock. NASA says these shelters would emit some residual heat that the resonance photos would pick up. But NASA said it clearly would not be what we are seeing here. So, what we think this means is that these feed boxes are decoys. We think they are exhaust vents for an underground complex. We believe there is some kind of entrance somewhere in the population center structures that leads to the underground lab back here."

He let it sink in for a few moments. Nobody asked any questions.

"Also," he said, "there is a—we have information from a confidential informant that there is a tunnel system. We believe it runs from the breeding center here to this complex—a business called EnviroBreed—here. We believe it has allowed Zorrillo to circumvent surveillance and is one of the possible means of moving product from the ranch to the border."

Ramos went on to detail the raid. The plan was to strike at midnight. The Mexican militia would have a two-part responsibility. A single unmarked car would be sent to the ranch gate, swerving as if driven by a drunk on the gravel road. Using this ruse, the three guardsmen in the car would take custody of the two gate sentries. After that, half of the remaining militia would move down the ranch road to the population center while the other half would advance to the EnviroBreed compound, surround it and await developments on the ranch.

"The success of the operation largely relies on the two men on the gate being taken before issuing a warning to the PC," Corvo said. His first words during the briefing. "If we fail that, we lose the element of surprise."

After the ground attack was underway, the three air squads would come. The two transport craft would put down on the north and east sides of the PC to drop the CLET team. The CLETs would perform initial entry to all structures. The third helicopter, the Lynx, would remain airborne and act as a flying command post.

Lastly, Ramos said, the ranch had two rovers, two-man Jeep patrols. Ramos said they followed no set patrol or pattern and they would be impossible to pinpoint until the raid began.

"They are the wild cards," Ramos said. "That is what we have a mobile air command for. They warn us when the Jeeps are spotted coming in or the Lynx will just take them out."

Ramos was pacing back and forth in front of the bulletin board, swinging the yardstick. Bosch could tell he liked this, the feeling of being in charge of something. Maybe it made up for Vietnam or Iraq.

"Okay, gentlemen, I've got a few more things here," Ramos said as he pinned another photo up. "Our target is the ranch. We have search warrants for drugs. If we find manufacturing apparatus we are gold. If we find narcotics we are gold. But the thing we really want is this man here."

The photo was a blowup from the mug book Bosch had looked at that morning.

"This is our main man," Ramos said. "Humberto Zorrillo. The pope of Mexicali. If we don't get him, this whole operation goes down the tubes. He's the mastermind. He's the one we want.

"It might interest you to know that in addition to his activities related to narcotics, he is a suspect in the killing of two L.A. cops, not to mention a couple other killings up there in the last month or so. This is a man who doesn't think twice about it. If he doesn't do it himself, he has plenty of people working for him who will. He's dangerous. Anybody we encounter on the ranch has to be considered armed and dangerous. Questions?"

One of the militia asked a question in Spanish.

"Good question," Ramos replied. "We are not going into Enviro-Breed initially because of two reasons. One, our prime target is the ranch and we would have to initially deploy more resources to EnviroBreed if we were to make simultaneous entry to the compound and the ranch. Secondly, our CI indicates the tunnel on that side may be rigged. Booby-trapped. We don't want to chance it. When we get the ranch secured, we'll go in then or we'll follow the tunnel over."

He waited for more questions. There was none. The men in front of him were shifting their weight from foot to foot or chewing their nails or flicking their thumbs on their knees. The adrenaline rush was just beginning to kick. Bosch had seen it before, in Vietnam and since. So he approached his own rising excitement with an uneasy sense of dread.

"All right then!" Ramos yelled. "I want everybody locked and loaded in one hour. At midnight we jam!"

The gathering broke up with some adolescent howls from the younger agents. Bosch moved toward Ramos as he was taking the photos off the board.

"Sounds like a plan, man."

"Yeah. Just hope it goes down close to the way we said it. They never go down exactly right."

"Right. Corvo told me you've got another plan. The one to get Zorrillo across the border."

"Yeah, we've got something cooked up."

"You gonna tell me?"

He turned around from the board, all the photos in a nice stack in his hands.

"Yeah, I'll tell you. You'll like this, Bosch, since it will get him up to L.A. to face trial on your guys. What's going to happen is that after the little fuck is captured he will resist arrest and injure himself. Probably facial injuries and they are going to look worse than they really are. But we will want to get him immediate medical attention. The DEA will offer the use of one of the helicopters. The commander of the militia unit will gratefully accept. But, you see, the pilot will become confused and mistake the lights of Imperial County Memorial Hospital on the other side of the border with the Mexicali General Clinic, which is just on this side of the border. When the chopper lands at the wrong hospital and Zorrillo gets off on the wrong side of the border, he will be subject to arrest and the American justice system. Tough break for him. We might have to put a notice of reprimand in the pilot's personnel file."

Ramos had that leering smile on his face again. He winked at Bosch and then walked away.

Twenty-Nine

THE LYNX WAS CROSSING OVER THE CARPET OF MEXI-cali's lights, heading southwest toward the dark shape of the Cuca-pah Mountains. The ride was smoother and quieter than anything he remembered from Vietnam or his dreams after.

Bosch was in the rear compartment huddled next to the left window. The cold night air was somehow getting in through a vent somewhere. Aguila was on the seat next to him. And in the forward compartment were Corvo and the pilot. Corvo was Air Leader, handling communications and directions on the ranch assault. Ramos was Ground One, in charge on the surface. Looking into the forward compartment, Bosch could see the dim reflection of the cockpit's green dials on the visor of Corvo's helmet.

The helmets of all four of the men in the chopper were connected through electronic umbilical cords to a center console port. The helmets had air-to-ground and on-board radio two-way and night-vision capabilities.

After they had flown for fifteen minutes the lights through the windows became fewer. Without the glare of the brightness from below, Harry could make out the silhouette of one of the other helicopters about two hundred yards to the left side. The other black ship would be on the right side. They were flying in formation.

"ETA two minutes," a voice said in his ear. The pilot.

Bosch took the Kevlar vest he held in his lap and slipped it underneath him, onto the seat. A protection against ground fire. He saw Aguila do the same thing with the DEA loaner.

The Lynx began a sharp descent and the voice in his ears said, "Here we go." Bosch snapped the night-vision apparatus down and looked into the lenses. The earth moved quickly below, a yellow river of scrub brush and little else. They passed over a road and then a turnoff. The helicopter banked in the direction of the turn. He saw a car, a pickup truck and a Jeep stopped on the road and then several other vehicles moving on the dirt road, yellow clouds of dust billowing behind them. The militia was in and speeding toward the population center. The battle had been engaged.

"Looks like our friends have already taken care of one of the patrol Jeeps," Corvo's voice said in Bosch's earpiece.

"That's a ten-four," came a returning voice, apparently from one of the other choppers.

The Lynx overtook the militia vehicles. Bosch was staring at open road in the night-vision scope. The craft's descent continued and then leveled off at what Bosch estimated was an elevation of about three hundred yards. In the yellow vision field he could now see the hacienda and the front of the bunker. He saw the other two helicopters, looking like black dragonflies, set down on their assigned sides of the house. Then he felt the Lynx pull up slightly as if hovering on an air pocket.

"One down!" a voice shouted in the headset.

"Two down!" came another.

Men in black began spilling from the side doors of the landed craft. One group of six went immediately to the front of the hacienda. The six-man group from the other helicopter moved toward the bunker building. Militia cars now began pulling into the field of view. Bosch saw more figures leap from the helicopters. That would be Ramos and the backup.

It all appeared surrealistic in the scope to Bosch. The yellow tint. The tiny figures. It seemed like a badly filmed and edited movie.

"Switching to ground com," Corvo said.

Bosch heard the click as the frequencies were switched. Almost immediately he began to pick up radio chatter and the heavy breathing of men running. Then there was a loud banging sound, but Bosch could tell it was not weapon fire. It was the ram used to open the door. Over the air there were now panicked shouts of "*Policia!* DEA!" Corvo's voice cut through a momentary lull in the shouting.

"Ground One, talk to me. What have we got? Let's talk to the mothership."

There was some static and then Ramos's voice came back.

"We have entry at Point A. We have—I'm going—"

Ramos was cut off. Point A was the hacienda. The plan had been to hit the hacienda and the bunker, Point B, at once.

"Ground Two, do we have entry yet at Point B?" Corvo asked.

No answer. It was a few long moments of silence and then Ramos came back up on the air.

"Air Leader, can't tell on Ground Two at this time. Target team has approached entry point and we—"

Before the transmission was cut off Bosch heard the unmistakable sound of automatic gunfire. He felt adrenaline begin to flood his body. Yet he could do nothing but sit and listen to the dead radio air and watch the murky yellow night vision display. He saw what he believed were muzzle flashes from the front of the bunker. Then Ramos came back up on the air.

"We're hot! We're hot!"

The helicopter lurched as the pilot took them up higher. As the craft rose, the night scope offered a larger view of the scene below. The entire PC became visible. Now Bosch could see figures on the roof of the bunker, moving toward the front of the structure. He pushed the switch on the side of his helmet and said into the mouthpiece, "Corvo, they've got people on the roof. Warn them."

"Stay off!" Corvo shouted. Then to below, he radioed, "Ground Two, Ground Two, you have weapons on the roof of the bunker. Count two positions approaching northside, copy?"

Bosch could hear no shooting over the sound of the rotor but he

could see the muzzle flash from automatic weapons from two locations at the front of the bunker. He saw sporadic flashes from the
vehicles but the militia was pinned down. He heard a radio transmission open and heard the sound of fire but then it was closed and
no one had spoken.

"Ground Two, copy?" Corvo said into the void. There was just
the initial strain of panic in his voice. There was no reply. "Ground
Two, do you copy?"

A hard-breathing voice came back. "Ground Two. Yeah. We're
pinned down in the Point B entry. We're in a crossfire here. Would
like some help."

"Ground One, report," Corvo barked.

There was a long moment of silence. Then Ramos came on the
air. His words were partially obscured by gunfire. "Here. We've...
the house...have three suspects down. No others present. Looks
like they're...fucking bunker."

"Get to the bunker. Two needs backup."

"—that way."

Bosch noticed how the voices on the radio were higher and more
urgent. The code words and formal language had been stripped
away. Fear did that. He had seen it in the war. He'd seen it on the
streets when he was in uniform. Fear, though always unspoken,
nevertheless stripped men of their carefully orchestrated poses. The
adrenaline roars and the throat gurgles with fear like a backed-up
drain. Sheer desire for survival takes over. It sharpens the mind,
pares away all the bullshit. A once-modulated reference to Point B
becomes the almost hysterical expletive.

From four hundred yards up and looking down through the
night scope, Bosch could also see the flaw in the plan. The DEA
agents had hoped to outrun the militia in their helicopters, charge
the population center and secure things before the ground troops
arrived. But that hadn't happened. The militia was there and now
one of the CLET groups was pinned down between the militia and
the people in the bunker.

There was a sudden increase in the shooting from the bunker. Bosch could tell this by the flaring of repeated muzzle flashes. Then on the scope he saw a Jeep suddenly begin speeding from the back of the bunker. It smashed through a gate in the wall that surrounded the compound and began moving across the scrubland in a southeasterly direction. Bosch pushed his transmit button again.

"Corvo, we have a runner. Jeep heading southeast."

"Have to let him go for now. It's going to shit down there and I can't move anybody. Stay off the fucking line."

The Jeep was now well out of the scope's field of vision. He flipped the lenses up off his face and looked out the window. There was nothing. Only darkness. The Jeep was running without lights. He thought of the barn and stables out near the highway. That was where the runner was going.

"Ramos," Corvo said over the radio. "Do you want lights?"

No return.

"Ground One? . . . Ground Two, do you want lights?"

". . . ights would be good but you'd be a sit . . . ," the Ground Two voice said. "Better hold it a few until we . . . eaned up."

"That's a copy. Ramos are you copying?"

There was no answer.

The shooting ended quickly after that. The pope's guardians put down their weapons after apparently determining that their odds of survival in a prolonged firefight were not good.

"Air Leader, give us that light now," Ramos radioed from below, the tone of his voice back to being calmly modulated and confident.

Three powerful beams from the belly of the Lynx then illuminated the ground below. Men with hands laced together on the tops of their heads were walking out of the bunker and into the hands of the militia. There were at least a dozen. Bosch saw one of the CLETs drag a body out of the bunker and leave it on the ground outside.

"We're secure down here," Ramos radioed.

Corvo signaled with his thumb to the pilot and the craft began to descend. Bosch felt tension drift out of him as they went down.

In thirty seconds they were on the ground next to one of the other helicopters.

In the yard in front of the bunker, the prisoners were kneeling while some of the militia officers used plastic disposable handcuffs to bind their wrists. Others were making a stack of confiscated weapons. There were a couple of Uzis and AK-47s but mostly shotguns and M-16s. Ramos was standing with the militia captain, who had his radio to his ear.

Bosch did not see a recognizable face among the prisoners. He left Aguila and went to Ramos.

"Where's Zorrillo?"

Ramos held up his hand in a do-not-disturb gesture and didn't answer. He was looking at the captain. Corvo walked up then, too. There was a report over the captain's radio and then he looked at Ramos and said, "Nada."

"Okay, nothing's happening at EnviroBreed," Ramos said. "Nobody in or out since this went down here. The militia is maintaining a watch over there."

Ramos saw Corvo and in a lower voice, meant just for him, said, "We've got a problem. We've lost one."

"Yeah, we saw him," Bosch said. "He was in the Jeep and headed southeast out of—"

He stopped when he realized what Ramos had meant.

"Who'd we lose?" Corvo asked.

"Kirth, one of the CLETs. But that's not the whole problem."

Bosch stepped back from the two men. He knew he had no place in this.

"What the fuck do you mean?" Corvo said.

"Come on, I'll show you."

The two agents headed off around the hacienda. Bosch trailed at a discreet distance behind. A covered porch ran the length of the rear of the house. Ramos crossed it to an open door. A CLET agent, his mask pulled up to expose his blood- and sweat-streaked face, was on the floor three feet inside the door. It looked to Bosch like four rounds: two in the upper chest, just above the vest, and two in the neck. A nice tight pattern, all of them through-and-through wounds. Blood was still leaking out from beneath the body into a pool. The dead agent's eyes and mouth were open. He had died quickly.

Bosch could see the problem. It was friendly fire. Kirth had been hit with fire from one of the 636s. The wounds were too big, too devastating and bunched too close together to have come from the weapons stacked near the prisoners.

"Looks like he came running out this back door when he heard the shooting," Ramos was saying. "Ground Two was already in a crossfire. Someone from Two's unit must have opened on the door, hit Kirth here."

"God damn it!" Corvo yelled. Then in a lower voice, he said, "All right, come over here, Ramos."

They huddled together and this time Bosch could not hear what was said but didn't have to. He knew what they would do. Careers were at stake here.

"Got it," Ramos said, returning to a normal voice and breaking away from Corvo.

"Good," Corvo said. "When you are done with that, I want you to get to a secure line and call L.A. Operations. We are going to need Public Info Officers down here and up there to work on this ASAP. The media is going to be crawling all over this. From all over."

"You got it."

Corvo started to go into the house but came back.

"Another thing, keep the Mexicans away from this."

He meant the militia. Ramos nodded and then Corvo stalked off. Ramos looked over at Bosch standing in the shadows of the porch. A silent acknowledgement passed between them. Bosch knew that the media would be told that Kirth had been fatally wounded by Zorrillo's men. Nobody would say anything about friendly fire.

"You got a problem?" Ramos said.

"I don't have a problem with anything."

"Good. Then I'm not going to have to worry about you. Right, Bosch?"

Bosch stepped to the door.

"Ramos, where's Zorrillo?"

"We're still searching. Still a lot of space in these buildings to cover. All I can tell you is we've cleared the hacienda and he isn't here. Only three inside are dead and he ain't one of them. So no one's talking. But your cop killer's in there, Bosch. The man with the tears."

Bosch silently stepped around Ramos and the body and into the hacienda. He was careful not to step into the blood. As he passed, he looked down into the dead man's eyes. They were already filming and looked like chips of dirty ice.

He followed a hallway to the front of the house, where he heard voices from a doorway at the bottom of the stairs in the front entry. As he approached he could see the room beyond was an office. There was a large polished wood desk, its center drawer open. Behind the desk was a wall of bookshelves.

Inside the room were Corvo and one of the CLET agents. And two bodies. One was on the floor next to an overturned couch. The other was in a chair near the room's only window, off to the right of the desk.

"C'mon in here, Bosch," Corvo said. "We can probably use your expertise here."

The body in the chair held Bosch's attention. The man's expensive black leather jacket was open, revealing a gun still holstered on the belt. It was Grena, though this was not easy at first to tell because a bullet fired into the police captain's right temple had obliterated much of the face when it exited beneath the left eye. Blood had flowed down both shoulders and ruined the jacket.

Bosch pulled his eyes away and looked at the man on the floor.

One leg was over the back of the couch, which had been knocked backwards. He had at least five holes in his chest that Bosch could make out in the blood. The three teardrops tattooed on the cheek were also unmistakable. Arpis. The man he had seen at Poe's. There was a chrome-plated forty-five on the floor next to his right leg.

"That your man?" Corvo asked.

"One of 'em, yeah."

"Good. Don't have to worry about him, then."

"The other one is SJP. He's a captain named Grena."

"Yeah, I just pulled the ID out of his pocket. He also had six grand in his wallet. Not bad, since SJP captains make about three hundred bucks a week. Take a look over here."

He moved to the other side of the desk. Bosch followed and saw that the rug had been folded back, exposing a floor safe about the size of a hotel refrigerator. Its thick steel door was propped open and the interior was empty.

"This is how it was found when the CLETs came in. What do you think? These stiffs don't look too old. I think we got here just a little late for the show, huh?"

Bosch studied the scene for a few moments.

"Hard to say. Looks like the end of a business deal. Maybe Grena got greedy. Asked for more than he deserved. Maybe he was making some kind of play with Zorrillo, some kind of scam, and it went to shit. I saw him a few hours ago at the bullfight."

"Yeah, what did he say? That he was heading over to the pope's for a shot?"

Corvo didn't laugh and neither did Bosch.

"No, he just told me to get out of town."

"So, who shot him?"

"Looks like a forty-five to me. Just guessing. That would make Arpis over here a likely candidate."

"Then who shot Arpis?"

"Got me. But if I was guessing, it looks like Zorrillo or whoever was behind the desk pulls a gun out of the drawer there and starts popping him right here in front of the desk. He goes backwards and over the couch."

"Why would he shoot him?"

"I don't know. Maybe Zorrillo didn't like what he did to Grena. Maybe Zorrillo was starting to get scared of him. Maybe Arpis made the same play Grena did. Could've been a lot of things. We'll never know. I thought Ramos said it was three bodies."

"Across the hall."

Bosch crossed the hall into a long and wide living room. It had deep-pile, white shag carpet and a white piano. There was a painting of Elvis on the wall above a white leather couch. The rug was stained with blood from the third man, who was lying in front of the couch. It was Dance. Bosch recognized him from the mug shot even with the bullet wound in his forehead and the blond hair now dyed black. The practiced sulk had been replaced on his face with a look of wonder. His eyes were open and almost seemed to be looking up at the hole in his forehead.

Corvo walked in behind him.

"What do you think?"

"I think it looks like the pope had to get out of here in a hurry. And he didn't want to leave these three behind to talk about it.... Shit, I don't know, Corvo."

Corvo raised the hand-held radio to his mouth.

"Search teams," he said. "Status."

"Search Leader here. We've got the underground lab. Entrance is through the bunker structure. It's major. We have product sitting in the drying pans. Multiweight. We're home. We're gold."

"What about the priority suspect?"

"Negative at this time. No suspects in the lab."

"Shit," Corvo said after signing off. He rubbed the edge of the Motorola against the scar on his cheek as he thought about what to do next.

"The Jeep," Bosch said. "We have to go after it."

"If he's heading to EnviroBreed, the militia is there waiting. At the moment, I can't cut people loose to go running around the ranch. It's six thousand fucking acres."

"I'll go."

"Wait a minute, Bosch. This is not your action."

"Fuck it, Corvo. I'm going."

Thirty

BOSCH CAME OUT OF THE HOUSE LOOKING IN THE dim light for Aguila and finally saw him standing near the prisoners and the militia. Bosch realized he probably felt more like an outsider here than Harry did himself.

"I am going after the Jeep we saw. I think it was Zorrillo."

"I am ready," the Mexican said.

Before they could move Corvo came running up. But it was not to stop them.

"Bosch, I've got Ramos in the chopper. It's all I can spare."

The silence that followed was punctuated by the sound from the other side of the hacienda of the helicopter's rotor beginning to turn.

"Go!" Corvo yelled. "Or he'll go without you."

They ran around the building and climbed back into their spots in the Lynx. Ramos was in the cockpit with the pilot. The craft abruptly lifted off and Bosch forgot about the seat belt. He was too busy putting on his helmet and night-vision equipment.

There was nothing in the scope yet. No Jeep. No runner. They were heading southwest from the ranch's population center. As he watched the yellow land go by in the night-vision lenses, Harry realized he still hadn't informed Aguila of his captain's demise. When we are done here, he decided.

In two minutes they came upon the Jeep. It was parked in a copse of eucalyptus trees and tall brush. A tumbleweed as big as a truck had blown up against it or been put up against it as a meager disguise. The vehicle was about fifty yards from the corrals and barn. The pilot put on the spots and the Lynx began circling. There was no sign of the driver, the runner, Zorrillo. Looking between the front seats, Bosch saw Ramos give the pilot the thumbs down sign and the craft began its descent. The lights were cut off and until Harry's eyes adjusted, it felt like they were dropping through the depths of a black hole.

He finally felt the impact of the ground and his muscles relaxed slightly. He heard the engine cut and there was just the chirping and whupping sound of the free-turning rotor winding down. Through the window Bosch could see the western side of the barn. There were no doors or windows on this exposure and he was thinking that they could approach with reasonable cover when he heard Ramos yell.

"What the—hold on!"

There was a hard impact and the helicopter lurched violently and began sliding. Bosch looked out his window and could only see that they were being pushed sideways. The Jeep. Someone had been hidden in the Jeep. The Lynx's landing rails finally caught on something in the earth and the craft tipped over. Bosch covered his face and ducked when he saw the still spinning rotor start biting into the ground and splintering. Then he felt Aguila's weight crash down on him and heard yelling in the cockpit that he could not decipher.

The helicopter rocked in this position for only a few seconds before there was another loud impact, this time from the front. Bosch heard tearing metal and shattering glass and gunfire.

Then it was gone. Bosch could feel the vibration in the ground dissipating as the Jeep sped away.

"I think I got him!" Ramos yelled. "Did you see that?"

All Bosch could think of was their vulnerability. The next hit would probably be from behind where they could not see to shoot.

He tried to reach his Smith but his arms were trapped under Aguila. The Mexican detective finally began to crawl off him and they both tentatively moved into crouches in the now sideways compartment. Bosch reached up and tried the door, which was now above them. It slid about halfway open before catching on something, a torn piece of metal. They took off their helmets and Bosch went out first. Then Aguila handed him the bullet-proof vests. Bosch didn't know why but took them. Aguila followed him out.

The smell of fuel was in the air. They moved to the crushed front of the helicopter where Ramos, gun in one hand, was trying to slide through the hole where the front window used to be.

"Help him," Bosch said. "I'll cover."

He pulled his gun and turned in a full circle but saw no one. Then he saw the Jeep, parked where he had seen it from the air, the tumbleweed still pressed against it. This made no sense to Bosch. Unless—

"The pilot is trapped," Aguila said.

Harry looked into the cockpit. Ramos was shining a flashlight on the pilot, whose blonde mustache was inked with blood. There was a deep slash on the bridge of his nose. His eyes were wide and Bosch could see the flight control apparatus was crushed in on his legs.

"Where's the radio?" Bosch said. "We've got to get help out here."

Ramos stuck his upper body back through the cockpit window and came back out with the hand-held radio.

"Corvo, Corvo, come up, we've got an emergency here." While waiting for a response, Ramos said to Bosch, "Do you believe this shit? That fucking monster comes outta nowhere. I didn't know what the—"

"What's happening?" Corvo's voice came back on the radio.

"We've got a situation here. We need a medevac out here. Tools. The Lynx is wrecked. Corcoran is pinned inside. Has injuries."

"—cation of the crash?"

"It's not a crash, man. A goddamn bull attacked it on the ground.

It's wrecked and we can't get Corcoran out. Our location is one hundred yards northeast of the breeding center, the barn."

"Stay there. Help's on the way."

Ramos clipped the radio to his belt, held the flashlight under his arm and reloaded his handgun.

"Let's each take a side of a triangle, the chopper in the middle and watch for this thing. I know I hit it but it didn't show a thing."

"No," Bosch said. "Ramos, you and Aguila take sides of it and wait for help. I'm going to clear the barn. Zorrillo's getting—"

"No, no, no, we don't do it like that, Bosch. You aren't calling any of the shots here. We wait here and when help—"

He stopped in midsentence and made a full turn. Then Bosch realized he heard it, too. Or, rather, felt it. A rhythmic vibration in the ground, growing stronger. It was impossible to place the direction. He watched Ramos turn in circles with the flashlight. He heard Aguila say, "El Temblar."

"What?" Ramos yelled. "What?"

And then the bull appeared at the edge of vision. A huge black beast, it came at them undeterred by their number. This was his turf to defend. The bull seemed to Bosch in that moment to have come from within the darkness, an apparition of death, its head down and jagged horns up. It was less than thirty feet away when it locked on a specific target. Bosch.

In one hand he held the Smith. In the other the vest, with the word POLICE on it in reflective yellow tape. In the seconds he had left he realized the tape had caught the beast's attention and singled him out. He also came to the conclusion that his gun was useless. He could not fell the animal with bullets. It was too big and powerful. It would take a perfect shot on a moving target. Wounding it, as Ramos had, would not stop it.

He dropped the gun and held the vest up.

Bosch heard yelling and shooting from his right side. It was Ramos. But the bull stayed on him. As it came closer he swept the vest to his right, its yellow letters catching the light of the moon. He let it go as the animal closed in. The bull, like a blur of black in darkness, hit the vest before it left his hand. Bosch tried to jump out of the way but one of the massive shoulders of the animal brushed him and sent him tumbling.

From the ground he looked up to see the animal cut to its left like a gifted athlete and close in on Ramos. The agent was still firing and Bosch could see the reflection of the moon off the shells as they were ejected from his gun. But the bullets did not stop the beast's charge. They did not even slow it. Bosch heard the gun's ejector go dry and Ramos was pulling the trigger on an empty chamber. His last cry was unintelligible. The bull hit him low in the legs and then raised its brutish and bloodied neck up, ejecting him into the air. Ramos seemed to tumble in slow motion before coming down headfirst and unmoving.

The bull tried to stop its charge but momentum and damage from bullets finally left it unable to control its huge weight. Its head dipped and it cartwheeled onto its back. It righted itself and prepared for another charge. Bosch crawled to his gun, picked it up and aimed. But the animal's front legs faltered and it went down. Then it slowly turned onto its side and lay unmoving, save for the hesitant rise and fall of its chest. Then that stopped, too.

Aguila and Bosch took off for Ramos at the same time. They huddled over him but did not move him. He was on his back and his eyes were still open and caked with dirt.

His head lolled at an unnatural angle. His neck appeared to have been cleanly broken in the fall. In the distance they could hear the sound of one of the Hueys flying their way. Bosch stood up and could see its spotlight sweeping over the scrubland, looking for them.

"I'm going to the tunnel," Bosch said. "When they land, come in with backup."

"No," Aguila said. "I'm going with you."

He said it in a way that invited no debate. He leaned down and took the radio off Ramos's belt and picked up the flashlight. He gave the radio to Bosch.

"Tell them we are both going."

Bosch radioed Corvo.

"Where's Ramos?"

"We just lost Ramos. Me and Aguila are going to the tunnel. Alert the militia at EnviroBreed that we are coming through. We don't want to get shot."

He turned the radio off before Corvo could reply and dropped it on the ground next to the dead DEA agent. The other helicopter was almost on them now. They ran to the barn, their weapons held up and ready, and moved slowly around the outside until they were at the front and could see the bay door had been slid open. Wide enough for a man to pass through.

They went through and crouched in the darkness. Aguila began to sweep the flashlight's beam around. It was a cavernous barn with stalls running along both sides to the back. There were crates used for trucking bulls to arenas stacked in the back along with towers made of bales of hay. Bosch saw a line of overhead lights running down the center of the building. He looked around and found the switch near the bay door.

Once the interior was lighted they moved down the aisle between the rows of stalls, Bosch taking the right and Aguila the left. The stalls were all empty, the bulls set free to roam the ranch. It was when they reached the back that they saw the opening to the tunnel.

A forklift was parked in the corner, holding a pallet of hay bales four feet off the ground. There was a four-foot-wide hole in the concrete floor where the pallet had sat. Zorrillo, or whoever the runner had been, had used the forklift to lift the pallet but there had been no one to drop it back down to hide his escape.

Bosch crouched down and moved to the edge of the hole and looked down. He saw a ladder leading about twelve feet down to a lighted passageway. He looked up at Aguila.

"Ready?"

The Mexican nodded.

Bosch went first. He climbed a few steps down the ladder and then dropped the rest of the way, bringing up his gun and ready to shoot. But there was no one in the tunnel as far as he could see. It wasn't even like a tunnel. It was more of a hallway. It was tall enough to stand in and an electrical conduit ran along the ceiling feeding lights in steel cages every twenty feet. There was a slight curve to the left and so he could not see where it ended. He moved into the passageway and Aguila dropped down behind him.

"Okay," Bosch whispered. "Let's stay to the right. If there is shooting, I'll go low and you go high."

Aguila nodded and they began to move quickly through the tunnel. Bosch, trying to figure his bearings, believed they were heading east and slightly north. They covered the ground to the curve quickly and then pressed themselves hard against the wall as they moved into the second leg of the passage.

Bosch realized that the bend in the passage was too wide for them to still be on line with EnviroBreed. He stared down the last segment of the tunnel and saw that it was clear. He could see the exit ladder maybe fifty yards ahead. And he knew they were going somewhere other than EnviroBreed. He wished he hadn't left the radio with Ramos's body.

"Shit," Harry whispered.

"What?" Aguila whispered back.

"Nothing. C'mon."

They began to move again, covering the first twenty-five yards quickly and then slowing to a cautious and quieter approach to the exit ladder. Aguila switched to the right wall and they came upon the opening at the same time, both with guns extended upward, sweat getting in their eyes.

There was no light from the opening above them. Bosch took the flashlight from Aguila and put its beam through the hole. He could see exposed wooden rafters of a low ceiling in the room above. No one looked down at them. No one shot at them. No one did a thing. Harry listened for any sound but heard nothing. He nodded to Aguila to cover and holstered his gun. He started climbing the ladder, one hand holding the flashlight.

He was scared. In Vietnam, leaving one of Charlie's tunnels always meant the end of fear. It was like being born again; you were leaving the darkness for safety and the hands of comrades. Out of the black and into the blue. But not this time; this time was the opposite.

When he reached the top, before rising through the opening, he flashed the beam around again but saw nothing. Then, like a turtle, he slowly moved his head out of the opening. The first thing he noticed in the beam was the sawdust everywhere on the floor. He climbed farther out, taking in the rest of the surroundings. It was some kind of storage room. There were steel shelves stocked with saw blades, boxes of sanding belts for industrial machinery. There were some hand tools and carpentry saws. One group of shelves were stacked with wooden dowel pegs, with different sizes on different shelves. Bosch immediately thought of the pegs attached to the baling wire that had been used to kill Kapps and Porter.

He moved fully into the room now and signaled to Aguila that it was safe to come up. Then Harry approached the storage room's door.

It was unlocked and it opened into a huge warehouse with lines of machinery and work benches on one side and the completed product—unfinished furniture, tables, chairs, chests of drawers— stacked on the other. Light came from a single bulb that hung from a cross support beam. It was the night-light. Aguila came up behind him then. They were in Mexitec, Bosch knew.

At the far end of the warehouse were sets of double doors. One of these was open and they moved to it quickly. It led to a loading-dock area that was off the back alley Bosch had walked through the night before. There was a puddle at the bottom of the parking bay and he saw wet tire tracks leading into the alley. There was no one in sight. Zorrillo was long gone.

"Two tunnels," Bosch said, unable to hide the dejection in his voice.

"Two tunnels," Corvo said. "Ramos's informant fucked us."

Bosch and Aguila were sitting on chairs of unfinished pine watching Corvo pacing and looking like shit, like a man in charge of an operation that had lost two men, a helicopter and its main target. It had been nearly two hours since they had come up through the tunnel.

"How d'you mean?" Bosch asked.

"I mean the CI had to have known about the second tunnel. How's he know about one and not the other? He set us up. He left Zorrillo the escape route. If I knew who he was I'd charge him with accessory in the death of a federal agent."

"You don't know?"

"Ramos didn't register this one with me. Hadn't gotten around to it."

Bosch breathed a little easier.

"I can't fucking believe this," Corvo was saying. "I might as well never go back. I'm done, man. Done...Least you got your cop killer, Bosch. I got a shit sandwich."

"Have you put out a telex?" Bosch said to change the subject.

"Already out. To all stations, all law enforcement agencies. But it doesn't matter. He's long gone. He'll probably go to the interior, lie low for a year and then start over. Right where he left off. Probably Michoacan, maybe farther down."

"Maybe he went north," Bosch said.

"No way he'd try to cross. He knows if we get him up there, he'll never see daylight again. He went south, where he's safe."

There were several other agents in the factory with clipboards, cataloging and searching. They had found a machine that hollowed out table legs so that they could be filled with contraband, recapped and sent across the border. Earlier they had found the second tunnel opening in the barn and followed it through to EnviroBreed. There had been no explosives on the trapdoor and they had gone in. The place was empty except for the two dogs outside. They killed them.

The operation had closed down a major smuggling network. Agents had left for Calexico to arrest the head of EnviroBreed, Ely. There were fourteen arrests made on the ranch. Others would follow. But all of that wasn't enough for Corvo or anybody. Not when agents were dead and Zorrillo was in the wind. Corvo had been wrong if he thought Bosch would be satisfied that Arpis was dead. Bosch wanted Zorrillo, too. He was the man who had called the hits.

Bosch got up so he wouldn't have to witness the agent's anguish anymore. He had enough of his own. Aguila must have felt the same. He, too, stood and began to walk listlessly around the machines and the furniture. Basically, they were waiting for one of the militia cars to take them back to the airport to Bosch's car. The DEA would be here until well after sunup. But Bosch and Aguila were finished.

Harry watched Aguila go back into the storage room and approach the tunnel entrance. He had told him about Grena and the Mexican had simply nodded. He hadn't shown a thing. Now Aguila dropped to his haunches and seemed to be studying the floor, as if the sawdust were a spread of tea leaves in which he could read Zorrillo's location.

After a few moments, he said, "The pope has new boots."

Bosch walked over and Aguila pointed to the footprints in the sawdust. There was one that was not from Aguila's or Bosch's shoes. It was very clear in the dust and Harry recognized the elongated heel of a bulldog boot. Inside it was the letter "S" formed by a curving snake. The edges of the print were sharp in the dust, the head of the snake clearly imprinted.

Aguila had been right. The pope had new boots.

Thirty-One

ALL THE WAY TO THE BORDER CROSSING, BOSCH CON-
templated how it had been done, how all the parts now seemed to
fit, and how it might have gone unnoticed if not for Aguila noticing
the footprint. He thought about the Snakes box in the closet of the
apartment in Los Feliz. A clue so obvious, yet he had missed it. He
had seen only what he wanted to see.

It was still early, just the first hint of dawn's light was fighting its
way up the eastern horizon, and there was not yet much of a line at
the crossing. Nobody was cleaning windshields. Nobody was selling junk. Nobody was there at all. Bosch badged the bored-looking
Border Patrol agent and was waved through.

He needed a phone and some caffeine. He drove two minutes to
the Calexico Town Hall, got a Coke from the machine in the police
department's cramped lobby and took it out to the pay phone on the
front wall. He looked at his watch and knew she would be at home,
probably awake and getting ready for work.

He lit a cigarette and dialed, charging the call to his own PacTel
card. While he waited for it to go through he looked across the street
into the fog. He saw the shapes of sleeping figures under blankets
scattered about the park. The ground fog gave the images a ghostly,
lonely resonance.

Teresa picked up after two rings. She sounded like she had been awake already.

"Hi."

"Harry? What is it?"

"Sorry to wake you up."

"You didn't. What's the matter?"

"Are you getting dressed up to go to Moore's funeral today?"

"Yes. What is this? You called me at ten minutes before six to ask—"

"That isn't Moore they'll be putting in the ground."

There was a long silence during which Bosch looked into the park and saw a man standing there, a blanket wrapped around his shoulders, staring back at him in the fog. Harry looked away.

"What are you saying? Harry, are you all right?"

"I'm tired but never better. What I'm saying is he's still alive. Moore. I just missed him this morning."

"Are you still in Mexico?"

"At the border."

"That doesn't make sense. What you said. There were matches made on the latents, we got dental, and his own wife ID'd a photograph of the tattoo on the body. His identification was confirmed."

"It's all bullshit. He set it up."

"Why, Harry, are you calling me now and telling me this?"

"I want you to help me, Teresa. I can't go to Irving. Only you. You help me and you'll help yourself. If I'm right."

"That's a big if, Harry."

Bosch looked back into the park and the man in the blanket was gone.

"Just tell me how it could be possible," she said. "Convince me."

Bosch was silent a moment, like a lawyer composing himself before a cross-examination. He knew that every word he spoke now had to stand the test of her scrutiny or he would lose her.

"Besides the prints and dental, Sheehan told me they also matched his handwriting to the I-found-out-who-I-was note. He said they compared it to a change-of-address card Moore had put in his personnel file a few months ago after he and his wife separated."

He took a deep drag on the cigarette and she thought he had finished.

"So? I don't see—what about it?"

"One of the concessions the protective league won a few years back during contract negotiations was guaranteed access to your personnel file. So cops could check if there were beefs on their record, commendations, letters of complaint, anything like that. So Moore had access to his P-file. He went into Personnel a few months back and asked for it because he had just moved and needed to update it with his new address."

Bosch held it there a moment, to compose the rest of it in his mind.

"Okay, okay," she said.

"The P-files also contain print cards. Moore had access to the print card Irving took to you on the day of the autopsy. That was the card your tech used to identify the prints. You see? While Moore had the file, he could have switched his card for someone else's. Then you used the bogus card to identify his body. But, see, it wasn't his body. It was the other person's."

"Who?"

"I think it was a man from down here named Humberto Zorrillo."

"This seems too farfetched. There were other IDs. I remember that day in the suite. What's his name, Sheehan, he got a call from SID saying they matched prints in the motel room to Moore. They used a different set than we did. It's a double-blind confirmation, Harry. Then we have the tattoo. And the dental. How do you explain all of that?"

"Look, Teresa, listen to me. It all can be explained. It all works. The dental? You told me you only found one usable fragment, part of a root canal. That meant no root was left. It was a dead tooth so you could not tell how long it had been out, only that it matched his dentist's charts. That's fine, but one of Moore's crew told me he once saw Moore get punched during a Boulevard brawl and he lost a tooth. That could've been it, I don't know."

"Okay, what about the prints in the room? Explain that?"

"Easy. Those were his prints. Donovan, the SID guy, told me he pulled prints from the Department of Justice computer. Those would have been Moore's real prints. That meant he was really in the room. It doesn't mean it's his body. Normally, one set of exemplars—the ones from the DOJ computer—would be used to do all the match work, but Irving screwed it up by going to the P-file. And that's the beauty of Moore's plan. He knew Irving or someone in the department would do it this way. He could count on it because he knew the department would put a rush on the autopsy, the ID, everything, because it was a fellow officer. It's been done before and he knew they would do it for him."

"Donovan never did a cross-match between our prints and the set he pulled?"

"Nope, because it wasn't the routine. He might've gotten around to it later when he thought about it. But things were happening too fast on this case."

"Shit," she said. He knew he was winning her over. "What about the tattoo?"

"It's a barrio insignia. A lot of people could have had them. I think Zorrillo had one."

"Who is he?"

"He grew up with Moore down here. They might be brothers, I don't know. Anyway, Zorrillo became the local drug kingpin. Moore went to L.A. and became a cop. But somehow Moore was working for him up there. The story goes on from there. The DEA raided Zorrillo's ranch last night. He got away. But I don't think it was Zorrillo. It was Moore."

"You saw him?"

"I didn't need to."

"Is anyone looking for him?"

"The DEA is looking. They're concentrating in interior Mexico. Then again, they're looking for Zorrillo. Moore may never turn up again."

"It all seems...You're saying Moore killed Zorrillo and then traded places with him?"

"Yeah. Somehow he got Zorrillo to L.A. They meet at the Hideaway and Moore puts him down—the trauma to the back of the head you found. He puts his boots and clothes on the body. Then he blows the face away with the shotgun. He makes sure to leave some of his own prints around to make Donovan bite and puts the note in the back pocket.

"I think the note worked on a number of levels. It was taken as a suicide note at first. Authenticating the handwriting helped add to the identification. On another level, I think it was something personal between Moore and Zorrillo. Goes back to the barrio. 'Who are you?' 'I found out who I was.' That part of it is a long story."

They were both silent for a while, rethinking all of what Bosch had just said. He knew there were still a lot of loose ends. A lot of deception.

"Why all the killings?" she asked. "Porter and Juan Doe, what did they have to do with anything?"

This is where he had few answers.

"I don't know. They were somehow in the way, I guess. Zorrillo had Jimmy Kapps killed because he was an informant. I think Moore was the one who told Zorrillo. After that Juan Doe—his name, by the way, is Gutierrez-Llosa—gets beaten to death down here and taken up there. I don't know why. Then Moore pops Zorrillo and takes his place. Why he had to do Porter, I don't know. I guess he thought Lou might figure it out."

"That's so cold."

"Yeah."

"How could it happen?" she asked then, more to herself than Bosch. "They are about to bury him, this drug dealer...full honors, the mayor and chief there. The media."

"And you'll know the truth."

She thought about that for a long time before asking the next question.

"Why did he do it?"

"I don't know. We're talking about different lives. The cop and the drug dealer. But there must've been something still between them, that bond—whatever it is—from the barrio. And somehow one day the cop crosses over, starts watching out for the dealer on the streets of L.A. Who knows what made him do it? Maybe money, maybe just something he had lost a long time ago when he was a kid."

"What do you mean?"

"I don't know. I'm still thinking."

"If they were that close, why did he kill him?"

"I guess we'll have to ask him. If we ever find him. Maybe he—maybe like you said it was just to take Zorrillo's place. All that money. Or maybe it was guilt. He got in too far and he needed a way to end it . . . . Moore was—or is—hung up on the past. His wife said that. Maybe he was trying to recapture something, go back. I don't know yet."

There was silence on the line again. Bosch took a last drag on his cigarette.

"The plan seems almost perfect," he said. "He leaves a body behind in circumstances he knew would make the department not want to come looking."

"But you did, Harry."

"Yeah."

And here I am, he thought. He knew what he had to do now. He had to finish it. He could see the ghostly figures of several people in the park now. They were waking to another day of desperation.

"Why did you call me, Harry? What do you want me to do?"

"I called because I have to trust someone. I could only think of you, Teresa."

"Then what do you want me to do?"

"You have access to the DOJ prints in your office, right?"

"That's how we make most of our IDs. That's how we will make all of them after this. I have Irving by the balls now."

"Do you still have the print card he brought over for the autopsy?"

"Um, I don't know. But I'm sure the techs made a copy of it to keep with the body. You want me to do the crosscheck?"

"Yeah, do a cross and you'll see they don't match."

"You're so sure."

"Yeah. I'm sure but you might as well confirm it."

"Then what?"

"Then, I guess, I'll see you at the funeral. I've got one more stop to make and then I'm heading up."

"What stop?"

"I want to check out a castle. It's part of the long story. I'll tell you later."

"You don't want to try to stop the funeral?"

Harry thought a few moments before answering. He thought of Sylvia Moore and the mystery she still held for him. Then he thought about the idea of a drug lord getting a cop's farewell.

"No, I don't want to stop it. Do you?"

"No way."

He knew her reasons were far different from his. But he didn't care about that. Teresa was well on her way to winning her assignment as permanent chief medical examiner. If Irving got in her way now, he'd end up looking like one of the customers in the autopsy suite. In that case, more power to her, he thought.

"I'll see you in a little bit," he said.

"Be careful, Harry."

Bosch hung up and lit another cigarette. The morning sun was up now and beginning to burn the ground fog off the park. People were moving around over there. He thought he heard a woman laughing. But at the moment he felt very much alone in the world.

Thirty-Two

BOSCH PULLED HIS CAR UP TO THE FRONT GATE AT
the end of Coyote Trail and saw that the circular driveway in front
of Castillo de los Ojos was still empty. But the thick chain that had
secured the two halves of the iron gate the day before hung loose
and the lock was open. Moore was here.

Harry left his car there, blocking the exit, and slipped through
the gate on foot. He ran across the brown lawn in a crouched,
uneasy trot, mindful that the windows of the tower looked down
at him like the dark accusing eyes of a giant. He pressed himself
against the stucco surface of the wall next to the front door. He was
breathing heavily and sweating, though the morning air was still
quite cool.

The knob was locked. He stood there unmoving for a long
period, listening for something but hearing nothing. Finally, he
ducked below the line of windows that fronted the first floor and
moved around the house to the side of the four-bay garage. There
was another door here and it, too, was locked.

Bosch recognized the rear of the house from the photographs
that had been in Moore's bag. He saw the sliding doors running
along the pool deck. One door was open and the wind buffeted the
white curtain. It flapped like a hand beckoning him to come in.

The open door led to a large living room. It was full of ghosts—

furniture covered by musty white sheets. Nothing else. He moved to his left, silently passing through the kitchen and opening a door to the garage. There was one car, which was covered by more sheets, and a pale green panel van. It said MEXITEC on the side. Bosch touched the van's hood and found it still warm. Through the windshield he saw a sawed-off shotgun lying across the passenger seat. He opened the unlocked door and took the weapon out. As quietly as he could, he cracked it open and saw both barrels were loaded with double-ought shells. He closed the weapon, holstered his own, and carried it with him.

He pulled the sheet off the front end of the other car and recognized it as the Thunderbird he had seen in the father-and-son photo in Moore's bag. Looking at the car, Bosch wondered how far back you have to go to trace the reason for a person's choices in life. He didn't know the answer about Moore. He didn't know the answer about himself.

He went back to the living room and stopped and listened. There was nothing. The house seemed still, empty, and it smelled dusty, like time spent slowly and painfully in wait for something or someone not coming. All the rooms were full of ghosts. He was considering the shape of a shrouded fan chair when he heard the noise. From above, like the sound of a shoe dropping on a wood floor.

He moved toward the front and in the entry area he saw the wide stone staircase. Bosch moved up the steps. The noise from above was not repeated.

On the second floor he went down a carpeted hallway, looking through the doors to four bedrooms and two bathrooms but finding each room empty.

He went back to the stairs and up into the tower. The lone door at the top landing was open and Harry heard no sound. He crouched and moved slowly into the opening, the sawed-off leading the way like a water finder's divining rod.

Moore was there. Standing with his back to the door and looking at himself in the mirror. The mirror was on the back of a closet door which was open slightly, angling the glass so that it did not catch Harry's reflection. He watched Moore unseen for a few moments, then looked around. There was a bed in the center of the room with an open suitcase on it. Next to it was a gym bag that was zipped closed and already appeared to be packed. Moore still had not moved. He was intently staring at the reflection of his face. He had a full beard now, and his eyes were brown. He wore faded blue jeans, new snakeskin boots, a black T-shirt and a black leather jacket with matching gloves. He was Melrose Avenue cool. From a distance he could easily pass for the pope of Mexicali.

Bosch saw the wood grips and chrome handle of an automatic tucked into Moore's belt.

"You going to say something, Harry? Or just stare."

Without moving his hands or head, Moore shifted his weight to the left and then he and Bosch were staring at each other in the mirror.

"Picked up a new pair of boots before you put Zorrillo down, didn't you?"

Now Moore turned completely to face him. But he didn't say anything.

"Keep your hands out front like that," Bosch said.

"Whatever you say, Harry. You know, I kinda thought that if somebody came, you'd be the one."

"You wanted somebody to come, didn't you?"

"Some days I did. Some days I didn't."

Bosch moved into the room and then took a step sideways so he was directly facing Moore.

"New contacts, beard. You look like the pope—from a distance. But how'd you convince his lieutenants, his *guardia*. They were just going to stand back and let you move in and take his place?"

"Money convinced them. They'd probably let you move in there if you had the bread, Harry. See, anything is negotiable when you have your hands on the purse strings. And I did."

Moore nodded slightly toward the duffel bag on the bed.

"How about you? I have money. Not much. About a hundred and ten grand there."

"I figured you'd be running away with a fortune."

"Oh, I am. I am. What's in the bag is just what I have on hand. You caught me a little short. But I can get you more. It's in the banks."

"Guess you've been practicing Zorrillo's signature as well as his looks."

Moore didn't answer.

"Who was he?"

"Who?"

"You know who."

"Half brother. Different fathers."

"This place. This is what it was all about, wasn't it? It's the castle you lived in before you were sent away."

"Something like that. Decided to buy it after he was gone. But it's falling apart on me. It's so hard to take care of something you love these days. Everything is a chore."

Bosch tried to study him. He looked tired of it all.

"What happened back at the ranch?" Bosch asked.

"You mean the three bodies? Yes, well, I guess you could say justice happened. Grena was a leech who had been sucking Zorrillo for years. Arpis detached him, you could say."

"Then who detached Arpis and Dance?"

"I did that, Harry."

He said it without hesitation and the words froze Bosch. Moore was a cop. He knew never to confess. You didn't talk until there was a lawyer by your side, a plea bargain in place, and a deal that was signed.

Harry adjusted his sweating hands on the sawed-off. He took a step forward and listened for any other sound in the house. There was only silence until Moore spoke again.

"I'm not going back, Harry. I guess you know that."

He said it matter-of-factly, as if it was a given, something that had been decided a long time ago.

"How'd you get Zorrillo up to L.A., and then into that motel room? How'd you get his prints for the personnel file?"

"You want me to tell you, Harry? Then what?"

Moore looked down at the gym bag briefly.

"Then nothing. We're going back to L.A. You haven't been advised—nothing you say now can be used against you. It's just you and me here."

"The prints were easy. I was making him IDs. He had three or four so he could come across when he liked. One time he told me he wanted a passport and full wallet spread. I told him I needed prints. Took 'em myself."

"And the motel?"

"Like I said, he crossed over all the time. He'd go through the tunnel and the DEA would be out there sitting on the ranch thinking he was still inside. He liked to come up to see the Lakers, sit down on court level near that blonde actress who likes to get on TV. Anyway, he was up there and I told him I wanted to meet. He came."

"And you put him down and took his place.... What about the old man, the laborer? What did he do?"

"He was just in the wrong place. Zorrillo told me he was there when he came up through the floor on the last trip. He wasn't sup- posed to be in that room. But I guess he couldn't read the signs. Zorrillo said he couldn't take the chance he'd tell someone about the tunnel."

"Why'd you dump him in the alley? Why didn't you just bury him out in Joshua Tree. Someplace he'd never be found."

"The desert would've been good but I didn't dump him, Bosch. Don't you see? They were controlling me. They brought him up here and dumped him there. Arpis did. That night I get a call from Zorrillo telling me to meet him at the Egg and I. He says park in the alley. I did and there was the body. I wasn't going to move the fucking thing. I called it in. You see it was one more way for him to keep his hold on me. And I went along. Porter caught the case and I made a deal with him to take it slow."

Bosch didn't say anything. He was trying to envision the sequence Moore had just described.

"This is getting boring, man. You going to try to cuff me, take me in, be the hero?"

"Why couldn't you let it go?" Bosch asked.

"What?"

"This place. Your father. The whole thing. You should have let the past go."

"I was robbed of my life, man. He kicked us right out. My mother—How do you let go of a past like that? Fuck you, Bosch. You don't know."

Bosch said nothing. But he knew he was allowing this to go on too long. Moore was taking control of the situation.

"When I heard he was dead, it did something," Moore said. "I don't know. I decided I wanted this place and I went to see my brother. That was my mistake. Things started small but they never stopped. Soon I was running the show for him up there. I had to get out from under it. There was only one way."

"It was the wrong way."

"Don't bother, Bosch. I know the song."

Bosch was sure Moore had told the story the way he believed it. But it was clear to Bosch he had fully embraced the devil. He had found out who he was.

"Why me?" Bosch asked.

"Why you what?"

"Why did you leave the file for me? If you hadn't done that, I wouldn't be here. You'd be in the clear."

"Bosch, you were my backup. You don't see? I needed something in case the suicide play didn't work. I figured you'd get that file and take it from there. I knew with just a little misdirection you would sound the alarm. Murder. Thing is, I never thought you'd get this far. I thought Irving and the rest of them would crush you because they wouldn't want to know what it was all about. They'd just want the whole thing to die with me."

"And Porter."

"Yeah, well, Porter was weak. He's probably better off now, anyway."

"And me? Would I be better off if Arpis had hit me with the bullet in the hotel room?"

"Bosch, you were getting too close. Had to take the shot."

Harry had nothing more to say or ask. Moore seemed to sense that they were at a final point. He tried one more time.

"Bosch, in that bag I have account numbers. They're yours."

"Not interested, Moore. We're going back."

Moore laughed at that notion.

"Do you really think anybody up there gives a rat's ass about all of this?"

Bosch said nothing.

"In the department?" Moore said. "No fucking way they care. They don't want to know about something like this. Bad for business, man. But, see, you—you're not in the department, Bosch. You're in it but not of it. See what I'm saying? There's the problem. There's—you take me back, man, and they're gonna look at you as being just as bad as me. Because you'll be pulling this wagon full of shit behind you.

"I think you're the only one who cares about it, Bosch. I really think you are. So just take the money and go."

"What about your wife? You think she cares?"

That stopped him, for a few moments, at least.

"Sylvia," he said. "I don't know. I lost her a long time ago. I don't know if she cares about this or not. I don't care anymore myself."

Bosch watched him, looking for the truth.

"Water under the bridge," Moore said. "So take the money. I can get more to you later."

"I can't take the money. I think you know that."

"Yeah, I guess I know that. But I think you know I can't go back with you, either. So where's that leave us?"

Bosch shifted his weight on to his left side, the butt of the shotgun against his hip. There was a long moment of silence during which he thought about himself and his own motives. Why hadn't he told Moore to take the gun out of his pants and drop it?

In a smooth, quick motion, Moore reached across his body with his right hand and pulled the gun out of his waistband. He was bringing the barrel around toward Bosch when Harry's finger closed over the shotgun's triggers. The double-barrel blast was deafening in the room. Moore took the brunt of it in the face. Through the smoke Bosch saw his body jerk backward into the air. His hands flew up toward the ceiling and he landed on the bed. His handgun fired but it was a stray shot, shattering one of the panes of the arched windows. The gun dropped onto the floor.

Pieces of blackened wadding from the shells floated down and landed in the blood of the faceless man. There was a heavy smell of burned gunpowder on the air and Bosch felt a slight mist on his face that he also knew by smell was blood.

He stood still for more than a minute, then he looked over and saw himself in the mirror. He quickly looked away.

He walked over to the bed and unzipped the duffel bag. There were stacks and stacks of money inside it, most of it in one-hundred-dollar bills. There was also a wallet and passport. He opened them and found they identified Moore as Henry Maze, age forty, of Pasadena. There were two loose photos held in the passport.

The first was a Polaroid that he guessed had come from the white bag. It was a photo of Moore and his wife in their early twenties. They were sitting on a couch, maybe at a party. Sylvia was not looking at the camera. She was looking at him. And Bosch knew why he had chosen this photo to take. The loving look on her face was beautiful. The second photo was an old black and white with discoloration around the edges, indicating it had come from a frame. It showed Cal Moore and Humberto Zorrillo as boys. They were play-fully wrestling, both shirtless and laughing. Their skin was bronze, blemished only by the tattoos. Each boy had the Saints and Sinners tattoo on his arm.

He dropped the wallet and passport back into the duffel bag but put the two photos in his coat pocket. He walked over to the window with the broken pane and looked out onto Coyote Trail and the lowlands leading to the border. No police cars were coming. No Border Patrol. No one had even called for an ambulance. The thick walls of the castle had held the sound of the man dying inside.

The sun was high in the sky and he could feel its warmth through the triangular opening in the broken glass.

Thirty-Three

BOSCH DID NOT BEGIN TO FEEL WHOLE AGAIN UNTIL he reached the smogged outskirts of L.A. He was back in the nastiness again but he knew that it was here that he would heal. He skirted downtown on the freeway and headed up through Cahuenga Pass. Midday traffic was light. Looking up at the hills he saw the charred path of the Christmas-night fire. But he even took some comfort in that. He knew that the heat of the fire would have cracked open the seeds of the wildflowers and by spring the hillside would be a riot of colors. The chaparral would follow and soon there would be no scar on the land at all.

It was after one. He was going to be too late for Moore's funeral mass at the San Fernando Mission. So he drove through the Valley to the cemetery. The burial of Calexico Moore, killed in the line of duty, was to be at Eternal Valley in Chatsworth, the police chief, the mayor and the media presiding. Bosch smiled as he drove. We gather here to honor and bury a drug dealer.

He got there before the motorcade but the media were already set up on a bluff near the entrance road. Men in black suits, white shirts and black ties, with funeral bands around their left arms, were in the cemetery drive and signaled him to a parking area. He sat in the car, using the rearview mirror to put on a tie. He was unshaven and looked crumpled but didn't care.

The plot was near a stand of oak trees. One of the armbands had pointed the way. Harry walked across the lawn, stepping around plots, the wind blowing his hair in all directions. He took a position a good distance away from the green funeral canopy and accompanying bank of flowers and leaned against one of the trees. He smoked a cigarette while he watched cars start to arrive. A few had beaten the procession. But then he heard the approaching sound of the helicopters—the police air unit that flew above the hearse and the media choppers that started circling the cemetery like flies. Then the first motorcycles cut through the cemetery gate and Bosch watched as the TV cameras on the bluff followed the long line in. There must have been two hundred cycles, Bosch guessed. The best day to run a red light, break the speed limit or make an illegal U-turn in the city was on a cop's funeral day. Nobody was left minding the store.

The hearse and attendant limousine followed the cycles. Then came the rest of the cars and pretty soon people were parking all over the place and walking across the cemetery from all directions toward the plot. Bosch watched one of the armbands help Sylvia Moore out of the limo. She had been riding alone. Though he was maybe fifty yards away, Harry could tell she looked lovely. She wore a simple black dress and the wind gusted hard against it, pressing the material against her and showing her figure. She had to hold a black barrette in place in her hair. She wore black gloves and black sunglasses. Red lipstick. He couldn't take his eyes off her.

The armband led her to a row of folding chairs beneath the canopy and alongside the hole that had been expertly dug into the earth. Along the way, her head turned slightly and Bosch believed she was looking at him but was not sure because the glasses hid her eyes and her face showed no sign. After she was seated, the pallbearers, composed of Rickard, the rest of Moore's narcotics unit, and a few others Bosch didn't know, brought the grayish-silver steel casket.

"So, you made it back," a voice said from behind.

Bosch turned to see Teresa Corazón walking up behind him.

"Yeah, just got in."

"You could use a shave."

"And a few other things. How's it going, Teresa?"

"Never better."

"Good to hear. What happened this morning after we talked?"

"About what you expected. We pulled DOJ prints on Moore and compared them to what Irving had given us. No match. Two different people. That isn't Moore in the silver bullet over there."

Bosch nodded. Of course, by now he didn't need her confirmation. He had his own. He thought of Moore's faceless body lying on the bed.

"What are you going to do with it?" he asked.

"I've already done it."

"What?"

"I had a little discussion with Assistant Chief Irving before the funeral mass. Wish you could have seen his face."

"But he didn't stop the funeral."

"He's playing the percentages, I guess. Chances are Moore, if he knows what's good for him, won't ever show up again. So he is hoping that all it costs him is a recommendation on the medical examiner's office. He volunteered to do it. I didn't even have to explain his position to him."

"I hope you enjoy the job, Teresa. You're in the belly of the beast now."

"I will, Harry. And thanks for calling me this morning."

"Does he know how you came up with all of this? Did you tell him I called?"

"No. But I'm not sure I had to."

She was right. Irving would know Bosch was in the middle of this somehow. He looked past Teresa to look at Sylvia again. She was sitting quietly. The chairs on either side of her empty. No one was going to come near her.

"I'm going over to the group," Teresa said. "I told Dick Ebart I would meet him here. He wants to set up a date to call for the commission's full vote."

Bosch nodded. Ebart was a county commissioner of twenty-five years in office and closing in on seventy years old. He was her informal sponsor for the job.

"Harry, I still want to keep things on just a professional basis. I appreciate what you did for me today. But I want to keep things at a distance, for a while at least."

He nodded and watched her walk toward the gathering, her footing unsteady in high heels on the cemetery turf. For a moment Bosch envisioned her in a carnal coupling with the aged commissioner whose photos in the newspaper were most notable because of his drooping, crepe-paper neck. He was repulsed by the image and by himself for imagining it. He blanked it out of his mind and watched Teresa mingling in the crowd, shaking hands and becoming the politician she would now have to be. He felt a sense of sadness for her.

The service was a few minutes away and people were still arriving. In the crowd he picked up the gleaming head of Assistant Chief Irvin Irving. He was in full uniform, carrying his hat under his arm. He was standing with the chief of police and one of the mayor's front men. The mayor was apparently late as usual. Irving then saw Bosch, broke away and started walking toward him. He seemed to be taking in the vista of the mountains as he walked. He didn't look at Bosch until he was next to him under the oak tree.

"Detective."

"Chief."

"When did you get in?"

"Just now."

"Could use a shave."

"Yeah, I know."

"So what do we do? What do we do?"

The way he said it was almost wistful and Bosch didn't know whether Irving wanted an answer from him or not.

"You know, Detective, yesterday when you did not come to my office as ordered, I opened a one-point-eighty-one on you."

"I figured you would, Chief. Am I suspended?"

"No action taken at the moment. I'm a fair man. I wanted to speak with you first. You spoke with the acting chief medical examiner this morning?"

Bosch wasn't going to lie to him. He thought this time he held all of the high cards.

"Yes. I wanted her to compare some fingerprints."

"What happened down there in Mexico to make you want to do that?"

"Nothing I care to talk about, Chief. I'm sure it will all be on the news."

"I'm not talking about that ill-fated raid undertaken by the DEA. I am talking about Moore. Bosch, I need to know if I need to walk over there and stop this funeral."

Bosch watched a blue vein pop high on Irving's shaven skull. It pulsed and then died.

"I can't help you there, Chief. It's not my call. We've got company."

Irving turned around to look back toward the gathering. Lieutenant Harvey Pounds, also in dress uniform, was walking toward them, probably wanting to find out how many cases he could close from Bosch's investigation. But Irving held up a hand like a traffic cop and Pounds abruptly stopped, turned and walked away.

"The point I am trying to make with you, Detective Bosch, is that it appears we are about to bury and eulogize a Mexican drug lord while a corrupt police officer is running around loose. Do you have any idea what embarrass—Damn it! I cannot believe I just spoke those words out loud. I cannot believe I spoke those words to you."

"Don't trust me much, do you, Chief?"

"In matters like these, I do not trust anyone."

"Well, don't worry about it."

"I am not worried about who I can and can not trust."

"I mean about burying a drug lord while a corrupt cop is running around loose. Don't worry about it."

Irving studied him, his eyes narrowing, as if he might be able to peer through Bosch's own eyes, into his thoughts.

"Are you kidding me? Don't worry about it? This is a potential embarrassment to this city and this department of unimaginable proportions. This could—"

"Look, man, I am telling you to forget about it. Understand? I am trying to help you out here."

Irving studied him again for a long moment. He shifted his weight to the other foot. The vein on his scalp pulsed with new life. Bosch knew it would not sit well with him, to have someone like Harry Bosch keeping such a secret. Teresa Corazón he could deal with because they both played on the same field. But Bosch was different. Harry rather enjoyed the moment, though the long silence was getting old.

"I checked with the DEA on that fiasco down there. They said this man they believe to be Zorrillo escaped. They don't know where he is."

It was a half-assed effort to get Bosch to open up. It didn't work.

"They never will know."

Irving said nothing to this but Bosch knew better than to interrupt his silence. He was working up to something. Harry let him work, watching as the assistant chief's massive jaw muscles bunched into hard pads.

"Bosch, I want to know right now if there is a problem on this. Even a potential problem. Because I have to know in the next three minutes whether to walk over there in front of the chief and the mayor and all of those cameras and put a stop to this."

"What's the DEA doing now?"

"What can they do? They are watching the airports, contacting local authorities. Putting his photo and description out. There is not a lot they can do. He is gone. At least, they say. I want to know if he is going to stay gone."

Bosch nodded and said, "They're never going to find the man they are looking for, Chief."

"Convince me, Bosch."

"Can't do that."

"And why not?"

"Trust goes two ways. So does the lack of trust."

Irving seemed to consider this and Bosch thought he saw an almost imperceptible nod.

Bosch said, "The man they are looking for, who they believe to be Zorrillo, is in the wind and he isn't coming back. That's all you need to know."

Bosch thought of the body on the bed at Castillo de los Ojos. The face was already gone. Another two weeks and the flesh would go. No fingerprints. No identification, other than the bogus credentials in the wallet. The tattoo would stay intact for a while. But there were plenty who had that tattoo, including the fugitive Zorrillo.

He had left the money there, too. An added precaution, enough there maybe to convince the first finder not to bother calling the authorities. Just take the money and run.

Using a handkerchief, he had wiped the shotgun of his prints and left it. He locked the house, wrapped the chain through the black bars of the gate and closed the hasp on the lock, careful to wipe each surface. Then he had headed home to L.A.

"The DEA, are they putting a nice spin on things yet?" he asked Irving.

"They're working on it," Irving said. "I am told the smuggling network has been closed down. They have ascertained that the drug called black ice was manufactured on the ranch, taken through tunnels to two nearby businesses, then moved across the border. The shipment would make a detour, probably in Calexico, where it would be removed and the delivery van would go on. Both businesses have been seized. One of them, a contractor with the state to provide sterile medflies, will probably prove embarrassing."

"EnviroBreed."

"Yes. By tomorrow they will finish comparisons between the bills of lading shown by drivers at the border and the receipt of cargo records at the eradication center here in Los Angeles. I am told these documents were altered or forged. In other words more sealed boxes passed through the border than were received at the center."

"Inside help."

"Most likely. The on-site inspector for the USDA was either dumb or corrupt. I don't know which is worse."

Irving brushed some imaginary impurity off the shoulder of his uniform. It could not be hair or dandruff since he had neither. He turned away from Bosch to face the coffin and the thick gathering of officers around it. The ceremony was about to begin. He squared his shoulders and without turning back, he said, "I don't know what to think, Bosch. I don't know whether you have me or not."

Bosch didn't answer. That would be one Irving would have to worry about.

"Just remember," Irving said. "You have just as much to lose as the department. More. The department can always come back, always recover. It might take a good long time but it always comes back. The same can't be said for the individual who gets tarred with the brush of scandal."

Bosch smiled in a sad way. Never leave a thing uncovered. That was Irving. His parting shot was a threat, a threat that if Bosch ever used his knowledge against the department, he, too, would go down. Irving would personally see to it.

"Are you afraid?" Bosch asked.

"Afraid of what, Detective?"

"Of everything. Of me. Yourself. That it won't hold together. That I might be wrong. Everything, man. Aren't you afraid of everything?"

"The only thing that I fear are people without a conscience. Who act without thinking their actions through. I don't think you are like that."

Bosch just shook his head.

"So let's get down to it, Detective. I have to rejoin the chief and I see the mayor has arrived. What is it you want, provided it is within my authority to provide?"

"I wouldn't take anything from you," Bosch said very quietly. "That's what you just don't seem to get."

Irving finally turned around to face him again.

"You are right, Bosch. I really don't understand you. Why risk everything for nothing? You see? It raises my concerns about you all over again. You don't play for the team. You play for yourself."

Bosch looked steadily at Irving and didn't smile, though he wanted to. Irving had paid him a fine compliment, though the assistant chief would never realize it.

"What happened down there had nothing to do with the department," he said. "If I did anything at all, I did it for somebody and something else."

Irving stared back blankly, his jaw flexing as he ground his teeth. There was a crooked smile below the gleaming skull. It was then that Bosch recognized the similarity to the tattoos on the arms of Moore and Zorrillo. The devil's mask. He watched as Irving's eyes lit on something and he nodded knowingly. He looked back at Sylvia and then returned his gaze to Bosch.

"A noble man, is that it? All of this to insure a widow's pension?"

Bosch didn't answer. He wondered if it was a guess or Irving knew something. He couldn't tell.

"How do you know she wasn't part of it?" Irving said.

"I know."

"But how can you be sure? How can you take the chance?"

"The same way you're sure. The letter."

"What about it?"

Bosch had done nothing but think about Moore on his way

back. He had had four hours of driving on the open road to put it together. He thought he had it.

"Moore wrote the letter himself," he began. "He informed on himself, you could say. He had this plan. The letter was the start. He wrote it."

He stopped to light a cigarette. Irving didn't say a word. He just waited for the story.

"For reasons that I guess go back to when he was a boy, Moore fucked up. He crossed and after he was already on the other side he realized there is no crossing back. But he couldn't go on, he had to get out. Somehow.

"His plan was to start the IAD investigation with that letter. He put just enough in the letter so Chastain would be convinced there was something to it, but not enough that Chastain would be able to find anything. The letter would just serve to cloud his name, put him under suspicion. He had been in the department long enough to know how it would go. He'd seen the way IAD and people like Chastain operate. The letter set the stage, made the water murky enough so that when he turned up dead at the motel the department, meaning you, wouldn't want to look too closely at it. You're an open book, Chief. He knew you'd move quickly and efficiently to protect the department first, find out what really happened second. So he sent the letter. He used you, Chief. He used me, too."

Irving turned toward the grave site. The ceremony was about to begin. He turned back to Bosch.

"Go ahead, Detective. Quickly, please."

"Layer after layer. Remember, you told me he had rented that room for a month. That was the first layer. If he hadn't been discovered for a month decomp would've taken care of things. There would have been no skin left to print. That would leave only the latents he left in the room and he'd've been home free."

"But he was found a few weeks early," Irving helpfully interjected.

"Yeah. That brings us to the second layer. You. Moore had been a cop a long time. He knew what you would do. He knew you'd go to personnel and grab his package."

"That's a big gamble, Bosch."

"You ask me, it was a better-than-even bet. Christmas night, when I saw you there with the file, I knew what it was before you said. So I can see Moore taking the gamble and switching the print cards. Like I said, he was gambling it would never come to that anyway. You were the second layer."

"And you? You were the third?"

"Yeah, the way I figure it. He used me as sort of a last backup. In case the suicide didn't wash, he wanted somebody who'd look at it and see a reason for Moore to have been murdered. That was me. I did that. He left the file for me and I went for it, thought he'd been killed over it. It was all a deflection. He just didn't want anybody looking too closely at who was actually on the tile floor in the motel. He just wanted some time."

"But you went too far, Bosch. He never planned on that."

"I guess not."

Bosch thought about his meeting with Moore in the tower. He still hadn't decided whether Moore had been expecting him, even waiting for him. Waiting for Harry to come kill him. He didn't think he'd ever know. That was Calexico Moore's last mystery.

"Time for what?" Irving asked.

"What?"

"You said he just wanted some time."

"I think he wanted time to go down there, take Zorrillo's place and then take the money and run. I don't think he wanted to be the pope forever. He just wanted to live in a castle again."

"What?"

"It's nothing."

They were silent a moment before Bosch finished up.

"Most of this I know you already have, Chief."

"I do?"

"Yeah, you do. I think you figured it out after Chastain told you that Moore sent the letter himself."

"And how did Detective Chastain know that?"

He wasn't going to give Bosch anything. That was okay, though. Harry found that telling the story helped clarify it. It was like holding it up to inspect for holes.

"After he got the letter, Chastain thought it was the wife who sent it. He went to her house and she denied it. He asked for her typewriter because he was going to make sure and she slammed the door in his face. But she didn't do it before saying she didn't even have a typewriter. So then, after Moore turns up dead, Chastain starts thinking about things and takes the machine out of Moore's office at the station. My guess is he matched the keys to the letter. From that point, it wouldn't be difficult to figure out the letter came from either Moore or somebody in the BANG squad. My guess is that Chastain interviewed them this week and concluded they hadn't done it. The letter was typed by Moore."

Irving didn't confirm any of it but didn't have to. Bosch knew. It all fit.

"Moore had a good plan, Chief. He played us like cheater's solitaire. He knew every card in the deck before it was turned over."

"Except for one," Irving said. "You. He didn't think you'd come looking."

Bosch didn't reply. He looked over at Sylvia again. She was innocent. And she would be safe. He noticed Irving turn his gaze on her, too.

"She's clear," Bosch said. "You know it. I know it. If you make trouble for her, I'll make trouble for you."

It wasn't a threat. It was an offer. A deal. Irving considered it a moment and nodded his head once. A blunt agreement.

"Did you speak to him down there, Bosch?"

Harry knew he meant Moore and he knew he couldn't answer.

"What did you do down there?"

After a few moments of silence Irving turned and walked as upright as a Nazi back to the rows of chairs holding the VIPs and top brass of the department. He took a seat his adjutant had been saving in the row behind Sylvia Moore. He never looked back at Bosch once.

Thirty-Four

THROUGH THE ENTIRE SERVICE BOSCH HAD WATCHED her from his position next to the oak tree. Sylvia Moore rarely raised her head, even to watch the line of cadets fire blanks into the sky or when the air squad flew over, the helicopters arranged in the missing-man formation. One time he thought she glanced over at him, or at least in his direction, but he couldn't be sure. He thought of her as being stoic. And he thought of her as being beautiful.

When it was over and the casket was in the hole and the people were moving away, she stayed seated and Bosch saw her wave away an offer from Irving to be escorted back to the limousine. The assistant chief sauntered off, smoothing his collar against his neck. Finally, when the area around the burial site was clear, she stood up, glanced once down into the hole, and then started walking toward Bosch. Her steps were punctuated by the slamming of car doors all across the cemetery. She took the sunglasses off as she came.

"You took my advice," she said.

This immediately confused him. He looked down at his clothes and then back at her. What advice? She read him and answered.

"The black ice, remember? You have to be careful. You're here, so I assume you were."

"Yes, I was careful."

He saw that her eyes were very clear and she seemed even stronger than the last time they had encountered each other. They were eyes that would not forget a kindness. Or a slight.

"I know there is more than what they have told me. Maybe you will tell me sometime?"

He nodded and she nodded. There was a moment of silence as they looked at each other that was neither long nor short. It seemed to Bosch to be a perfect moment. The wind gusted and broke the spell. Some of her hair broke loose from the barrette and she pushed it back with her hand.

"I would like that," she said.

"Whenever you want," he said. "Maybe you'll tell me a few things, too."

"Such as?"

"That picture that was missing from the picture frame. You knew what it was, but you didn't tell me."

She smiled as if to say he had focused his attention on something unnecessary and trivial.

"It was just a picture of him and his friend from the barrio. There were other pictures in the bag."

"It was important but you didn't say anything."

She looked down at the grass.

"I just didn't want to talk or think about it anymore."

"But you did, didn't you?"

"Of course. That's what happens. The things you don't want to know or remember or think about come back to haunt you."

They were quiet for a moment.

"You know, don't you?" he finally said.

"That that wasn't my husband buried there? I had an idea, yes. I knew there was more than what people were telling me. Not you, especially. The others."

He nodded and the silence grew long but not uncomfortable. She turned slightly and looked over at the driver standing next to the limo, waiting. There was nobody left in the cemetery.

"There is something I hope you will tell me," she said. "Either now or sometime. If you can, I mean...Um, is he...is there a chance he will be back?"

Bosch looked at her and slowly shook his head. He studied her eyes for reaction. Sadness or fear, even complicity. There was none. She looked down at her gloved hands, which grasped each other in front of her dress.

"My driver...," she said, not finishing the thought. She tried a polite smile and for the hundredth time he asked himself what had been wrong with Calexico Moore. She took a step forward and touched her hand to his cheek. It felt warm, even through the silk glove, and he could smell perfume on her wrist. Something very light. Not really a smell. A scent.

"I guess I should go," she said.

He nodded and she backed away.

"Thank you," she said.

He nodded. He didn't know what he was being thanked for but all he could do was nod.

"Will you call? Maybe we could...I don't know I—"

"I will call."

Now she nodded and turned to walk back to the black limousine. He hesitated and then spoke up.

"You like jazz? The saxophone?"

She stopped and turned back to him. There was sharpness in her eyes. That need for touch. It was so clear he could feel it cut him. He thought maybe it was his own reflection.

"Especially the solos," she said. "The ones that are lonely and sad. I love those."

"There is...is tomorrow night too soon?"

"It's New Year's Eve."

"I know. I was thinking...I guess it might not be the right time. The other night—that was...I don't know."

She walked back to him and put her hand on his neck and pulled his face down to hers. He went willingly. They kissed for a long time and Bosch kept his eyes closed. When she let him go he didn't look to see if anyone was watching. He didn't care.

"What is a right time?" she asked.

He had no answer.

"I'll be waiting for you."

He smiled and she smiled.

She turned for the last time and walked to the car, her high heels clicking on the asphalt once she left the carpet of grass. Bosch leaned back against the tree and watched the driver open the door for her. Then he lit a cigarette and watched as the sleek black machine carried her out through the gate and left him alone with the dead.

About the Author

MICHAEL CONNELLY is the author of thirty-five previous novels, including the *New York Times* bestsellers *The Law of Innocence*, *Fair Warning*, and *The Night Fire*. His books, which include the Harry Bosch series, the Lincoln Lawyer series, and the Renée Ballard series, have sold more than eighty million copies worldwide. Connelly is a former newspaper reporter who has won numerous awards for his journalism and his novels. He is the executive producer of *Bosch*, starring Titus Welliver, and the creator and host of the podcast *Murder Book*. He spends his time in California and Florida.

Has a killer lain dormant for years only to
strike again on New Year's Eve?

LAPD Detective Renée Ballard and Harry Bosch
team up to find justice for an innocent victim in the
new thriller from #1 *New York Times* bestselling
author Michael Connelly.

THE DARK HOURS

Available November 2021

Please turn the page for a preview.

1

IT WAS SUPPOSED TO RAIN FOR REAL AND THAT would have put a damper on the annual rain of lead. But the forecast was wrong. The sky was blue-black and clear. And Ballard braced for the onslaught, positioning herself on the north side of the division under the shelter of the Cahuenga overpass. She would have preferred being alone but was riding with a partner, and a reluctant partner at that. Detective Lisa Moore of the Hollywood Division Sexual Assault Unit was a day-shift veteran who just wanted to be home with her girlfriend. But it was always all hands on deck on New Year's Eve. Tactical alert: everyone in the department in uniform and working twelves. Ballard and Moore had been working since six p.m. and it had been quiet. But it was now about to strike midnight on the last day of the year and the trouble would begin. Added to that, the Midnight Men were out there somewhere. Ballard and her reluctant partner needed to be ready to move quickly when the call came in.

"Do we have to stay here?" Moore asked. "I mean, look at these people. How can they live like this?"

Ballard surveyed the makeshift shelters made of discarded tarps and construction debris that lined both sides of the underpass. She saw a couple of Sterno cook fires and people milling about at their meager encampments. It was so crowded that some shanties were even pressed up against the mobile toilets the city had put on the sidewalks to preserve some semblance of dignity and sanitation in the area. North of the overpass was a residential zone of apartments fronting the hillside area known as the Dell. After multiple reports of people defecating in the streets and yards of the neighborhood, the city came through with the portable toilets. A "humanitarian effort," it was called.

"You ask that like you think they all want to be living under an overpass," Ballard said. "Like they have a lot of choices. Where are they going to go? The government gives them toilets. It takes their shit away but not much else."

"Whatever," Moore said. "It's such a blight—every overpass in the fucking city. It's so third world. People are going to start leaving this place because of this."

"They already have," Ballard said. "Anyway, we're staying here. I've spent the last four New Year's Eves under here and it's the safest place to be when the shooting starts."

They were quiet for a few moments after that. Ballard had thought about leaving herself, maybe going back to Hawaii. It wasn't because of the intractable problem of homelessness that gripped the city. It was everything. The city, the job, the life. It had been a bad year with the pandemic and social unrest and violence. The police department had been vilified, and she along with it. She'd been spat on, figuratively and literally, by the people she thought she stood for. It was a hard lesson, and a sense of futility had set upon her and was deep in the marrow now. She needed some kind of a break. Maybe to go track down her mother in the mountains of Maui and try to reconnect after so many years.

She took one of her hands off the wheel and held her sleeve to her nose. It was her first time back in uniform since the protests. She could make out the smell of tear gas. She had dry-cleaned the uniform twice but the odor was baked in, permanent. It was a good reminder of the year that had been.

The pandemic and protests had changed everything. The department went from being proactive to reactive. And the change had somehow cast Ballard adrift. She had found herself more than once thinking about quitting. That is, until the Midnight Men came along. They had given her purpose.

Moore checked her watch again. Ballard noticed and glanced at the dashboard clock. It was off by an hour, but doing the math told her it was two minutes till midnight.

"Oh, here we go," Moore said. "Look at this guy."

She was looking out her window at a man approaching the car. It was below 60 degrees but he wore no shirt and was holding his dirt-caked pants up with his hand. He wore no mask either. Moore had her window cracked but now hit the button and closed and sealed the car.

The homeless man knocked on her window. They could hear him through the glass.

"Hey, officers, I got a problem here."

They were in Ballard's unmarked car but she had engaged the flashing grille lights when they parked in the median under the overpass. Plus they were in full uniform.

"Sir, I can't talk to you without a mask," Moore said loudly. "Go get a mask."

"But I been ripped off," the man said. "That sumbitch o'er there took my shit when I was sleepin'."

"Sir, I can't help you until you get a mask," Moore said.

"I don't have no fucking mask," he said.

"Then I'm sorry, sir," she said. "No mask, no ask."

The man punched the window, his fist hitting the glass in front of Moore's face. She jerked back even though it had not been a punch intended to break the glass.

"Sir, step back from the car," Moore commanded.

"Fuck you," he said.

"Sir, if I have to get out, you're going to County," Moore said. "If you don't have corona now, you'll get it there. You want that?"

The man started to walk away.

"Fuck you," he said again. "Fuck the police."

"Like I never heard that before," Moore said.

She checked her watch again and Ballard looked back at the dash clock. It was now the final minute of 2020, and for Moore and most people in the city and the world, the year couldn't end soon enough.

"Jesus Christ, can we move to another spot?" Moore complained.

"Too late," Ballard said. "I told you, we're safe under here."

"Not from these people," Moore said.

2

IT WAS LIKE A BAG OF POPCORN COOKING IN A MICRO-wave. A few pops during the final countdown of the year and then the barrage as the frequency of gunfire made it impossible to separate it into individual discharges. A gunshot symphony. For a solid five minutes, there was an unbroken onslaught as revelers of the new year fired their weapons into the sky, following a Los Angeles tradition of decades.

It didn't matter that what goes up must come down. Every new year in the City of Angels began with risk.

The gunfire of course was joined by legitimate fireworks and fire-crackers, creating a sound unique to the city and as reliable through the years as the changing of the calendar. The over/under at roll call was 18 in terms of calls related to the rain of lead. Windshields mostly would be the victims, though the year before, Ballard caught a report of a bullet falling through a skylight and hitting a stripper on the shoulder who was toiling on a stage below. The falling bullet didn't even break the skin. But a jagged piece of falling skylight glass did give a customer sitting close to the stage a new part in his hair. He chose not to make a police report, because it would reveal that where he was didn't match where he had said he would be.

Whatever the number was, patrol would handle most of the calls unless a detective was warranted. Ballard and Moore were mostly waiting for one call. The Midnight Men. It was a painful reality that sometimes you needed predators to strike again in hopes of a mistake or a new piece of evidence that could lead to a solve.

.The Midnight Men was the unofficial moniker Ballard had bestowed on the tag team rapists who had assaulted two women in a five-week span. Both assaults had occurred on holiday nights— Thanksgiving night and Christmas Eve. The cases were linked by modus operandi and not DNA. The Midnight Men were careful not to leave DNA behind. Each attack started shortly after midnight and lasted as long as four hours while the predators took turns assaulting women in their own beds, ending the torture by cutting a large hank of each victim's hair off with the knife held to her throat during the ordeal. Other humiliations were included in the attacks and helped link the cases beyond the rarity of a two-man rape team.

Ballard, as the third watch detective, had been the responding detective on both cases. She had then called in day-watch detectives from the Hollywood Division Sexual Assault Unit. Lisa Moore was a member of that three-detective unit.

In past years, a pair of serial rapists would have immediately drawn the attention of the Sex Crimes Unit that worked out of the Police Administration Building downtown as part of the elite Robbery-Homicide Division. But City Hall cutbacks in police funding had seen the unit disbanded, and sex assault cases were now handled by the divisional detective squads. It was an example of how protesters demanding the defunding of the police department had achieved their goal through unintended means. The move to defund was turned away by the city's politicians, but the police department had burned through its budget in dealing with the protests that followed the death of George Floyd at the hands of police in Minneapolis. After weeks of tactical alert and associated costs, the department was out of money and the result was freezes on hiring, the disbanding of units, and the end of several programs. In effect, the department had been defunded in several key areas.

Lisa Moore was a perfect example of how all of this led to a downgrade in service to the community. Rather than the Midnight Men investigation going to a specialized unit with many resources and detectives with extra training and experience in serial investigations, it had gone to the overworked and understaffed Hollywood Division sex crime team that was responsible for investigating every rape, attempted rape, assault, groping, indecent exposure, and claim of pedophilia in a vast geographic and population-dense area. And Moore was like many in the department since the protest, looking to do as little as possible between now and her retirement four years away. She was looking at the Midnight Men case as a time suck taking her away from her normal eight-to-four existence, where she dutifully filed paperwork the first half of the day and conducted minimal investigative work after that, leaving the station only if there was no way the work could be done by phone and computer. She had greeted her assignment to work the midnight shift with Ballard over the New Year's holiday as a major insult and inconvenience. Ballard, on the other side of that coin, had seen it as a chance to get closer to taking down two predators who were out there hurting women.

"What do you hear about the vax?" Moore asked.

Ballard shook her head.

"Probably the same as you hear," she said. "Next month—maybe."

Now Moore shook her head.

"Assholes," she said. "We're first-fucking-responders and should get it with the fire department. Instead we're with the grocery workers."

"The fire guys are considered health-care providers," Ballard said. "We're not."

"I know, but it's the principle of it. Our union is shit."

"It's not the union. It's the governor, the health department, a lot of things."

"Fuckin' politicians..."

Ballard let it go. It was a complaint heard often at roll calls and in police cars across the city. Like many in the department, Ballard had already contracted COVID-19. She had been knocked down for three weeks in November and now just hoped she had enough antibodies to see her through to the vaccine's arrival.

During the brooding silence that followed, a patrol car pulled up next to them on Moore's side, in one of the two southbound lanes.

"You know these guys?" Moore asked as she reached for the window button.

"Unfortunately," Ballard said. "Pull your mask up."

It was a team of P2s named Smallwood and Vitello, who always had too much testosterone running in their blood. They also thought they were "too healthy" to contract the virus and eschewed the department-mandated mask requirement.

Moore lowered the window after pulling her mask up.

"How's things in the tuna boat?" Smallwood said, a wide smile on his face.

Ballard pulled up her department-issued mask. It was navy blue with LAPD embossed in silver along the jaw line.

"You're blocking traffic there, Smallwood," Ballard said.

Moore looked back at Ballard.

"Really?" she whispered. "Small wood?"

Ballard nodded.

Vitello hit the switch for the light bar on the patrol car's roof. Flashing blue lit up the graffiti on the concrete walls above the tents and shanties on both sides of the overpass. Various versions of "Fuck the Police" and "Fuck Trump" had been whitewashed by city crews but the messages came through under the penetrating blue light.

"How's that?" Vitello asked.

"Hey, there's a guy over there, wants to report a theft of property," Ballard responded. "Why don't you two go take a report?"

"Fuck that," Smallwood said.

"Sounds like detective work to me," Vitello added.

The conversation, if it could be called that, was interrupted by the voice of a com center dispatcher coming up on the radio in both cars, asking for any 6-William unit, "6" being the designation for Hollywood, and "William" for detective.

"That's you, Ballard," Smallwood said.

Ballard pulled the radio out of its charger in the center console and responded.

"Six-William-twenty-six. Go ahead."

The dispatcher asked her to respond to a shooting with injury on Gower.

"The Gulch," Vitello called over. "Need backup down there, ladies?"

Hollywood Division was broken into seven different patrol zones called Basic Car Areas. Smallwood and Vitello were assigned to the area that included the Hollywood Hills, where crime was low and most of the residents they encountered were white. This was a move designed to keep them out of trouble and away from confrontational enforcement with minorities. However, that had not always worked. Ballard had heard about them roughing up teenagers in cars parked illegally on Mulholland Drive, where there were spectacular views of the city at night.

"I think we can handle it," Ballard called across. "You boys can go back up to Mulholland and watch for kids throwing their condoms out the window. Make it safe up there, guys."

She dropped the car into drive and hit the gas before either Smallwood or Vitello could manage a comeback.

"Poor guy," Moore said without sympathy in her voice. "Officer Smallwood."

"Yeah," Ballard said. "And he tries to make up for it every night on patrol."

Moore laughed as they sped south on Cahuenga.

3

THE GOWER GULCH WAS THE NAME AFFIXED BY Hollywood lore to the intersection of Sunset Boulevard and Gower Street, where almost a hundred years ago it was a pickup spot for day laborers. These laborers waited at the corner for work as extras on the westerns the movie studios were turning out by the week. Many of the Hollywood cowboys waited at the intersection in full costume—dusty boots, chaps, vests, ten-gallon hats—so it became known as the Gower Gulch. It was said that a young actor named Marion Morrison picked up work here. He was better known as John Wayne.

The Gulch was now a shopping plaza with the fading facade of an Old West town and portraits of the Hollywood cowboys—from Wayne to Gene Autry—hanging on the outside wall of the Rite Aid drugstore. Going south from the Gulch, a stretch of studio stages as big as gymnasiums lined the east side all the way down to the crown jewel of Hollywood, Paramount Studios. The storied studio was surrounded by twelve-foot-high walls and iron gates, like a prison. But these barriers were constructed to keep people out, not in.

The west side of Gower was a contradiction. It was lined with a stretch of car repair shops sharing space with aging apartments where burglar bars guarded all windows and doors. The west side was marked heavily by the graffiti of a local gang called Las Palmas 13, but the east-side walls of the studios were left unmarred, as if those with the spray paint knew by some intuition not to mess with the industry that built the city.

The shooting call took Ballard and Moore to a street party in the tow yard of an auto body shop. Several people were milling about in the street, most without masks, most watching officers from two patrol cars who were taping off a crime scene inside the gated and asphalt-paved yard lined with vehicles in different stages of repair and restoration.

"So we have to do this, huh?" Moore said.

"I do," Ballard said.

She opened the door and got out of the car. She knew her answer would shame Moore into following. Ballard was pretty sure she was going to need Moore to help with this.

Ballard ducked under yellow tape stretched across the entrance to the business and quickly ascertained that the victim of the shooting was not on scene and had been transported. She saw Sergeant Dave Byron and another officer trying to corral a group of potential witnesses in one of the business's open garages. Two other uniforms were stringing an inner boundary around the actual crime scene, which was marked by a pool of blood and debris left behind by the paramedics. Ballard walked directly to Byron.

"Dave, what do you have for me?" she asked.

Byron looked over his shoulder at her. He was masked but she could tell by his eyes that he was smiling.

"Ballard, I have a shit sandwich for you," he said.

She signaled him away from the citizens so they could talk privately.

"Folks, you all stay right here," Byron said, holding his hands up in a stay-put motion to the witnesses, a sign that they might not understand English.

He joined Ballard by the front of the rusting body of an old VW bus. He looked at what he had jotted down in a small notebook.

"Your victim is supposedly Javiar Raffa, owner of the business," he said. "Lives about a block from here."

He pointed a thumb over his shoulder, indicating the neighborhood west of the body shop.

"For what it's worth, he has tats indicating an affiliation with Las Palmas," Byron added. "Old tattoos."

"Okay," Ballard said. "Where'd they transport him?"

"Hollywood Pres. He was circling."

"What did the wits tell you?"

"Not much. Left them for you. Raffa apparently has the gates open and puts out a keg every New Year's Eve. It's for the neighborhood but a lot of Las Palmas shows up. After the countdown, there was some shooting of firearms into the sky, and then suddenly Raffa was on the ground. So far, nobody is saying they actually saw him get hit. And you've got shell casings all over the place. Good luck with that."

Ballard shot her chin toward a camera mounted on the roof eave over the corner of the garage.

"What about cameras?" she asked.

"The cameras outside are dummies," Byron said. "Cameras inside are legit but I have not checked them. I'm told they are not in a position to be of much help."

"Okay. You get here before the EMTs?"

"I did not. But the basic car did. Finley and Watts. They said it was a head wound. They're over there and you can go talk to them."

"Will do."

Ballard checked to see if either of the uniforms who were marking the boundary was a Spanish speaker. Ballard knew basic Spanish but was not skilled enough to conduct witness interviews. She saw that one of the officers tying the crime scene tape to the sideview mirror of an old pickup was Victor Rodriquez.

"You mind if I keep V-Rod to translate?" she asked.

Ballard thought she saw the lines of a frown form on Byron's mask.

"How long?" he asked.

"Preliminary with the witnesses and then maybe the family when we go to the house," Ballard said. "I'll get somebody from detective services if we transport anybody back to the station."

"All right, but anything else comes up, I'm going to need to pull him back out."

"Roger that. I'll move fast."

Ballard walked over to Rodriquez, who had been with the division for about a year after transferring from Rampart.

"Victor, you're with me," Ballard said.

"I am?" he said.

"Let's go talk to witnesses."

"Cool."

Moore caught up to Ballard in step toward the group of witnesses.

"I thought you were staying in the car," Ballard said.

"What do you need?" Moore said.

"I could use someone at Hollywood Pres to check on the victim. You want to take the car and head over?"

"Shit."

"Or you can interview witnesses and family while I go."

"Give me the keys."

"I thought so. Keys are still in the car. Let me know what you find out."

Ballard briefed Rodriquez in a whisper as they approached the witnesses.

"Don't lead them," she said. "We just want to know what they saw, what they heard, anything they remember before they saw Mr. Raffa on the ground."

"Roger that."

They spent the next forty minutes doing quick interviews with the collected witnesses, none of whom saw the victim get shot. In separate interviews, each described a crowded, chaotic scene in the lot during which most people were looking up at the stroke of midnight as fireworks and bullets cut through the sky. Though no one admitted doing it themselves, they acknowledged that there were those in the neighborhood crowd who had fired guns into the air.

None of these witnesses revealed enough to make them important enough to transport to the station for another round of questioning. Ballard copied their addresses and phone numbers into her notebook and told them to expect follow-up contact from homicide investigators.

As she was wrapping up with the last witness, she got a call from Moore, who was at Hollywood Presbyterian Medical Center.

"The victim's family is all here, and they are about to get the word that he didn't make it," she said. "What do you want me to do?"

I want you to act like a trained detective, Ballard thought but didn't say.

"Keep the family there," she said instead. "I'm on my way."

"I'll try," Moore said.

"Don't try, do it," Ballard said. "I'll be there in ten. Do you know if they speak English?"

"I'm not sure."

"Okay, find out and text me. I'll bring somebody in case."

"What's it looking like over there?"

"Too early to tell. If it was an accident, the shooter didn't stick around. And if it wasn't, I've got no camera and no witnesses."

Ballard disconnected and walked over to Rodriquez.

"Victor, you need to drive me to Hollywood Pres," she said.

"Roger that."

Ballard informed Byron of where she was going and asked him to keep the crime scene secured until she got back.

As she crossed the lot, following Rodriquez to his car, she saw the first drops of rain hitting the asphalt amid the bullet casings.

4

RODRIQUEZ USED THE LIGHTS BUT NOT THE SIREN to speed their drive to the hospital. Ballard used the minutes to call her lieutenant at home to update him. Derek Robinson-Reynolds, the OIC of Hollywood detectives, picked up immediately, having texted Ballard a request for the update.

"Ballard, I was expecting to hear from you sooner than this."

"Sorry, L-T. We had several witnesses to talk to before we could get a handle on this. I also just heard that our victim is DOA."

"Then I'll have to get West Bureau out. I know they are already running full squad on a two-bagger from yesterday."

Homicides were handled out of West Bureau. Robinson-Reynolds was ready to pass the investigation off but knew it would not be well received by his counterpart at West Bureau homicide.

"Sir, you can do that, of course, but I haven't determined what this is yet. There were a lot of people shooting guns at midnight. Not sure if this was accidental or intentional. I'm heading to the hospital now to get a look at him."

"Well, didn't any of the witnesses see it?"

"Not the witnesses who stuck around. None of them said they saw it. They just saw the victim on the ground. Anybody who saw it scrammed out of there before the unies got on scene."

There was a pause as the lieutenant considered his next move.

They were a block from the hospital. Ballard spoke before Robinson-Reynolds responded.

"Let me run with it, L-T."

Robinson-Reynolds remained silent. Ballard made her case.

"West Bureau is running on the two-bagger. We don't even know what this is yet. Let me stay with it and we'll see where it stands in the morning when you come in."

The lieutenant finally spoke.

"I don't know, Ballard. Not sure I want you capering out there on your own."

"I'm not alone. I'm with Lisa Moore, remember?"

"Right, right. Nothing on that tonight?"

He was asking about the Midnight Men.

"Not so far. We're pulling into Hollywood Pres now. The family of the victim is here."

It pushed Robinson-Reynolds to make a decision.

"Okay, I'll hold off on West Bureau. For now. Keep me informed. No matter the hour, Ballard."

"Roger that."

"Okay, then."

Robinson-Reynolds disconnected. Ballard's phone buzzed with a text as Rodriquez was pulling to a stop behind Ballard's car, which had been left by Moore in an ambulance bay.

"Was that Dash?" Rodriquez asked. "What did he say?"

He was using the short name ascribed to Robinson-Reynolds by most in the division when not addressing the lieutenant personally. Ballard checked the text. It had come in from Moore: No English spoken here.

"He gave us the green light," Ballard said.

"Us?" Rodriquez said.

"I'm probably going to need you in here again."

"Sergeant Byron told me to double-time back."

"Sergeant Byron's not in charge of the investigation. I am, and you're with me until I say otherwise."

"Roger that—as long as you tell him."

"I will."

Ballard found Moore in the ER waiting room, surrounded by a group of crying women and one teenage boy. Raffa's family had just gotten the bad news about their husband and father. A wife, three adult daughters, and the son were all exhibiting various degrees of shock, grief, and anger.

"Oh, boy," Rodriquez said as they approached.

Nobody liked intruding on the kind of trauma unexpected death brings.

"I heard you want to be a detective someday, V-Rod," Ballard asked.

"Roger that," Rodriquez responded.

"Okay, I want you to help Detective Moore interview the family. Do more than translate. Ask the questions. Any known enemies, his association with Las Palmas, who else was at the shop tonight. Get names."

"Okay, what about you? Where are—"

"I need to check the body, then I'll be joining you."

"Got it."

"Good. Let Detective Moore know."

Ballard split off from him and went to the check-in counter. Soon she was led back to the nursing station that was in the middle of the ER. It was surrounded by multiple examination and treatment spaces separated by curtain walls. She asked a nurse if the body of the gunshot victim had been moved yet from a treatment space. She was told that the hospital was waiting for a coroner's team to pick it up. She was pointed to a closed curtain.

Ballard pulled back the pastel green curtain, entered the single-bed examination space, and then pulled the curtain closed behind her. Javier Raffa's body was faceup on the bed. There had been no attempt to cover him. His shirt—a blue work shirt with his name on an oval patch—was pulled open and his chest still showed conduit ointment, likely from paddles that had been used to revive him.

His eyes were open and there was a rubber device extending from the mouth. Ballard knew it was placed in the mouth of patients exhibiting seizures.

There was a bullet entry wound below the right eye and close to the bridge of the nose.

Ballard pulled a pair of black rubber gloves out of a compartment on her equipment belt and stretched them on. Using both hands, she gently turned the dead man's head to check for an exit wound. She noticed a discolored area of skin on the right side of the neck. She turned the head fully to confirm there was no exit wound. The bullet was still inside.

She turned the head back and then leaned farther over the bed to look closely at the wound. She guessed that it had been made by a small-caliber bullet and noticed that the wound was outlined by a ring of darkened skin. It was tattooing from burnt gunpowder discharged from the barrel of the weapon that fired the bullet into Javier Raffa's head.

In that moment, Ballard knew this had been no accident. Raffa had been murdered. A killer had used the moment when all eyes were cast upward to the midnight sky and there was gunfire all around to press the muzzle of a gun to Raffa's face and pull the trigger. And in that moment, Ballard knew she wanted the case, that she would find a way to keep this conclusion to herself until she was too deeply embedded to be removed.

She knew this could be the solve she needed to save herself.

5

BALLARD PULLED THE CURTAIN CLOSED AFTER STEP-
ping out of the treatment bay. She stepped over to the nursing station so she would not block traffic in the busy ER. She pulled her
phone and called the number for the Hollywood Division Gang
Intelligence Unit. No one picked up. She then called the inside line
in the watch office. Sergeant Kyle Dallas answered and Ballard asked
him who was working second twelves from GIU.

"That would be Janzen and Cordero," Dallas said. "And I think
Sergeant Davenport is around too."

"Out or in?" Ballard asked.

"I just saw Cordero in the break room, so I guess they may have
all come in now that the witching hour is passed."

"Okay, if you see them, tell them to stay put. I need to talk to
them. I'll be in soon."

"You got it."

Ballard went through the automatic doors to the waiting room
and saw Moore and Rodriquez sitting in the corner with the Raffa
family in a group interview. Renée was annoyed that Moore had
not conducted individual interviews but then she reminded herself
that Moore was used to investigating sexual assaults, which usually
involved solo interviews of victims. Moore was out of her league
here and Rodriquez just didn't know any better.

Ballard saw that the son was sitting outside the inner huddle and looking over the shoulders of two of his sisters at Moore. She walked up and tapped him on the shoulder.

"Do you speak English?" she whispered.

The boy nodded.

"Come with me, please," Ballard said.

She led him over to another corner. The waiting room was surprisingly uncrowded. Surprising for any night of the week but particularly so for post-midnight on New Year's Eve. She pointed to a chair for the boy to take and then pulled a second chair away from the wall and positioned it so they could talk face-to-face.

They both sat down.

"What's your name?" Ballard asked.

"Gabriel," the boy said.

"You are Javier's son?"

"Yes."

"I'm sorry for your loss. We are going to find out what happened and who did it. I'm Detective Ballard. You can call me Renée."

Gabriel eyed her uniform.

"Detective?" he asked.

"We had to be in uniform for New Year's Eve," Ballard said. "Everybody out on the street, that sort of thing. How old are you?"

"Fifteen."

"What school do you go to?"

"Hollywood."

"And you were at the shop's tow yard tonight at midnight?"

"Yes."

"Were you with your father?"

"Uh, no, I was . . . over by the Caddy."

While at the crime scene, Ballard had seen a rusting old Cadillac parked in the lot. Its trunk was open and there was a beer keg sitting in a bed of ice inside it.

"Were you with anyone by the Caddy?" Ballard asked.

"My girlfriend," Gabriel said.

"What's her name?"

"I don't want to get her in trouble or nothing."

"She's not in trouble. We're just trying to figure out who all was there tonight, that's all."

Ballard waited.

"Lara Rosas," Gabriel finally said.

"Thank you, Gabriel," Ballard said. "Do you know Lara from school or the neighborhood?"

"Uh, both."

"And she went home?"

"Yeah, she left when we came here."

"Did you see what happened to your father?"

"No, I just saw after. Him laying there."

Gabriel was exhibiting no emotion and Ballard saw no tear lines on his face. She knew this meant nothing. People process and express shock and grief in different ways. No behavior or lack of shown emotion should be considered suspicious.

"Did you see anybody at the party that you thought was strange or didn't belong?" Ballard asked.

"Not really," Gabriel said. "There was a guy there at the keg who didn't look like he belonged. But it was a street party. Who could say."

"Was he asked to leave?"

"No, he was just there. He got his beer and then I guess he left. I didn't see him no more."

"Was he from the neighborhood?"

"I doubt it. I never saw him before."

"What made you say that he didn't look like he belonged?"

"Well, he was a white guy, plus he seemed kind of dirty, you know. His clothes and stuff."

"You think he was homeless?"

"I don't know, maybe. That's what I thought."

"And this was before the shooting that you saw him?"

"Yeah, before. Definitely. It was before everyone started looking up."

"You said his clothes were dirty. What was he wearing?"

"A gray hoodie and blue jeans. His pants were dirty."

"Was it dirt or grease?"

"Like dirt, I think."

"What about his shoes, do you remember them?"

"Nah, I don't know about his shoes."

Ballard paused and tried to commit the details of the stranger to memory. She was not writing anything down. She thought it would be better to maintain eye contact with Gabriel and not possibly spook him by taking out a notebook and pen.

"Who else did you notice who wasn't right?" she asked.

"Nobody," Gabriel said. "That was it."

"And you're not sure if the guy in the hoodie hung around after getting his beer?"

"I didn't see him again."

"So, when you last saw him, how long was that before midnight and all the shooting started?"

"I don't know, a half hour. Maybe longer."

Ballard nodded. It was now time to ask more difficult questions and hold this kid to her side as long as she could.

"Did you fire any weapons tonight, Gabriel?" she asked.

"No, no way." Gabriel said.

"Okay, good. Are you associated with Las Palmas Thirteen?"

"What are you asking me? I'm no gangster. My parents said no way."

"Don't get upset. I'm just trying to figure out what is what. I need to know who I'm dealing with. You're not associated, that's good. But your father was. I just saw the tattoos on his neck."

"He quit that shit a long time ago. He was totally legit."

"Okay, that's good to know. But I heard there were guys from Las Palmas in the shop yard for the party. Is that true?"

"I don't know, maybe. My father grew up with these people. He didn't just throw them in the trash. But he was legit, his business was legit, he even had a white man as his partner. So don't go starting no shit about 'gang related.' That's bullshit."

Ballard nodded.

"Good to know, Gabriel. Can you tell me, was his partner there?"

"I didn't see him. Are we done here?"

"Not yet, Gabriel. What is the partner's name?"

"I don't know. He's a doctor up out in Malibu or some shit. I only seen him once when he came in with a bent frame."

"A bent frame?"

"His Mercedes. He backed into something and bent the frame."

"Got it. Okay, I need two more things from you, Gabriel."

"What?"

"I need your girlfriend's phone number and I need you to step outside to my car for a minute."

"Why should I go with you? I want to see my father."

"They're not going to let you see your father, Gabriel. Not till later. I want to help you. I want this to be the last time you have to talk to the police about this. But to do that, I need to wipe your hands to make sure you're telling the truth."

"What?"

"You said you didn't fire a gun tonight. I wipe your hands with something I have in my car and we'll know for sure. After that, you'll only hear from me when I come by to tell you we caught the person who did this to your father."

Ballard waited while Gabriel considered the options.

"If you won't do it, I have to assume you lied to me. You don't want that, do you?"

"All right, whatever, let's do it."

Ballard walked over to the group first to ask Moore for the car keys. She was told they were in the car. She then led Gabriel out to the ambulance bays. She got his girlfriend's cell number, then got the keys and opened her car's trunk. She had a packet of wipe pads for gunshot-residue testing. She used separate pads to wipe both Gabriel's hands, then sealed them in plastic bags to be submitted to the lab.

"See, no gunpowder, right?" Gabriel said.

"The lab will confirm that," Ballard said. "But I already believe you, Gabriel."

"So, what do I do now?"

"You go in and be with your mother and your sisters. They're going to need you to be strong for them."

Gabriel nodded and his face contorted. It was as though telling him to be strong had kicked his strength out from beneath him.

"You okay?" Ballard asked.

She touched his shoulder.

"You're going to catch this guy, right?" he said.

"Yeah," Ballard said. "We're going to catch him."

6

BALLARD DIDN'T GET BACK TO THE STATION UNTIL almost three a.m. She went up the stairs off the back hallway and into the room shared by the Gang Intel and Vice units. It was long and rectangular and usually empty because both units worked the streets. But the room now was crowded. Officers from both squads, in uniforms like Ballard, sat behind desks and at work tables going down the length of the room. The large crowd could be explained in a number of ways. First, it was difficult to work vice and gangs in full uniform, as dictated by the department's tactical alert. It could also mean that, because it was beyond the witching hours of midnight to two a.m., everyone had returned to the house on break. But Ballard knew that it could also be that this was the new LAPD—officers stripped of the mandate of proactive enforcement and waiting to be reactive, to hit the streets only when it was requested and required, and only then doing the minimum that was required so as not to engender a complaint or controversy.

To Ballard, much of the department had fallen into the pose of a citizen caught in the middle of a bank robbery. Head down, eyes averted, adhering to the warning; nobody move and nobody gets hurt.

She spotted Sergeant Davenport at the end of one of the work tables and headed toward him. He looked up from a cell phone to see her coming, and a smile of recognition creased his face. He was mid-forties and had been working gangs in the division for over a decade.

"Ballard," he said. "I hear El Chopo got it tonight."

Ballard stopped at the table.

"El Chopo?" she asked.

"That's what we called Javier back in the day," Davenport said. "When he was a gangster and using his padre's place as a chop shop."

"But not anymore?"

"He supposedly went straight after his wife started dropping kids."

"I was surprised I didn't see you out at the scene tonight. That why?"

"That and other things. Just doin' what the people want."

"Which is staying off the street?"

"It's pretty clear if they can't defund us, they want to de-see us. We're just giving the people what they want, right, GoGo?"

Davenport looked for affirmation to a gang cop named Gomez.

"Right, Sergeant," Gomez said.

Ballard pulled out the empty chair to Davenport's right side and sat down. She decided to drop the questioning of Davenport's motives and current views of policing the city.

"So, what can you tell me about Javier?" she asked. "Do you believe he went straight? Would Las Palmas even allow that?"

"The word is that twelve or fifteen years ago, he bought his way out," Davenport said. "And as far as we know, he's been clean and legit ever since."

"Or too smart for you?"

"There's always that possibility."

Davenport laughed.

"Well, do you still have a file on the guy?" Ballard asked. "Shake cards, anything?"

"Oh, we got a file," Davenport said. "It's probably a little dusty. GoGo, pull the file on Javier Raffa and bring it to Detective Ballard."

Gomez got up and walked to the line of four-drawer file cabinets that ran the length of one side of the room.

"That's how far this guy goes back," Davenport said. "He's in the paper files."

"So, not on your radar anymore?" Ballard pressed.

"Nope. And we would have known if he was active. We follow some of the OGs. If they were meeting, we would have seen it."

"How far up was Raffa before he dropped out?"

"Not far. He was a soldier. We never made a case on the guy but we knew he was chopping stolen cars for the team."

"How did you hear he bought his way out?"

Davenport shook his head like he couldn't remember.

"Just the grapevine," he said. "I can't name you the snitch offhand—it was a long time ago. But that was what was said, and as far as we could tell, it was accurate."

"How much does something like that cost?" Ballard asked.

"Can't remember. It might be in the file."

Gomez returned from the cabinets and handed a file to Davenport instead of Ballard. He in turned handed it to Ballard.

"Knock yourself out," he said.

"Can I take this?" Ballard asked.

"As long as you bring it back."

"Roger that."

Ballard took the file, got up, and walked out. She had the feeling that several of the men were watching as she left the room.

She went down the stairs and into the detective bureau, where she saw Lisa Moore at her desk. She was typing on her computer.

"You're back," Ballard said.

"No thanks to you," Moore said. "You left me with those people and that kid cop."

"Rodriquez? He probably has five years on. He's been in the division longer than I have."

"Doesn't matter, he looks like a kid."

"Did you get anything good from the wife and daughters?"

"No, but I'm writing it up, anyway. Where is this going, anyway?"

"I'm going to keep it for a bit. Send whatever you've got to me."

"Not to West Bureau?"

"They're running all teams on a double murder. So I'll work this until they're ready to take it."

"And Dash is okay with that?"

"I talked to him. It's not a problem."

"What do you have there?"

She pointed to the file Ballard was carrying.

"An old gang file on Raffa," Ballard said. "Davenport said he hasn't been active in years, that he bought his way out when he started a family."

"Aw, isn't that sweet," Moore said.

The sarcasm was clear in her voice. Ballard had long realized that Moore had lost her empathy. Working sex cases full time probably did that. Losing empathy for victims was a protective measure, but Ballard hoped it never happened to her. Police work could easily hollow you out. But she believed that losing one's empathy was losing one's soul.

"Send me your reports when you're ready to file," Ballard said.

"Will do," Moore said.

"And nothing on the Midnight Men, right?"

"Not yet. Maybe they're lying low tonight."

"It's still early. On Thanksgiving, we didn't get the call out till dawn."

"Wonderful. Can't wait till dawn."

The sarcasm again. Ballard ignored it and grabbed an empty desk nearby. Because she worked the late show, she didn't have an assigned desk. She was expected to borrow a desk in the room whenever she needed one. She looked at a few of the knickknacks on the one shelf in the cubicle where she sat and quickly realized it was the workstation of a dayside CAPs detective named Tom Newsome. He loved baseball, and there were several souvenir balls on little pedestals on the shelf. They had been signed by Dodgers players past and present. The gem of the collection was in a small plastic cube to protect it. It wasn't signed by a player. Instead the signature was from the man who had called Dodgers games on radio and TV for more than fifty years. Vince Scully was revered as the voice of the city because he transcended baseball. Even Ballard knew who he was and she thought that Newsome was risking the theft of the ball, even in a police station.

Opening the file, Ballard was greeted by a booking photo of Javier Raffa as a young man. He had died at age thirty-eight, and the photo was from a 2003 arrest for receiving stolen property. She read the details on the arrest report the photo was clipped to. It said Raffa had been pulled over in a 1977 Ford pickup truck with several used auto parts in the bed. One of these parts—a trans-axle—still had the manufacturing serial number embossed on it, and it was traced to a Mercedes G Wagon reported stolen in the San Fernando Valley the month before.

According to the records in the file, Raffa's lawyer, listed as Michael Haller, negotiated a disposition that got the twenty-one-year-old Javier probation and community service in exchange for a guilty plea. The case was then expunged from Raffa's record when he completed probation and 120 hours of community service without issue. The file noted that his community service included painting over gang graffiti affixed to freeway overpasses throughout the city.

It was the one and only arrest record in the file, although there were several field interview cards paper-clipped together in the file. These were all dated before the arrest and went back through the years to when Raffa was sixteen years old. Most of these came out of basic gang rousts. Patrol breaking up parties or Hollywood Boulevard cruise lines. Officers taking down names and associates, tattoos, and other descriptors to be fed into Gang Intel files and databases. As the son of a body shop owner, Raffa was always driving classic and restored cars or low riders that were also described on the shake cards.

From early on in the cards Raffa had the nickname El Chopo ascribed to him. It was an obvious take on the moniker of one of the biggest cartel kingpins, known as El Chapo, which translated from Spanish to mean "Shorty." One note that caught Ballard's eye and was repeated on the four cards written and filed between 2000 and 2003 was a descriptor of a tattoo on the right side of Raffa's neck. It depicted a white billiard ball with an orange stripe and the number 13—a reference to Las Palmas 13 and its association with and deference to la eMe, the prison gang also known as the Mexican Mafia. The 13 was a reference to M, the thirteenth letter of the alphabet.

Ballard thought about the discoloration she had seen on Raffa's neck. She realized it was laser scarring from when he'd had the tattoo removed.

There was an intel report in the file dated October 25, 2005, that was a bullet-point recounting of multiple nuggets of unsubstantiated bits of gossip and information from a confidential informant identified as LP3. Ballard assumed that the informant was a Las Palmas insider. She scanned through the separate entries and found one entry about Raffa.

- Javier Raffa (El Chopo) DOB 02/14/82—said to have paid Humberto Viera $25K cash tribute for no-strings separation from the gang.

Ballard had never heard of someone buying their way out of a gang. She had always known of the "blood in, blood out, till death do us part" rule of gang law. She picked up the desk phone. Newsome had taped a station phone directory to it. She called the extension next to GIU and asked for Sergeant Davenport. While she waited for him to come on the line, she picked one of the baseballs off its pedestal and tried to make out the signature scribbled on it. She knew little about baseball or the Dodgers or the players on the team past and present. To her, the first name on the signature looked like Mookie but she thought she had to have that wrong.

Davenport came on the line.

"It's Ballard, got a question."

"Go ahead."

"Humberto Viera of Las Palmas, is he still around?"

Davenport chuckled.

"Depends on what you mean by 'around,'" he said. "He's been up in Pelican Bay for at least eight, ten years. And he isn't coming back."

"Your case?" Ballard asked.

"I was part of it, yeah. Got him on a couple of one-eight-sevens of White Fence guys. We flipped the getaway driver, and that was it for Humberto. Bye-bye on him."

"Okay. Anyone else I could talk to about Javier Raffa buying his way out of the gang?"

"Hmm. I don't think so. That goes pretty far back, as far as I remember. I mean, there are always OGs around but they're original gangsters because they toe the line. But for the most part, these gangs turn over membership every eight or ten years. Nobody's going to talk to you about Raffa."

"What about LP-three?"

There was a pause before Davenport answered.

"What do you think you'll get out of her?"

"So it's a woman?"

"I didn't say that. What do you think you will get out of him?"

"I don't know. I'm looking for a reason somebody put a bullet in Javier Raffa's head."

"Well, LP-three is long gone. That's a dead end."

"You're sure now?"

"I'm sure."

"Thanks, Sergeant. I'll catch you later."

Ballard put the phone in its cradle. It was clear to her from Davenport's gaffe that LP3 was a woman and possibly still active as an informant. Otherwise he would not have been so clumsy in trying to cover up his slip of the tongue. Ballard didn't know what it meant in terms of her case, considering that Raffa had apparently separated from the gang more than fifteen years earlier. But it was good to know that if the case turned toward the gang, the GIU had an insider who could provide insight and information.

"What was that about?" Moore asked.

She was sitting across the aisle from Ballard.

"Gang Intel," Ballard said. "They don't want me talking to their Las Palmas CI."

"Figures," Moore said.

Ballard wasn't sure what that meant but didn't respond. She knew Moore was one and done on the late show. Her involvement in the case would end when the sun came up and her shift was over, the tactical alert was ended, and all officers returned to their normal schedules. Moore would be back on dayside, but Ballard would be left alone to work in the dark hours.

It was exactly the way she wanted it.

7

BALLARD BEGAN PUTTING TOGETHER THE MURDER book on the Raffa case. This effort started with the tedious job of writing out the incident report, which described the killing and identified the victim but also included many mundane details such as time of the initial call, names of responding patrol officers, ambient temperature, next-of-kin notification, and other details that were important in documenting but not solving the case. She then wrote summaries of the witness interviews she had conducted and collected from Lisa Moore, though Moore's documentation was short and perfunctory. A summary of the interview with Raffa's youngest daughter had only one line: "This girl knows nothing and can contribute nothing to the investigation."

All of this was put into a three-ring binder. Lastly, Ballard started a case chrono that documented her movements by time and included mention of her discussion with Davenport. She then made copies of the documents in the GIU file and put them in the binder as well. She got all of this done by five a.m. and then got up and approached Moore, who was looking at email on her phone. Their shift ended in an hour but that didn't matter to Ballard.

"I'm going to go downtown to see what Forensics collected," Ballard said. "You want to stay or go?"

"I think I'll stay," Moore said. "There is no way you'll be back by six."

"Right. Then do you mind taking the GIU file back up to Davenport?"

"No, I'll take it. But why are you doing this?"

"Doing what?"

"Running with the case. It's a homicide. You're just going to turn it over to West Bureau as soon as everybody wakes up over there."

"Maybe. But maybe they'll let me work it."

"You're giving the rest of us a bad name, Renée."

"What are you talking about?"

"Just stay in your lane. Nobody moves, nobody gets hurt, right?"

Ballard shrugged.

"You didn't say that about me jumping on the Midnight Men case," she said.

"That's rape," Moore said. "You're talking about a homicide case."

"I don't see the difference. There's a victim and there's a case."

"Well, put it this way: West Bureau will see a difference. They're not going to be nice about you trying to take away one of theirs."

"Well, we'll see. I'm going. Let me know if our two assholes hit again."

"Oh, I will. And you do the same."

Ballard went back to her borrowed desk, closed her laptop, and collected her things. She pulled up her mask and then headed out. After leaving the station, she took the 101 toward downtown, driving through the pre-dawn grays toward the towers that always seemed lit at any hour of darkness. Traffic had generally been cut in half during the pandemic, but the city at this hour was dead, and Ballard made it to the 10 east interchange in less than fifteen minutes. From there it was only another five minutes before the exit to the Cal State L.A. campus. The Forensic Science Center, the five-story lab shared by the LAPD and the L.A. County Sheriff's Department, was at the south end of the vast campus.

The building seemed just as quiet as the streets. Ballard took the elevator up to the third floor, where the crime scene techs worked. She buzzed her way in and was met by a criminalist named Anthony Manzano, who had been out at the Javier Raffa crime scene.

"Ballard," he said. "I was wondering who I was going to hear from."

"It's me, for now," Ballard said. "West Bureau is running with a double and it's all hands on deck for now."

"You don't have to tell me. Everybody but me is working it. Come on back."

"Must be a hairy case."

"More like a TV case and they don't want to look bad."

Ballard had been curious about why no media had turned up at the Gower Gulch case. She had thought that the initial theory, that someone had been killed by a falling bullet, would have been catnip to the media, but so far, there had been no calls and no show-ups from the media that she was aware of.

Manzano led her through the lab to his workstation. She saw three other criminalists at work in other pods and assumed they were on the West Bureau case.

"What is the case out there?" she asked casually.

"Elderly couple robbed and murdered," Manzano said.

After a pause he delivered the kicker.

"They were set on fire," he said. "While alive."

"Jesus Christ," Ballard said.

She shook her head but immediately thought, yes, the media would be all over that case, and the department would want to give the appearance of no stone unturned and would throw several bodies on the case. That meant she stood a good chance of being able to keep the Raffa case if she could get the approval of her boss, Lieutenant Robinson-Reynolds.

There was a light table in Manzano's pod, and spread across it was a wide piece of graph paper on which he had been in the process of sketching the crime scene.

"This is your scene right here and I've been plotting the locations of the casings we collected," Manzano said. "It looked like the shootout at the O.K. Corral out there."

"You mean the firing into the sky, right?" Ballard said.

"I do, and it's interesting. We have thirty-one shells recovered and I think it adds up to only three guns in play—including the murder weapon."

"Show me."

To the side of the graph paper was a clipboard with Manzano's notes and drawings from the scene. There was also an open cardboard box containing the thirty-one bullet casings in individual plastic evidence bags.

"Okay, so thirty-one shots produced thirty-one shells on the ground," Manzano said. "We have three separate calibers and ammunition brands, so this becomes pretty easy to figure out."

He reached into the box, rooted around in it, and came out with one of the bagged bullet casings.

"We have identified seventeen casings as nine-millimeter PDX1 rounds produced by Winchester," Manzano said. "You will have to get confirmation from FU but to me, as a nonexpert, the firing-pin marks on these look alike, and that would suggest they all came from a nine-millimeter weapon that would hold sixteen rounds in the clip and one in the chamber if fully loaded."

Manzano had referenced the Firearms Unit, which was no longer called that because of the meaning associated with the acronym. It had been updated to Firearms Analysis Unit.

"I think you are probably looking at a Glock seventeen or similar weapon there," Manzano said. "Then we have thirteen casings that were forty-caliber and manufactured by Federal. I looked at our ammo catalog and these likely were jacketed hollow points, but FU would have an opinion on that. And of course these could have been fired by any number of firearms. Twelve in the clip, one in the chamber."

"Okay," Ballard said. "That leaves one casing."

Manzano reached into the box and found the bag containing the last bullet.

"Yes," he said. "And this is a Remington twenty-two."

Ballard took the evidence bag and looked at the brass casing. She was sure it was from the bullet that killed Javier Raffa.

"This is good, Anthony," she said. "Show me where you found it?"

Manzano pointed to an X on the crime scene schematic that had the marker number 1 next to it and was inside the rectangular outline of a car. To the right of the car was a stick figure that Ballard took be Javier Raffa.

"Of course, the victim was transported before we got there, but the blood pool and EMT debris marked that spot," he said. "The casing was nine feet, two inches from the blood and located under one of the wrecks in the tow yard. The Chevy Impala, I believe."

Ballard realized that they had caught a break. The ejected shell had gone under the car and that made it difficult for the gunman to retrieve it before people started to notice that Raffa was down.

She held up the evidence bag.

"Can I take this to Firearms?" she asked.

"I'll write a COC," Manzano said.

He was talking about a chain-of-custody receipt.

"Do you know if anyone is over there?" Ballard asked.

"Should be somebody," Manzano said. "They're on tac alert like everybody else."

Ballard pulled her phone and checked the time. Tactical alert would end in fifteen minutes. It was Friday and the January 1 holiday. The Firearms Analysis Unit might possibly go dark.

"Okay, let me sign the COC and get over there before they leave," she said.

The FAU was just down the hall and Ballard entered with ten minutes to spare. At first she thought she was too late. She didn't see anyone and then she heard someone sneeze.

"Hello?"

"Sorry," someone said. "Coming out."

A man in a black polo shirt with the FAU logo stepped out from one of the gun storage racks that lined one wall of the unit. The unit had collected so many varieties of firearms over the years that they were displayed in rows of racks that could be closed together like an accordion.

The man was carrying a feather duster.

"Just doing a little housekeeping," he said. "We wouldn't want Sirhan's gun to get dusty. It's part of history."

Ballard just stared for a moment.

"Mitch Elder," the man said. "What can I do for you?"

Ballard identified herself.

"Are you about to leave at the end of the tac alert?" she asked.

"Supposed to," Elder said. "But . . . whaddaya got?"

It had been Ballard's experience that gun nuts always liked a challenge.

"We had a homicide this morning. Gunshot. I have a casing and was looking for a make on the weapon used, maybe a NIBIN run."

The National Integrated Ballistic Information Network was a database that stored characteristics of bullets and casings used in crimes. Each carried markings that could be matched to specific weapons and compared crime to crime. Casings were the better bet because bullets often fragmented or mushroomed on impact, making comparisons more difficult.

Ballard held up the clear evidence bag with the casing in it as bait. Elder's eyes fixed on it. He didn't take long.

"Well, let's see what you got," he said.

Ballard handed him the bag and then followed him to a workstation. He put on gloves, removed the casing, and studied it under a lighted magnifying glass. He turned it in his fingers, studying first the primer and then the rim for marks left by the weapon that had fired it.

"Good extractor marking," he finally said. "I think you are looking for a Walther . . . but we'll see. This will take a little time for me to encode. If you want to go get breakfast, I'll be here when you get back."

"No, I'm good," Ballard said. "I have to make a call."

"Then maybe we can get breakfast after we're done."

"Uh . . . I think I'll probably need to keep moving with the case. But thanks."

"Suit yourself."

"I'm going to find an extra desk."

She walked away, almost shaking her head. She was annoyed with herself for adding the thanks at the end of the rejection.

She found a workspace that was completely empty except for a phone on the desk. She pulled her phone and called Robinson-Reynolds, clearly waking him up.

"Ballard, what is it?"

He seemed annoyed.

"You told me to update you no matter the time."

"I did. Whaddaya got?"

"I think our shooting was a homicide—a murder—and I want to stick with it."

"Ballard, you know it needs to go to—"

"I know the protocol but West Bureau is running with a big media case and I think they would welcome me taking it off their hands—at least until they come up for air on the double they've got."

"You're not a homicide detective."

"I know, but I was. I can handle this, L-T. We've already conducted witness interviews and I've been to Forensics and now I'm at Firearms running NIBIN on the shell we found."

"You shouldn't have done any of that. You should have turned it over as soon as you knew it wasn't an accidental."

"West Bureau was busy; I ran with it. We can turn it over now but they won't jump on it, and hours and maybe days will go by before they do."

"It's not my call, Ballard. It's their call. Lieutenant Fuentes over there."

"Can you call him and grease this for me, L-T? He'll probably be happy we want to take it off his hands."

"There is no 'we' on this, Ballard. Besides, you are supposed to be off duty starting ten minutes ago. I got no overtime for you."

"I'm not doing this for OT. No greenies on this."

"Greenies" was a reference to the color of the 3 x 5 cards that had to be filled out and signed by a supervisor authorizing overtime work.

"No greenies?" Robinson-Reynolds asked.

"No greenies," Ballard promised.

"What about the Midnight Men, and where is Moore in all of this? You are supposed to be working together."

"She stayed at the station to start putting together the murder book and writing witness statements. Nothing came up on the Midnight Men but I'll still be working that. I'm not dropping it."

"Then that's a lot of your plate."

"I wouldn't ask for this if I couldn't handle my plate."

There was a pause before Robinson-Reynolds made a decision.

"Okay, I'll make the call to Fuentes. I'll let you know."

"Thanks, L-T."

The lieutenant disconnected first and Ballard walked back over to Elder's workstation. He was gone. She looked around and saw him sitting at a computer terminal by the window that looked out on the 10 Freeway. It meant he was on the NIBIN database. She walked over.

"Ballard, you've got something here," Elder said.

"Really?" Ballard said. "What?"

"Another case. The bullet is linked to another case. Nine years ago up in the Valley. A guy got shot in a robbery. The shells match. Same gun was used."

"Wow."

Ballard felt a cold finger go down her spine.

"What's the case number?" she asked.

Elder dictated a number off the computer screen. Ballard grabbed a pen out of a cup next to the computer terminal and wrote the number on her hand.

"It's an open case?" she asked.

"Open-unsolved," Elder said. "An RHD case."

Robbery-Homicide Division, Ballard's old unit before she was unceremoniously shipped out to the late show in Hollywood. But nine years ago went back before her time there.

"Does it say there who the contact is?" she asked.

"It does but it's out of date," Elder says. "Says here the lead on it is Harry Bosch. But I knew him and he's been retired a while."

Ballard froze for just a moment before managing to speak.

"I know," she then said.